W. C. Green

Aristophanes

The Wasps

W. C. Green

Aristophanes
The Wasps

ISBN/EAN: 9783741166433

Manufactured in Europe, USA, Canada, Australia, Japa

Cover: Foto ©Andreas Hilbeck / pixelio.de

Manufactured and distributed by brebook publishing software
(www.brebook.com)

W. C. Green

Aristophanes

ARISTOPHANES

EDITED BY

W. C. GREEN, M.A.

LATE FELLOW OF KING'S COLLEGE, CAMBRIDGE
CLASSICAL LECTURER AT QUEENS' COLLEGE

THE WASPS

RIVINGTONS

London, Oxford, and Cambridge

1868

INTRODUCTION TO THE WASPS.

THE play of *The Wasps* was exhibited in the spring of B.C. 422, in the archonship of Aminias, probably at the Lenaean festival. It gained the second prize, a play called Προάγων being first, and one of Leucon called Πρέσβεις third.

According to the Greek "Didascalies" it was exhibited in the name of Philonides; and these, as Ranke thinks, are upon the whole the safest guides. He therefore infers that Aristophanes on account of his failure with the *Clouds* returned to his old plan of sheltering himself behind another name, and that the *Proagon*, as well as the *Wasps*, was a play of Aristophanes. On the other hand Richter (who has investigated and edited this play with great care) considers the Didascalies untrustworthy, especially this one; and assigns the *Wasps* to the Great Dionysia, the *Proagon* to the Lenaea. Philonides, he thinks, was merely the principal actor. But this is a matter of no great moment as far as the *Wasps* is concerned; since, whether Philonides were nominal author or actor, Aristophanes was doubtless known to be the real author as well as he is now.

In the *Proagon* Euripides was ridiculed: in the *Wasps* the Athenian litigiousness is the object of satire. According to Ranke, with the *Clouds* ends the first period of Aristophanes' dramatic poetry. And this is a convenient division, borne out in a great measure by a change in the poet's style. For though he is still tolerably consistent, attacking Cleon and the

litigious spirit which he had before ridiculed (e.g. *Nub.* 208),
yet his style seems less strict and severe: there is more of the
ludicrous, more broad fun.   And therefore naturally there is
less completeness and connexion of parts in this play.   It is
not so political as the *Knights*, not so personal as the *Clouds.*
The *Wasps*, in fact, consists of two distinct parts: the first,
which contains the madness of the old dicast and the ridiculous means used to cure him, ending with the parabasis; the
second, in which he is converted to fashionable life, being as
it were an afterpiece, and deemed by some critics unnecessary.
Thus Schlegel calls the *Wasps* Aristophanes' feeblest play; and
few critics rank it very high.   But it may be said in defence of
our poet, that the last scenes form a very striking contrast to the
early part, and so enhance its effect.   They are perhaps drawn
out to a somewhat tedious length, but possibly some certain
time had to be filled up.   And Aristophanes, after exposing
the absurdities of a life devoted to the law-courts, may well
have meant to shew the evil of the other extreme—probably
too common among the young fashionables at Athens—in the
tipsy frolics of the old ex-juryman.   Weak in connexion and
plot the play may be, but it is brilliant and amusing in particular scenes.

The *Wasps* gave to Racine the idea of *Les Plaideurs*, and
several whole scenes may be compared with advantage.   On
the details of Athenian law, with which the play abounds,
Schoemann, Richter in his long and elaborate Prolegomena,
and the Dictionary of Antiquities, furnish ample information.

ΑΡΙΣΤΟΦΑΝΟΥΣ ΣΦΗΚΕΣ

TABLE OF THE READINGS OF DINDORF'S AND MEINEKE'S TEXTS.

	Dindorf.	Meineke.
3	προὔφειλεις	πρῶφειλεν
7	ταῖν	ταῖν
	ὕπνου	ἤδη
16	καταπτάμενον	καταπτόμενον
21	πῶς δὴ, προσερεῖ τις	Ζ. πῶς δή; Σ. προερεῖ τις
25	τοιοῦτον	τοιοῦτ’
36	ἐμπεπρημένη	ἐμπεπρημένη
53	οὕτωσι	οὕτω σ’
55	πρῶτον	πρότερον
68	ἄνω	ἄνω
74	Ἀμωίας	Σ. Ἀμυνίας
75	εἶναι...λέγει	εἶναι φ. ἀ. Ζ. ἀλλ’ οὐδὲν λέγει
76	Σ. μὰ	μὰ
77	Ζ. οὐκ	Ζ. οὐκ post lacunam Sosiani versus
	ἀρχὴ	ἀρχὴ
78	ὁδὶ	Σ. ὁδὶ
79	ἰ. φ. ἀ. Σ. οὐδαμῶς γ’	ἰ. φ. ἀ. Ζ. οὐδαμῶς γ’
81	Ζ. Νικόστρατοι	Σ. Νικόστρατοι
83	Σ. μὰ	Ζ. μὰ
94	γ’ ἔχειν	φέρειν
100	ὅτι	ὡς
105	προσεχόμενοι	προσισχόμενοι
121	δῆτα	δὴ δὲ
125	ἐξεφρίομεν	ἐξεφρείομεν
136	ἔχων...τινδι,	post v. 110 locat
136	φρυαγμοσεμνάκους τινὰς	φρυαγμοσεμνακουστίνους
147	οὔκ * ἐρρήσεις	οὐ γὰρ ἐρρήσεις
151	* * τὴν θ. ὤθει	ὅδε τὴν θ. ὠθεῖ
154	μοχλοῦ·	μοχλοῦ
160	ἀποσκλῆναι	ἀποσκλῆν’ ἂν
176	ταύτη γ’	αὕτη γ’
177	ἐξάγειν δοκῶ	ἔξαγ’ ἐνδοθεν
183	Βῶμαι ΖΑ. τουτονί, ΒΔ. τουτὶ	Βῶι, καὶ τουτονί. τουτὶ
190	ἥσυχον	ἡσύχωι
198	κεκλεισμένη	κεκλημένη
202	προσεκυλιἀ γ’	προσεκυλῖσον
217	τάρ’...νῦν	νῦν...γὰρ
220	μελησιἀ.	μελισιἀ.

	Dindorf.	Meineke.
234	'ταῦθ' ἢ Σάβῃ	' νταῦθ Σάβῃ θ'
244	ἠδίκησεν	ἠδίκηκεν
247	. λαθὼν τις	λίθος τις
251	μαθὼν	παθὼν
259	βόρβοροι	μάρμαροι
274	ἀπολώλεκε	ἀπολώλεκεν
282	καὶ λέγων	λέγων ὥς
283	ὡι	καὶ
302	σὺ δέ	Ι Ι. σὺ δέ
311	ὁπόθεν γε	ὁπόθεν δή
312	ἰὼ'...παρέχῃ	ΧΟ. ἰὼ'...παρέχῃ
317	ὑπακούων	ἐπακούων
318	ἀλλ' οὐ γὰρ οἷόν τ' ἔτ'	ἀλλὰ γὰρ οὐχ οἷόν τ'
323	μέγα βρωτήσαι	μεγαβρόντα
334	ὁ ταῦτά σ'	οὕτ ταῦθά σ'
335	τὰς θύρας	τῇ θύρᾳ
339	τίνα	ἢ τίνα
343	λέγεις τι	λέγεις σύ τι
350	διορύξαι	διαλέξαι
378	τῶν θεῶν	τοῖν θεοῖν
383	ἅπαντες καλέσαντες	ἅπαντ' ἐκκαλέσαντες
384	τὰ τοιαῦτα	τοιαῦτα
396	διαδύεται αὖ	διαδὺν ἔλαθεν
397	μιαρώτατε	μιάρ' ἀνδρῶν
407	ἐντέτατ' ὀξύ	ἐντετάμεθ' ὀξύ
414	ὡι χρή	om.
415	κεκράγετε	κεκράγατε
416	ὡς τίνδ'...μαθήσομαι	ΒΔ. ὡς τοῦδ'...μαθήσομαι
418	θεοσεχθρία	θεοσεχθρία
419	ὑμῶν	ἡμῶν
422	αὖθις	αὐταῖς
	ἀλλ' ἅπας	ἀλλὰ πᾶς
432	κύκλῳ	'ν κύκλῳ
442	δηλαδή· καί	δῆλα δ', εἰ καί
452	ἄφες	ἄφες
457	σὺ τῦφε	σύ. ΒΔ. τῦφε
458	Σ. οὐχί	οὐχί
459	Ξ. καὶ σύ	καὶ σύ
460	ἆρ' ἐμ.	Ξ. ἆρ' ἐμ.
463	αὐτὰ δῆλα	αὐτόθηλα
465	λάθρα γ' ἐλάνθαν' ὑπιοῦσά με	λάθρᾳ μ' ἐλάμβαν' ὑπιοῦσα
472	ἔλθωμεν	ἔλθοιμεν
473	σοί	σούν
	ἐρῶν	ἐραστά
480	οὐδὲ μὲν γ' οὐδ' ἐν	οὐδὲ μὴν οὔτω 'ν
483	ταὐτὰ ταῦτα	ταῦτα ταῦτα
	ξυνωμόται	ξυνωμότην
485	μοι	σοι
486	οὐδέποτέ γ'	οὐδέπω γ'
487	δῖ' ἐστάλης	ἐξεστάλης
493	θέλῃ	'θέλῃ
504	νῦν	νῦν γ'
522	καὶ ξίφος	ΦΙ. καὶ ξίφος

	Dindorf.	Meineke.
514	εἰπέ μοι	ΒΔ. εἰπέ μοι
525	ἀκράτου	ἄκρατον
526	νῦν δὲ	νῦν δὴ
527	λέγειν τι δεῖ	δᾶ τι λέγειν.
530	ΦΙ. ἀτὰρ	ἀτὰρ
532	λέγειν	λέγων
542	δ' ἐν ταῖς ὁδοῖς	δ' ἂν ταισὶν ἐν
		ταῖσιν ὁδοῖς ἁπάσαις
543	καλούμεθ'	καλοίμεθ'
558	ἀπόφυξιν	ἀπόφευξιν
565	ἀνιών	ἀνιών
570	συγκύπτωσθ' ἅμ βλ.	συγκύπτοντα βλ.
577	καί...ἄρχειν	om.
578	αἰδοῖα	τὰ δαῖα
588	σεμνόν	σε μόνον
599	Εὐφημίου	Εὐφημίδου
600	σπόγγον	σφάγγον
601	τῶν...οἵων	τῶνθ'...οἵων μ'
602	χὐπηρεσίαν	καὶ ὑπηρεσίαν
605	ἐπιλελήσμην	'πελελήσμην
606	εἰσήκονθ' ἅμα	εἰσήκοντά με
608	φιλήσῃ	φιλῇ με
609	παππάζουσ'	παππίζουσ'
612	καὶ μή	κοὐ μή
614	ἀλλην	ἀλλ' ἤν
615—618	τάδε...κατέκαρθεν	om.
620	καὶ τῆς τοῦ	καὶ τοῦ
627	μ'	γ'
634	οὐκ, ἀλλ'	οὔκουν
636	ὡς δ' ἐπὶ πάντ' ἐλήλυθεν	ὡς ὅδε πάντ' ἐπῆλθε κοὐ-
637	κοὐδὲν παρῆλθεν	δὲν τι παρῆλθεν
642	ὦσθ'	ὡς
645	ἀπόφυξιν	ἀπόφευξιν
661	τούτων	τούτου
665	μὰ Δί' οὐ μέντοι· καὶ	μὰ Δί' οὐ μέντοι. ΦΙ. καὶ
666	ΦΙ. ἐς τούτους κ.τ.λ.	ΒΔ. ἐς τούτους κ.τ.λ.
667	ΒΔ. σὺ γὰρ	σὺ γὰρ
671	δώσεις	οἴσεις
674	λαγαρυζόμενος	λαγαριζόμενος
694	πρίον'	πρίονθ'
695	κωλακρέτην	κωλαγρέτην
698	καὶ ταῖσιν ἅπασιν	καὶ τοισίδ' ἅπασιν
701	ἀκαρῆ	ἀκαρές
704	ἐπισίξῃ	ἐπισίξῃ
710	πύῳ	πυῷ
713	ποθ' ὥσπερ νάρκη μου κατὰ	πέπονθ' ; ὥσπερ νάρκη μου
749	πειθόμενοι	πιθόμενοι
758	μὴ νῦν	μὴ νυν
765	ἐνθάδε	ἐνθαδὶ
767	ταῦθ'	πρᾶτθ'
770	γε	δέ
772	εἵλη	ἔλη
773	καθήμενοι,	καθήμενοι

	Dindorf.	Meineke.
795	καθέψαι	κατασπέψαι
	λέγων	γελῶν
808	ἀπὸ	ἀπὸ
813	κᾶν γάρ...λήψομαι	post v. 797 locat
816	ἵνα γ'	ἵ' ἂν
819	εἴ των ἐκομίσαις	οὕτω' ξεκόμισας
821	οἷόσπερ κ.τ.λ.	ΒΔ. οἷόσπερ κ.τ.λ.
826	εἰσαγάγω	εἰσάγω
827	τί τις	τί τις
833, 4	ἔνδοθεν. τί ποτε τὸ χρῆμα';	ἔνδοθεν ὅ τι ποτὲ χρῆμι
837	ἀρπάσας	ὑφαρπάσας
849	διατρίψεις	διατρίβας
858	δὴ τίς ἐστιν; οὐχὶ	δὴ τις ἐστὶν οὐχὶ
867	ξυνέβητον	ξυνεβήτην
868	ΒΔ. εὐφημία κ.τ.λ.	εὐφημία κ.τ.λ.
875	προθύρου προστύλαια	προστύλου πάρος αὐλᾶς
885	σοι * * κάπᾴδομεν	ταῦτά σοι κάπᾴδομεν
888	ἠσθόμεσθα	ἠσθήμεσθα
890	τῶν γ. ν.	τῶν γ. ν. ἱῆς παιδν
893	τίς...ἁλώσεται	τίς...ΒΔ. οὕτοι. ΦΙ. ὅσσι ἁλώσεται
894—7	Ξ. ἀκούετ'...σύκισσι	ΒΔ. ἀκούετ'...σύκισσι
901	ποῦ δ' ὁ διώκων	ποῦ ποῦ δ' ὁ διώκων
903	ΒΔ. πάρεστιν...Λάβητ	ΒΔ. πάρεστιν οὗτοι. ΦΙ. ἰ. ἰ. αὖ Λάβητ
905	Ξ. σίγα	σίγα
907	ἦν	ἦς
917	ΦΙ. οὐδέν μ.; Ξ. οὐδ. τ.κ.ἐ.	ΦΙ. οὐδέν μ....ἐμοί
921	ἀφῆτέ γ' αὐτὸν	ἀφῆτ' ἔτ' αὐτὸν
924	θυσίαν	θυσίαν
929	κεκλάγχω	κεκλάγγω
935	ὁ θεσμοθέτηι. ποῦ' σθ' οὗτοι;	ὁ θεσμοθέτηι ποῦ' σθ'; οὗτοι,
939	προσκεκαυμένα	προσκεκλημένα
957	ὅτι σοῦ	ὅ τι; σοῦ
961	ὑπέγραφ'	ἐγραφεν
967	ἕλει	ἕλει
968	τραχήλι'	τὰ τραχήλι'
970	οἰκουρὸς	οἰκουρῶ
973	ΦΙ. αἰβοῖ...μαλάττομαι	ΦΙ. αἰβοῖ. ΒΔ. τί τὸ κακόν; ΦΙ. ἔσθ' ὁ. μ.
974	περιμένει	περιβαίνει
978	αἰτεῖτε	αἰτεῖσθε
981	ἐξηπάτησιν	ἐξηπάτησεν
983	ἀπεδάκρυσα	ἀπεδάκρυσα
991	'πτευθενί	'πταθθ' ἔτι
993	ΒΔ. φερ'...ἠγωνίσμεθα;	ΒΔ. φ. ἐ. ΦΙ. πῶς d. ἠ.
997	ἀπέφυγεν	πέφευγεν
1011	νῦν μὲν τὰ	νῦν τὰ
1019	πρῶτον γ'	πρῶτιστ'
	ἀνθρώποις	ἀνθρωρίοις
1030	ἐπιχειρεῖν	ἐπεχείρει
1037	μετ' αὐτοῦ	μετ' αὐτὸν
1062	ἀνδρικώτατοι	ἀλκιμώτατοι
1064	κύκνου τ' ἔτι	κύκνου τε

	Dindorf.	Meineke.
1076	Ἀττικαί…αὐτόχθονες	om.
1083	ἀπωσάμεσθα	ἐσωζόμεσθα
1085	πρὸς ἐσπέρᾳ	πρὸς ἑσπέραν
1087, 8		inverso ordine legit
1091	πάντα μὴ	πάντες ἐμὲ
1110	πυκνὸν	Πυκνὸς
1114	ἐγκαθήμενοι	οἱ καθήμενοι
1115	οὐκ…φόρου	om.
1116	γόνον	πόνον
1133	καὶ τρέφειν	κἀκτρέπειν
1138	θυμαιτίδα	θυμαιτίδα
1141	ἐοικέναι	προσεικέναι
1157	ἀποδίου	ὑπολόου
1158	ὑπόδυθι	ὑποδοῦ τι
1159	ὑποδύσασθαι	ὑποδήσασθαι
1161	πόδ'	ποτ'
1167	γήρᾳ	γήρως
1168	ὑποδυσάμενος	ὑποδησάμενος
1169	διασαλακώνισοι	διασαλπώνισον
1172	δοθῆρι	Δοθῆρι
1190	ἐμάχετό γ' αὐτίκα	ἆρ' ἐμάχετ' αὐτίκα
1193	λαγῶας τε	καὶ λαγῷα
1195	πῶς δ' ἂν	πῶς ἂν
1208	προσμάνθανε	προμάνθανε
1219	αὐλητρίς	αὐλητρίς
1222	σκόλι' ὅπως δέξει καλῶς	σκόλια πῶς δέξει; Φ. καλῶς
1223	ἀληθες, ὡς οὐδεὶς	ΒΔ. ἀληθες; Φ. ὡς οὐδ' εἰ
1225	δέξει	δέξει
1226	ἐγένετ' Ἀθηναῖος	Ἀθηναῖός γε
1227	κλέπτης	ὡς σὺ κλέπτης.
1228	τουτὶ σὺ δράσεις; π.	τοῦτ' εἰ σὺ δράσεις, π.
1231	ἕτερον ᾄσομαι	ἕτερ' ἀντᾴσομαι
1239	τούτῳ…ἐγώ.	om.
1244	κᾆτ' ᾄσεται	κᾀντᾴσεται
1245	βίαν	βίον
1248	δὴ ἀκεκόμισας	νὴ Δι' ἐκόμπασας
1252	μεθυσθῶμεν	μεθύωμεν
	μηδαμῶς	μὴ, μηδαμῶς
1262	ἀποίχεται	ἀπέρχεται
1268	ῥοιᾶς	ῥοᾶς
1274	ἐλάττων	ἔλαττον
1287	οὐκτὸς	ἐκτὸς
1303	ὑβριστότατοι	ὑβρίστατοι
1305, 6		inverso ordine legit
1310	ἀχυρῶσαι	ἀχυρμὸν
1324	ὁδὶ δὲ δὴ καὶ	ὁδὶ δὲ καὐτὸς
1338	ἀντέχομαι	οὐκέτ' ἀντέχομαι
1339	ἰαμβοῖ αἰβοῖ	αἰβοῖ
1340	* * ποῦ 'στιν	ποῦ 'στιν ἡμῖν
1350	αὖτ'	ταῦτ'
1356	υἱίδιον	υἱίδιον
1360	καὐτὸς ἐπὶ	καὐτόσ' ἐπὶ
1380	νομίσαι	νομίσαι σ'

	Dindorf.	*Meineke.*
1387	νἡ...Ὀλυμπίαν	om.
1391	ἐδ πιθήσῃ	κἀπιθήσαι
1414	πρὸς ποδῶν	προσπολῶν
1418	καλέσῃ	καλέσῃ
1423	δευρὶ πρότερον, ἐπιτρέπαι	δευρί· πότερον ἐπιτρέπαι
1432	οὕτω...Πιττάλου	post v. 1440 locat.
1434	αὐτὸς	οὗτος
1443	ἐγώ σε	ἔγωγε
1449	ἀπολῶ σ'	ἀπόλοι'
	τοῖσι	ταῖς σαῖς
1454	πείσεταί τι	τι μεταπεσεῖται
1461	μετεβάλλοντο	μετεβάλοντο
1473	κατακοσμῆσαι	κατακομῆσαι
1481	διορχησόμενος	διορχησάμενος
1487	ῥώμῃ	ῥύμῃ
1507	οὐδέν γ'	οὐδὲν
1510	τινοτήρῃ	τινοτήρῃ
1514	ψίυρά	μοι· σὺ δὲ
1519	θαλασσίοιο	θαλασσίου θεοῦ

ΥΠΟΘΕΣΙΣ.

I.

Φιλοκλέων Ἀθηναῖος φιλόδικσι ὢν τὴν φύσιν ἐφαίνα περὶ τὰ δικαστήρια συνεχῶς. Βδελυκλέων δὲ ὁ τούτου παῖς ἀχθόμενοι ταύτῃ τῇ νόσῳ καὶ πειρώμενοι τὸν πατέρα παύειν, ἐγκαθείρξας τοῖς οἴκοις καὶ δίκτυα περιβαλὼν ἐφύλαττε νύκτωρ καὶ μεθ᾽ ἡμέραν. ὁ δὲ ἐξόδου αὐτῷ μὴ προκειμένης ἔκραζεν. οἱ δὲ συνδικασταὶ αὐτοῦ σφηξὶν ἑαυτοὺς ἀφομοιώσαντες παρεγένοντο, βουλόμενοι διὰ ταύτῃ τῆς τέχνης ὑποκλέπτειν τὸν συνδικαστήν· ἐξ ὧν καὶ ὁ χορὸς συνέστηκε καὶ τὸ δρᾶμα ἐπιγέγραπται. ἀλλ᾽ οὐδὲν ἤνυον οὐδὲ οὗτοι. πέρας δὲ τοῦ νεανίσκου θαυμάζοντος τίνος ἕνεκα ὁ πατὴρ οὕτωσι ἥττηται τοῦ πράγματος, ἔφη ὁ πρεσβύτης εἶναι τὸ πρᾶγμα σπουδαῖον καὶ σχεδὸν ἀρχὴν τὸ διαέζειν. ὁ δὲ παῖς ἐπειρᾶτο τὰς ὑποψίας ἐξαιρεῖν τοῦ πράγματος, νουθετῶν τὸν γέροντα. ὁ δὲ πρεσβύτης μηδαμῶς νουθετούμενοι οὐ μεθίει τοῦ πάθους· ἀλλ᾽ ἀναγκάζεται ὁ νέοι ἐπιτρέπειν φιλοδικεῖν, καὶ ἐπὶ τῆς οἰκίας τοῦτο ποιεῖ, καὶ τοῖς κατὰ τὴν οἰκίαν δικάζει. καὶ δύο κύνες ἐπεισάγονται πολιτικῶς παρ᾽ αὐτῷ κρινόμενοι· καὶ κατὰ τοῦ φεύγοντος ἐκφέρειν συνεχῶς τὴν ψῆφον μέλλων ἀπατηθεὶς ἅμα τὴν ἀποδικάζουσαν φέρει ψῆφον. περιέχει δὲ καὶ δικαιολογίαν τινὰ τοῦ χοροῦ ἐκ τοῦ ποιητοῦ προσώπου, ὡς σφηξὶν ἐμφερεῖς εἰσιν οἱ τοῦ χοροῦ, ἐξ ὧν καὶ τὸ δρᾶμα. οἳ ὅτε μὲν ἦσαν νέοι, πικρῶς τοῖς δίκαις ἐφήδρευον, ἐπεὶ δὲ γέροντες γεγόνασιν, κεντοῦσι τοῖς κέντροις, ἐπὶ τέλει δὲ τοῦ δράματος ὁ γέρων ἐπὶ δεῖπνον καλεῖται, καὶ ἐπὶ ὕβριν τρέπεται, καὶ κρίνει αὐτὸν ὕβρεως ἀρτόπωλις· ὁ δὲ γέρων πρὸς αὐλὸν καὶ ὄρχησιν τρέπεται, καὶ γελωτοποιεῖ τὸ δρᾶμα.

Τοῦτο τὸ δρᾶμα πεποίηται αὐτῷ οὐκ ἐξ ὑποκειμένης ὑποθέσεως, ἀλλ᾽ ὡσανεὶ γενομένης· πέπλασται γὰρ τὸ ὅλον. διαβάλλει δὲ Ἀθηναίους ὡς φιλοδικοῦντας, καὶ σωφρονίζει τὸν δῆμον ἀποστῆναι τῶν δικῶν. καὶ διὰ τοῦτο καὶ τοὺς δικαστὰς σφηξὶν ἀπεικάζει κέντρα ἔχουσι καὶ πλήττουσι. πεποίηται δ᾽ αὐτῷ χαριέντως. ἐδιδάχθη ἐπὶ ἄρχοντος Ἀμεινίου διὰ Φιλωνίδου [ἐν τῇ πθʹ ὀλυμπιάδι]. βʹ ἦν, εἰς Λήναια. καὶ ἐνίκα πρῶτος Φιλωνίδης Προάγωνι, Λεύκων Πρέσβεσι τρίτος.

II.

ΑΡΙΣΤΟΦΑΝΟΥΣ ΓΡΑΜΜΑΤΙΚΟΥ.

Φιλοῦντα διαέζειν πατέρα παῖς εἴρξας ἄφνω
αὐτός τ᾽ ἐφύλαττεν ἔνδον οἰκέται θ᾽, ὅπως
μὴ λαθεῖν μηδ᾽ ἐξίῃ διὰ τὴν νόσον.
ὁ δ᾽ ἀντιμάχεται παντὶ τρόπῳ καὶ μηχανῇ.
εἶθ᾽ οἱ συνήθεις καὶ γέροντες, λεγόμενοι
σφηκές, παραγίνονται βοηθοῦντες σφόδρα
ἐπὶ τῷ δύνασθαι κέντρα ἐνιέναι τισὶ
φράσοντες ἱκανόν. ὁ δὲ γέρων τηρούμενος
συμπείθεθ᾽ ἔνδον διαδικάζειν καὶ βιοῦν,
ἐπεὶ τὸ διαέζειν κέκριτεν ἐκ παντὸς τρόπου.

ΤΑ ΤΟΤ ΔΡΑΜΑΤΟΣ ΠΡΟΣΩΠΑ

ΣΩΣΙΑΣ } οἰκέται Φιλοκλέωνος.
ΞΑΝΘΙΑΣ }
ΒΔΕΛΤΚΛΕΩΝ.
ΦΙΛΟΚΛΕΩΝ.
ΧΟΡΟΣ ΓΕΡΟΝΤΩΝ ΣΦΗΚΩΝ.
ΠΑΙΔΕΣ.
ΚΤΩΝ.
ΑΡΤΟΠΩΛΙΣ.
ΧΑΙΡΕΦΩΝ, κωφὸν πρόσωπον.
ΚΑΤΗΓΟΡΟΣ.

ΣΦΗΚΕΣ.

ΣΩΣΙΑΣ

ΟΥΤΟΣ, τί πάσχεις, ὦ κακόδαιμον Ξανθία;

ΞΑΝΘΙΑΣ

φυλακὴν καταλύειν νυκτερινὴν διδάσκομαι.

ΣΩΣΙΑΣ

κακὸν ἄρα ταῖς πλευραῖς τι προὔφειλες μέγα.
ἆρ' οἶσθά γ' οἷον κνώδαλον φυλάττομεν;

ΞΑΝΘΙΑΣ

οἶδ'· ἀλλ' ἐπιθυμῶ σμικρὸν ἀπομερμηρίσαι.   5

1—53. Xanthias and Sosias, who are set to watch Philocleon, tell each other their troubles and their dreams.

1 φυλακὴν καταλύειν.] Cf. Arist. *Polit.* v. 8, Ἵνα φυλάττωσι καὶ μὴ καταλύωσιν, ὥσπερ νυκτερινὴν φυλακὴν, τὴν τῆς πόλεως τήρησιν. As this verb is used in many phrases, with βίον, πόλεμον, εἰρήνην, βουλήν, and other nouns, it may probably have been with φυλακὴν the common word for coming off guard when relieved. Hence Xanthias in his sleepiness says, 'Oh! I am just taking a lesson at coming off guard.' The watchman in Aesch. *Agam.* 12—17, is described as suffering from his long watch, and having a hard task to keep off sleep.

3 προὔφειλες.] 'You had then an old score to pay off on your sides (when you allowed yourself to become sleepy, for it is they that will

suffer if you sleep).' The imperfect is far preferable to the present tense here. The MSS. have προὔφειλες, and the scholiast says, ἐχρεώστεις τι κακὸν ταῖς πλευραῖς σου καὶ ἀποδοῦναι θέλεις.

4 κνώδαλον.] Cf. *Lysistr.* 476, τί ποτε χρησόμεθα τοῖσδε ταῖς κνωδάλοις; said of women. There seems to be hardly an animal to which κνώδαλον cannot be applied; and no one English equivalent for it as a term of abuse; for we should vary the species of animal to suit the circumstances. Thus, here we might render it 'serpent,' with reference to the dicast's wiliness, and power of wriggling away: in the Lysistrata (looking to the context), 'these very hornets.'

5 ἀπομερμηρίσαι.] Only used (as far as lexicons tell) here. μερμηρίζειν is common in Homer. μέρμηρα ἡ μέριμνα καὶ ἡ φροντίς. Schol.

κἂν τῇ θαλάττῃ θηρίον τὴν ἀσπίδα;

ΞΑΝΘΙΑΣ

οἴμοι, τί δῆτά μοι κακὸν γενήσεται
ἰδόντι τοιοῦτον ἐνύπνιον;

ΣΩΣΙΑΣ

μὴ φροντίσῃς.   25
οὐδὲν γὰρ ἔσται δεινὸν, οὐ μὰ τοὺς θεούς.

ΞΑΝΘΙΑΣ

δεινόν γέ τοῦστ' ἄνθρωπος ἀποβαλὼν ὅπλα.
ἀτὰρ σὺ τὸ σὸν αὖ λέξον.

ΣΩΣΙΑΣ

ἀλλ' ἐστὶν μέγα.
περὶ τῆς πόλεως γάρ ἐστι τοῦ σκάφους ὅλου.

ΞΑΝΘΙΑΣ

λέγε νυν ἀνύσας τι τὴν τρόπιν τοῦ πράγματος.   30

ΣΩΣΙΑΣ

ἔδοξέ μοι περὶ πρῶτον ὕπνον ἐν τῇ πυκνὶ
ἐκκλησιάζειν πρόβατα συγκαθήμενα,
βακτηρίας ἔχοντα καὶ τριβώνια·
κἄπειτα τούτοις τοῖσι προβάτοις μοὐδόκει
δημηγορεῖν φάλαινα πανδοκεύτρια,   35

the supposition that the riddle ought to begin in the orthodox English fashion, with a Why or a What. ἀσπὶς would sound ambiguous in the riddle till the answer was seen.

25 τοιοῦτον.] With τοιοῦτ' ἐν, the αι in τοιοῦτ' would have to be scanned·long: which is not so well; for the υ in ἐνύπνιον should certainly be short. Cf. Eq. 940, and the note there on ἐνατοππιγάτῃ.

27 δεινόν γέ.] Xanthias takes up the word δεινὸν more in its sense of 'monstrous, strange,' than 'to be feared,' as Sosias had meant it. But 'terrible' will tolerably do duty for both senses.

29 σκάφους.] Cf. Aesch. S. C. Theb. 2, ὅστις φυλάσσει πρᾶγος ἐν

τρόμπῃ πόλεως οἴακα νωμῶν: and Soph. Antig. 190, ταύτῃ ἔτι πλέοντες ὀρθῆς τοὺς φίλους ποιούμεθα. Xanthias, to keep up the metaphor, asks for the 'keel' of the matter. ὡσανεὶ ἔλεγε τὴν ῥίζαν, Schol., because the keel was laid first. If there is allusion to τρόπον (as Bergler thinks), the equivoque might be kept by 'let us get at once to the bittom of the matter.'

33 βακτηρίας κ. τριβ.] Apparently the usual equipment of the older men. Cf. vv. 117, 1131, and Ach. 184, 343; also Nub. 541.

34—36. The Athenians listen like silly sheep to a devouring monster.

35 πανδοκεύτρια.] τοῦτα δεχομένη, Schol. Cf. Eq. 238, φάραγγα καὶ χάρυβδιν ἁρπαγῆς. The word

ἔχουσα φωνὴν ἐμπεπρημένης ὑός.

ΞΑΝΘΙΑΣ

αἰβοῖ.

ΣΩΣΙΑΣ

τί ἐστι;

ΞΑΝΘΙΑΣ

παῦε παῦε, μὴ λέγε·
ὄζει κάκιστον τοὐνύπνιον βύρσης σαπρᾶς.

ΣΩΣΙΑΣ

εἶθ' ἡ μιαρὰ φάλαιν' ἔχουσα τρυτάνην
ἵστη βόειον δημόν.

ΞΑΝΘΙΑΣ

οἴμοι δείλαιος·   40
τὸν δῆμον ἡμῶν βούλεται διιστάναι.

ΣΩΣΙΑΣ

ἐδόκει δέ μοι Θέωρος αὐτῆς πλησίον
χαμαὶ καθῆσθαι, τὴν κεφαλὴν κόρακος ἔχων.
εἶτ' Ἀλκιβιάδης εἶπε πρός με τραυλίσας·

usually means 'hostess' (as in *Ran.*
114); here it is 'receiver general
of all bribes,' perhaps 'one who
never shuts the door 'gainst those
who come and pay their score.'
36 ἐμπεπρημένης.] ἐμπεφυσημέ-
νης καὶ παχείας, Schol., 'of a fat,
bloated sow.' But MSS. R, V,
have ἐμπεπρημένης, ἐμπεπρησμένην.
Whether 'inflamed voice' or 'in-
flated' be better, is doubtful. Either
is curious. Richter renders the
common text, 'the voice of a singed
sow.' But the time after the singeing is an odd one to choose for describing the animal's voice. Cleon's
voice Aristophanes elsewhere calls
κυκλοβόρου φωνήν, and φωνὴν χαρά-
δρας ὀλεθρον τετοκυίας (*Eq.* 137,
Vesp. 1034).
38 βύρσης.] With reference to
Cleon's trade, see *The Knights*,
passim.

40—41 δημόν...δῆμον.] A similar play on the word is in *Eq.* 954,
where Demus' seal is δημοῦ βοείου
θρίον ἐξωπτημένον. Whether βόειον
here implies ἀναίσθητον, as a scholiast says, is very doubtful. I know
of no such use of βόειος. Some pun
on 'fat of bull's flesh,' and 'John
Bull' might be suggested as a modern equivalent.
41 διιστάναι.] There is no need
to fix on any particular disturbance
for this 'setting the people by the
ears.' The pun on ἱστάναι, 'to
weigh,' and διιστάναι is the chief
thing aimed at.
44 τραυλίσας.] Alcibiades' lisp is
mentioned by Plutarch. οἱ δὲ τραυ-
λοὶ τὸ λ ἀντὶ τοῦ ρ λέγουσιν. Schol.
It was perhaps affectation. 'Lab-
dacismum, quem scriptores notant
in Alcibiade, deliciis, non naturae
tribuendum arbitror.' Erasmus,

ὁλᾷς; Θέωλος τὴν κεφαλὴν κόλακος ἔχει.   45

ΞΑΝΘΙΑΣ

ὀρθῶς γε τοῦτ' Ἀλκιβιάδης ἐτραύλισεν.

ΣΩΣΙΑΣ

οὔκουν ἐκεῖν' ἀλλόκοτον, ὁ Θέωρος κόραξ
γιγνόμενος;

ΞΑΝΘΙΑΣ

ἥκιστ', ἀλλ' ἄριστον.

ΣΩΣΙΑΣ

πῶς;

ΞΑΝΘΙΑΣ

ὅπως;

ἄνθρωπος ὢν εἶτ' ἐγένετ' ἐξαίφνης κόραξ·
οὔκουν ἐναργὲς τοῦτο συμβαλεῖν, ὅτι   50
ἀρθεὶς ἀφ' ἡμῶν ἐς κόρακας οἰχήσεται;

ΣΩΣΙΑΣ

εἶτ' οὐκ ἐγὼ δοὺς δύ' ὀβολὼ μισθώσομαι
οὕτω σ' ὑποκρινόμενον σοφῶς ὀνείρατα;

ΞΑΝΘΙΑΣ

φέρε νυν κατείπω τοῖς θεαταῖς τὸν λόγον,

Colloq. de Ræl. Pron. Similar affectation in the way of drawls and
lazy slurring of the liquids is not
unknown among the Alcibiadeses
of our own time.

45 Θέωλος.] As if from θεὸς and
ὄλλυμι: cf. v. 418, Θεώρου θεοισεχθρία.

46 ὀρθῶς γε.] Alcibiades' lisp led
him to Theorus' right name, κόλαξ.
An epigram is quoted from the An-
thology: Ρῶ καὶ λάμβδα μόνον κόρακας κολάκων διορίζει· λοιπὸν ταὐτὸ
κόραξ βωμολόχος τε κόλαξ. τοὔνεκά
μοι, βέλτιστε, τόδε ζῶον πεφύλαξο,
εἰδὼς καὶ ζώντων τοὺς κόλακας κόρακας: which might be freely imitated:
'Twixt fowls and fools in northern
tongue small difference is heard;
There's chattering fowls, and prating

fools; the man's much like the bird.
And those who of this feather be,
'twere best, my friend, to shun,
Sure that for any useful end such
fowls and fools are one.'

51 ἐς κόρακας.] To the point
perhaps is Diogenes' apophthegm:
κρεῖττόν ἐστιν ἐς κόρακας ἀπελθεῖν ἢ
ἐς κόλακας. 'Better join the fowls
than the fools.' Here 'it is plain
that we shall lose him, and the fowls
(pronounced 'fules') will get him.'

53 οὕτω σ' ὅτι.] This (for vulg.
οὕτως) commends itself. It is due
to Geel and Bergk, and adopted by
Richter.

53 ὑποκρινόμενον.] Cf. Hom. Od.
XIX. 535, 555, for exactly the same
use.

54—135. Xanthias lays the mat-

ὀλίγ' ἄτθ' ὑπειπὼν πρῶτον αὐτοῖσιν ταδί,   55
μηδὲν παρ' ἡμῶν προσδοκᾶν λίαν μέγα,
μηδ' αὖ γέλωτα Μεγαρόθεν κεκλεμμένον.
ἡμῖν γὰρ οὐκ ἔστ' οὔτε κάρυ' ἐκ φορμίδος
δούλω διαρριπτοῦντε τοῖς θεωμένοις,
οὔθ' Ἡρακλῆς τὸ δεῖπνον ἐξαπατώμενος,   60
οὐδ' αὖθις ἐνασελγαινόμενος Εὐριπίδης·

ter, before the audience, praying
them not to expect too much, but
promising something new. He and
his fellow-slave have (he says) to
guard for their young master his old
father, who is sick of a law fever, is
always getting up early, going off to
the courts; who dreams of nothing
but law-suits, and has a mania for
condemning every one. They have
tried mild remedies in vain, and now
have to shut him up and guard
strictly every hole by which he might
slip out.

In the opening scene of Racine's
Les Plaideurs (which indeed is
founded on *The Wasps*), Petit Jean's
description of his master's doings
presents several points of similarity
to that of Xanthias.

54 κατείπω τ. θ.] So in *Eq.* 36 the
matter is put before the audience.

55 ὑπειπὼν.] Used nearly as
in Dem. *c. Arist.* 637, καὶ γέγραφεν,
οὐδὲν ὑπειπὼν ὅπως ἂν τις ἀποστείρη,
τὴν τιμωρίας: where οὐδὲν ὑπ. means
'with no reservation.' Here 'with
this short preface or saving clause.'
ὑπὸ expresses the quiet insertion of
the clause, which is to save them
from any after charge of having promised more than they performed.

57 Μεγαρόθεν.] ὡς ποιητῶν ὄν-
των τινῶν ἀπὸ Μεγαρίδος ἀμούσων
καὶ ἀφυῶς σκωπτόντων. Schol. who
quotes also from Eupolis τὸ σκῶμμ'
ἀσελγὲς καὶ Μεγαρικὸν σφόδρα. Aristotle (*Poet.* c. 3) says that the Me-
garians claimed the invention of
comedy. In the *Acharnians* the
Megarian calls the dressing up of
his daughters Μεγαρικὰν μηχανάν.

58 κάρυ' ἐκ φορμίδος.] Such scat-
terings for a scramble among the
audience seem to have been common.
Cf. *Plut.* 797, οὐ γὰρ πρεπῶδές ἐστι
τῷ διδασκάλῳ ἰσχάδια καὶ τρωγάλια
τοῖς θεωμένοις προβαλόντ' ἀεὶ τούτων
οὖν ἐνασαγεάζειν γελᾶν. Cf. also
Pac. 962, where Trygaeus does something of the sort, perhaps in parody
of other comic writers. In *Nub.*
540—552, Aristophanes disclaims
such tricks and repetitions, much as
he does here.

60 Ἡρακλῆς.] In the *Alcestis*
of Euripides Hercules' unseemly
eagerness for his meal is described
(v. 753—760, 773—802): and Aristophanes afterwards represents him
as greedy when in Hades: cf. *Ran.*
549, &c. Hence Ἡρακλῆς ξενίζεται
had passed into a proverb of any
one impatient. But there is probably a reference here to some particular exhibition of Hercules miss-
ing his meal, either by another
comedian, or (as Richter thinks) by
our poet himself in a former play.

61 αὖθις...Εὐριπίδης.] As in the
Acharnians (v. 400—478) and, acc.
to the Scholiast, in the *Proagon*. Of
course the *Thesmophoriazusae* is out
of the question, as it was exhibited
at a later date than this play.

ἐνασελγαινόμενος.] ὑβριζόμενοι.
Schol. L. and S. also take it as passive here; but refer to Diodorus Si-
culus as using it active. It may just
as well here mean ἀσελγῶν πράττων,
'acting outrageously.' ἐν means 'in
the play.' Aristophanes would hardly call his own chastisement of Euripides ἀσελγεία.

οὐδ' εἰ Κλέων γ' ἰλαμψε τῆς τύχης χάριν,
αὖθις τὸν αὐτὸν ἄνδρα μυττωτεύσομεν.
ἀλλ' ἔστιν ἡμῖν λογίδιον γνώμην ἔχον,
ὑμῶν μὲν αὐτῶν οὐχὶ δεξιώτερον, 65
κωμῳδίας δὲ φορτικῆς σοφώτερον.
ἔστιν γὰρ ἡμῖν δεσπότης ἐκεινοσὶ
ἄνω καθεύδων, ὁ μέγας, οὑπὶ τοῦ τέγους.
οὗτος φυλάττειν τὸν πατέρ' ἐπέταξε νῷν,
ἔνδον καθείρξας, ἵνα θύραζε μὴ 'ξίῃ. 70
νόσον γὰρ ὁ πατὴρ ἀλλόκοτον αὐτοῦ νοσεῖ,
ἣν οὐδ' ἂν εἷς γνοίη ποτ' οὐδ' ἂν ξυμβάλοι,
εἰ μὴ πύθοιθ' ἡμῶν· ἐπεὶ τοπάζετε.
Ἀμυνίας μὲν ὁ Προνάπους φήσ' οὑτοσὶ
εἶναι φιλόκυβον αὐτόν·

ΣΩΣΙΑΣ
ἀλλ' οὐδὲν λέγει 75
μὰ Δί', ἀλλ' ἀφ' αὐτοῦ τὴν νόσον τεκμαίρεται.

62 Ἰλαμψε. τῆς τύχης χάριν.]
Reiske interprets 'si comoedia. in
qua Cleo fuit exagitatus, placuit et
splendido applausu fuit excepta.'
Rather 'if Cleon came out brilliant-
ly, thanks to good luck (rather than
to good management).' So the
Scholiast : ὡς τοῦ Κλέωνος ἀπὸ δυσ-
γενῶν ἐκλάμψαντος. Though Cleon
did owe his name to good luck,
the Knights, Aristophanes says, was
enough of a dressing for him. In
Nub. 549, the poet claims credit
for not trampling on him when
down.
63 μυττωτεύσομεν.] Cf. Eq. 771,
κατακνησθείην ἐν μυττωτῷ μετὰ τυροῦ and Pac. 247, ὡς ἐπιτετρίψεσθ'
αὐτίκα ἀναξάναντα καταμεμυττωτευ-
μένα.
65—66 δεξιώτερον ... φορτικῆς.]
In a former parabasis, Nub. 524—
527, φορτικαὶ are similarly opposed
to δεξιαί.
67 ἔστιν γάρ.] This is to be
connected in sense with κατεῖπω τὸν
λόγον in v. 54. Cf. Eq. 40, λέγοιμ'
him.

ἂν ἤδη. νῷν γάρ ἐστι δεσπότης
κ.τ.λ.
74—84. There are various ways
of dividing this dialogue. Dindorf's
text makes Xanthias collect the
guesses of the audience, and Sosias
remark upon them. Meineke re-
verses this, and, following Bergk,
supposes that a line spoken by Sosias, telling of another guess, has
been lost before οὐκ, ἀλλὰ φ. μ. In
Dindorf's text the οὐκ comes rather
awkwardly, having nothing in Sosias' μὰ Δί' ἀλλ ... τεκμαίρεται to
refer to. Hence Richter's text, beginning Sosias' part with ἀλλ' οὐδὲν
λέγει, seems preferable. Everything
then follows naturally, and no loss
of a line need be supposed. And
the Scholiast says (on the word φι-
λόκυβοι) τινὲς ἀμοιβαῖα, which suggests a division of that line.
74 Ἀμυνίας.] Satirized by Cratinus as a flatterer, braggart, and
informer. Schol. Cf. Nub. 686,
for a charge of cowardice against
him.

ΞΑΝΘΙΑΣ

οὐκ, ἀλλὰ φίλο μέν ἐστιν ἀρχὴ τοῦ κακοῦ.
ὁδὶ δέ φησι Σωσίας πρὸς Δερκύλον
εἶναι φιλοπότην αὐτόν.

ΣΩΣΙΑΣ

οὐδαμῶς γ᾽, ἐπεὶ
αὕτη γε χρηστῶν ἐστιν ἀνδρῶν ἡ νόσος   80

ΞΑΝΘΙΑΣ

Νικόστρατος δ᾽ αὖ φησιν ὁ Σκαμβωνίδης
εἶναι φιλοθύτην αὐτὸν ἢ φιλόξενον.

ΣΩΣΙΑΣ

μὰ τὸν κύν᾽, ὦ Νικόστρατ᾽, οὐ φιλόξενος,
ἐπεὶ καταπύγων ἐστὶν ὅ γε Φιλόξενος.

ΞΑΝΘΙΑΣ

ἄλλως φλυαρεῖτ᾽· οὐ γὰρ ἐξευρήσετε.   85
εἰ δὴ 'πιθυμεῖτ᾽ εἰδέναι, σιγᾶτε νῦν.
φράσω γὰρ ἤδη τὴν νόσον τοῦ δεσπότου.
φιληλιαστής ἐστιν ὡς οὐδεὶς ἀνήρ,
ἐρᾷ τε τούτου, τοῦ δικάζειν, καὶ στένει
ἢν μὴ 'πὶ τοῦ πρώτου καθίζηται ξύλου.   90
ὕπνου δ᾽ ὁρᾷ τῆς νυκτὸς οὐδὲ πασπάλην.

78 Σωσίας.] Some spectator is meant: Sosias was a common name. But our Sosias thinks with Demosthenes (cf. Eq. 85, &c.) that tippling is an honest man's failing; and perhaps means to defend himself as well as his namesake; as if of himself it were also implied that ἀφ᾽ αὐτοῦ τὴν ν. τ. Dercylus is another of the same habits.

81 φιλοθύτην.] This probably means 'superstitious,' too much given to sacrifices, omens, and the like. It recals Nicias' character. φιλόξενος is meant by Nicostratus as praise, and might follow rather naturally on φιλοθύτηι, sacrifices entailing feasts. But Sosias takes it of Philoxenus an effeminate rascal.

83 κύν᾽.] One of Socrates' oaths; and his favourite of the three (κύνα, χῆνα, πλάτανον); but perhaps there is not much reference to him here.

88 φιληλιαστής.] He coins a word beginning, as he said at v. 77, with φιλ. The Heliaea was Philocleon's favourite court. Cf. below, v. 772, and for details about the court see Dict. Ant.

90 τοῦ πρώτου ξύλου.] Cf. Ach. 25, ὡστιοῦνται...περὶ τοῦ πρώτου ξύλου. Schömann hence infers that there were wooden seats in the Pnyx, perhaps in the middle of it, though most were of stone. And that there would be benches for the Heliasts seems tolerably certain.

91 πασπάλην.] Analogous is

ἢν δ' οὖν καταμύσῃ κἂν ἄχνην, ὅμως ἐκεῖ
ὁ νοῦς πέτεται τὴν νύκτα περὶ τὴν κλεψύδραν.
ὑπὸ τοῦ δὲ τὴν ψῆφόν γ' ἔχειν εἰωθέναι
τοὺς τρεῖς ξυνέχων τῶν δακτύλων ἀνίσταται,   95
ὥσπερ λιβανωτὸν ἐπιτιθεὶς νουμηνίᾳ.
καὶ νὴ Δί' ἢν ἴδῃ γέ που γεγραμμένον
υἱὸν Πυριλάμπους ἐν θύρᾳ Δῆμον καλὸν,
ἰὼν παρέγραψε πλησίον "κημὸς καλός."
τὸν ἀλεκτρυόνα δ', ὃς ᾖδ' ἀφ' ἑσπέρας, ἔφη   100
ὄψ' ἐξεγείρειν αὐτὸν ἀναπεπεισμένον,
παρὰ τῶν ὑπευθύνων ἔχοντα χρήματα.
εὐθὺς δ' ἀπὸ δορπηστοῦ κέκραγεν ἐμβάδας,
κἄπειτ' ἐκεῖσ' ἐλθὼν προκαθεύδει πρῲ πάνυ,

the use of ἄχνη. κέγχραι Ἀλευρον Schol. and on ἄχνην the Scholiast refers to Hom. *Il.* ε. 499, ὡς δ' ἄνεμος ἄχνας φορέει ἱερὰς κατ' ἀλωάς. ἄχνη has other significations, but the idea of something fine and light is in all.

93 ὁ νοῦς κ.τ.λ.] So in *Nub.* 27, Phidippides dreams of horses.

95 τοὺς τρεῖς.] i.e. the thumb, forefinger, and middle-finger. Schol.

96 λ. ἐπιτιθεὶς.] Cf. *Ran.* 888, *Nub.* 426, οὐδ' ἐπιθείην λιβανωτόν.

98 υἱὸν Πυριλάμπους.] Demus son of Pyrilampes was a beautiful youth. Cf. Plat. *Gorg.* 482, λέγω δὲ ἐννοήσας ὅτι ἐγώ τε καὶ σὺ νῦν τυγχάνομεν ταυτόν τι πεπονθότες, ἐρῶντε δύο ὄντε δυοῖν ἑκάτερος· ἐγὼ μὲν Ἀλκιβιάδου τε τοῦ Κλεινίου καὶ φιλοσοφίας, σὺ δὲ δυοῖν, τοῦ τε Ἀθηναίων δήμου καὶ τοῦ Πυριλάμπους. In *Ach.* 143, this lovers' habit of writing up the name of a favourite is mentioned: καὶ θῆτα φιλαθήναιος ἦν ὑπερφυῶς, ὑμῶν τ' ἐραστὴς ἦν ἀληθῶς, ὥστε καὶ ἐν τοῖσι τοίχοις ἔγραφ' Ἀθηναῖοι καλοί.

99 κημός.] The point is in the rhyme. For the word cf. *Eq.* 1150.

100 ἀλεκτρυόνα κ.τ.λ.] Racine in *Les Plaideurs* has 'Il fit coucher la tête à son coq, de colère, pour

l'avoir éveillé plus tard qu'à l'ordinaire; Il disoit qu'un plaideur, dont l'affaire alloit mal, Avoit graissé la patte à ce pauvre animal.' And Plautus has something similar, *Aul.* 3. 4. 10, 'Obtrunco gallum furem manifestarium, Credo ego edepol illi mercedem gallo pollicitos coquos, Si id palam fecisset.'

ἀφ' ἑσπέρας.] So MS. *Rav.* acc. to Cobet, and it seems preferable to ἀφ' ἑσπ. ἀπὸ ἑσπ. ' from evening' = 'after evening, towards night-fall,' is a common phrase. This cock-crowing, though much earlier than the usual time, did not content the old man. ἐν ὑπερβολῇ τοῦτο. Schol. The time of cock-crowing (ἀλεκτοροφωνία) is sometimes put with tolerable definiteness for three o'clock in the morning: as in ὀψέ, ἢ μεσονυκτίου, ἢ ἀλεκτοροφωνίας, ἢ πρωΐ. St Mark xiii. 35. Here ἀφ' ἑσπέρας might perhaps mean about 9 p.m., which seemed late to Philocleon who was ready to start directly after his supper (v. 103). The Latin 'de' seems to answer to ὡρὸ in this use. Cf. Juv. xiv. 190, Media de nocte supinum clamosus juvenem pater excitat.

103 δορπηστοῦ.] So δειπνηστὸς from δεῖπνον Hom. *Odyss.* ρ. 120.

ὥσπερ λεπὰς προσεχόμενος τῷ κίονι.   105
ὑπὸ δυσκολίας δ᾽ ἅπασι τιμῶν τὴν μακρὰν
. ὥσπερ μέλιττ᾽ ἢ βομβυλιὸς εἰσέρχεται
ὑπὸ τοῖς ὄνυξι κηρὸν ἀναπεπλασμένος.
ψήφων δὲ δείσας μὴ δεηθείη ποτέ,
ἵν᾽ ἔχοι δικάζειν, αἰγιαλὸν ἔνδον τρέφει.   110
τοιαῦτ᾽ ἀλύει· νουθετούμενος δ᾽ ἀεὶ
μᾶλλον δικάζει. τοῦτον οὖν φυλάττομεν
μοχλοῖσιν ἐνδήσαντες, ὡς ἂν μὴ ᾽ξίῃ.
ὁ γὰρ υἱὸς αὐτοῦ τὴν νόσον βαρέως φέρει.
καὶ πρῶτα μὲν λόγοισι παραμυθούμενος   115
ἀνέπειθεν αὐτὸν μὴ φορεῖν τριβώνιον
μηδ᾽ ἐξιέναι θύραζ᾽· ὁ δ᾽ οὐκ ἐπείθετο.
εἶτ᾽ αὐτὸν ἀπέλου κἀκάθαιρ᾽, ὁ δ᾽ οὐ μάλα.
μετὰ ταῦτ᾽ ἐκορυβάντιζ᾽· ὁ δ᾽ αὐτῷ τυμπάνῳ
ᾁξας ἐδίκαζεν ἐς τὸ Καινὸν ἐμπεσών.   120

105 τῷ κίονι.] A pillar at the
entrance of the court probably, but
no other mention of it is noticed.
The comparison of a limpet sticking
to a rock is found also in *Plut.* 1096,
ὥσπερ λεπὰς τῷ μειρακίῳ προσίσχεται.
106 τὴν μακρὰν.] A long line
drawn on the tablet (τίνδειον, cf. v.
167) meant condemnation: a short
line acquittal. Schol.
107—108. By his constant habit
of drawing the long line he has got
his nails permanently stuffed with
wax.
110 ἔχοι.] ἔχῃ Bekk. and vulg.
ἔχοι R, V, Dind. Mein. &c. This
last, being better on critical grounds,
is certainly not to be objected to on
grounds of sense, the reference being to a past intention, though τρέφει
is pres. tense. And indeed δείσας
and μὴ δεηθείη make the opt. ἔχοι
quite natural. 'And, as he feared
he might be short of voting-pebbles
some day, that he might have where-
with to give his vote as dicast, he
keeps a whole beach of shingle in-

doors.'
113 ἐνδήσαντες.] Vulg. ἐγκλεί-
σαντες.
118 ἀπέλου.] Cf. *Nub.* 1044, λού-
σθαι. *Plut.* 657, ἐλοῦμεν.
ὁ δ᾽ οὐ μάλα.] 'But he would
none of this;' supply ἀνελούετο, or
ἐκαθαίρετο. The imperfect of the
active expresses here 'he was for
doing the washing or cleansing,' the
imperf. pass. with οὐ 'he was not
for having it done.'
119 ἐκορυβάντιζ᾽.] A course of
Corybantic orgies and phrenzy might
drive away his judicial madness.
120 Καινόν.] The Scholiast
names four courts, Παράβυστον, Καινόν, Τρίγωνον, Μέσον. Pausanias
mentions Παράβυστον and Τρίγωνον:
the first as being in an obscure part
of the town—perhaps it was a court-
house built on to the side of some
building or temple—the second as
named from its shape. Καινόν and
Μέσον, the 'New Court' and 'Cen-
tral Court,' are intelligible enough:
but of their exact site we know nothing.

ὅτε δῆτα ταύταις ταῖς τελεταῖς οὐκ ὠφέλει,
διέπλευσεν εἰς Αἴγιναν εἶτα ξυλλαβὼν
νύκτωρ κατέκλινεν αὐτὸν εἰς Ἀσκληπιοῦ·
ὁ δ' ἀνεφάνη κνεφαῖος ἐπὶ τῇ κιγκλίδι.
ἐντεῦθεν οὐκέτ' αὐτὸν ἐξεφρίομεν.   125
ὁ δ' ἐξεδίδρασκε διά τε τῶν ὑδορροῶν
καὶ τῶν ὁπῶν· ἡμεῖς δ' ὅσ' ἦν τετρημένα
ἐνεβύσαμεν ῥακίοισι κἀπακτώσαμεν·
ὁ δ' ὡσπερεὶ κολοιὸς αὑτῷ παττάλους
ἐνέκρουεν ἐς τὸν τοῖχον, εἶτ' ἐξήλλετο.   130
ἡμεῖς δὲ τὴν αὐλὴν ἅπασαν δικτύοις
καταπετάσαντες ἐν κύκλῳ φυλάττομεν.
ἔστιν δ' ὄνομα τῷ μὲν γέροντι Φιλοκλέων,
ναὶ μὰ Δία, τῷ δ' υἱεῖ γε τῳδὶ Βδελυκλέων,

---

123 Ἀσκληπιοῦ.] Cf. Plut. 411, κατακλίνειν αὐτὸν εἰς Ἀσκληπιοῦ πρώτιστόν ἐστι. Similar attempts at a cure are made in the Plutus (v. 655, &c.).

124 κνεφαῖοι.] Cf. Ran. 1350, ὅπως κνεφαῖοι εἰς ἀγορὰν φέρουσ' ἀπολοίμαν. The darkness of early morning is meant in both places. In Les Plaideurs (Act II. Sc. 1) L'Intimé tells Léandre that his disguise will not be penetrated for that 'Ile! lorsqu'à votre père ils vont faire leur cour, A peine seulement savez-vous s'il est jour.'

125 ἐξεφρίομεν.] Cf. v. 156, 892. A third compound from the same verb is διαφρίω, used in Av. 193, and (acc. to some texts) in Thuc. VII. 32.

126 ἐξεδίδρασκε...ἐξήλλετο.] Imperf. of attempts.

ὑδορροῶν.] κοῖλοι τόποι, δι' ὧν χωρεῖ τὸ ὕδωρ τὸ ἐξ ὑετῶν. Schol. and on Ach. 922, ὑδορροόα καλεῖται τὸ μέρος τῆς στεφανίδος δι' οὗ τὸ ἀπὸ τοῦ ὄμβρου ὕδωρ συναγόμενον κατέρχεται. Hence it is plain that they were waterpipes forming a regular part of the internal arrangement of the house. Of course it does not follow that they were really large enough to admit of a man's passage

through them: for there is an intended absurdity and exaggeration here. In Ach. 922 they may be the same as here (not 'canals' as L. and S. say), and the communication may be by them through the roofs of the ship-sheds (νεώσοικοι). But this will depend on the view taken of τίφη there. In Ach. 1186 an open channel seems meant, but that passage abounds in absurdities, and is by some editors rejected.

128 κἀπακτώσαμεν.] Cf. Soph. Aj. 579, καὶ δῶμα πάκτου. It is of making all fast by closing doors and the like; whereas ἐμβῦσαι is to 'stuff up,' of such holes and ends of pipes, channels, &c. as would usually be open, but now needed stoppers, to keep in the indefatigable dicast.

129 ὁ δ' ὡσπ. κολοιὸς κ.τ.λ] 'And he, jackdaw-like, was always knocking him pegs into the wall, and so trying to hop out.' Tame jackdaws used (says the Scholiast) to have perches put to hop on to. Of course they did not make their own perches, though Philocleon did.

133 Φιλοκλέων......Βδελυκλέων.] Cleon appears as the κηδίμων of the dicasts in v. 242, cf. v. 596, αὐτὸς δὲ Κλέων κ.τ.λ.

ἔχων τρόπους φρυαγμοσεμνάκους τινάς.   135

BΔEΛΤKΛEΩN

ὦ Ξανθία καὶ Σωσία, καθεύδετε;

ΞΑΝΘΙΑΣ

οἴμοι.

ΣΩΣΙΑΣ

τί ἔστι;

ΞΑΝΘΙΑΣ

Βδελυκλέων ἀνίσταται.

BΔEΛΤKΛEΩN

οὐ περιδραμεῖται σφῷν ταχέως δεῦρ' ἄτερος;
ὁ γὰρ πατὴρ ἐς τὸν ἱπνὸν εἰσελήλυθεν
καὶ μυσπολεῖ τι καταδεδυκώς. ἀλλ' ἄθρει,   140
κατὰ τῆς πυέλου τὸ τρῆμ' ὅπως μὴ 'κδύσεται·
σὺ δὲ τῇ θύρᾳ πρόσκεισο.

ΣΩΣΙΑΣ.

ταῦτ', ὦ δέσποτα.

135 φρυαγμοσεμνάκους.] Rendered by Florens Christianus 'capero-fronti-pervicos.' It is compounded of φρύαγμα and σεμνός. But φρυαγμοσεμμακουστίνους is one reading: and the Scholiast seems to think ὀφρύν part of the compound, which would require ὀφρυαγμ., but what the precise elements would then be, is not plain. Meineke (following Hamaker) puts this line after v. 110, αἴγ. ἔνδον τρέφει. ·. This avoids the awkward construction of the nom. ἔχων after υἱεῖ; and it is not plain how Bdelycleon's manners were 'haughty and pretentious,' which appears about the meaning of the word. If φρυαγμοσεμμακουστίνους be put of Philocleon as v. 111, the end of the word might come from ἀκούω and the meaning be 'having the temper of a proud stern listener,' who was sure to condemn the accused. 136—129. Philocleon makes several attempts to escape: through the outlet of the water from the bath; through the chimney; by holding

on under the donkey; by the roof. At last he is quiet; and the two slaves prepare to receive with stones his peppery fellow-dicasts, whom they expect to come and look for their leader.

137 Βδελυκλέων ἀνίσταται] Racine borrows a little of what follows for Sc. 2 and 3 of the first Act in Les Plaideurs: but with scarcely any of the fun or liveliness of his original.

139 ἱπνόν.] ἱπνὸς κυρίως ἡ κάμινος, νῦν δὲ τὸ μαγειρεῖον φησιν. Schol. And in v. 837 it seems certainly 'the kitchen.' Here L. and S. take it for the stove by which the bath was heated; and it may well be so, for v. 141 seems to require something of the sort.

140 μυσπολεῖ.] If (as L. and S. say) there be reference to μυστιπολεύω, we should render 'is at his mouse-tricks' for 'mysteries.'

141 τῆς πυέλου τὸ τρῆμ'.] A hole for letting out the hot water. Schol.

ΒΔΕΛΤΚΛΕΩΝ

ἄναξ Πόσειδον, τί ποτ' ἄρ' ἡ κάπνη ψοφεῖ;
οὗτος, τίς εἶ σύ;

ΦΙΛΟΚΛΕΩΝ

καπνὸς ἔγωγ' ἐξέρχομαι.

ΒΔΕΛΤΚΛΕΩΝ

καπνός; φέρ' ἴδω ξύλου τίνος σύ.

ΦΙΛΟΚΛΕΩΝ

συκίνου.   145

ΒΔΕΛΤΚΛΕΩΝ

νὴ τὸν Δί' ὅσπερ γ' ἐστὶ δριμύτατος καπνῶν.
ἀτάρ, οὐ γὰρ ἐρρήσεις γε, ποῦ 'σθ' ἡ τηλία;
δύου πάλιν· φέρ' ἐπαναθῶ σοι καὶ ξύλον.
ἐνταῦθά νυν ζήτει τιν' ἄλλην μηχανήν.
ἀτὰρ ἄθλιός γ' εἶμ' ὡς ἑτερός γ' οὐδεὶς ἀνήρ,   150
ὅστις πατρὸς νῦν Καπνίου κεκλήσομαι.

ΣΩΣΙΑΣ.

* * τὴν θύραν ὤθει· πίεζέ νυν σφόδρα,
εὖ κἀνδρικῶς· κἀγὼ γὰρ ἐνταῦθ' ἔρχομαι.

---

145 **συκίνου.**] With reference to συκοφάντη; but also κατσπουδὸ τὸ σύκινον ξύλον. Schol.

146 **δριμύτατος.**] This fact is (says the Scholiast) attested by Aristotle. But Philocleon is δριμὺς much as Demus was to be in *Eq.* 808, εἴθ' ἥξει σοι δριμὺς ἄγροικοι κατὰ σοῦ τὴν ψῆφον ἰχνεύων.

147 **οὐ γὰρ ἐρρήσεις.**] So Dindorf (in his notes), Hermann, and Meineke. Vulg. ἀσερρήσεις. MS. Rav. οὐκ ἐρρήσεις. Elmsl. οὐκέτ' ἐρρήσεις. The ἐι does not seem the preposition wanted, but rather ἐξ. Dindorf compares *Ach.* 487, ἀτάρ, φίλαι γάρ αἱ παρόντες,...τί ταῦτα τοὺς Λάκωνας αἰτιώμεθα; **τηλία.**] This seems a general word for any board. ταυτὶ βαθεῖα ἐν ᾗ ἄλφιτα ἐπίπρασκον. Schol.

Though used to stop the chimney it may be 'flour-tray, flour-board' here, rather than 'chimney-board:' the flour-board being taken as the nearest thing at hand to clap upon the top of the chimney. Then a log was to be put on this to weigh it down and make matters more safe.

151 **Καπνίου.**] κατσίας was a kind of wine, but the reference to this (if there be any) has not much point. Nor is it plain what pre-eminent wretchedness there was in being the son of a 'smoky' father.

152 **τὴν θ. ὤθει.**] Vulg. ταῖ, τὴν. MSS. R, V, have nothing before τὴν θ. Meineke reads ὅδε τὴν θ. ὤθει. Hirschig gives this line and what follows to Sosias: so does Richter, with σὺ δὲ to fill the gap.

καὶ τῆς κατακλεῖδος ἐπιμελοῦ καὶ τοῦ μοχλοῦ
φύλαττέ θ' ὅπως μὴ τὴν βάλανον ἐκτρώξεται.   155

ΦΙΛΟΚΛΕΩΝ

τί δράσετ'; οὐκ ἐκφρήσετ', ὦ μιαρώτατοι,
δικάσοντά μ', ἀλλ' ἐκφεύξεται Δρακοντίδης;

ΒΔΕΛΤΚΛΕΩΝ

σὺ δὲ τοῦτο βαρέως ἂν φέροις;

ΦΙΛΟΚΛΕΩΝ

         ὁ γὰρ θεὸς
μαντευομένῳ μοὔχρησεν ἐν Δελφοῖς ποτέ,
ὅταν τις ἐκφύγῃ μ', ἀποσκλῆναι τότε.   160

ΒΔΕΛΤΚΛΕΩΝ

Ἄπολλον ἀποτρόπαιε, τοῦ μαντεύματος.

ΦΙΛΟΚΛΕΩΝ

ἴθ, ἀντιβολῶ σ', ἔκφρες με, μὴ διαρραγῶ.

ΒΔΕΛΤΚΛΕΩΝ

μὰ τὸν Ποσειδῶ, Φιλοκλέων, οὐδέποτέ γε.

ΦΙΛΟΚΛΕΩΝ

διατρώξομαι τοίνυν ὀδὰξ τὸ δίκτυον.

ΒΔΕΛΤΚΛΕΩΝ

ἀλλ' οὐκ ἔχεις ὀδόντας.

154 κατακλεῖδος.] The exact
nature of this part of the fastening
does not appear. The μοχλὸς and
βάλανος we often meet with, e.g. in
Thuc. II. 4, a passage which well
illustrates the construction and fastening of doors in ancient time.
Richter interprets κατακλεῖς to mean
the whole apparatus of fastening:
but it looks more like a part; perhaps it is the hole into which the
βάλανος went.

155 φύλαττέ θ' ὅπως.] Nothing
seems gained by the change φύλατθ'
ὅπως, which, as Dindorf has it,
wants a conjunction. Meineke
punctuates μοχλοῦ φύλαθ' ὅπως
κ.τ.λ.: but, though the βάλανος cer-

tainly did go through the μοχλὸς
into its socket, there seems no need
to change the common text, by
which, as Richter notes, the brief
and hurried orders of the slave seem
better given.

160 ἀποσκλῆναι.] The ἂν which
Meineke adds seems unnecessary.
The infinitive follows χρῆσαι in such
sentences as ἔχρησα πέμψαι (Aesch.
Eum. 203); and, though this may
be rather a telling of 'what shall
be' than an ordaining of a thing 'to
be,' an oracle is always a sort of
decree or command.

161 Ἄπολλον κ.τ.λ.] Cf. Av. 61,
Ἄπολλον ἀποτρόπαιε,τοῦχασμήματος.
164 τὸ δίκτυον.] Cf. v. 131.

26 ΑΡΙΣΤΟΦΑΝΟΥΣ [165

ΦΙΛΟΚΛΕΩΝ

οἴμοι δείλαιος·   165
πῶς ἄν σ' ἀποκτείναιμι; πῶς; δότε μοι ξίφος
ὅπως τάχιστ', ἢ πινάκιον τιμητικόν.

ΒΔΕΛΤΚΛΕΩΝ

ἄνθρωπος οὗτος μέγα τι δρασείει κακόν.

ΦΙΛΟΚΛΕΩΝ

μὰ τὸν Δί' οὐ δῆτ', ἀλλ' ἀποδόσθαι βούλομαι
τὸν ὄνον ἄγων αὐτοῖσι τοῖς κανθηλίοις·   170
νουμηνία γάρ ἐστιν.

ΒΔΕΛΤΚΛΕΩΝ

οὐκοῦν κἂν ἐγὼ
αὐτὸν ἀποδοίμην δῆτ' ἄν;

ΦΙΛΟΚΛΕΩΝ

οὐχ ὥσπερ γ' ἐγω.

ΒΔΕΛΤΚΛΕΩΝ

μὰ Δί', ἀλλ' ἄμεινον. ἀλλὰ τὸν ὄνον ἔξαγε.

ΞΑΝΘΙΑΣ

οἵαν πρόφασιν καθῆκεν, ὡς εἰρωνικῶς,
ἵν' αὐτὸν ἐκπέμψειας.

167 πινάκιον τιμητικόν.] On which to draw the long line: cf. v. 106. It occurs to the old dicast as his own peculiar and most deadly weapon.

170 αὐτοῖσι τοῖς κανθηλίοις.] Of such phrases Elmsley has collected instances in his note on Eur. Med. 160. The preposition ξὺν is rarely added. The explanation of the phrase seems to be this: ἡ ναῦς διεφθάρη αὐτοῖς ἀνδράσι, 'the ship was lost with the men themselves, with the very men, with even the men,' and, as they would be the last things to be lost if any escape were possible, everything else belonging to the ship was necessarily lost. Hence αὐτοῖς ἀνδράσιν = 'men and all.'

171 νουμηνία.] On which day

there would be a fair. Demus bought the Paphlagonian slave on this day (Eq. 43). Dr Primrose (in The Vicar of Wakefield) sent his son Moses to sell the horse at a neighbouring fair: and Philocleon pretends in v. 172 to distrust his son's powers at a bargain, fearing a result like that in Goldsmith's story. κἂν...ἄν.] Cf. note on Nub. 783 for the repetition of ἄν.

174 καθῆκεν.] This word suggests Bdelycleon's answer, for καθιέναι ἄγκιστρον is an angling term: cf. Theocr. Id. XXI. 42, ἰδάκινον ἰχθύας, ἐκ καλάμων δὲ πλάνον κατέσειον ἐδωδάν. Similar is the use κατεῖναι κάλων, κατιεμένην καταπειρητηρίην, of a sounding line. Herod. II. 28.

ΒΔΕΛΤΚΛΕΩΝ

ἀλλ' οὐκ ἔσπασεν   175
ταύτῃ γ'· ἐγὼ γὰρ ᾐσθόμην τεχνωμένου.
ἀλλ' εἰσιών μοι τὸν ὄνον ἐξάγειν δοκῶ,
ὅπως ἂν ὁ γέρων μηδὲ παρακύψῃ πάλιν.
κάνθων, τί κλάεις; ὅτι πεπράσει τήμερον;
βάδιζε θᾶττον. τί στένεις, εἰ μὴ φέρεις   180
'Οδυσσέα τιν';

ΞΑΝΘΙΑΣ

ἀλλα ναὶ μὰ Δία φέρει
κάτω γε τουτονί τιν' ὑποδεδυκότα.

ΒΔΕΛΤΚΛΕΩΝ

ποῖον; φέρ' ἴδωμαι.

ΞΑΝΘΙΑΣ

τουτονί.

175—6 οὐκ ἔσπασεν ταύτῃ γ'.] 'He caught nothing with this line.' Cf. *Thesm.* 928, αὐτῇ μὲν ἢ μήρυθοι οὐδὲν ἔσπασεν. In Euripides (*Elatr.* 582) ἦν δ' ἐασπάσωμαί γ' ὃν μετέρχομαι βόλον is of net-fishing. Such metaphors are frequent in Greek. There is no sufficient reason for changing ταύτῃ to αὐτῇ. Aristophanes was not bound to quote the proverb with exactly the same words.

177 ἐξάγειν δοκῶ.] Elmsley would read ἐξάξειν; Meineke adopts from Cobet, ἐξαγ' ἔνδοθεν. No change is needed. Cf. Aesch. *Agam.* 16, ὅταν δ' ἀείδειν ἢ μινύρεσθαι δοκῶ; also Plat. *Prot.* 340, δοκῶ παρακαλεῖν; in illustration of which Wayte has quoted several other passages for δοκῶ, 'I am minded,' followed by infinitive of present and aorist.

178 παρακύψῃ.] Cf. *Pac.* 982, *Thesm.* 797, *Ach.* 16. To these Aristophanic passages may be added from the Septuagint, Prov. vii. 6, ἀπὸ γὰρ θυρίδος ἐκ τοῦ οἴκου αὐτῆς εἰς τὰς πλατείας παρακύπτουσα, κ.τ.λ.

Cant. ii. 9, παρακύπτων διὰ τῶν θυρίδων. Not very different is 2 Kings ix. 30, 'Ιεζάβελ ἐστιμμίσατο τοὺς ὀφθαλμοὺς αὐτῆς, καὶ ἠγάθυνε τὴν κεφαλὴν αὐτῆι, καὶ διέκυψε διὰ τῆς θυρίδος. In this passage Bdelycleon says that the old man will have no excuse (when the ass is brought out) for peeping out again. He had evidently been peeping out of a window through the netting (v. 164). It is probable that in *Ach.* 16 παρέκυψεν is of the sly peeping of Chaeris before entrance; not of any stooping posture afterwards, as the Scholiast takes it.

179 κάνθων, τί κλάεις.] So Polyphemus asks his ram, why, contrary to his wont, he is so slow? This whole scene is a comic parody on Ulysses' escape beneath the ram's belly, and his assumption of the name Οὔτις (*Odyss.* ix. 425, &c.).

183 ἴδωμαι.] Hirschig, to avoid the use of the middle ἴδωμαι in iambic dialogue, reads ἴδω Ζ. ναὶ τουτωι. But ναὶ seems weak. Richter has ἴδωμεν with τουτωι, given to

ΒΔΕΛΤΚΛΕΩΝ

τουτὶ τί ἦν;

τίς εἶ ποτ', ὦνθρωπ', ἐτεόν;

ΦΙΛΟΚΛΕΩΝ

Οὖτις νὴ Δία.

ΒΔΕΛΤΚΛΕΩΝ

Οὖτις σύ; ποδαπός;

ΦΙΛΟΚΛΕΩΝ

Ἴθακος Ἀποδρασιππίδου.   185

ΒΔΕΛΤΚΛΕΩΝ

Οὖτις μὰ τὸν Δί' οὔ τι χαιρήσων γε σύ.
ὕφελκε θᾶττον αὐτόν. ὢ μιαρώτατος,
ἵν' ὑποδέδυκεν ὥστ' ἔμοιγ' ἰνδάλλεται
ὁμοιότατος κλητῆρος εἶναι πωλίῳ.

ΦΙΛΟΚΛΕΩΝ

εἰ μή μ' ἐάσεθ' ἥσυχον, μαχούμεθα.   190

Xanthias. Meineke follows Hirschig, but gives the whole line to
Bdelycleon.

185 Ἴθακος Ἀποδρασιππίδου.]
Of Ithaca, because Ulysses was so;
but perhaps there may be some idea
of a derivation from Ἴθι. Ἀποδρ.
a name coined from ἀποδρᾶναι; cf.
διαδρασιπολῖτος, Ran. 1014. Imita-
ting Bunyan's coinage of names we
might represent these significant
Greek titles by ' Mr Nobody, from
the land of Go, son of Mr Ready-
to-run.'

186 οὖτις...σύ τι.] He plays on the
words; cf. Hom. Odyss. ι. 408, ᾦ
φίλοι οὖτίς με κτείνει δόλῳ, to which
his comrades answer, εἰ μὲν δὴ μήτις
σε βιάζεται...νοῦσόν γ' οὔτως ἔστι
Διὸς μεγάλου ἀλέασθαι.

188 ἵν' ὑποδέδυκεν.] Ἵνα is best
taken not as an exclamation, but
rather in close connexion with μιαρώτατος, 'abominable wretch, in
having crept under there!' This use
of relatives and relative particles is
common in Greek. Cf. Nub. v.
1157, θ, οὐδὲν ἐργάσαισθ'...οἷσι ἐμοὶ
τρίφεται υἱόs, and 1206—θ, μάκαρ...
αὐτὸν ἐφὺς ὡς σοφὸs χοῖον τὸν υἱὸν
τρέφεις. But though, in strictness
of construction, οἷσι, ὡς, &c. are relative, we turn them by a separate
definite clause in English; e.g. Plat.
Theaet. 161, τὸ δὲ δὴ ἐμόν τε καὶ
τῆ ἐμῆ τέχνη σιγῶ ὅσον γέλωτα
ὀφλισκάνομεν, 'but of myself and
my art I say nothing, such utter
ridicule do we incur.' Cf. note on
Nub. 394.

189 κλητῆρος πωλίῳ.] His position suggests that he is a ' sucking
foal:' his litigious tastes that he is
the foal of a κλητήρ. But κλητῆρος
comes in oddly. Is it a comic substitution for ὄνθωνος? It answers
to it in quantity and in the initial
consonant, and that appears to be
about what Aristophanes requires
when putting one word παρὰ προσδο-
κίαν for another.

ΒΔΕΛΤΚΛΕΩΝ

περὶ τοῦ μαχεῖ νῷν δῆτα;

ΦΙΛΟΚΛΕΩΝ

περὶ ὄνου σκιᾶς.

ΒΔΕΛΤΚΛΕΩΝ

πονηρὸς εἶ πόρρω τέχνης καὶ παράβολος.

ΦΙΛΟΚΛΕΩΝ

ἐγὼ πονηρός; οὐ μὰ Δί᾽, ἀλλ᾽ οὐκ οἶσθα σὺ
νῦν μ᾽ ὄντ᾽ ἄριστον ἀλλ᾽ ἴσως, ὅταν φάγῃς
ὑπογάστριον γέροντος ἡλιαστικοῦ.   195

ΒΔΕΛΤΚΛΕΩΝ

ὤθει τὸν ὄνον καὶ σαυτὸν ἐς τὴν οἰκίαν.

ΦΙΛΟΚΛΕΩΝ

ὦ ξυνδικασταὶ καὶ Κλέων, ἀμύνατε.

ΒΔΕΛΤΚΛΕΩΝ

ἔνδον κέκραχθι τῆς θύρας κεκλεισμένης.
ὤθει σὺ πολλοὺς τῶν λίθων πρὸς τὴν θύραν,
καὶ τὴν βάλανον ἔμβαλλε πάλιν ἐς τὸν μοχλόν,   200

191 **περὶ ὄνου σκιᾶς.**] Of this proverb for 'a mere nothing' the Scholiast gives as origin a tale of a man who, having hired an ass to carry his goods, was for shading himself behind the animal at noonday. To this the owner of the ass objected, saying that he had let out the ass, but not its shadow. The cause was brought into court. And, in after times, Demosthenes is said to have used the story to shame his audience into attention.

191 **πόρρω τέχνης.**] 'Far advanced in craftiness,' very sly. This suits far better with Bdelycleon's tricks and attempts to escape, than 'without art,' as some unaccountably render it.

193—5. Philocleon replies that he is not πονηρὸς, but ἄριστος to the taste; and that, when they come to taste and know him, they will find

him so. He is ὑπογάστριον because of his position. The ass that suckles him, which above was ἐλητήρ, is now γέρων Ἡλιαστικός. The Athenians ἐχρῶντο τοῖς ὀνείοις, says the Scholiast. Indeed from *Eq.* 1399, τὰ κύπεια μιγνὺς τοῖς ὀνείοις πράγμασιν, we might infer that they ate such food; but then Cleon's sausages were probably not to be of the first order. However, granting that they ate both dog and donkey, the wit of this passage will still sound rather flat to English ears.

197 **ὦ ξυνδικασταί, κ.τ.λ.**] So Cleon calls the heliasts to his aid in *Eq.* 255.

198 **κέκραχθι.**] Cf. *Ach.* 335, ὡς ἀποκτενῶ εἴραχθι.

199. Here he turns to the servant with orders to make all fast.

200 **βάλανον...ἐς τὸν μοχλόν.**]

καὶ τῇ δοκῷ προσθεὶς τὸν ὅλμον τὸν μέγαν
ἀνύσας τι προσκύλιέ γ'.

ΣΩΣΙΑΣ

οἴμοι δείλαιος·
πόθεν ποτ' ἐμπέπτωκέ μοι τὸ βώλιον;

ΞΑΝΘΙΑΣ

ἴσως ἄνωθεν μῦς ἐνέβαλέ σοί ποθεν.

ΣΩΣΙΑΣ

μῦς; οὐ μὰ Δί', ἀλλ' ὑποδυόμενός τις οὑτοσὶ   205
ὑπὸ τῶν κεραμίδων ἡλιαστὴς ὀροφίας.

ΞΑΝΘΙΑΣ

οἴμοι κακοδαίμων, στρουθὸς ἀνὴρ γίγνεται·
ἐκπτήσεται. ποῦ ποῦ 'στί μοι τὸ δίκτυον;
σοῦ σοῦ, πάλιν σοῦ.

ΒΔΕΛΥΚΛΕΩΝ

νὴ Δί' ἦ μοι κρεῖττον ἦν
τηρεῖν Σκιώνην ἀντὶ τούτου τοῦ πατρός.   210

ΣΩΣΙΑΣ

ἄγε νυν, ἐπειδὴ τουτονὶ σεσοβήκαμεν,
κοὐκ ἔσθ' ὅπως διαδὺς ἂν ἡμᾶς ἔτι λάθοι,
τί οὐκ ἀπεκοιμήθημεν ὅσον ὅσον στίλην;

Cf. v. 154. The βάλανος went through the μοχλός, and into a socket behind it; and this verse partly justifies, and certainly explains, Meineke's punctuation at v. 154.

201 δοκῷ.] This beam was plainly distinct from the μοχλός, or ordinary bar. It was probably a large wooden beam put across the whole door, only perhaps to be used when the house was to be permanently shut up, or barricaded, as here.

202—210. This dialogue Meineke makes between Xanthias and Bdelycleon to v. 206, giving 207—210 to Bdelycleon.

206 ὀροφίας.] λέγονται μῦς ὀροφίαι καὶ ὄφεις οἱ περὶ τὰς ὀροφὰς διάγοντες καὶ ταύτας περιτρώγοντες. A mouse is rather thought of here than a snake; cf. v. 140: but in India and hot climates a snake dropping from the roof would be natural enough.

209 σοῦ σοῦ.] From the Scholiast's ἀποσοβοῦσι τὸν γέροντα ὡς στρουθὸν we may conclude that this word σοῦ was in use merely as an exclamation to scare away birds.

210 Σκιώνην.] Cf. Thuc. IV. 120. Scione had revolted to Brasidas in the year before this play was exhibited.

213 ἀπεκοιμήθημεν.] 'Why don't we at once sleep?' Cf. Plat. Prot. 310, τί οὖν οὐ διηγήσω ἡμῖν τὴν

ΒΔΕΛΤΚΛΕΩΝ

ἀλλ', ὦ πονήρ', ἥξουσιν ὀλίγον ὕστερον
οἱ ξυνδικασταὶ παρακαλοῦντες τουτονὶ   215
τὸν πατέρα.

ΣΩΣΙΑΣ

τί λέγεις; ἀλλὰ νῦν ὄρθρος βαθύς.

ΒΔΕΛΤΚΛΕΩΝ

νὴ τὸν Δΐ, ὀψὲ γάρ' ἀνεστήκασι νῦν.
ὡς ἀπὸ μέσων νυκτῶν γε παρακαλοῦσ' ἀεί,
λύχνους ἔχοντες καὶ μινυρίζοντες μέλη
ἀρχαιομελησιδωνοφρυνιχήρατα,   220
οἷς ἐκκαλοῦνται τοῦτον.

ΣΩΣΙΑΣ

οὐκοῦν, ἢν δέῃ,
ἤδη ποτ' αὐτοὺς τοῖς λίθοις βαλλήσομεν.

ΒΔΕΛΤΚΛΕΩΝ

ἀλλ', ὦ πονηρὲ, τὸ γένος ἤν τις ὀργίσῃ
τὸ τῶν γερόντων, ἔσθ' ὅμοιον σφηκιᾷ.
ἔχουσι γὰρ καὶ κέντρον ἐκ τῆς ὀσφύος   225
ὀξύτατον, ᾧ κεντοῦσι, καὶ κεκραγότες
πηδῶσι καὶ βάλλουσιν ὥσπερ φέψαλοι.

ξυνωσίαν; and Soph. Oed. Tyr.
1003, τί δῆτ' ἔγωγ' οὐ τοῦδε τοῦ
φόβου σ', ἄναξ, ἐπείπερ εὕρων ἦλθον,
ἐξελυσάμην; To these instances
Wayte, in his note on the passage
first quoted, adds several.
ὅσον ὅσον.] Cf. Nub. 1288, πλέον
πλέον.
217 γάρ' ἀνεστήκασι νῦν.] The
MSS. have γάρ...νῦν: Porson γ' ἀρ'
...νῦν; Meineke νῦν...γάρ, which
gives a late position to γάρ. The
meaning is that ὄρθρος βαθὺς is not
too early for them, nay, that they
are rather late this time; since
generally they come soon after mid-
night, in the small hours.
220 ἀρχαιομελησ.] Whether μέλοι or μέλι be the second element in
this compound is rather doubtful.

If μέλι, as the Scholiast and Ari-
starchus say, then Meineke's ἀρχαιο-
μελισιδ. is to be preferred. But
Dindorf quotes from Av. 750, ἔνθεν,
ὥσπερεὶ μέλιττα, Φρύνιχος ἀμβροσίων
μελέων ἀπεβόσκετο καρπὸν ἀεὶ φέρων
γλυκεῖαν ᾠδάν. Phrynichus wrote
a play named the Phoenissae, in
which Sidonians were frequently
mentioned. Songs from this play
are meant here.
225 κέντρον.] Bergler quotes from
Phrynichus, the comic poet, ἔστιν δ'
αὐτοὺς τὸ φυλάττεσθαι τῶν νῦν χαλε-
πώτατον ἔργον· ἔχουσι γάρ τι κέντρον
ἐν τοῖς δακτύλοις.
227 φέψαλοι.] So the chorus of
old Acharnians (Ach. 666) invoke
their muse to come fiery and spark-
ling like φέψαλοι.

ΣΩΣΙΑΣ

μὴ φροντίσῃς· ἐὰν ἐγὼ λίθους ἔχω,
πολλῶν δικαστῶν σφηκιὰν διασκεδῶ.

ΧΟΡΟΣ

χώρει, πρόβαιν' ἐρρωμένως. ὦ Κωμία, βραδύνεις;   230
μὰ τὸν Δί', οὐ μέντοι πρὸ τοῦ γ', ἀλλ' ἦσθ' ἱμὰς κύνειος·
νυνὶ δὲ κρείττων ἐστὶ σοῦ Χαρινάδης βαδίζειν.
ὦ Στρυμόδωρε Κονθυλεῦ, βέλτιστε συνδικαστῶν,
Εὐεργίδης ἆρ' ἐστί που 'νταῦθ', ἢ Χάβης ὁ Φλυεύς;
πάρεσθ', ὃ δὴ λοιπόν γ' ἔτ' ἐστὶν, ἀππαπαῖ παπαιάξ,   235
ἥβης ἐκείνης, ἡνίκ' ἐν Βυζαντίῳ ξυνῆμεν
ῤρουροῦντ' ἐγώ τε καὶ σύ· κᾆτα περιπατοῦντε νύκτωρ
τῆς ἀρτοπώλιδος λαθόντ' ἐκλέψαμεν τὸν ὅλμον,
κᾆθ' ἥψομεν τοῦ κορκόρου, κατασχίσαντες αὐτόν.

228 ἐὰν ἐγώ.] Dindorf has plainly
shewn, In a note on this line, that
the second syllable of ἐὰν is long,
and that the Insertion of γε has
been owing to copyists' ignorance
of this. Cf. v. 1231 of this play
for one of the many examples.

230—315. The Chorus now en-
ter: they are old men, attired in
some way to resemble wasps, perhaps in the colour of their dress,
but certainly in their stings. They
stir each other up, recount their
youthful exploits, and look forward
to condemning any who are brought
before them. Some boys bearing
torches attend them, and they carefully pick their way to Strepsiades'
house. Surprised at his non-appear-
ance, they halt, and try to rouse him
with their song ; imagining possible
causes for his delay, reminding him
of his severity, and calling him to
share in the spoil of a rich man who
is to be condemned. A short dispute follows between the old men
and their young link-bearers, who
threaten to strike work if they do
not get figs, but soon find that they
may be thankful if they get even
their breakfast.

231 ἱμὰς κύνειος.] Whether this
be 'a thong of dogskin,' or (as
Dindorf and Schneider prefer) 'a
thong with which dogs are fastened,'
or 'a dog whip,' as some think, it
is any way meant as a proverb for
toughness. Cf. ἱμάντας ἐκ Δειρῶν
(Ach. 724).

232 Χαρινάδης.] One of the
name is mentioned in Pac. 1155 ;
but hardly one of the same character, as he is there a rather jovial
countryman invited to feast and
make merry.

233 Στρυμόδωρε.] Cf. Ach. 272,
Lys. 259. Conthyla was an Attic
deme.

235—9. As in Ach. 210, &c. the
old men recal the deeds of their
youth.

236 ἐν Βυζαντίῳ.] Forty-seven
years before: cf. Thuc. 1. 94.

239 κορκόρου.] Genitive of part :
'some of the pimpernel.' But it is
the ordinary case to use of eatables
and drinkables. So the French
almost always use 'du, de la' in
like phrases.

αὐτόν.] Sc. τὸν ὅλμον. They were
short of wood; so stole and broke
up a wooden mortar. Others, not

ἀλλ᾽ ἐγκονῶμεν, ὦνδρες, ὡς ἔσται Λάχητι νυνί·		240
σίμβλον δέ φασι χρημάτων ἔχειν ἅπαντες αὐτόν.
χθὲς οὖν Κλέων ὁ κηδεμὼν ἡμῖν ἐφεῖτ᾽ ἐν ὥρᾳ
ἥκειν ἔχοντας ἡμερῶν ὀργὴν τριῶν πονηρὰν
ἐπ᾽ αὐτὸν, ὡς κολωμένους ὧν ἠδίκησεν. ἀλλὰ
σπεύδωμεν, ὦνδρες ἥλικες, πρὶν ἡμέραν γενέσθαι.		245
χωρῶμεν, ἅμα τε τῷ λύχνῳ πάντη διασκοπῶμεν,
μή που λίθος τις ἐμποδὼν ἡμᾶς κακόν τι δράσῃ.

ΠΑΙΣ

τὸν πηλὸν, ὦ πάτερ πάτερ, τουτονὶ φύλαξαι.

ΧΟΡΟΣ

κάρφος χαμᾶθέν νυν λαβὼν τὸν λύχνον πρόβυσον.

ΠΑΙΣ

οὐκ, ἀλλὰ τῳδί μοι δοκῶ τὸν λύχνον προβύσειν.		250

ΧΟΡΟΣ

τί δὴ μαθὼν τῷ δακτύλῳ τὴν θρυαλλίδ᾽ ὠθεῖς,
καὶ ταῦτα τοὐλαίου σπανίζοντος, ὠνόητε;

so well, take αὐτὸν to be of the
κόρκοροι. But αὐτὸν would not have
been expressed at all if that had
been the meaning; ἤψομεν τοῦ κ.
κατασχίσαντες, 'we split up and
boiled the pimpernel,' would have
been sufficient.
240 ἔσται Δάχητι.] ἡ δίκη ἡ τι-
μωρία ἢ τοιοῦτόν τι. Schol.
241 σίμβλον.] Cf. the use of
βλίττειν in Eq. 794. Laches had
stored up his plunderings like a bee.
His peculations in Sicily are further
alluded to in v. 895, &c., where the
dog Labes is tried.
243 ἡμ. τριῶν.] A military provision was στί᾽ ἡμερῶν τριῶν. Cf.
Pac. 312, Eq. 1079. In Racine's
play (Act I. Sc. 4) Dandin, when
going out, says, 'Je ne veux de trois
mois rentrer dans la maison. De
sacs et de procès j'ai fait provision.'
244 κολωμένους.] Cf. Eq. 456,
χώσω κολᾷ τὸν ἄνδρα. The middle
form of the future is the true Attic

form.
247 λίθος.] Better than vulg.
λαθών: they are looking well to
their footsteps, and avoiding mud
and stones, in the dark morning.
And λίθοι is in MS. V.
248. The boys are beside the
regular chorus. Dindorf thinks
there were perhaps six. They are
sent to bear a message to Cleon at
v. 408.
248—272. Of these lines the
copyists ingeniously made tetrameter
iambics, by insertions here and there
of σύ, γε, νῦν, τι, που, δὴ, δδ᾽, ἐξ.
The lines are called, 'versus asyn-
arteti:' each is composed of a dimeter iambic and a dimeter trochaic
cataleclic.
251 μαθών.] 'Urit me prurĭtus
emendandi, et nescio quo modo
malim hic legere τί δὴ ταθών, non
μαθών.' Florens Chr. The same
complaint takes Meincke, wherever
the phrase τί μαθών occurs.

οὐ γὰρ δάκνει σ', ὅταν δέῃ τίμιον πρίασθαι.

ΠΑΙΣ

εἰ νὴ Δί' αὖθις κονδύλοις νουθετήσεθ' ἡμᾶς,
ἀποσβέσαντες τοὺς λύχνους ἄπιμεν οἴκαδ' αὐτοί·   255
κἄπειτ' ἴσως ἐν τῷ σκότῳ τουτουὶ στερηθεὶς
τὸν πηλὸν ὥσπερ ἀτταγᾶς τυρβάσεις βαδίζων.

ΧΟΡΟΣ

ἦ μὴν ἐγὼ σοῦ χἀτέρους μείζονας κολάζω.
ἀλλ' οὑτοσί μοι βόρβορος φαίνεται πατοῦντι·
κοὐκ ἔσθ' ὅπως οὐχ ἡμερῶν τεττάρων τὸ πλεῖστον   260
ὕδωρ ἀναγκαίως ἔχει τὸν θεὸν ποιῆσαι.
ἔπεισι γοῦν τοῖσιν λύχνοις οὑτοιὶ μύκητες·
φιλεῖ δ', ὅταν τοῦτ' ᾖ, ποιεῖν ὑετὸν μάλιστα.
δεῖται δὲ καὶ τῶν καρπίμων ἄττα μή 'στι πρῷα
ὕδωρ γενέσθαι κἀπιπνεῦσαι βόρειον αὐτοῖς.   265
τί χρῆμ' ἄρ' οὐκ τῆς οἰκίας τῆσδε συνδικαστὴς

253 δάκνει σ'.] For σὲ elided, even when emphatic, cf. *Νυβ.* 916, and the note there. And Soph. *Oed.Tyr.* 329, ἐγὼ δ' οὐ μήποτε τἀμ' ὡς ἂν εἴπω μὴ τὰ σ' ἐκφήνω κακά is an analogous elision, for the possessive σὰ must there have some stress laid on it, as opposed to τἀμά. There is a similar complaint of wastefulness in oil in *Νυβ.* 56—9, where the old men enforce their reproof with blows.

254 κονδ. κ.] Cf. *Eq.* 1236, κονδύλοις ἡρμοττόμην.

257. When the light is gone, the old men will flounder about in the mud like sand-pipers. For ἀτταγᾶς cf. note on *Ach.* 875.

259 βόρβορος.] Meineke takes μάρμαρος from Hermann. MS. Ven. has βάρβαρος. Hermann argues that 'as the old man says there must be rain within four days at most, it is hard and dry ground that he ought to be complaining of.' But then what force have πηλὸς and ἀτταγᾶς above? And μάρμαρος is an uncommon word to admit on

conjecture for 'stony ground, &c.' It seems better to take vv. 261, 262 of past rain, and then τὸ πλεῖστον must be taken with ὕδωρ. The prophecy of rain 'within four days at most' from the signs of the lamp-wicks would be curious. The old men's talk will run about thus: 'You talk of mud: why here is mud beneath my feet—enough to shew that heaven has been raining its hardest for four days—and then look too at the lamp-wicks: they have fungi on them: that shews rain is about; and we shall have some more.' Their first inferring from the mud how much rain there has been, and then passing on to the consideration of rain to come, may be a little rambling, but is not out of character with old men.

262 μύκητες.] Cf. Virg. *Georg.* I. 391, testa cum ardente viderent Scintillare oleum et putres concrescere fungos.

264 δεῖται δὲ, κ.τ.λ.] And this rain (they go on to say) is wanted for the later fruits.

πέπονθεν, ὡς οὐ φαίνεται δεῦρο πρὸς τὸ πλῆθος;
οὐ μὴν πρὸ τοῦ γ' ἐφολκὸς ἦν, ἀλλὰ πρῶτος ἡμῶν
ἡγεῖτ' ἂν ᾄδων Φρυνίχου· καὶ γάρ ἐστιν ἀνὴρ
φιλῳδός. ἀλλά μοι δοκεῖ στάντας ἐνθάδ', ὦνδρες,	270
ᾄδοντας αὐτὸν ἐκκαλεῖν, ἤν τί πως ἀκούσας
τοὐμοῦ μέλους ὑφ' ἡδονῆς ἑρπύσῃ θύραζε.
τί ποτ' οὐ πρὸ θυρῶν φαίνετ' ἄρ' ἡμῖν ὁ γέρων οὐδ' ὑπα-
κούει;
μῶν ἀπολώλεκεν τὰς
ἐμβάδας, ἢ προσέκοψ' ἐν	275
τῷ σκότῳ τὸν δάκτυλόν που,
εἶτ' ἐφλέγμηνεν αὐτοῦ
τὸ σφυρὸν γέροντος ὄντος;
καὶ τάχ' ἂν βουβωνιῴη.
ἦ μὴν πολὺ δριμύτατός γ' ἦν τῶν παρ' ἡμῖν,
καὶ μόνος οὐκ ἂν ἐπείθετ',
ἀλλ' ὁπότ' ἀντιβολοίη
τις, κάτω κύπτων ἂν οὕτω,
λίθον ἕψεις, ἔλεγεν.	280
τάχα δ' ἂν διὰ τὸν χθιζινὸν ἄνθρωπον, ὃς ἡμᾶς διεδύετ'
ἐξαπατῶν, λέγων ὡς
καὶ φιλαθήναιος ἦν καὶ

268 ἐφολκὸς.] Cf. Aesch. Supp.
200, καὶ μὴ πρόλεσχοι μηδ' ἐφολκὸς
ἐν λόγῳ γένῃ. The Scholiast says
ἐφολκὶς is the boat towed astern of a
ship. This adjective we more often
find active; e.g. in Thuc. IV. 108,
τοῦ Βρασίδου ἐφολκὰ καὶ οὐ τὰ ὄντα
λέγοντος.
269 Φρυνίχου.] Cf. above, v. 220.
270 ἀλλά μοι δοκεῖ στάντας.]
Cf. Eq. 1311, καθῆσθαί μοι δοκεῖ ἐς
τὸ Θησεῖον πλεούσας. The Chorus
having picked their way to Philocleon's house halt there, and chant
their summons.
274 ἀπολώλεκεν τὰς.] Hermann
corrected to ἀπολώλεκεν τὰς to agree
with λέγων ὡς as he has it in v. 283.
Richter's ἐξαπατῶν τε λέγων δ' in v.
283 seems as good, retaining here

the vulg. ἀπολώλεκε.
276 δάκτυλον.] Sc. ποδός.
278 δριμύτατός γ'.] Cf. note on
Eq. 808, εἴ ποτέ ἥξει σοι δριμὺς ἄγροικος,
κ.τ.λ.
279 κάτω κύπτων.] To show in-
attention, or to avoid being moved
by the defendant's piteous appearance.
280 λίθον ἕψεις.] The Scholiast
gives similar proverbs : πλίνθον πλύ-
νεις, χύτραν ποικίλλεις, εἰς ὕδωρ γρά-
φεις, Αἰθίοπα λευκαίνεις, κατὰ θα-
λάττης σπείρεις.
281. Perhaps grief at the escape
of a defendant has made him ill.
282 φιλαθήναιος.] To be pronounced with the diphthong short,
for the line answers to ἐμβάδας ἢ
προσέκοψ' εν.

τἀν Σάμῳ πρῶτος κατείποι,
διὰ τοῦτ' ὀδυνηθεὶς
εἶτ' ἴσως κεῖται πυρέττων.
ἔστι γὰρ τοιοῦτος ἀνήρ.   285
ἀλλ', ὠγάθ', ἀνίστασο μηδ' οὕτως σεαυτὸν
ἔσθιε, μηδ' ἀγανάκτει
καὶ γὰρ ἀνὴρ παχὺς ἥκει
τῶν προδόντων τἀπὶ Θράκης·
ὃν ὅπως ἐγχυτριεῖς.
ὕπαγ', ὦ παῖ, ὕπαγε.   290

ΠΑΙΣ

ἐθελήσεις τι μοι οὖν, ὦ πάτερ, ἥν σου τι δεηθῶ;

---

283 τἀν Σάμῳ.] The accused man claimed to have done the state service by early information which enabled them to get a footing in Samos. The Athenians helped Miletus against Samos under Pericles, about twenty years before this play was exhibited. They reduced the island in nine months. Thuc. I. 115—117.

287 ἔσθιε.) Cf. Hom. *Il.* ζ. 202, ὃν θυμὸν κατέδων. It is a favourite metaphor. Bergler quotes from Alcæus ἔδωδ' ἐμαυτὸν ὡς πολύπους.

288 παχὺς.] So *Pac.* 639, τῶν δὲ συμμάχων ἔσειον τούς παχεῖς καὶ πλουσίους, αἰτίας ἂν προστιθέντες ὡς φρονεῖ τὰ Βρασίδου. To be a traitor in the matter of the Thrace-ward parts, and to favour Brasidas, amount to about the same, since Brasidas took a leading part in the campaigns there. For the operations cf. Thuc. IV. 102.

289 ἐγχυτριεῖς.] 'Put in the pot,' add 'him to the 'stock' for soup. One of our poet's frequent metaphors from cookery. Cf. *Eq.* 745, ἥψωτοι ἑτέρου τὴν χύτραν ὑφειλόμην, where χύτρα is plainly the 'stock-pot' boiling on the fire with the meat in it: and *Eq.* 1136—40, τούτῳ δ' ἐπίτηδες...τρέφεις, κᾆθ', ὅταν μή σοι τύχῃ ὄψον ὦ, τούτων δὲ ἂν

ἢ παχὺς θύσας ἐπιδειπνεῖς. Being plump and fat (παχὺς), he would be a savoury morsel to add to the pot. Our own slang will supply 'pot' or 'dish' as equivalents. The Scholiast's explanation of ἐγχ. as referring to exposure of infants in χύτραι seems to me quite unnecessary here. Being recognized by Hesychius it deserves some respect, but where Aristophanes can be so easily explained from himself, it appears better so to explain him.

290 ὕπαγ', ὦ παῖ] Hermann supplies this line to the end of the strophe (after v. 280, λ. ἐ. ἔλεγεν) for the sake of symmetry. There seems no strong reason to give why the chorus should not say it only once, after the completion of both parts of their song. Why may not the chorus have halted, and deferred their 'lead on' to the end ? Cf. above, v. 270, στάντες ἐνθάδ' ἐκκαλεῖν.

291—302. These lines metrically are answered by 303—315. The metre in the first five lines is 'Ionicum a minore,' $\smile\smile--\ |\ \smile\smile--\ |$. Instances of this metre are Aesch. *Pers.* 65—112, and in Latin, Hor. *Od.* III. 13, Miserarum est neque amori dare ludum, &c.

ΧΟΡΟΣ

πάνυ γ', ὦ παιδίον. ἀλλ' εἰπὲ τί βούλει με πρίασθαι
καλόν; οἶμαι δέ σ' ἐρεῖν ἀστραγάλους δήπουθεν, ὦ παῖ. 295

ΠΑΙΣ

μὰ Δί', ἀλλ' ἰσχάδας, ὦ παππία· ἥδιον γάρ.

ΧΟΡΟΣ

                              οὐκ ἂν
μὰ Δί', εἰ κρέμαισθέ γ' ὑμεῖς.

ΠΑΙΣ

μὰ Δί' οὐ τἄρα προπέμψω σε το λοιπόν

ΧΟΡΟΣ

ἀπὸ γὰρ τοῦδέ με τοῦ μισθαρίου   300
τρίτον αὐτὸν ἔχειν ἄλφιτα δεῖ καὶ ξύλα κὦψον
σὺ δὲ σῦκά μ' αἰτεῖς.

ΠΑΙΣ

ἄγε νυν, ὦ πάτερ, ἢν μὴ τὸ δικαστήριον ἄρχων
καθίσῃ νῦν, πόθεν ὠνησόμεθ' ἄριστον; ἔχεις ἐλ-   305
πίδα χρηστήν τινα νῷν ἢ πόρον "Ελλας ἱρὸν εἰπεῖν;

ΧΟΡΟΣ

ἀπαπαῖ, φεῦ, ἀπαπαῖ, φεῦ, μὰ Δί' οὐκ ἔγωγε νῷν οἶδ' 309
ὁπόθεν γε δεῖπνον ἔσται.   311

---

298 ἥδιον γάρ.] The ι is scanned
short, the answering line being μὰ
Δί' οὐκ ἔγωγε νῷν οἶδ'.

300 μισθαρίου.] The τριώβολον,
which had to find three (husband
wife and child) in the necessaries of
life. The diminutive μισθάριον expresses the paltriness of the pay.

302. Hermann adds δ' ἔ here to
balance v. 315. But it might be
'extra metrum' there. Cf. note at
v. 190.

303—308. Seeing that figs are
quite out of the question, the boy
begins to be anxious about his
breakfast, if the court should not sit.

305 καθίσῃ.] Cf. v. 1441, ἔστ' ἂν
τὴν δίκην ἄρχων καλῇ. It appears
that the archon had the power of
determining whether the court
should sit, and that it was not sure
to sit every day. Cf. Thesm. 78,
ἐπεὶ νῦν γ' οὔτε τὰ δικαστήρια μέλλει
δικάζειν οὔτε βουλῆς ἐσθ' ἕδρα.

308 πόρον "Ελλας ἱρόν.] From
Pindar, acc. to Scholiast. Having
used πόρον, 'way,' i.e. means of getting money, he adds ridiculously
enough the other words which he
remembers come with πόρον in Pindar. The sacred πόρος "Ελλας is
there the Hellespont.

ΠΑΙΣ

τί με δῆτ᾽, ὦ μελέα μῆτερ, ἔτικτες,

ΧΟΡΟΣ

ἵν᾽ ἐμοὶ πράγματα βόσκειν παρέχῃς;

ΠΑΙΣ

ἀνόνητον ἄρ᾽ ὦ θυλάκιόν σ᾽ εἶχον ἄγαλμα.   314

ἒ ἒ

πάρα νῷν στενάζειν.

ΦΙΛΟΚΛΕΩΝ

φίλοι, τήκομαι μὲν   317
πάλαι διὰ τῆς ὀπῆς
ὑμῶν ὑπακούων.
ἀλλ᾽ οὐ γὰρ οἷός τ᾽ ἔτ᾽ εἰμ᾽
ᾄδειν. τί ποιήσω;
τηροῦμαι δ᾽ ὑπὸ τῶνδ᾽, ἐπεὶ
βούλομαί γε πάλαι μεθ᾽ ὑ-   320
μῶν ἐλθὼν ἐπὶ τοὺς καδί-

311 τί μα, κ.τ.λ.] From the Theseus of Euripides. The Scholiast gives both lines to the boy, and says that in the play they were spoken by those destined to be eaten by the Minotaur. I do not see what good sense can be made of v. 313 thus given to the boy. It seems better to follow Meineke and Cobet, who give v. 313 to the chorus. 'Why,' laments the boy, 'didst thou bear me!' 'To be a plague to me to keep, of course,' replies the old man. However, v. 313 may in some way resemble the line in Euripides that follows τί με κ.τ.λ.

314 ἀνόνητον, κ.τ.λ.] Hippolytus says (in the Theseus), ἀνόνητον ἄγαλμα, πάτερ, οἴοισι τεκών. The wallet here was to put the meal in, which the dicasts would buy if they got their pay. Cf. Eccl. 380, B. τὸ τρώβολον δῆτ᾽ ἔλαβες; Χ. εἰ γὰρ ὤφελον. ἀλλ᾽ ὕστεροι ἦλθον νὴ Δι᾽ ὥστ᾽ αἰσχύνομαι μὰ Δι᾽ οὐδὲν ἄλλο

μᾶλλον ἢ τὸν θύλακον. The boy is here carrying the father's wallet.

315 πάρα νῷν στ.] 'We may both make our moan.' Perhaps, as Richter thinks, both young and old unite to say this. It is no doubt another Euripidean scrap.

316—394. Philocleon hears the chorus, and tells them his hard case. They are indignant. After some talk about ways of escape, the old man hits on the plan of gnawing through the net, and letting himself down by a cord.

318 ὑπακούων.] Meineke's ἀνακούων is in no respect better than this. Cf. Nub. 263. Of Philocleon listening at the window ὑπ. seems correctly said. as it is so frequently used of a door-keeper listening to and answering a knock at the door.

321 καδίσκους.] He would fain be off to his dear balloting-urns, and be doing some mischief. Cf. v. 340, οὐκ ἐᾷ με...δρᾶν οὐδὲν κακόν.

σκους κακόν τι ποιῆσαι.
ἀλλ', ὦ Ζεῦ Ζεῦ, μέγα βροντήσας
ἤ με ποίησον καπνὸν ἐξαίφνης,
ἤ Προξενίδην, ἤ τὸν Σέλλου   325
τοῦτον τὸν ψευδαμάμαξυν.
| τόλμησον, ἄναξ, χαρίσασθαί μοι,
πάθος οἰκτείρας·
ἤ με κεραυνῷ διατινθαλέῳ
σπόδισον ταχέως·
κἄπειτ' ἀνελὼν μ' ἀποφυσήσας   330
εἰς ἐξάλμην ἔμβαλε θερμήν·
ἤ δῆτα λίθον με ποίησον ἐφ' οὗ
τὰς χοιρίνας ἀριθμοῦσιν.

323 dλλ' ὦ Zεῦ, κ.τ.λ.] These
wishes are in a sort of half-tragic
style. Cf Aesch. *Prom. Vinct.*
1043—1053: which passage Aristophanes possibly had in his mind
here. The metre (anapaestic) is the
same.
μέγα βροντήσας.] Vulg. μέγα
βρόντα, which Meineke reads as one
word, Hirschig as imperative, following it by ἐδμί ιν. It seems well
to commence the anapaestic system
with ἀλλ' ὦ Zεῦ, and therefore Dindorf's text is preferable, for the pa-
roemiac verse should not be at the
beginning.
325 Προξενίδην.] Having spoken of smoke, he adds these as
beggarly braggarts (πτωχαλαζόναι),
called 'smokes,' Proxenides, and
Aeschines, son of Sellus. Schol. Cf.
Av. 1126, Προξενίδης ὁ κομπασεύς,
and below, v. 457.
326 ψευδαμάμαξυν.] The ἀμά-
μαξυς is a kind of vine, whose wood
crackles loud in the fire. Hence
the whole word means that Aeschines is false and noisy. Schol. ψευ-
δατράφαξυν in *Eq.* 630 is a similar
compound, used also metaphorically.
327 τόλμησον χαρίσασθαι.]
'Bring thy heart to grant me the
boon.' 'Id est χαρίσαι,' Brunck,
from which note not much is gained.

More to the point is Bergler's quotation from Soph. *Trach.* 1070, τὸ·
ὦ τέκνον, τόλμησον, οἰκτειρόν τί με.
τολμᾶν, τλῆναι, τλήμων express 'en-
durance' of various kinds, from bold-
ness and hardihood' to 'patience
and misery.'
328 κεραυνῷ.] Cf. Soph. *Trach.*
1087, ἐποτεῖσαν, ὦναξ, ἐγκαταςκηψον
βέλοι, πάτερ, κεραυνοῦ.
329 διατινθαλέῳ.]διαπύρῳ Hesych.
Suidas quotes τινθαλέοισι καταμή-
ναντο λοετροῖς. And ποτῷ τινθαλέῳ
occurs in Nicand. *Alexipharm.* 445.
Hence it seems used of hot liquid:
and the thunderbolt may be con-
ceived of as liquid fire.
330 ἀποφυσήσας.] Men blow
off the ashes of fish baked on the
coals. Schol. The word σπόδισον
suggests this culinary metaphor,
which is rather a coming down after
the tragic style of the preceding
lines.
332 λίθον, κ.τ.λ.] 'Or turn me
to stone—so it be that whereon they
count the voting-shells.' For χοιρίναι
cf. *Eq.* 1332. The prayer that he
might be turned to stone suggests
Niobe: and it is possible that this
may have reference to some play of
that name. We know that there
was a *Niobe* of Aeschylus, and also
one of Sophocles. Cf. v. 580.

ΧΟΡΟΣ

τίς γάρ ἐσθ᾽ ὁ ταῦτά σ᾽ εἴργων
κἀποκλείων τὰς θύρας; λέ-
ξον· πρὸς εὔνους γὰρ φράσεις.   335

ΦΙΛΟΚΛΕΩΝ

οὑμὸς υἱός. ἀλλὰ μὴ βοᾶτε· καὶ γὰρ τυγχάνει
οὑτοσὶ πρόσθεν καθεύδων. ἀλλ᾽ ὕφεσθε τοῦ τόνου.

ΧΟΡΟΣ

τοῦ δ᾽ ἔφεξιν, ὦ μάταιε, ταῦτα δρᾶν σε βούλεται;
ἢ τίνα πρόφασιν ἔχων;

ΦΙΛΟΚΛΕΩΝ

οὐκ ἐᾷ μ᾽, ὦνδρες, δικάζειν οὐδὲ δρᾶν οὐδὲν κακόν,   340
ἀλλά μ᾽ εὐωχεῖν ἕτοιμός ἐστ᾽· ἐγὼ δ᾽ οὐ βούλομαι.

ΧΟΡΟΣ

τοῦτ᾽ ἐτόλμησ᾽ ὁ μιαρὶς χα-
νεῖν ὁ Δημολογοκλέων ὕδ᾽,

---

335 **πρὸς εὔνους γ. φ.**] The chorus sympathize with him in his prison, much as the ocean nymphs do with Prometheus in his strait. Cf. Aesch. *Prom. Vinct.* 128, &c.

337 **τόνου.**] Met. from ships, says the Scholiast: *i. e.* from their ropes. It might be from stringed instruments: 'loosen the tension,' and so 'lower the tone.' There is the same doubt as to the metaphor in *Eq.* 532. Herodotus uses the word of the tension of the ropes in the bridge across the Hellespont, VII. 36.

338 **ἔφεξιν.**] For the accusative see note on *Eq.* 783. For the sense, τίνος ἕνεκα (Schol. R.) is the best Greek comment. ἔφεξις should be taken in the sense of 'aim, intent,' from ἐπέχειν, in such uses as ἐπέχειν τόξον, ἐπέχειν τὸν νοῦν. 'With what aim, aiming at what, does he wish, &c.' It is generally interpreted as =πρόφασις=ἐπισχεσίη (Hom. *Odyss.* φ. 71), 'grounds,' 'something to rest upon.' The gloss of Hesychius

χάρω, ἕνεκα, ἐποχὴν, πρόφασιν, is not decisive against the sense of 'final aim;' and we get thus some distinction between ἔφεξις and πρόφασις in our text. 'What is his aim in this? What fair grounds has he to go upon?'

339 **ἢ τίνα π. ἔ.**] This line some would eject. But vv. 334—345 =vv. 365—378, and ἢ—ἔχων answers tolerably to ἀλλ᾽...γνάθον, if we take Meineke's ἢ τίνα for τίνα.

342 **Δημολογοκλέων.**] 'Quasi sui oblitus hoc dicit chorus.' Bergl. Dindorf calls this 'inepta interpretatio.' But it seems about right. The chorus probably, in their anger, are meant to use a word that shall end like Bdelycleon, the man's true name, without looking to the force of that termination. They mean δημολόγοι in a bad sense, not reflecting that it will apply to their friends more than to their foes. δημοκλοναοκλέων or δημογελοκλέων, conj. Reisk. The Scholiast explains by τύραννος καὶ ἀρχοντικῶν.

ὅτι λέγεις τι περὶ τῶν νε-   343
ῶν ἀληθές. οὐ γὰρ ἄν ποθ᾽
οὗτος ἀνὴρ τοῦτ᾽ ἐτόλμη-
σεν λέγειν, εἰ
μὴ ξυνωμότης τις ἦν.   345
ἀλλ᾽ ἐκ τούτων ὥρα τινά σοι ζητεῖν καινὴν ἐπίνοιαν,
ἥτις σε λάθρα τἀνδρὸς τουδὶ καταβῆναι δεῦρο ποιήσει.

ΦΙΛΟΚΛΕΩΝ

τίς ἂν οὖν εἴη; ζητεῖθ᾽ ὑμεῖς, ὡς πᾶν ἂν ἔγωγε ποιοίην·
οὕτω κιττῶ διὰ τῶν σανίδων μετὰ χοιρίνης περιελθεῖν.

ΧΟΡΟΣ

ἔστω ὀπὴ δῇθ᾽ ἥντιν᾽ ἂν ἔνδοθεν οἷός τ᾽ εἴης διορύξαι, 350
εἶτ᾽ ἐκδῦναι ῥάκεσιν κρυφθείς, ὥσπερ πολύμητις Ὀδυσσεύς;

ΦΙΛΟΚΛΕΩΝ

πάντα πέφρακται κοὐκ ἔστιν ὀπῆς οὐδ᾽ εἰ σέρφῳ διαδῦναι.
ἀλλ᾽ ἄλλο τι δεῖ ζητεῖν ὑμᾶς· ὀπίαν δ᾽ οὐκ ἔστι γενέσθαι.

ΧΟΡΟΣ

μέμνησαι δῇθ᾽, ὅτ᾽ ἐπὶ στρατιᾶς κλέψας ποτὲ τοὺς ὀβελίσκους

---

345 ξυνωμότης.] Cleon is always charging 'conspiracy' on his enemies. Cf. Eq. 236, 257: and below vv. 483, 488, 495, 507.

349 σανίδων.] τῶν περιεχουσῶν τὰ δώματα τῶν εἰσαχθησομένων εἰς τὸ δικαστήριον, Schol. He wants to go the round of these notices, that he may know what suits are coming on, and so may come into court prepared for the business he has to do. Some however (with another explanation of the Scholiast) take σανίδων here = δρυφάκτων, the rails or barriers. But cf. below, R₄θ, where the σανίδες and γραφαί are brought out together: which makes for the first interpretation.

350 διορύξαι.] Meineke's διαλέξαι is from Hesychius: who however when he explains διαλέξαι by διορύξαι may only have been referring to Lysistr. 720, διαλέγουσαι τὴν ὀπήν,

'widening the hole,' and may not have meant to imply that the exact infinitive διαλέξαι was in Aristophanes.

351 ῥάκεσιν, κ.τ.λ.] Cf. Hom. Od. λ. 245, στεῖρα τάα' ἀμφ' ὤμοισι βαλὼν, οἰκῆι ἐοικὼς, ἀνδρῶν δυσμενέων κατέβη πόλιν εὐρυάγυιαν, and Eur. Hec. 239, οἶσθ᾽ ἡνίκ᾽ ἦλθες Ἰλίου κατάσκοπος, δυσχλαινίᾳ τ᾽ ἄμορφος, ὄμμάτων τ᾽ ἄπο φόνου σταλαγμοὶ σὴν κατέσταζον γένυν. And his later appearance in the beggar character in the Odyssey may also be meant.

353 ὀπήν.] There is a pun on the double derivation from ὀπὸς or ὀπή; and possibly (as Florens thinks) an allusion to the sourness of the dicast in ὀπίας from ὀπός. He cannot get out through the hole; and he cannot be as sharp and sour as he would fain be with those brought before him.

ἵεις σαυτὸν κατὰ τοῦ τείχους ταχέως, ὅτε Νάξος ἑάλω; 355

ΦΙΛΟΚΛΕΩΝ

οἶδ'· ἀλλὰ τί τοῦτ'; οὐδὲν γὰρ τοῦτ' ἐστὶν ἐκείνῳ προσ-
    όμοιον.
ἥβων γὰρ κἀδυνάμην κλέπτειν, ἰσχυόν τ' αὐτὸς ἐμαυτοῦ,
κοὐδείς μ' ἐφύλαττ', ἀλλ' ἐξῆν μοι
φεύγειν ἀδεῶς. νῦν δὲ ξὺν ὅπλοις
ἄνδρες ὁπλῖται διαταξάμενοι   360
κατὰ τὰς διόδους σκοπιωροῦνται,
τὼ δὲ δύ' αὐτῶν ἐπὶ ταῖσι θύραις
ὥσπερ με γαλῆν κρέα κλέψασαν
τηροῦσιν ἔχοντ' ὀβελίσκους.

ΧΟΡΟΣ

ἀλλὰ καὶ νῦν ἐκπόριζε   365
μηχανὴν ὅπως τάχισθ'· ἕ-
ως γὰρ, ὦ μελίττιον.

ΦΙΛΟΚΛΕΩΝ

διατραγεῖν τοίνυν κράτιστον ἐστί μοι τὸ δίκτυον.
ἡ δέ μοι Δίκτυννα συγγνώμην ἔχοι τοῦ δικτύου.

ΧΟΡΟΣ

ταῦτα μὲν πρὸς ἀνδρός ἐστ' ἄνοντος ἐς σωτηρίαν.

---

355 Νάξος ἑάλω.] By Cimon (cf. Thuc. i. 98), about fifty years before this play. Cf. v. 283. From such references we may infer the chorus to be old men of about seventy years.

357 ἰσχυόν τ' αὐτὸς ἐμαυτοῦ.] Either 'I had my own proper strength,' was not the weakling I now am; or 'was lord of my own limbs and body.' Mitchell. In this latter case ἰσχύειν would govern a genitive after the analogy of ἄρχειν, κρατεῖν, and such verbs. That ἰσχυον = ἰσχυρότερος ἦν (as L. and S. say) is unlikely. Besides, would not ἰσχυρότερος ἦν αὐτὸς ἐμαυτοῦ mean naturally, 'I was stronger than my former self, than I was *before* that

time,' not 'than my present self, than I am *now*'?

363 γαλῆν.] Cf. *Pax.* 1151, where the wife is bidden to bring out the meat, εἴ τι μὴ 'ξήνεγκεν αὐτῶν ἡ γαλῆ τῆι ἑσπέρας. For the arrangement ὥσπερ με γαλῆν cf. *Nub.* 257, ὥσπερ με τὸν 'Αθάμανθ' ὅπως μὴ θύσετε.

364 τηροῦσιν ἔχοντ'.] For dual with plural cf. *Nub.* 1506, παθόντε... ὑβρίζετε.

368 Δίκτυννα, κ.τ.λ.] May the patroness of nets excuse me for tearing this net.

369 ἄνοντος.] Cf. Aesch. *Fr.* 145, οὔτ' ἂν τι θύων οὔτ' ἐπισπένδων ἄνοις; and Eur. *Andr.* 1132, ἀλλ' οὐδὲν ἦνεν.

ἀλλ' ἔπαγε τὴν γνάθον.   370

ΦΙΛΟΚΛΕΩΝ

διατέτρωκται τοῦτό γ'. ἀλλὰ μὴ βοᾶτε μηδαμῶς,
ἀλλὰ τηρώμεσθ' ὅπως μὴ Βδελυκλέων αἰσθήσεται.

ΧΟΡΟΣ

μηδὲν, ὦ τᾶν, δέδιθι, μηδέν·
ὡς ἐγὼ τοῦτόν γ', ἐὰν γρύ-
ξῃ τι, ποιήσω δακεῖν τὴν
καρδίαν καὶ τὸν περὶ ψυ-   375
χῆς δρόμον δραμεῖν, ἵν' εἰδῇ
μὴ πατεῖν τὰ
τῶν θεῶν ψηφίσματα.

ἀλλ' ἐξάψας διὰ τῆς θυρῖδος τὸ καλῴδιον εἶτα καθίμα
δήσας σαυτὸν καὶ τὴν ψυχὴν ἐμπλησάμενος Διοπείθους. 380

ΦΙΛΟΚΛΕΩΝ

ἄγε νυν, ἢν αἰσθομένω τούτω ζητητόν μ' ἐσκαλαμᾶσθαι
κἀνάσπαστον ποιεῖν εἴσω, τί ποιήσετε; φράζετε νυνί.

ΧΟΡΟΣ

ἀμυνοῦμέν σοι τὸν πρινώδη θυμὸν ἅπαντες καλέσαντες,
ὥστ' οὐ δυνατόν σ' εἴργειν ἔσται· τοιαῦτα ποιήσομεν ἡμεῖς.

---

374 Δακεῖν τ. κ.] 'To gnaw his heart' in vexation. Cf. *Nub.* 1369.

378 τῶν θεῶν.] Vulg. ταῖς θεαῖν; which would mean Ceres and Proserpine. ψηφίσματα seems by way of surprise for μυστήρια. The Scholiast has the dual. Meineke, Cobet, and some others τοῖν θεοῖν. Probably whether dual or plural be in the text, Ceres and Proserpine are specially meant. Schömann (*De Com. Ath.* p. 249) says, 'τὰ ταῖν θεαῖν ψηφίσματα dici facete pro τοῖν τ. θ. νόμοι, de pietate erga parentes, quae ideo earum dearum Cereris atque Proserpinae, lex dici poterat, quoniam omnem in vita et moribus iis acceptam referebant, mysteriaque iis etiam in hujus rei memoriam celebrabant.'

380 Διοπείθους.] The Scholiast

on *Av.* 989, ὁ μέγας Διοπείθης, quotes from Phrynichus ἀνὴρ χορεύει, καὶ τὰ τοῦ θεοῦ καλά. βούλει Διοπείθη μεταδράμω καὶ τύμπανα; and from Amipsias Διοπείθει τῷ παραμαινομένῳ. Hence it is plain that ψυχὴν ἐμπλ. Δ. means 'having filled your soul with raging fury.' Cf. *Ach.* 484, κατασιῶν Εὐριπίδην. The Scholiast further says that Diopithes was an orator; and in the *Knights* (v. 1085) he, or a namesake, is spoken of as maimed (κυλλός), or as bribed.

381 ἐσκαλαμᾶσθαι.] Below, at v. 609, ἐσκαλαμᾶται is used, but not so literally. 'arundo' in Latin bears the same sense as κάλαμος in this use.

383 πρινώδη.] Cf. *Ach.* 180, στιπτοὶ γέροντες, πρίνινοι, ἀτεράμονες.

ΦΙΛΟΚΛΕΩΝ

δράσω τοίνυν ὑμῖν πίσυνος· καὶ μανθάνετ'· ἤν τι πάθω
'γώ,   385
ἀνελόντες καὶ κατακλαύσαντες θεῖναί μ' ὑπὸ τοῖσι δρυφάκτοις.

ΧΟΡΟΣ

οὐδὲν πείσει· μηδὲν δείσῃς. ἀλλ', ὦ βέλτιστε, καθίει
σαυτὸν θαρρῶν κἀπευξάμενος τοῖσι πατρῴοισι θεοῖσιν.

ΦΙΛΟΚΛΕΩΝ

ὦ Λύκε δέσποτα, γείτων ἥρως· σὺ γὰρ οἷσπερ ἐγὼ κε-
χάρησαι,
τοῖς δακρύοισιν τῶν φευγόντων ἀεὶ καὶ τοῖς ὀλοφυρμοῖς· 390
ᾤκησας γοῦν ἐπίτηδες ἰὼν ἐνταῦθ', ἵνα ταῦτ' ἀκροῷο,
κἀβουλήθης μόνος ἡρώων παρὰ τὸν κλάοντα καθῆσθαι.
ἐλέησον καὶ σῶσον νυνὶ τὸν σαυτοῦ πλησιόχωρον·
κοὔ μή ποτέ σου παρὰ τὰς κάννας οὐρήσω μηδ' ἀποπάρδω.

ΒΔΕΛΥΚΛΕΩΝ

οὗτος, ἐγείρου.

ΣΩΣΙΑΣ

τί τὸ πρᾶγμ';

---

386 **δρυφάκτοις.**] Even in death he would be in the court. Cf. *Eq.* 675 for δρύφακτοι.

387 **οὐδὲν πείσει.**] 'You'll come to no harm = you'll not die:' ἤν τι πάθω 'γώ above is the common euphemism, ' If anything should happen to me'='If I should die.'

389 **Λύκε.**] The hero Lycus, son of Pandion, had a statue close to the court, and appears to have been a, patron of the courts generally. Cf. below, v. 819. Also Pollux names a special court as τὸ ἐπὶ Λύκῳ δικαστήριον.

390 **τοῖς δακρύοισιν, κ.τ.λ.**] Generally tears and wailings were thought out of place and displeas-

ing at shrines and temples: but Lycus, he argues, must delight in such, as he has settled himself there.

394 **κάννας.**] 'reed-mats,' ψιάθους. Schol. Others think it simply means 'a wattled fence.' And a protecting enclosure round the statue of Lycus, whether of mats hung up, or of lattice work, seems to suit the passage.

395—470. Bdelycleon discovers his father escaping, raises the alarm, and they keep him back. The Chorus come to his rescue; Bdelycleon summons more slaves; and, after a scuffle, the Chorus are beaten back, exclaiming loudly at the conspiracy and tyranny.

ΒΔΕΛΤΚΛΕΩΝ

ὥσπερ φωνή μέ τις ἐγκεκύκλωται. 395

ΣΩΣΙΑΣ

μῶν ὁ γέρων πη διαδύεται αὖ;

ΒΔΕΛΤΚΛΕΩΝ

μὰ Δί᾽ οὐ δῆτ᾽, ἀλλὰ καθιμᾷ
αὑτὸν δήσας.

ΣΩΣΙΑΣ

ὦ μιαρώτατε, τί ποιεῖς; οὐ μὴ καταβήσει;

ΒΔΕΛΤΚΛΕΩΝ

ἀνάβαιν᾽ ἀνύσας κατὰ τὴν ἑτέραν καὶ ταισιν φυλλάσι παῖε,
ἤν πως πρύμνην ἀνακρούσηται πληγεὶς ταῖς εἰρεσιώναις.

ΦΙΛΟΚΛΕΩΝ

οὐ ξυλλήψεσθ᾽ ὁπόσοισι δίκαι τῆτες μέλλουσιν ἔσεσθαι, 400
ὦ Σμικυθίων καὶ Τισιάδη καὶ Χρήμων καὶ Φερέδειπνε;
πότε δ᾽, εἰ μὴ νῦν, ἐπαρήξετέ μοι, πρίν μ᾽ εἴσω μᾶλλον
ἄγεσθαι;

ΧΟΡΟΣ

εἰπέ μοι, τί μέλλομεν κινεῖν ἐκείνην τὴν χολὴν,
ἥνπερ, ἡνίκ᾽ ἄν τις ἡμῶν ὀργίσῃ τὴν σφηκιάν;
νῦν ἐκεῖνο νῦν ἐκεῖνο   405

---

395 **ἐγκεκύκλωται.**] Rather a
curious use of this verb. Euripides
uses it of the ether, τοῦ χθόν᾽ ἐγκυ-
κλουμένου αἰθέρος, *Bacch.* 292. Perhaps Aristophanes took it from
some poet, Euripides or another,
who had spoken of 'a circum-am-
bient voice.'

396 **διαδύεται αὖ.**] Dindorf adds
the αὖ for the metre. Brunck added
οὐ before μὰ Δί'. Porson reads διαδὺς
ἔλαθεν for διαδύεται: this last Meineke and Hirschig admit.

397 **μιαρώτατε, τί ποιεῖς;**] μιάρ᾽
ἀνδρῶν, Porson, to avoid the sequence of anapaests after dactyl. It
is a nice point to settle whether
such a sequence was so utterly in-

admissible to an Athenian that we
are justified in leaving MSS. in
order to avoid it. Cf. notes on *Nub.*
663 and 1407.

398 **ἑτέραν.**] Sc. θυρίδα. Philocleon was getting down from a
window.

399 **εἰρεσιώναις.**] For these cf.
Scholiast on *Eq.* 729.

400—403. He calls on several
of his fellow dicasts by name. The
names Τισιάδῃ, from τίσασθαι, and
Φερέδειπνοι (v. 311, ὁπόθιν τὸ δαῖτνον
ἔσται) are significant.

403, 4 **τί μέλλομεν.**] 'Why do
we delay to rouse, &c.' After ἥνπερ
supply κινοῦμεν.

405—414. These lines probably

τοὐξύθυμον, ᾧ κολαζό-
μεσθα, κέντρον ἐντέτατ᾽ ὀξύ.
ἀλλὰ θαἰμάτια βαλόντες ὡς τάχιστα, παιδία,
θεῖτε καὶ βοᾶτε, καὶ Κλέωνι ταῦτ᾽ ἀγγέλλετε,
καὶ κελεύετ᾽ αὐτὸν ἥκειν   410
ὡς ἐπ᾽ ἄνδρα μισόπολιν
ὄντα κἀπολουμενον, ὅτι
τόνδε λόγον ἐσφέρει,
[ὡς χρὴ] μὴ δικάζειν δίκας.

BΔΕΛΤΚΛΕΩΝ

ὠγαθοί, τὸ πρᾶγμ᾽ ἀκούσατ᾽, ἀλλὰ μὴ κεκράγετε.   415

ΧΟΡΟΣ .

νὴ Δί᾽ ἐς τὸν οὐρανὶν γ᾽· ὡς τοῦδ᾽ ἐγὼ οὐ μεθήσομαι.

ought to correspond metrically to
vv. 463—470: but they do not do
so exactly, and it is hardly safe to
alter the text to produce a strict
agreement.
406 κολαζόμεσθα.] Cf. Plat.
Prot. 324 C, τιμωροῦνται καὶ κολά-
ζονται. A rare use of the middle
form in the present, though in the
future tense the middle is the proper
Attic form. Cf. above, v. 244.
407 ἐντέτατ᾽ ὀξύ.] This does not
content Dindorf, but as the antistrophic verse is also uncertain, he
offers no correction. Hermann
reads ἐντέταται ὀξύ. Meineke makes
this agree with v. 465, by ἐντετά-
μισθ᾽ ὀξύ here and ἐλάμβαν᾽ ὀπισθ᾽σα
there.
414 ὡς χρή.] Most editors throw
these words out; and so the verse
would answer to αὐτὸς ἀρχων μόνος.
415 ὠγαθοί, κ.τ.λ.] This scene
between Bdelycleon and the enraged
Chorus is rather like that between
Dicaeopolis and the Acharnian col-
liers, *Ach.* 284, &c.
416 ὡς τοῦδ᾽ ἐγὼ οὐ μεθήσομαι.]
Whether this be given to Bdelycleon, or to the Chorus (and it will
make tolerable sense either way,
though perhaps the actual holder

is more correctly said 'to loose his
hold of,' than is he who will not
give up his attempt to seize a person), it seems certain that τοῦδε for
τόνδε is a proper correction. Dawes
pointed out that μεθύναι, 'to set
loose, send from you,' governed the
accusative—μεθίεσθαι, 'to loose one-
self from, let go one's hold of,' a
genitive. The passages which some
have brought to support the accus.
after μεθίεσθαι are: Soph. *El.* 1277,
μή μ᾽ ἀποστερήσῃς τῶν σῶν πρόσω-
πων ἡδονὰν μεθέσθαι. Eur. *Med.* 736,
τούτοις…ἀγουσιν οὐ μεθῶ᾽ ἂν ἐκ γαίας
ἐμέ. In neither of these passages
is the accusative governed by the
verb in question (see Elmsley and
Porson on the *Medea*, and Jebb on
the *Electra*). Brunck also brings
Eur. *Iph. in Aul.* 309, ἄφες δὲ τήνδ᾽
ἐμοί. ME. οὐκ ἂν μεθείμην; which
proves nothing; and Eur. *Phoen.*
519, where no doubt ἐκείνου should
be read for ἐκεῖνον. The principle
of Dawes' rule is so plain, that a
few copyists' errors need not weigh
against it.
ἐγὼ οὐ.] Cf. *Nub.* 901, ἐγὼ αὐτά:
which Dindorf there writes in one
word, as by crasis. Editors have
not been thoroughly consistent in

ταῦτα δῆτ' οὐ δεινὰ καὶ τυραννίς ἐστιν ἐμφανής;
ὦ πόλις καὶ Θεώρου θεοισεχθρία,
κεἴ τις ἄλλος προέστηκεν ὑμῶν κόλαξ.

ΞΑΝΘΙΑΣ

Ἡράκλεις, καὶ κέντρ' ἔχουσιν. οὐχ ὁρᾷς, ὦ δέσποτα; 420

ΒΔΕΛΤΚΛΕΩΝ

οἷς γ' ἀπώλεσαν Φίλιππον ἐν δίκῃ τὸν Γοργίου.

ΧΟΡΟΣ

καὶ σέ γ' αὖθις ἐξολοῦμεν· ἀλλ' ἅπας ἐπίστρεφε
δεῦρο κἀξείρας τὸ κέντρον εἶτ' ἐπ' αὐτὸν ἵεσο,
ξυσταλεὶς, εὔτακτος, ὀργῆς καὶ μένους ἐμπλήμενος,
ὡς ἂν εὖ εἰδῇ τὸ λοιπὸν σμῆνος οἷον ὤργισεν. 425

ΞΑΝΘΙΑΣ

τοῦτο μέντοι δεινὸν ἤδη νὴ Δί', εἰ μαχούμεθα·
ὡς ἔγωγ' αὐτῶν ὁρῶν δέδοικα τὰς ἐγκεντρίδας.

ΧΟΡΟΣ

ἀλλ' ἀφίει τὸν ἄνδρ'· εἰ δὲ μὴ, φήμ' ἐγὼ

---

their manner of writing such combinations of vowel sounds; and possibly the original writers were no
more so; a rigid uniformity in or-
thography being a modern refine-
ment.

418 θεοισεχθρία.] The reproach-
ful expression, θεοῖς ἐχθρός, had
almost come to be considered one
adjective; and from it was formed
a noun in -ia. Other readings are
θεοσεχθρία, θεοσχθρία, but they do
not seem so good; nor do they
appear to suit the metre. The lines
are composed of four cretics.

421 ἐν δίκῃ.] ἀντὶ τοῦ δικαίωτες.
Schol. The prevailing sense of ἐν
δίκῃ in Aristophanes (as elsewhere)
is 'justly.' Cf. Eq. 257, ἐν δίκῃ γ',
ἐπεὶ τὰ κοινὰ πρὶν λαχεῖν κατεσθίεις.
And it is not quite certain that here,
if the Philippus mentioned was, as
the Scholiast says, a traitor and
barbarian, Bdelycleon may not

mean to hint that his judicial punishment served him right. When this
man was condemned does not appear. A passage in The Birds (v.
1700), βάρβαροι δ' εἰσὶν γένος, Γοργίου τε καὶ Φιλίππου, apparently
refers to the same person.

422 αὖθις.] 'In another trial, as
a second instance,' Holden reads
αὑτοῖς, which Meineke adopts.

423 ἱσο [ξυσταλείς.] Cf. Eccl. 93,
ξυστειλάμεναι θαἰμάτια, and 486,
πρὶν ταῦτα συστέλλον σεαυτήν. Not
very unlike this use, though more
specially nautical, is Eq. 432, ἐγὼ
δὲ συστελλῶ γε τοὺς ἀλλᾶντας εἶτ'
ἀφήσω κατὰ εὖμ' ἐμαυτὸν οὔριον
ἐλάειν σε μακρὰ κελεύσας.

424 ἐμπλήμενος.] For the form
cf. Eccl. 51, τριχίδων ἐμπλήμενος.

428. The metre is the same as
that of 418, 419, each line being
composed of four cretics. In v. 429
-ρας μακαρι- is an equivalent for a

τὰς χελώνας μακαριεῖν σε τοῦ δέρματος.

ΦΙΛΟΚΛΕΩΝ

εἶά νυν, ὦ ξυνδικασταί, σφῆκες ὀξυκάρδιοι,　　　430
οἱ μὲν ἐς τὸν πρωκτὸν αὐτῶν ἐσπέτεσθ' ὠργισμένοι,
οἱ δὲ τὠφθαλμὼ 'ν κύκλῳ κεντεῖτε καὶ τοὺς δακτύλους.

ΒΔΕΛΥΚΛΕΩΝ

ὦ Μίδα καὶ Φρὺξ βοήθει δεῦρο καὶ Μασυντία,
καὶ λάβεσθε τουτουὶ καὶ μὴ μεθῆσθε μηδενί·
εἰ δὲ μή, 'ν πέδαις παχείαις οὐδὲν ἀριστήσετε.　　　435
ὡς ἐγὼ πολλῶν ἀκούσας οἶδα θρίων τὸν ψόφον.

ΧΟΡΟΣ

εἰ δὲ μὴ τοῦτον μεθήσεις, ἔν τί σοι παγήσεται.

ΦΙΛΟΚΛΕΩΝ

ὦ Κέκροψ ἥρως ἄναξ, τὰ πρὸς ποδῶν Δρακοντίδη,

cretic in time, two short syllables being in place of one long.

429 χελώνας, κ.τ.λ.] This prophecy is fulfilled later on in the play, when Xanthias comes in (at v. 1292) exclaiming, ἰὼ χελῶναι μακάριαι τοῦ δέρματος, after being beaten by his master.

431 τὠφθαλμὼ 'ν.] Cf. *Nub.* 943, τὠφθαλμὼ κεντούμενος ὥσπερ ὑπ' ἀνθηνῶν...ἀπολεῖται. Elmsley's 'ν κύκλῳ for κύκλῳ seems worthy of acceptation, because MS. Rav. has τὠφθαλμῶν: otherwise the simple dative κύκλῳ might be confirmed by many examples, and would be satisfactory.

433 Μίδα.] Midas, Phryx, and Masyntias are names of slaves.

435 εἰ δὲ μή.] 'Else,' if you do not (obey me and not let him go). Instances like this are frequent, where, a prohibition having gone before, we cannot render εἰ δὲ μή literally without some ambiguity, because of the preceding negative.

οὐδὲν ἀριστήσετε.] Breakfast seems to have been the meal on the absence of which the Greeks most comment as a hardship. Cf. Theocr. *Idyll.* I. 51, πρὶν ἢ 'κρατίστως ἐπὶ ξηροῖσι καθίξῃ, where some read 'νάριστον (ἀνάριστον), 'breakfastless,' and the tense comes out much the same with either reading. Cf. also Aesch. *Ag.* 351, πόνοι νήσται πρὸς ἀρίστοισιν ὧν ἔχει πόλις τάσσει.

436 θρίων.] There was a proverb, πολλῶν ἐγὼ θρίων ψόφων ἀκήκοα. Fig-leaves crackle loudly when burnt: hence the proverb, of empty and noisy threats. Schol.

437 τοῦτον μεθήσεις.] See above, at v. 416, for μεθεῖναι and μεθέσθαι.

ἔν τί σοι.] For the tmesis cf. *Nub.* 792, ἀπὸ γὰρ ὀλοῦμαι. *Ach.* 295, κατά σε χώσομεν.

438 Δρακοντίδη.] The fable of Cecrops' serpent shape below is found in Ov. *Met.* 255, and elsewhere. But Richter explains Δρακ. differently: 'the poet compares the oft invoked god to the oft accused Dracontides,' for whom cf. v. 157. But the older explanation seems the better; and the reference to Dracontides very doubtful.

περιορᾷς οὕτω μ' ὑπ' ἀνδρῶν βαρβάρων χειρούμενον,
οὓς ἐγὼ 'δίδαξα κλάειν τέτταρ' ἐς τὴν χοίνικα;   440

ΧΟΡΟΣ

εἶτα δῆτ' οὐ πόλλ' ἔνεστι δεινὰ τῷ γήρᾳ κακά;
δηλαδή· καὶ νῦν γε τούτω τὸν παλαιὸν δεσπότην
πρὸς βίαν χειροῦσιν, οὐδὲν τῶν πάλαι μεμνημένοι
διφθερῶν κἀξωμίδων, ἃς οὗτος αὐτοῖς ἠμπόλα,
καὶ κυνᾶς· καὶ τοὺς πόδας χειμῶνος ὄντος ὠφέλει,   445
ὥστε μὴ ῥιγῶν ἑκάστοτ'· ἀλλὰ τούτοις γ' οὐκ ἔνι
οὐδ' ἐν ὀφθαλμοῖσιν αἰδὼς τῶν παλαιῶν ἐμβάδων.

ΦΙΛΟΚΛΕΩΝ

οὐκ ἀφήσεις οὐδὲ νυνί μ', ὦ κάκιστον θηρίον;
οὐδ' ἀναμνησθεὶς ὅθ' εὑρὼν τοὺς βότρυς κλέπτοντά σε
προσαγαγὼν πρὸς τὴν ἐλάαν ἐξέδειρ' εὖ κἀνδρικῶς,   450
ὥστε σε ζηλωτὸν εἶναι, σὺ δ' ἀχάριστος ἦσθ' ἄρα.
ἀλλ' ἄνες με καὶ σὺ καὶ σύ, πρὶν τὸν υἱὸν ἐκδραμεῖν.

ΧΟΡΟΣ

ἀλλὰ τούτων μὲν τάχ' ἡμῖν δώσετον καλὴν δίκην,
οὐκέτ' ἐς μακρὰν, ἵν' εἰδῆθ' οἷόν ἐστ' ἀνδρῶν τρόπος

439 βαρβάρων.] He calls to the national hero to aid him against the foreign slaves, Mida, Phryx, and the rest.

440 κλάειν τέτταρ' ἐς τὴν χοίνικα.] 'To weep four times to the choenix,' that is, while kneading four loaves to the choenix of flour, which the Scholiast says was the regular proportion. The slave worked at kneading four loaves to the choenix, bemoaning his hard labour the while with a gush of tears for each loaf. But χοῖνιξ also means a kind of stocks, cf. *Plut.* 176, τὰς χοίνικας καὶ τὰς πέδας ποθοῦσαι. A pun on the two senses may possibly be intended; but the exact meaning of 'weeping four times (when put) into the stocks' is not clear. With κλάειν, τέτταρα, *Ach.* 2, ἥσθην τέτταρα, may be compared.

442 δηλαδή.] Cobet's δῆλα δ', εἰ καὶ νῦν γε (accepted by Meineke),

if not necessary, is very neat.

443 οὐδὲν κ.τ.λ.] The Chorus upbraid the slaves with want of gratitude for clothes given to them. Their master afterwards reckons even the beatings that they got as grounds for gratitude.

444 κἀξωμίδων.] ἱμάτια δουλικὰ καὶ ἑτερομάσχαλα, Schol.

445 πόδας ὠφέλει.] Cf. *Eq.* 874. εὐποδώτατόν τε τῇ πόλει καὶ τᾶσι δακτύλοισι, of the sausage-seller, after his gift to Demus of a pair of shoes.

450 προσαγαγὼν κ.τ.λ.] The culprit was tied up to an olive-tree, and received such a thrashing as any one might envy. εὖ κἀνδρικῶς occurs in the same collocation in *Eq.* 379.

451 ἀχάριστος ἦσθ' ἄρα.] 'You *after all* were thankless?' I was not earning the gratitude I had a right to expect, and thought at the time I should get.

ὀξυθύμων καὶ δικαίων καὶ βλεπόντων κάρδαμα.   455

ΒΔΕΛΤΚΛΕΩΝ
παῖε παῖ', ὦ Ξανθία, τοὺς σφῆκας ἀπὸ τῆς οἰκίας.

ΞΑΝΘΙΑΣ
ἀλλὰ δρῶ τοῦτ'· ἀλλὰ καὶ σὺ τῦφε πολλῷ τῷ καπνῷ.

ΣΩΣΙΑΣ
οὐχὶ σοῦσθ'; οὐκ ἐς κόρακας; οὐκ ἄπιτε; παῖε τῷ ξύλῳ.

ΞΑΝΘΙΑΣ
καὶ σὺ προσθεὶς Αἰσχίνην ἔντυφε τὸν Σελλαρτίου.
ἆρ' ἐμέλλομέν ποθ' ὑμᾶς ἀποσοβήσειν τῷ χρόνῳ.   460

ΒΔΕΛΤΚΛΕΩΝ
ἀλλὰ μα Δί' οὐ ῥᾳδίως οὕτως ἂν αὐτοὺς διέφυγες,
εἴπερ ἔτυχον τῶν μελῶν τῶν Φιλοκλέους βεβρωκότες.

ΧΟΡΟΣ
ἆρα δῆτ' οὐκ αὐτὰ δῆλα
τοῖς πένησιν, ἡ τυραννὶς
ὡς λάθρα μ' ἐλάμβαν' ὑπιοῦσα;   465

455 βλεπόντων κάρδαμα.] So πᾶσιν βλέπειν, πυρρίχην βλέπειν (Av. 1169), ναύφρακτον βλέπων (Ach. 95), &c.

456. Bdelycleon has been away for a short time, and now comes out again, encouraging the slaves to drive away the assailants.

457 ἀλλὰ καὶ σὺ.] To Sosias. Meineke arranges the dialogue differently, without Sosias.

458 σοῦσθ'.] Nearly as σοῦ σοῦ above at v. 209. But Aeschylus and Sophocles both use this word of 'haste,' without any notion of driving away; e.g. Aesch. S. c. Theb. 31, σοῦσθε σὺν παντευχίᾳ: and Soph. Aj. 1414, σούσθω, βάτω.

459 Αἰσχίνην.] The same as the son of Sellus mentioned above at v. 325. He was καττώδης διὰ τὴν ἀλαζονείαν. Also the Scholiast finds a reference to σέλας, 'blaze,' in the altered name of the man's father (which he spells Σελλάρτιοι): ὁ γὰρ

καττὸς τοῦ σέλαος γέννημα, 'smoke is born of blazing fire:' and therefore the smoky Aeschines is fitly 'son of Blazius.'

460 ἆρ' ἐμέλλομεν.] Cf. Ach. 347, Nub. 1301.

461 Φιλοκλέους.] ὡς Φιλοκλέους ἀγρίου ὄντος ἐν τῇ μελοποιΐᾳ. εἴπερ τὴν πικρίαν αὐτοῦ εἶχον, οὐκ ἂν ῥᾳδίως αὐτοὺς διέφυγες. Schol. The phrase κατασπῶν Εὐριπίδην, Ach. 484, expresses the same idea of imbibing a poet's spirit. Cf. also above, v. 360. And Homer's δράκων βεβρωκὼς κακὰ φάρμακ' (Il. χ. 94) may be added in illustration: as the serpent 'got venom from his food, and bitter fury within him,' so were this company to be bitter and keen on Philoclean diet. For Philocles cf. Thesm. 168, ταῦτ' ἆρ' ὁ Φιλοκλέης αἰσχρὸς ὢν αἰσχρῶς ποιεῖ.

465 ὡς λάθρα μ' ἐλάμβαν' ὑπιοῦσα.] This line has to agree with v. 407 in metre. MSS. and editors

εἰ σύ γ', ὦ πόνῳ πονηρὲ καὶ κομηταμυνία,
τῶν νόμων ἡμᾶς ἀπείργεις ὧν ἔθηκεν ἡ πόλις,
οὔτε τιν' ἔχων πρόφασιν
οὔτε λόγον εὐτράπελον,
αὐτὸς ἄρχων μόνος.   470

ΒΔΕΛΤΚΛΕΩΝ
ἔσθ' ὅπως ἄνευ μάχης καὶ τῆς κατοξείας βοῆς
ἐς λόγους ἔλθοιμεν ἀλλήλοισι καὶ διαλλαγάς;

ΧΟΡΟΣ
σοὺς λόγους, ὦ μισόδημε καὶ μοναρχίας ἐρῶν,
καὶ ξυνὼν Βρασίδᾳ, καὶ φορῶν κράσπεδα   475
στεμμάτων, τὴν θ' ὑπήνην ἄκουρον τρέφων;

ΒΔΕΛΤΚΛΕΩΝ
νὴ Δί' ἦ μοι κρεῖττον ἐκστῆναι τὸ παράπαν τοῦ πατρὸς
μᾶλλον ἢ κακοῖς τοσούτοις ναυμαχεῖν ὁσημέραι.

vary in the details: the above is Meincke's. λάθρᾳ γ' ἐλάνθαν, the common reading, seems tautological. 466 πόνῳ πονηρὶ.] Cf. Lys. 350, ὤνδρες πόνῳ πονηροί. Such alliterations pleased the Greek ear. Cf. note on Nub. 6. κομηταμυνία.] κομᾶν = μέγα φρονᾶν: of Amynias we shall have more at v. 1267. 469 εὐτράπελον.] 'Ready, ingenious,' and so 'plausible.' Possibly the chorus of dicasts would have borne resignedly being tyrannized over, had their enemy defeated them by some dexterous plea, such as they were wont to admire in court. But εὐτράπελος is not always used in a bad sense: cf. Thuc. II. 41, where it is Pericles' boast that to the Athenian beyond all the world it belongs ἐπὶ πλεῖστα εἴδη μάλιστ' εὐτραπέλως τὸ σῶμα αὔταρκες παρέχεσθαι. 470—547. Bdelycleon proposes a conference, to settle matters amicably. At first the chorus will have no compromise with conspirators;

but after some talk it is agreed that Philocleon shall advocate the cause of the dicasts, and shew that their life is the most desirable. The chorus encourage him to do his best in their defence. 473 ἐρῶν.] With the vulg. ἐρᾷ· τὰ this line did not correspond to the trochaic v. 417. Yet, for the sense, ἐραστὰ comes better after μισόδημε, and the correction in these cases to perfect the metrical correspondence is often a doubtful matter. 475 ξυνὼν Βρασίδᾳ.] Cf. Pac. 640, φοροῖ τὰ Βρασίδου. Hems or edgings of wool were worn, says the Scholiast, by the Laconians. The beard and moustache they also allowed to grow in some manner peculiar to themselves. Hence all these particulars denote τὸ λακωνίζειν. 479 κακοῖς τ. ναυμαχεῖν.] 'Face such a broadside of troubles' we might say. Naval metaphors are of course rife at Athens.

ΧΟΡΟΣ

οὐδὲ μὲν γ᾽ οὐδ᾽ ἐν σελίνῳ σοῦστὶν οὐδ᾽ ἐν πηγάνῳ· 480
τοῦτο γὰρ παρεμβαλοῦμεν τῶν τριχοινίκων ἐπῶν.
ἀλλὰ νῦν μὲν οὐδὲν ἀλγεῖς, ἀλλ᾽ ὅταν ξυνήγορος
ταὐτὰ ταὐτά σου καταντλῇ καὶ ξυνωμότας καλῇ.

ΒΔΕΛΤΚΛΕΩΝ

ἆρ᾽ ἄν, ὦ πρὸς τῶν θεῶν, ὑμεῖς ἀπαλλαχθεῖτέ μου;
ἢ δέδοκταί σοι δέρεσθαι καὶ δέρειν δι᾽ ἡμέρας.   485

ΧΟΡΟΣ

οὐδέποτέ γ᾽, οὐχ, ἕως ἄν τι μου λοιπὸν ᾖ,
ὅστις ἡμῶν ἐπὶ τυραννίδ᾽ ὧδ᾽ ἐστάλης.

480 σελίνῳ.] Parsley and rue were planted as a border to gardens; those who had not advanced beyond them were only at the entrance or threshold: hence 'you are only at the parsley,' or 'not yet at the parsley,' is a proverb meaning 'you have only just begun,' or 'you have not yet begun.'

481 τοῦτο γὰρ ... τριχοινίκων ἐπῶν.] 'For this three-quart phrase will we throw in,' i.e. the phrase οὐδὲ μέν γ᾽...πηγάνῳ. Cf. Pac. 521, ῥῆμα μυριάμφορον. The expressions in the former verse may have been taken from some bad poet. Archippus the Scholiast thinks is here attacked. τριχοίνικος evidently means 'capacious, big;' and the chorus are probably led to use their fine phrase by Bdelycleon's expressions before, ναυμαχῖν δσημέραι, and (perhaps) ἐκστῆναι τοῦ πατρός. Richter thinks all these may have been phrases used by Archippus. This poet wrote a play called ὄνου σκία, which some think is referred to above at v. 191.

482 ἀλλ᾽ ὅταν.] 'But (you will feel it) when.'

483 καταντλῇ.] Cf. Plat. Rep. 344 A. ταῦτα εἰπὼν ὁ Θρασύμαχος ἐν νῷ εἶχεν ἀπιέναι, ὥσπερ βαλανεὺς ἡμῶν καταντλήσας κατὰ τῶν ὤτων

ἀθρόον καὶ πολὺν τὸν λόγον.

483 ξυνωμότας.] So MS. V: MS. Rav. has an abbreviation which might equally stand for plural or singular. But, on the score of sense, the plural seems better. The orator would use the word in the plural, ξυνωμόται, associating Bdelycleon with accomplices; cf. v. 488, ξυνωμόται, and Eq. 628, ξυνωμόται λέγων πιθανώταθ᾽, in a very similar case.

484 ἀπαλλαχθεῖτέ μου.] 'Will you or won't you keep clear of me?' The leading idea of course is that he is to be rid of them rather than they rid of him, though the Greek at first sight looks as if the reverse were the case.

485 σου.] Thus Bergk reads for vulg. μοι. The Chorus are addressed in the singular in the person of their leader. δ. μοι means 'is it decreed for me?' A curious use of the dative after such a verb.

485 δέρεσθαι καὶ δέρειν.] Berg-ler compares Ran. 861, δάκνειν, δά-κνεσθαι.

487 ὧδ᾽ ἐστάλης.] The deficient syllable in MSS. before ἐστάλη is supplied in various ways. ἐπὶ τυραννίδι διεστάληι Bentl. ὧδ᾽ is due to Hermann. Either this or Meineke's ἐξεστάλης makes the line agree with v. 439.

ΒΔΕΛΤΚΛΕΩΝ

ὡς ἅπανθ' ὑμῖν τυραννίς ἐστι καὶ ξυνωμόται,
ἥν τε μεῖζον ἥν τ' ἔλαττον πρᾶγμά τις κατηγορῇ,
ἧς ἐγὼ οὐκ ἤκουσα τοὔνομ' οὐδὲ πεντήκοντ' ἐτῶν·   490
νῦν δὲ πολλῷ τοῦ ταρίχους ἐστὶν ἀξιωτέρα·
ὥστε καὶ δὴ τοὔνομ' αὐτῆς ἐν ἀγορᾷ κυλίνδεται.
ἥν μὲν ὠνῆταί τις ὀρφὼς, μεμβράδας δὲ μὴ θέλῃ,
εὐθέως εἴρηχ' ὁ πωλῶν πλησίον τὰς μεμβράδας·
οὗτος ὀψωνεῖν ἔοιχ' ἄνθρωπος ἐπὶ τυραννίδι.   495
ἥν δὲ γήτειον προσαιτῇ ταῖς ἀφύαις ἡδύσματα,
ἡ λαχανόπωλις παραβλέψασά φησι θατέρῳ·
εἰπέ μοι, γήτειον αἰτεῖς πότερον ἐπὶ τυραννίδι;
ἢ νομίζεις τὰς Ἀθήνας σοὶ φέρειν ἡδύσματα;

488 τυραννίς.] The Athenians, remembering the Pisistratids, were ever on their guard against 'tyranny.' The mutilation of the Hermae in Alcibiades' time was thought ἐπὶ ξυνωμοσίᾳ νεωτέρων πραγμάτων καὶ δήμου καταλύσεως γεγενῆσθαι. Thuc. VI. 27. And Demosthenes (de Syntaxi, p. 170) rebukes this suspiciousness, giving instances which, though of course not so absurd as those of Aristophanes, are absurd enough.

490 πεντήκοντ' ἐτῶν.] Fifty years is put as a round number for a long time. The expulsion of the Pisistratids would be considerably more than fifty years before this play; later disturbances and anti-democratical movements would be less than fifty years ago.

491 ἀξιωτέρα.] Cf. Eq. 645, 672, for this market sense of ἄξιος.

493—5. If any purchaser prefer one kind of anchovy to another, an absurd political charge is made out of it. The ὀρφὼς was the more delicate kind.

496 ταῖς ἀφύαις ἡδύσματα.] Various are the readings adopted here: ταῖς ἀφ. ἡδυσμά τι, ταῖς ἀφ. ἡδυσμά τις, ταῖς ἀφ. ἡδύσματα, τις ἀφ. ἡδυ-

σμά τι, τις ἀφ. ἡδύσματα. The substitution of τις for ταῖς is to avoid the dactyl in the fifth place; for which, however, cf. Ach. 318, τὴν κεφαλὴν ἔχων λέγειν: which some editors alter there. ταῖς ἀφύαις ἡδύσματα seems to square best with Eq. 678, ἔπειτα ταῖς ἀφύαις ἐδίδουν ἡδύσματα. Of course τις is not necessary as subject to προσαιτῇ; for the same purchaser may be supposed to go on from the fish stall to the vegetable stall. Indeed, the πρὸς in the compound verb rather implies that it is a further demand of the man who has just bought his anchovies.

497 θατέρῳ.] τῷ ἑτέρῳ ὀφθαλμῷ χαλεπῶς ὑποβλεψαμένη, ὡς οὐκ ἄξιον ἡγουμένη τὸν τυχόντα φαγεῖν γήτειον. Schol. Leeks were, the herb-seller meant, a dish for a king; it was not for the like of him to be wanting them, or to expect Athens to supply him therewith. Perhaps in the next line φέρειν contains a notion of paying as tribute (φόρον), and the line might be paraphrased, 'are you a king, and is Athens bound to pay you tribute of leeks to relish your anchovies?'

ΞΑΝΘΙΑΣ

κἀμέ γ' ἡ πόρνη χθὲς εἰσελθόντα τῆς μεσημβρίας,   500
ὅτι κελητίσαι 'κέλευον, ὀξυθυμηθεῖσά μοι
ἤρετ' εἰ τὴν Ἱππίου καθίσταμαι τυραννίδα.

ΒΔΕΛΤΚΛΕΩΝ

ταῦτα γὰρ τούτοις ἀκούειν ἡδέ', εἰ καὶ νῦν ἐγὼ
τὸν πατέρ' ὅτι βούλομαι τούτων ἀπαλλαχθέντα τῶν
ὀρθροφοιτοσυκοφαντοδικοταλαιπώρων τρόπων   505
ζῆν βίον γενναῖον ὥσπερ Μόρυχος, αἰτίαν ἔχω
ταῦτα δρᾶν ξυνωμότης ὢν καὶ φρονῶν τυραννικά.

ΦΙΛΟΚΛΕΩΝ

νὴ Δί' ἐν δίκῃ γ'· ἐγὼ γὰρ οὐδ' ἂν ὀρνίθων γάλα
ἀντὶ τοῦ βίου λάβοιμ' ἂν οὗ με νῦν ἀποστερεῖς·
οὐδὲ χαίρω βατίσιν οὐδ' ἐγχέλεσιν, ἀλλ' ἥδιον ἂν   510
δικίδιον σμικρὸν φάγοιμ' ἂν ἐν λοπάδι πεπνιγμένον.

502 Ἱππίου.] Aristophanes does not fall into the mistake about Hippias, which Thucydides remarks on (1. 20). He mentions Hippias as the tyrant in Eq. 447—9, Λ. τὸν πάντα εἶναί φημί σου τῶν δορυφόρων. Κ. τοίων; φράσον. Δ. τῶν Βυρσίνης τῆς Ἱππίου.

505 ὀρθροφ.] His life was wretched and toilsome (ταλαίπωροι), with early rising and trudging to the courts (ὀρθροφοιτία), and with pettifogging and suits (συκοφαντία, δίκαι). Mitchell calls him 'a home-forsaker, morning-trudger, a suit and cause-distracted man.' The ταλαιπωρία of his present life is contrasted with the joviality of that proposed.

506 Μόρυχος.] Of course it is only in irony that Morychus' life is termed γενναῖος. For this luxurious gourmand cf. Ach. 887, Pac. 1008, and below, v. 1142. Bdelycleon had promised εὐωχία to his father, cf. above, v. 341.

508 ὀρνίθων γάλα.] A proverb for the utmost luxury. It is promised as such in Av. 733, by the

chorus of birds (who ought to know all about it), and again at v. 1673.

510 βατίσιν.] Cf. Pac. 810, βατιδοσκόποι. Eels (in the next line) were the delight of Morychus, cf. Ach. 887, where the Copaic eel is welcomed as φίλη Μορύχῳ.

511 πεπνιγμένον.] The operation of πνίξις is best described by Herodotus, II. 92, when he is telling how the Egyptians prepare the edible byblus: οἱ δὲ ἂν καὶ κάρτα βούλωνται χρηστῇ τῇ βύβλῳ χρᾶσθαι, ἐν κλιβάνῳ διαφανεῖ πνίξαντες οὕτω τρώγουσι. It is plain that the operation was performed without water, in a close-covered vessel, of earthenware probably, and was nearly what cooks now call 'braising,' and was not 'stewing' or 'seething.' There is also a further metaphorical sense in πεπνιγμένον, because, as Reigler says, 'in judiciis innocentes saepe misere vexarentur et paene enecarentur.' The λοπὰς is the dish in which the meat is served after the cooking: but has not apparently any judicial meaning.

ΒΔΕΛΤΚΛΕΩΝ

νὴ Δί᾽ εἰθίσθης γὰρ ἤδεσθαι τοιούτοις πράγμασιν·
ἀλλ᾽ ἐὰν σιγῶν ἀνάσχῃ καὶ μάθῃς ἀγὼ λέγω,
ἀναδιδάξειν οἴομαί σ᾽ ὡς πάντα ταῦθ᾽ ὑμαρτάνεις.   515

ΦΙΛΟΚΛΕΩΝ

ἐξιμαρτάνω δικάζων;

ΒΔΕΛΤΚΛΕΩΝ

καταγελώμενος μὲν οὖν
οὐκ ἐπαίεις ὑπ᾽ ἀνδρῶν, οὓς σὺ μόνον οὐ προσκυνεῖς.
ἀλλὰ δουλεύων λέληθας.

ΦΙΛΟΚΛΕΩΝ

παῦε δουλείαν λέγων,
ὅστις ἄρχω τῶν ἁπάντων.

ΒΔΕΛΤΚΛΕΩΝ

οὐ σύ γ᾽, ἀλλ᾽ ὑπηρετεῖς
οἰόμενος ἄρχειν· ἐπεὶ δίδαξον ἡμᾶς, ὦ πάτερ,
ἥτις ἡ τιμή 'στί σοι καρπουμένῳ τὴν Ἑλλάδα.   520

ΦΙΛΟΚΛΕΩΝ

πάνυ γε· καὶ τούτοισί γ᾽ ἐπιτρέψαι θέλω.

ΒΔΕΛΤΚΛΕΩΝ

καὶ μὴν ἐγώ.
ἄφετε νῦν ἅπαντες αὐτόν.

512. It is all habit, says the son; I can easily shew you that you are quite wrong, and are making yourself a miserable slave.

516 καταγ. μὲν οὖν.] Nay, to say you are wrong is not enough; you are, though you don't see it, a laughing-stock to the demagogues and orators.

518 ἄρχω.] See the passage in *The Knights* (1111—1150), where the Chorus chide Demus for being duped by the orators and demagogues, and he strives to shew that he is not such a fool as he looks.

They allow, however, at the outset ὦ Δῆμε καλὴν γ᾽ ἔχεις ἀρχήν, ὅτι πάντες ἄνθρωποι δεδίασί σ᾽ ὥσπερ ἄνδρα τύραννον.

520 καρπουμένῳ.] What good do you, as a dicast, get (asks the son) from the revenues coming in from Greece? you only have your paltry three-obol piece: the demagogues take the lion's share.

521 πάνυ γε.] An assent to δίδαξον: 'with all my heart (I will inform you).'

522 ἄφετε.] Spoken to the slaves, who were still guarding him.

ΦΙΛΟΚΛΕΩΝ

καὶ ξίφος γέ μοι δότε·
ἢν γὰρ ἡττηθῶ λέγων σου, περιπεσοῦμαι τῷ ξίφει.

ΒΔΕΛΤΚΛΕΩΝ

εἰπέ μοι, τί δ' ἦν τὸ δεῖνα τῇ διαίτῃ μὴ 'μμένῃς ;

ΦΙΛΟΚΛΕΩΝ

μηδέποτε πίοιμ' ἄκρατον μισθὸν ἀγαθοῦ δαίμονος.   525

ΧΟΡΟΣ

νῦν δὴ τὸν ἐκ θἡμετέρου
γυμνασίου δεῖ τι λέγειν
καινόν, ὅπως φανήσει

καὶ ξίφος γέ.] This line is wrongly given to Bdelycleon in some editions. Bergler corrected the arrangement of speakers. Cf. v. 714, where Philocleon has the sword now asked for. And the καὶ ξίφος γέ μοι δότε, 'Ay, and give me a sword,' plainly shews that it is the beginning of another person's speech. Philocleon will, in tragic fashion, like Ajax, fall on his sword, if defeated.

524 τὸ δεῖνα.] Cf. *Lys.* 921, καίτοι τὸ δεῖνα ψίαθός ἐστ' ἐξοιστέα, 916, καίτοι τὸ δεῖνα προσκεφάλαιον οὐκ ἔχεις. Also *Pac.* 268, τὸ δεῖνα γὰρ ἀπόλωλ' Ἀθηναίοισιν ἀλετρίβανος. From all these passages it is plain that τὸ δεῖνα is used when a speaker, suddenly recollecting something that hinders or affects the matter in hand, cannot at once in his hurry find words for it, but explains his meaning in the following clause. Thus in the *Lysistrata* we might render it: 'And yet there's what's-its-name still wanted—a mat, I mean, must be brought;' and so too in the other passage. In the *Peace* it is: 'You don't bring the pestle? No, for what's-its-name prevented —I mean, the Athenians' pestle is dead.' And so here, 'And what if what's-its-name were to happen—

if, I mean, you were not to abide by the arbitration.' This explanation appears better than that of L. and S., who take τὸ δεῖνα to be a vocative of address to the person; an explanation which seems not applicable satisfactorily to any of the Aristophanic passages, and impossible in some. *Lys.* 1168 may be added, and will be found to be like those above quoted.

525 ἄκρατον μισθόν.] Cf. *Eq.* 85, ἄκρατον οἶνον ἀγαθοῦ δαίμονος. The dicast's mind thinks of 'wage' rather than 'wine.' I have not hesitated with Meineke to accept ἄκρατον for ἄκρατον, due to Richter. The confusion of υ and ρ is frequent in MSS. The converse change from τεττώβολον to τεττωβόλου is to be accepted in *Eq.* 798. Cf. also *Pac.* 254.

526 νῦν δή, κ.τ.λ.] To vv. 526 —545 correspond metrically vv. 631 —647; but some words have been lost near the end of the antistrophe.

528 φανήσει.] This is to be taken with μὴ κατά τ. ν. τ. λέγειν. Bdelycleon interrupts to ask for his desk (κίστην), that he may take notes: he then says to the chorus, with reference apparently to their words 'that you may appear' 'But what sort of a man will you appear, if

ΒΔΕΛΤΚΛΕΩΝ

ἐνεγκάτω μοι δεῦρο τὴν κίστην τις ὡς τάχιστα.
ἀτὰρ φανεῖ ποῖός τις ὤν, ἢν ταῦτα παρακελεύῃ;   530

ΧΟΡΟΣ

μὴ κατὰ τὸν νεανίαν
τόνδε λέγειν. ὁρᾷς γὰρ ὡς
σοὶ μέγας ἐστὶν ἀγὼν
καὶ περὶ τῶν ἁπάντων,
εἴπερ, ὃ μὴ γένοιθ᾽, οὗ-   535
τός σ᾽ ἐθέλει κρατῆσαι.

ΒΔΕΛΤΚΛΕΩΝ

καὶ μὴν ὅσ᾽ ἂν λέξῃ γ᾽ ἁπλῶς μνημόσυνα γράψομαι ᾽γώ.

ΦΙΛΟΚΛΕΩΝ

τί γὰρ φάθ᾽ ὑμεῖς, ἢν ὁδί με τῷ λόγῳ κρατήσῃ;

ΧΟΡΟΣ

οὐκέτι πρεσβυτῶν ὄχλος   540
χρήσιμος ἔστ᾽ οὐδ᾽ ἀκαρῆ·
σκωπτόμενοι δ᾽ ἂν παισὶν ἐν
ταῖσιν ὁδοῖς ἁπάσαις

you urge him on in this way?' meaning probably that the chorus, as well as their champion, will cut a very different figure after the contest from what they expect. Then the chorus, ignoring his interruption, go on with their directions to Philocleon.

532 λέγειν.] Meineke adopts Hirschig's λέγων. ὅπως φανήσει λέγων, ' that you may appear speaking, be proved to speak,' is perhaps a little better than φ. λέγειν, 'you may appear to speak:' but the construction with infinitive seems admissible, and has all the MS. authority.

533, 4 ἀγὼν...περὶ τῶν ἁπάντων.] A kind of phrase frequent in exhortations, e.g. Thuc. VII. 61, ὁ μὲν ἀγὼν ὃ μέλλων ἔσται περί τε σωτηρίας καὶ πατρίδοι ἑκάστοις.

535 ὃ μὴ γένοιθ᾽.] This refers only to κρατῆσαι, not to the whole phrase, ἐθέλει κρατῆσαι.
537 ὅσ᾽ ἂν λέξῃ γ᾽ ἁπλῶς.] 'Of every word he says.'
541 ἀκαρῆ.] Cf. Av. 1649, τῶν γὰρ πατρῴων οὐδ᾽ ἀκαρῆ μέτεστί σοι. The word is used of time in Nub. 496. The singular is found in Plut. 244, ἐν ἀκαρεῖ χρόνῳ (or χρόνου). And below, at v. 701, ἀκαρῆς is read by many editors, as countenanced by Suidas.
542—5. The very gamins in the street will mock at us. Street boys seem to have been an institution in all lands. Cf. Horace's 'vellunt tibi barbam lascivi pueri.' Meineke's text has been adopted: for Dindorf's is as far from the MSS. by omission as is Meineke's by the conjectural insertion of ταισίν.

θαλλοφόροι καλούμεθ', ἀν-
τωμοσιῶν κελύφη.   545
ἀλλ' ὦ περὶ τῆς πάσης μέλλων βασιλείας ἀντιλογήσειν
τῆς ἡμετέρας, νυνὶ θαρρῶν πᾶσαν γλῶτταν βασάνιζε.

ΦΙΛΟΚΛΕΩΝ

καὶ μὴν εὐθύς γ' ἀπὸ βαλβίδων περὶ τῆς ἀρχῆς ἀποδείξω
τῆς ἡμετέρας ὡς οὐδεμιᾶς ἥττων ἐστὶν βασιλείας.
τί γὰρ εὔδαιμον καὶ μακαριστὸν μᾶλλον νῦν ἐστὶ δικα-
σтοῦ,   550
ἢ τρυφερώτερον, ἢ δεινότερον ζῶον, καὶ ταῦτα γέροντος;
ὃν πρῶτα μὲν ἕρποντ' ἐξ εὐνῆς τηροῦσ' ἐπὶ τοῖσι δρυφάκτοις
ἄνδρες μεγάλοι καὶ τετραπήχεις· κᾆπειτ' εὐθὺς προσιόντι
ἐμβάλλει μοι τὴν χεῖρ' ἁπαλήν, τῶν δημοσίων κεκλοφυῖαν·

544 **θαλλοφόροι.**] Old men were employed to carry branches of olive at the Panathenaic procession, as being useless for any other service. SchoI.

545 **ἀντωμοσιῶν κελύφη.**] For ἀντ. cf. *Dict. Antiq.* p. 55. **κελύφη,** 'mere husks, empty shells:' their kernel, force, and virtue being now gone.

547 **βασάνιζε.**] 'Test your full powers of tongue;' *i.e.* do all you know in the way of speech.

548—649. Philocleon describes how he is courted and flattered by the powerful, that they may ensure acquittal when brought before him as a dicast: how he receives all kinds of presents and indulgences; how he and his fellows do what they will, and give account to none: how he is quite worshipped and petted at his own home, and is a very Zeus to the multitude. When he has ended this speech, during which Bdelycleon takes a few notes, and throws in a few remarks, the Chorus, and Philocleon himself, think that the day is won.

548 **βαλβίδων.**] A favourite metaphor. Cf. *Eq.* 1159, ἄφες ἀπὸ βαλβίδων ἐμέ τε καὶ τουτονί: also *Lys.* 1000, ἀπὸ μιᾶς ὑσπλαγίδος,

551 **τρυφερώτερον.**] 'Better found in all luxuries, means of gratifying appetite, &c.' The Scholiast's τρυφῆς δεόμενος is a curious mistake. The word is illustrated in detail in vv. 607—619.

δεινότερον.] 'More feared.' Cf. vv. 612—630. The more frequent sense perhaps of δεινός in Attic Greek, when used of persons, is 'clever, cunning:' but the context is decisive for the other meaning here. δεινός is first 'fearful,' then by easy transition 'wonderful;' then, of persons, such fear or wonder at them is grounded on their possession of great powers, especially knowledge or cunning.

κ. τ. γέροντος.] 'Even though he be old,' and the old (as the Scholiast notes) are generally incapable of pleasure, fear, and weak.

553 **τετραπήχεις.**] Used by way of praise in *Ran.* 1014, γενναίους καὶ τετραπήχεις: here rather of great hulking fellows, who have to cringe to the (probably) insignificant-looking little judge. In Theocr. *Id.* xv. 17, ἀνὴρ τρισκαιδεχάπηχυς is contemptuous. Persius' 'Fulfennius ingens' (*Sat.* v. 190) is of this six-foot type.

554 **τὴν χεῖρ' ἁπαλήν.**] Meineke

ἱκετεύουσίν θ᾿ ὑποκύπτοντες, τὴν φωνὴν οἰκτροχοοῦντες· 555
οἴκτειρόν μ᾿, ὦ πάτερ, αἰτοῦμαί σ᾿, εἰ καὐτὸς πώποθ᾿ ὑφείλου
ἀρχὴν ἄρξας ἢ ᾿πὶ στρατιᾶς τοῖς ξυσσίτοις ἀγοράζων·
ὃς ἔμ᾿ οὐδ᾿ ἂν ζῶντ᾿ ᾔδειν, εἰ μὴ διὰ τὴν προτέραν ἀπόφυξιν.

ΒΔΕΛΥΚΛΕΩΝ
τουτὶ περὶ τῶν ἀντιβολούντων ἔστω τὸ μνημόσυνόν μοι.

ΦΙΛΟΚΛΕΩΝ
εἶτ᾿ εἰσελθὼν ἀντιβοληθεὶς καὶ τὴν ὀργὴν ἀπομορχθεὶς, 560
ἔνδον τούτων ὧν ἂν φάσκω πάντων οὐδὲν πεποίηκα,
ἀλλ᾿ ἀκροῶμαι πάσας φωνὰς ἰέντων εἰς ἀπόφυξιν.
φέρ᾿ ἴδω, τί γὰρ οὐκ ἔστιν ἀκοῦσαι θώπευμ᾿ ἐνταῦθα δι-
καστῇ;
οἱ μέν γ᾿ ἀποκλάονται πενίαν αὑτῶν καὶ προστιθέασιν
κακὰ πρὸς τοῖς οὖσιν, ἕως ἀνιὼν ἂν ἰσώσῃ τοῖσιν ἐμοῖσιν·

doubtingly proposes τις for τὴν. But surely ἀπαλὴ is an indirect predicate: 'he puts his hand in mine (so as to be) soft,' or 'he puts his hand in mine softly.' For the sense, it is much the same as if the adverb had been used. The transition from plural to singular need cause no difficulty: cf. vv. 564, 565, and *Pac.* 639, ἔσειον...τοὺς ταχεῖς, αἰτίαι ἂν προστιθέντες ὡς φρασοῖ τὰ Βρασίδου. To illustrate the general sense of this passage, Bergler quotes from Xen. *de Rep. Ath.* 1. 18, νῦν δ᾿ ἠνάγκασται τὸν δῆμον κολακεύειν τῶν Ἀθηναίων εἰς ἕκαστος τῶν συμμάχων ...καὶ ἀντιβολῆσαι ἀναγκάζεται ἐν τοῖς δικαστηρίοις καὶ εἰσιόντος τοῦ ἐπιλαμβάνεσθαι τῆς χειρόί. διὰ τοῦτο οὖν οἱ σύμμαχοι δοῦλοι τοῦ δήμου τῶν Ἀθηναίων καθεστᾶσι μᾶλλον.

557 στρατιᾶς.] For thefts on service cf. above, v. 354: also vv. 236—8. But here is rather meant a fraudulent embezzlement of money intrusted to the soldier to purchase provisions for the mess; as ὑφείλου and ἀγοράζων prove: the ὑπὸ denoting a quietness and secrecy in the transaction.

558 ᾔδειν.] For the form cf.

Nub. 380, ἐλελήθειν.

560 εἰσελθὼν κ.τ.λ.] 'Then, having gone into court and taken my seat as dicast, after these entreaties, &c.' The ἀντιβολίαι came before the going into court. For εἰσελθὼν compare εἰσιόντος in the passage of Xenophon quoted above.
ἀπομορχθεὶς.] No other metaphorical use of this word is given. ἀποβαλὼν Schol. but it seems to mean 'having had my anger smoothed away,' having been stroked, patted, &c. into lenity.
561. The defendants will say anything and everything to gain acquittal.
565 ἕως ἀνιὼν.] Dindorf supplies ἀνιὼν from MS. V, in which the syllable ων is written. But the ι is long in ἀνιῶν in *Eq.* 349, which makes for Meineke's view, who (with Hermann) writes ἀνιῶν: 'till, ascending in the scale of miseries, (= making his woes ever greater and greater) he makes his equal to mine.' In illustration of this, in connection with προστιθέασιν in v. 564, may be quoted from Thuc. III. 45, ἐπεὶ διεξεληλύθασί γε διὰ π τῶν ζημιῶν οἱ ἄνθρωποι προστι

οἱ δὲ λέγουσιν μύθους ἡμῖν, οἱ δ' Αἰσώπου τι γέλοιον· 566
οἱ δὲ σκώπτουσ', ἵν' ἐγὼ γελάσω καὶ τὸν θυμὸν κατά-
θωμαι.
κἂν μὴ τούτοις ἀναπειθώμεσθα, τὰ παιδάρι' εὐθὺς ἀνέλκει,
τὰς θηλείας καὶ τοὺς υἱεῖς, τῆς χειρός, ἐγὼ δ' ἀκροῶμαι·
τὰ δὲ συγκύψανθ' ἅμ βληχᾶται· κἄπειθ' ὁ πατὴρ ὑπὲρ
αὐτῶν 570
ὥσπερ θεὸν ἀντιβολεῖ με τρέμων τῆς εὐθύνης ἀπολῦσαι·
εἰ μὲν χαίρεις ἀρνὸς φωνῇ, παιδὸς φωνὴν ἐλεήσαις·
εἰ δ' αὖ τοῖς χοιριδίοις χαίρω, θυγατρὸς φωνῇ με πιθέσθαι.
χἠμεῖς αὐτῷ τότε τῆς ὀργῆς ὀλίγον τὸν κόλλοπ' ἀνεῖμεν.
ἆρ' οὐ μεγάλη τοῦτ' ἔστ' ἀρχὴ καὶ τοῦ πλούτου καταχήνη;

εἴπων ἦσσον ἀδικοῦντο ὑπὸ τῶν κακούρ-
γων. καὶ ἐλεὴ τὸ πάλαι τῶν μεγίστων
ἀδικημάτων μαλακωτέρας κεῖσθαι αὐ-
τάι, ταραβαινομένων δὲ τῷ χρόνῳ
δι τὸν θάνατον αἱ πολλαὶ ἀνήκουσιν,
'Men have gone through the whole
list of punishments, ever adding
punishment to punishment (= with
continual increase in severity) if by
any means they might less suffer
from evil-doers. And punishments
enacted in old time were milder,
naturally enough, even for heinous
offences, but, as these in time were
defied by transgressors, the more
part have now reached the severity
of death.' The use of προστιθέναι
is similar, also ἀνήκουσι may be
compared with ἀνιών here.
566 Αἰσώπου.] A tragic actor
of the name is meant, says the Scholiast; and this would make the Αἰσώπου τι γέλοιον more distinct from
the 'fables' just mentioned. Yet
Αἰσωπικὸν γέλοιον is supposed to
refer to a different Aesop, namely the
writer of fables, in v. 1259: whence
it does not seem certain that the
fable-writer is not meant here as
well. The μῦθοι first mentioned
might be longer and more elaborate
apologues, and so considered distinct from Aesop's short and funny
fables about birds, beasts, &c.

570 ἅμ βληχᾶται.] Dindorf says:
'formam monosyllabam restitui,
annotatam ab Hesychio.' συγκύ-
πτοντα βληχᾶται l'orson. Richter
reads συγκύψανθ' from MSS. R
and V: and the aorist participle is
quite as good as the present, if not
better: cf. Herod. III. 42, συγκύψαν-
τες τοιεῦσι.
κἄπειθ' ὁ πατὴρ κ. τ. λ.] Cf.
Demosth. c. Mid. 574, where Midias
is said to intend thus to excite com-
miseration.
574 κόλλοπ' ἀνεῖμεν.] Cf. v.
337, ὕφεσθε τοῦ τόνου. The κόλλο-
πες are the small pegs of the lyre to
which the strings are fastened, and
by turning which they can be tight-
ened. Schol. This passage rather
supports the interpretation of v. 337
as a metaphor from a stringed instrument.
575 πλούτου καταχήνη.] Cf.
Eccl. 631, καταχήνη τῶν σεμνοτέρων
ἔσται πολλή. It seems to strike
Blepyrus as a curious phrase, for
he at once jots it down. ἐγχανεῖν
is a common word for 'to mock at,
have the laugh against,' but the
noun καταχήνη, as thus used, hardly
finds a literal English equivalent.
'Am I not herein a mighty king,
and cannot I snap my fingers at your
wealthy men?' is the sense.

ΒΔΕΛΥΚΛΕΩΝ

δεύτερον αὖ σου τουτὶ γράφομαι, τὴν τοῦ πλούτου κατα-
            χήνην   576
καὶ τἀγαθά μοι μέμνησ' ἄχεις φάσκων τῆς Ἑλλάδος ἄρχειν.

ΦΙΛΟΚΛΕΩΝ

παίδων τοίνυν δοκιμαζομένων αἰδοῖα πάρεστι θεᾶσθαι.
κἂν Οἴαγρος εἰσέλθῃ φεύγων, οὐκ ἀποφεύγει πρὶν ἂν ἡμῖν
ἐκ τῆς Νιόβης εἴπῃ ῥῆσιν τὴν καλλίστην ἀπολέξας.   580
κἂν αὐλητής γε δίκην νικᾷ, ταύτης ἡμῖν ἐπίχειρα
ἐν φορβειᾷ τοῖσι δικασταῖς ἔξοδον ηὔλησ' ἀπιοῦσιν.
κἂν ἀποθνῄσκων ὁ πατήρ τῳ δῷ καταλείπων παῖδ' ἐπί-
            κληρον,
κλάειν ἡμεῖς μακρὰ τὴν κεφαλὴν εἰπόντες τῇ διαθήκῃ

---

579 **Οἴαγρος.**] A tragic actor; whether of Aeschylus or Sophocles is doubtful, and matters little. Aeschylus and Sophocles wrote each a play called *Niobe:* that of Aeschylus is mentioned in *Ran.* 912.

580 **ῥῆσιν.**] Cf. *Nub.* 1371, Εὐριπίδου ῥῆσίν τιν'. The dicasts get something out of both actor and flutist, before giving them a verdict.

582 **φορβειᾷ.**] The object of the mouth-piece was, according to the Scholiast, ὅπως ἂν σύμμετρον τὸ πνεῦμα πεμπόμενον ἡδεῖαν τὴν φωνὴν τοῦ αὐλητοῦ ποιήσῃ, to make the stream of breath through the instrument regular and even, and so sweeten the tone. φορβειᾶς ἄτερ came to be a proverb for 'without regulation or control.' Hence Cicero to Atticus (*Epist.* II. 16) says of Pompey, 'Cnaeus quidem noster jam plane quid cogitet nescio; φυσᾷ γὰρ οὐ σμικροῖσιν αὐλίσκοις ἔτι, ἀλλ' ἀγρίαις φύσαισι φορβειᾶς ἄτερ:' quoting what we know to be a fragment of Sophocles. A crow is ridiculously introduced in *The Birds* (v. 861) with such a mouthpiece on.

ἔξοδον ηὔλησ' ἀπιοῦσιν.] 'Plays us out of court.' But the playing out was perhaps to be with the concluding piece of music from some well-known play: the end of a tragedy being called ἔξοδος.

583—6. If a father die, leaving one daughter sole heiress, and have betrothed her already, we set the will aside, and take upon ourselves to give away the bride to our favourite.

583 **ἐπίκληρον.**] The later name, according to the Scholiast, was μονοκληρονόμος: and it is curious that ἐπίκληρος should in Attic Greek have come to be so specially used of a *daughter* inheriting, and that too an *only* daughter and child. Such an heiress was also called πατροῦχος παρθένος (Herod. VI. 57), and it was a matter to settle by law, who, as next of kin, should have her to wife, if her father had not, before his death, betrothed her.

584 **κλάειν...τὴν κεφαλήν.**] The construction is curious. In *Pltt.* 612, σὺ δ' ἐὰν κλάειν μακρὰ τὴν κεφαλὴν, the second accusative τὴν κ. appears to be in apposition to σέ: 'and to let you—your head (= your person, yourself) go weep.' Here the construction probably is 'b▓▓▓ told the will that its head (▓▓

καὶ τῇ κόγχῃ τῇ πάνυ σεμνῶς τοῖς σημείοισιν ἐπούσῃ,   585
ἔδομεν ταύτην ὅστις ἂν ἡμᾶς ἀντιβολήσας ἀναπείσῃ.
καὶ ταῦτ᾽ ἀνυπεύθυνοι δρῶμεν τῶν δ᾽ ἄλλων οὐδεμί᾽ ἀρχή.

ΒΔΕΛΤΚΛΕΩΝ

τουτὶ γάρ τοί σε μόνον τούτων ὧν εἴρηκας μακαρίζω·
τῆς δ᾽ ἐπικλήρου τὴν διαθήκην ἀδικεῖς ἀνακογχυλιάζων.   589

ΦΙΛΟΚΛΕΩΝ

ἔτι δ᾽ ἡ βουλὴ χὠ δῆμος ὅταν κρῖναι μέγα πρᾶγμ᾽ ἀπορήσῃ,
ἐψήφισται τοὺς ἀδικοῦντας τοῖσι δικασταῖς παραδοῦναι·
εἶτ᾽ Εὔαθλος χὠ μέγας οὗτος κολακώνυμος ἀσπιδαποβλὴς
οὐχὶ προδώσειν ἡμᾶς φασὶν, περὶ τοῦ πλήθους δὲ μαχεῖσθαι.
κἂν τῷ δήμῳ γνώμην οὐδεὶς πώποτ᾽ ἐνίκησεν, ἐὰν μὴ
εἴπῃ τὰ δικαστήρι᾽ ἀφεῖναι πρώτιστα μίαν δικάσαντας·   595
αὐτὸς δ᾽ ὁ Κλέων ὁ κεκραξιδάμας μόνον ἡμᾶς οὐ περιτρώγει,

may go weep;' but there may be
(as Florens supposes) another meaning implied in κεφαλὴν, 'the head
or beginning of the will,' *prima
cera d caput testamenti.* The passages quoted by Dergler with κλάειν
μακρά do not help us in explaining
the construction of κεφαλὴν either
in the *Plutus* or here. The explanation of one Scholiast on the *Plutus*,
that τὐντουσαι is understood, is not
satisfactory.

585 καὶ τῇ κόγχῃ.] Supply ἐλ-
πόντες ἐλάειν. They used to put
shells over the seals for greater
security. Schol.

πάνυ σεμνῶς.] 'Most preten-
tiously,' with a great fuss, and show
of care.

587 καὶ ταῦτ᾽...ἀρχή.] And we
do all this with no account to render
afterwards: which is more than any
other magistrate can do, since he
has to submit to the εὐθύνη on going
out of office.

588 οὐ μόνον.] Reiske, Porson,
Dindorf, Meineke, read it thus.
σεμνὸν vulg., σεμνῶν MS. Rav. σεμνῶν might do, 'Why on this point
of your grand privileges I do con-

gratulate you.' τουτὶ refers to τὸ
ἀνυπευθύνους δρᾶν.

590. Philocleon goes on with his
tale, regardless of his son's remark;
shewing how the most important
public matters are referred to the
dicasts, and how the demagogues
all court them.

592 Εὔαθλος.] Cf. *Ach.* 710, and
the note there. The comic writers,
Plato and Cratinus, both mention
him. Schol.

κολακώνυμος.] For Cleonymus cf.
Nub. 353, and above, vv. 20—1.
His name is slightly changed so as
to include the word (κόλαξ) that best
describes his nature.

593 οὐχὶ προδώσειν.] Cf. below,
v. 666. In *Eq.* 1048 Cleon represents himself by a lion, ὃς περὶ τοῦ
δήμου πολλάκις εὐρώψε μαχεῖται.

595 ἀφεῖναι κ.τ.λ.] Cf. *Eq.* 50,
ὦ Δῆμε, λοῦσαι πρῶτον ἐκδικάσας
μίαν.

596 κεκραξιδάμας.] Cf. *Eq.* 137,
κεκράκτηι. His voice is often remarked on as loud: cf. above, v. 36.
Α φωνὴ μιαρά (*Eq.* 218) was one of
the requisites for a demagogue.

ἀλλὰ φυλάττει διὰ χειρὸς ἔχων καὶ τὰς μυίας ἀπαμύνει.
σὺ δὲ τὸν πατέρ' οὐδ' ὁτιοῦν τούτων τὸν σαυτοῦ πώποτ'
            ἔδρασας.
ἀλλὰ Θέωρος, καίτοὐστὶν ἀνὴρ Εὐφημίου οὐδὲν ἐλάττων,
τὸν σπόγγον ἔχων ἐκ τῆς λεκάνης τἀμβάδι' ἡμῶν περικωνεῖ.
σκέψαι δ' ἀπὸ τῶν ἀγαθῶν οἵων ἀποκλείεις καὶ κατερύκεις,
ἣν δουλείαν οὖσαν ἔφασκες χὐπηρεσίαν ἀποδείξειν.

ΒΔΕΛΤΚΛΕΩΝ
ἔμπλησο λέγων· πάντως γάρ τοι παύσει ποτὲ κἀναφανήσει
πρωκτὸς λουτροῦ περιγιγνόμενος τῆς ἀρχῆς τῆς περισέμνου.

ΦΙΛΟΚΛΕΩΝ
ὃ δέ γ' ἥδιστον τούτων ἐστὶν πάντων, οὗ 'γὼ 'πιλελή-
            σμην,   605
ὅταν οἴκαδ' ἴω τὸν μισθὸν ἔχων, κᾆτ' εἰσήκονθ' ἅμα πάντες
ἀσπάζωνται δια τἀργύριον, καὶ πρῶτα μὲν ἡ θυγάτηρ με

---

597 τὰς μυίας ἀπαμύνει.] As is
said in *Eq.* 59, δεισποῦντος ἐστὼτ
ἀπεσοβεῖ τοὺς ῥήτορας. Homer (*Il.*
8. 130) has a curious simile about
Athene keeping off the arrow from
Menelaus : ἡ δὲ τόσον μὲν ἔεργεν ἀπὸ
χροὸς ὡς ὅτε μήτηρ παιδὸς ἔργει
μυῖαν, ὅθ' ἡδεῖ λέξεται ὕπνῳ.

599 Εὐφημίου.] Euphemius and
Theorus were evidently of the same
stamp. Of the former we know
nothing; the latter is frequently
ridiculed.

600 περικωνεῖ.] κυρίως τὸ πωσσώ-
σαι τὰ κεράμια. Schol.

602 χὐπηρεσίαν.] καὶ ὑπηρεσίαν
MS. Rav., which Bentley and Meineke also read. Dindorf rather approves it, but notes that the Ravenna
MS. has καὶ οὐδὲν for κοὐδὲν in v.
741, and other similar readings,
'crasi non raro neglecta.' It is
difficult to lay down any invariable
rule how such sequences or blend-
ings of vowel-sounds were written.
Possibly the Greeks themselves had
no fixed rule. They were pronounced so as to satisfy the require-
ments of metre, &c., and the audience

would be in no doubt about them,
while the language was living and
in its prime: the method of writing
them was for later grammarians to
settle and reduce to uniformity.

603, 4. Bdelycleon thinks that
his father will turn out but a sorry
figure, for all his grand 'empire,' as
he calls it : a sow will return to her
wallowing in the mire.

606 ὅταν οἴκαδ' ἴω.] All the
conjunctives depend on ὅταν: so
either the sentence is not strictly regular, having no apodosis to ὃ δέ γ'
ἥδιστόν ἐστιν; or the apodosis must
be at once supplied before οὗ 'γὼ
'πιλελήσμην : ' what is most sweet
(is that) which I had well-nigh for-
got; viz. when I go home, &c.' But
there is most probably an anacolu-
thon : the sentence was first meant
to run thus : ὃ δέ γ' ἥδιστόν ἐστιν,
ὅταν οἴκαδ' ἴω, πάντες ἀσπάζωνται:
then the verbs were put in the sub-
ordinate clause introduced by ὅταν,
and, owing to the length of this
clause, the regular apodosis required
by strictness of grammar was
gotten.

ἀπορίζῃ καὶ τὼ πόδ' ἀλείφῃ καὶ προσκύψασα φιλήσῃ,
καὶ παππίζουσ' ἅμα τῇ γλώττῃ τὸ τριώβολον ἐκκαλαμᾶται,
καὶ τὸ γύναιόν μ' ὑποθωπεῦσαν φυστὴν μᾶζαν προσε-
νέγκῃ,   610
κἄπειτα καθεζομένη παρ' ἐμοὶ προσαναγκάζῃ, φάγε τουτί,
ἔντραγε τουτί· τούτοισιν ἐγὼ γάνυμαι, κοὐ μή με δεήσῃ
ἐς σὲ βλέψαι καὶ τὸν ταμίαν, ὁπότ' ἄριστον παραθήσει
καταρασάμενος καὶ τονθορύσας. ἀλλ' ἢν μή μοι ταχὺ μάξῃ...
τάδε κέκτημαι πρόβλημα κακῶν, σκευὴν βελέων ἀλεωρήν·
κἂν οἶνόν μοι μὴ 'γχῇς σὺ πιεῖν, τὸν ὄνον τόνδ' ἐσκεκό-
μισμαι   616
οἴνου μεστὸν, κᾆτ' ἐγχέομαι κλίνας· οὗτος δὲ κεχηνὼς
βρωμησάμενος τοῦ σοῦ δίνου μέγα καὶ στράτιον κατέπαρδεν.
ἆρ' οὐ μεγάλην ἀρχὴν ἄρχω
καὶ τῆς τοῦ Διὸς οὐδὲν ἐλάττω,   620
ὅστις ἀκούω ταῦθ' ἅπερ ὁ Ζεύς;
ἢν γοῦν ἡμεῖς θορυβήσωμεν,

609 ἐκκαλαμᾶται.] Cf. v. 381.
610 φυστήν.] ἐξ ἀλφίτων καὶ οἴνου. Schol.
611—14. He does not depend for his supplies on his son or the steward who will grumble all the while.
612 κοὐ μή.] Vulg. καὶ μή; which is hardly defensible, 'and let me not need to look, &c.' Elmsley proposed κεἰ μή με δεήσει. The correction κοὐ is Hermann's, approved by Meineke and Richter.
614 ἀλλ' ἢν μή μοι.] This is Meineke's reading, adopted by Holden. It is best understood as an aposiopesis, 'and if he do not—woe be to him.' Or, as Hirschig punctuates, we may make τάδε κέκτημαι, κ.τ.λ. the apodosis to ἢν μή. Meineke rejects the four lines 615—618. The vulg. ἄλλην μή, 'lest he may soon have to knead me another,' is not satisfactory.
615 πρόβλημα...ἀλεωρήν.] Homeric: cf. Hom. Il. μ. 57, δῄων ἀνδρῶν ἀλεωρήν.
616 ὄνον.] There is probably a

play on the similarity of sound in οἶνος and ὄνος; and on the double sense of ὄνος. The vessel may have been so named from having two long ears; being a sort of 'diota.'
617 κεχηνώς.] 'Wide-mouthed;' applicable both to the wine-vessel, and to the animal, when braying out his contempt.
618 βρωμησάμενος.] Of the vessel this might refer to the noise of the wine as it was poured in; as Bergler suggests. The general sense of the passage is that Philocleon gets his wine-vessel, fills it for himself, and with his ὄνος laughs to scorn his son's δῖνος.
στράτιον.] τὸ εἰς πολλοὺς διῆκον. Schol. πολεμικὸν ἢ φοβερόν. Hesych. The shout of Ares in Homer (Il. ε. 859), ὁ δ' ἔβραχε χάλκεος Ἄρης ὅσσον τ' ἐννεάχιλοι ἐπίαχον ἢ δεκάχιλοι ἀνέρες ἐν πολέμῳ, was decidedly στράτιον.
620—25. A dicast is as sovereign as Zeus; the thunders of the court are spoken of, and feared.

πᾶς τίς φησιν τῶν παριόντων,
οἶον βροντᾷ τὸ δικαστήριον,
ὦ Ζεῦ βασιλεῦ.   625
κἂν ἀστράψω, ποππύζουσιν,
κἀγκεχόδασίν μ᾽ οἱ πλουτοῦντες
καὶ πάνυ σεμνοί.
καὶ σὺ δέδοικάς με μάλιστ᾽ αὐτός·
νὴ τὴν Δήμητρα, δέδοικας. ἐγὼ δ᾽
ἀπολοίμην, εἰ σὲ δέδοικα.   630

ΧΟΡΟΣ

οὐπώποθ᾽ οὕτω καθαρῶς
οὐδενὸς ἠκούσαμεν οὐ-
δὲ ξυνετῶς λέγοντος.

ΦΙΛΟΚΛΕΩΝ

οὔκ, ἀλλ᾽ ἐρήμας ᾤεθ᾽ οὗτος ῥᾳδίως τρυγήσειν·
καλῶς γὰρ ᾔδειν ὡς ἐγὼ ταύτῃ κράτιστός εἰμι.   635

ΧΟΡΟΣ

ὡς δ᾽ ἐπὶ πάντ᾽ ἐπῆλθε κοὐδέν τι παρῆλθεν, ὥστ᾽ ἔγωγ᾽
ηὐξανόμην ἀκούων,

---

616 ποππύζουσιν.] This sound
is here meant by way of charm
against evil : cf. Plin. *Hist. Nat.*
XXVIII. 5, fulget ras poppysmate ado-
rare consensus gentium est. There
are various other uses of the word,
which is evidently onomatopoetic.

629 νὴ τ. Δ.] The old man probably repeats his assertion thus
strongly, not only to impress it on
his son (who perhaps makes some
gesture of dissent), but to convince
and assure himself.

631 καθαρῶς.] 'Clearly;' the
adverb is to be taken with λέγοντος.

634 οὔκ, ἀλλ᾽.] The proverbial
phrase ἐρήμας (ἀμπέλους) τρυγήσειν
is again used in *Eccl.* 885. It is
from those who guard vines care-
lessly, according to the Scholiast :
and a somewhat similar proverb
seems γλυκεῖ᾽ ὀπώρα φύλακος ἀπλι-

λοιπότοι. For the watching of vines,
see a pleasing picture in Theocritus
(*Id.* 1. 45—51) of a boy set to
watch the ripe grapes, from whom
a fox successfully manages τρυγᾶν
ἐρήμας. But to the dicast ἔρημοι
would also suggest δίκη, 'a case un-
defended'; where judgment goes by
default. The whole sense of the
speech is 'No (you never did hear
any speak better), yet this man
thought to win an easy victory,
(absurd!) for he knew forensic argument to be my strong point.' Or the
ellipse before γάρ may be rendered
by 'why, he knew, &c.'

636—641. In these lines Meineke's
readings square better with the cor-
responding verses 531—536 and are
about as near to MSS.

638 ηὐξανόμην.] 'Felt myself
bigger.' Cf. Plat. *Menex.* 235, ὥστ᾽

5

κἂν μακάρων δικάζειν
αὐτὸς ἔδοξα νήσοις,   640
ἡδόμενος λέγοντι.

ΦΙΛΟΚΛΕΩΝ

ὡς οὗτος ἤδη σκορδινᾶται κἄστιν οὐκ ἐν αὑτοῦ.
ἦ μὴν ἐγώ σε τήμερον σκύτη βλέπειν ποιήσω.

ΧΟΡΟΣ

δεῖ δέ σε παντοίας πλέκειν
εἰς ἀπόφυξιν παλάμας.   645
τὴν γὰρ ἐμὴν ὀργὴν πεπᾶ-
ναι χαλεπὸν .   .   .
.   .   .   .   .   .
μὴ πρὸς ἐμοῦ λέγοντι.
πρὸς ταῦτα μύλην ἀγαθὴν ὥρα ζητεῖν σοι καὶ νεόκοπτον,
ἢν μή τι λέγῃς, ἥτις δυνατὴ τὸν ἐμὸν θυμὸν κατερεῖξαι.

ΒΔΕΛΥΚΛΕΩΝ

χαλεπὸν μὲν καὶ δεινῆς γνώμης καὶ μείζονος ἢ 'πὶ τρυ-
                γῳδοῖς,   650
ἰάσασθαι νόσον ἀρχαίαν ἐν τῇ πόλει ἐντετοκυῖαν.
ἀτάρ, ὦ πάτερ ἡμέτερε Κρονίδη

ἔγωγε γενναίως διατίθεμαι ... ἡγούμε-
νος ἐν τῷ παραχρῆμα μεῖζων καὶ καλ-
λίων γεγονέναι, ... τέως δὲ οἶμαι μόνον
οὐκ ἐν μακάρων νήσοις οἰκεῖν.
639 δικάζων.] They cannot
imagine, even in the isles of the
blessed, life without lawsuits.
641 σκορδινᾶται.] Yawning or
gaping is a token of weariness in
Ach. 30. Here the dicast takes it
to mean confusion and loss of pre-
sence of mind. The Scholiast explains it as ὃ ποιοῦσιν ἐξ ὕπνου ἀνι-
στάμενοι καὶ μετὰ χάσμης τὰ μέλη
ἐκτείνοντες.
643 σκύτη βλέπων.] A proverb,
used also in Eupolis, according
to the Scholiast: εἴρηται δὲ ἐπὶ τῶν
ὑποψιαστικῶς διακειμένων πρὸς τὰ
μέλλοντα κακά. If so, it is not quite
analogous to βλέπειν νᾶπυ and the
like; for it then ought to mean 'to

look as if going to whip,' rather than
'to be whipt.'
647 χαλεπόν.] Some syllables
have been lost here: the amount
will differ, as we take Dindorf's text
or Meineke's.
649 κατερεῖξαι.] Cf. *Ran.* 505,
κατερικτῶν χύτρας ἕτνους δύ' ἢ τρεῖς.
650—724. Bdelycleon in reply
gives some account of the state revenues; shews how large a part of
these is absorbed by self-interested
demagogues, while the people get
but little, and follow blindly and
slavishly these leaders.
651 ἐντετοκυῖαν.] ἐγγεννηθεῖσαν.
Schol.
652 πάτερ.] Cf. Hom. *Od.* α.
45, ὦ πάτερ ἡμέτερε Κρονίδη, ὕπατε
κρειόντων. Philocleon was led to
use the phrase by his father's boast
that he and his fellow dicasts had

ΦΙΛΟΚΛΕΩΝ

παῦσαι καὶ μὴ πατέριζε.
εἰ μὴ γὰρ ὅπως δουλεύω 'γώ, τουτὶ ταχέως με διδάξεις,
οὐκ ἔστιν ὅπως οὐχὶ τεθνήξεις, κἂν χρῇ σπλάγχνων μ'
ἀπέχεσθαι.

ΒΔΕΛΥΚΛΕΩΝ

ἀκρόασαί νυν, ὦ παππίδιον, χαλάσας ὀλίγον τὸ μέτωπον·
καὶ πρῶτον μὲν λόγισαι φαύλως, μὴ ψήφοις, ἀλλ' ἀπὸ
χειρός, 656
τὸν φόρον ἡμῖν ἀπὸ τῶν πόλεων συλλήβδην τὸν προσιόντα·
κἄξω τούτου τὰ τέλη χωρὶς καὶ τὰς πολλὰς ἑκατοστάς,
πρυτανεῖα, μέταλλ', ἀγοράς, λιμένας, μισθοὺς καὶ δημιόπρατα.
τούτων πλήρωμα τάλαντ' ἐγγὺς δισχίλια γίγνεται ἡμῖν. 660
ἀπὸ τούτων νυν κατάθες μισθὸν τοῖσι δικασταῖς ἐνιαυτοῦ,
ἐξ χιλιάσιν, κοὔπω πλείους ἐν τῇ χώρᾳ κατένασθεν,
γίγνεται ἡμῖν ἑκατὸν δήπου καὶ πεντήκοντα τάλαντα.

---

the titles of Zeus: vv. 620—25.
The father stops him with 'don't be
fathering me,' and brings him to the
point.

654 σπλάγχνων μ' ἀπέχεσθαι.]
Cf. *Eq.* 410, ἦ μήποτ' ἀγοραίου Διὸς
σπλάγχνοισι παραγενοίμην. He
would be excluded from the sacrifices, if stained with the crime of
homicide.

656 λόγισαι φαύλως.] 'Do an
easy sum:' one that needs no peb-
bles or counters, but can be done
on the fingers, off-hand. This is of
course the sense of φαύλως, as indeed the Scholiast and Suidas explain it. Florens not so well explains
it 'do the sum badly,' inexactly,
'quia certior computatio per calcu-
los quam digitos.' But the sum
is done exactly enough in what follows.

658 τὰ τέλη, κ.τ.λ.] Schömann
de Com. Athen. p. 286 explains

these items. τέλη are taxes paid by
aliens and freedmen, by particular
trades, &c.: ἑκατοσταί, harbour dues
in the Piraeus: ἀγοραί, λιμένες represent duties paid on exports, im-
ports, and wares sold : μισθοί probably are rents from public lands
or houses let out to private indivi-
duals : πρυτανεῖα, court-fees, equivalent nearly to the Roman 'sa-
cramenta:' δημιόπρατα, confiscated
goods, or the money produced by
their sale.

660—663. These make up in all
2000 talents. But each dicast is to
have 3 obols a day, or half a
drachma: therefore 15 drachmae in
a month of 30 days, 150 drachmae
in a year of ten months. Then
6000 × 150 dr. = 150 × 60 × 100 dr.
= 150 talents. As the Scholiast remarks, the judicial year had but
10 months, 2 months being spent in
holiday.

ΦΙΛΟΚΛΕΩΝ

οὐδ᾽ ἡ δεκάτη τῶν προσιόντων ἡμῖν ἆρ᾽ ἐγίγνεθ᾽ ὁ μισθός.

ΒΔΕΛΤΚΛΕΩΝ

μὰ Δί᾽ οὐ μέντοι.

ΦΙΛΟΚΛΕΩΝ

καὶ ποῖ τρέπεται δὴ ᾽πειτα τὰ χρήματα τἆλλα; 665

ΒΔΕΛΤΚΛΕΩΝ

ἐς τούτους τοὺς, οὐχὶ προδώσω τὸν Ἀθηναίων κολοσυρτὸν,
ἀλλὰ μαχοῦμαι περὶ τοῦ πλήθους ἀεί. σὺ γὰρ, ὦ πάτερ,
αὑτοὺς
ἄρχειν αἱρεῖ σαυτοῦ, τούτοις τοῖς ῥηματίοις περιπεφθείς.
κᾆθ᾽ οὗτοι μὲν δωροδοκοῦσιν κατὰ πεντήκοντα τάλαντα
ἀπὸ τῶν πόλεων, ἐπαπειλοῦντες τοιαυτὶ κἀναφοβοῦντες, 670
δώσετε τὸν φόρον, ἢ βροντήσας τὴν πόλιν ὑμῶν ἀνατρέψω.
σὺ δὲ τῆς ἀρχῆς ἀγαπᾷς τῆς σῆς τοὺς ἀργελόφους περι-
τρώγων.
οἱ δὲ ξύμμαχοι ὡς ἤσθηνται τὸν μὲν σύρφακα τὸν ἄλλον

664 δεκάτη.] Being but 150 out of 1000.

665 καὶ ποῖ.] Meineke's and Bothe's arrangement of the speakers seems preferable. Philocleon says, 'Then after all we don't get a tenth of the whole. Bd. No, that you don't. Phi. What then becomes of the rest? Bd. Oh! it goes to those braggart demagogues, who cajole you with such fine promises.' The phrase τοὺς οὐχὶ πρ. κ.τ.λ. is much better as said in scorn by Bdelycleon, than as a serious confession on Philocleon's part.

666 κολοσυρτόν.] Of the lowest rabble: cf. Plut. 536. It is a word rather supplied by Bdelycleon to express what the stump-orators virtually meant, than the real word that they would have used, when thus making their showy professions of republicanism.

668 περιπεφθείς.] A peculiar use. In Plut. 159, ὀνόματι περιπέττουσι

τὴν μοχθηρίαν, as also in Plat. Legg. 886 E, λόγοισιν εὖ πως εἰς τὸ πιθανὸν περιπεπεμμένα, the word is of conduct or theories made plausible and smooth to outward view by specious words; but of its application to a person deceived by such means, this seems to be the only instance. But there is something rather analogous in Eq. 215, τὸν δῆμον προσποιοῦ ὑπογλυκαίνων ῥηματίοις μαγειρικοῖς: for there the 'sugaring' or 'sweetening' would, strictly, be applied to the viands, but the participle governs the person won over by such skill in cookery.

672 ἀργελόφους.] τὰ περιττὰ καὶ ἄχρηστα, ἀργίλοφοι γὰρ τῆ μηλωτῆ οἱ πόδες. Schol. 'refuse, leavings.'

673—77. These rascals get the best of everything: and the allies soon find that out, and court them, but scorn you.

ἐκ κηθαρίου λαγαριζόμενον καὶ τραγαλίζοντα τὸ μηδὲν,   674
σὲ μὲν ἡγοῦνται Κόννου ψῆφον, τούτοισι δὲ δωροφοροῦσιν
ὄρχας, οἶνον, δάπιδας, τυρὸν, μέλι, σήσαμα, προσκεφάλαια,
φιάλας, χλανίδας, στεφάνους, ὅρμους, ἐκπώματα, πλουθυ-
            γίειαν·
σοὶ δ᾽ ὧν ἄρχεις, πολλὰ μὲν ἐν γῇ πολλὰ δ᾽ ἐφ᾽ ὑγρᾷ πιτυ-
            λεύσας,
οὐδεὶς οὐδὲ σκορόδου κεφαλὴν τοῖς ἐψητοῖσι δίδωσιν.

ΦΙΛΟΚΛΕΩΝ

μὰ Δί᾽ ἀλλὰ παρ᾽ Εὐχαρίδου καὐτὸς τρεῖς γ᾽ ἀγλίθας μετέ-
            πεμψα.   680
ἀλλ᾽ αὐτήν μοι τὴν δουλείαν οὐκ ἀποφαίνων ἀποκναίεις.

673 σύρφακα.] Bergler quotes from Euphron, ὅταν μὲν ἔλθῃ εἰς τοιοῦτον συρφετὸν, Δρόμωνα καὶ Κέρδωνα καὶ Σωτηρίδην. It is much the same as κολοσυρτὸς, v. 666.

674 ἐκ κηθαρίου.] πλέγμα ἐστὶ κανισκῶδες ἐπιτιθέμενον τῇ πληρωτρίδι τῶν ψήφων. Schol. It was also called πήθιον: and the κημὸς seems to have been a similar vessel. The word here stands for law-business generally.

λαγαριζόμενον.] The explanation of this word, from λαγαρός, seems certainly preferable to that of the Scholiast, τὰ λάγαρα ἐσθίοντα, ὅ ἐστιν εὔθραυστα καὶ εὐτελῆ ὄντα. The general sense then will be: 'when the allies see that you, as a result of your lawsuits, become thin and starved.'

675 Κόννου ψῆφον.] That this means 'a mere cipher,' is tolerably certain; but the origin of the phrase is doubtful. A Connas is mentioned in Eq. 534, a worn out musician probably. The Connas, or Connas, of this passage may be the same, or he may be some other man of no account. The Scholiast tells us that Κόννου θρῖον was the proverb; where θρῖον is by Florens taken to mean 'inanis sonus,' cf. v. 436, πολλῶν...οἶδα θρίων τὸν ψό-

φων. And ψῆφοι seems used because a dicast is the subject: but it is uncertain whether Κ. ψῆφοι is 'the vote given by Connas,' (of no use or validity we may suppose,) or whether it means 'they think that you are but of the account of Connas,' you, as an item in the reckoning, are but of the value of Connas, viz. worth nothing.

676 ὄρχας.] κεράμινα ἀγγεῖα, ὑποθεκτικὰ ταρίχων, δύο ὦτα ἔχοντα. Schol. Cf. Pers. Sat. III. 76, Maenaque quod prima nondum defecerit orca: where the satirist is speaking of presents given by provincial clients to their legal advocates.

676 σήσαμα.] Cakes made of this were favourites at Athens: cf. Ach. 1092, σησαμοῦντες.

678 πιτυλεύσας.] πίτυλοι ἡ καταβολὴ τῆς κώπης. Schol. πιτυλεύσας here belongs properly to ἐφ᾽ ὑγρᾷ, some ordinary word = πονήσας being understood with ἐν γῇ. A similar zeugma is in Eq. 545, σωφρονικῶς κοὐκ ἀνοήτως ἐσπηδήσαι ἐφλυάρει. References to the Athenians' labours on the sea are frequent, e.g. in Eq. 785, τὴν ἐν Σαλαμῖνι.

681 αὐτήν τ. δ.] 'You do not exactly make out the slavery (that you spoke of).' Cf. v. 318.

ΒΔΕΛΤΚΛΕΩΝ

οὐ γὰρ μεγάλη δουλεία 'στὶν τούτοις μὲν ἅπαντας ἐν ἀρχαῖς
αὐτούς τ' εἶναι καὶ τοὺς κόλακας τοὺς τούτων μισθοφο-
ροῦντας;
σοὶ δ' ἦν τις δῷ τοὺς τρεῖς ὀβολούς, ἀγαπᾷς οἷς αὐτὸς
ἐλαύνων
καὶ πεζομαχῶν καὶ πολιορκῶν ἐκτήσω, πολλὰ πονήσας. 685
καὶ πρὸς τούτοις ἐπιταττόμενος φοιτᾷς, ὃ μάλιστά μ' ἀ-
πάγχει,
ὅταν εἰσελθὸν μειράκιόν σοι καταπῦγον, Χαιρέου υἱὸς,
ὡδὶ διαβὰς, διακινηθεὶς τῷ σώματι καὶ τρυφερανθείς,
ἥκειν εἴπῃ πρῷ κἂν ὥρᾳ δικάσονθ', ὡς ὅστις ἂν ὑμῶν
ὕστερος ἔλθῃ τοῦ σημείου τὸ τριώβολον οὐ κομιεῖται· 690
αὐτὸς δὲ φέρει τὸ συνηγορικὸν, δραχμὴν, κἂν ὕστερος ἔλθῃ·
καὶ κοινωνῶν τῶν ἀρχόντων ἑτέρῳ τινὶ τῶν μεθ' ἑαυτοῦ,
ἤν τίς τι διδῷ τῶν φευγόντων, ξυνθέντε τὸ πρᾶγμα δύ' ὄντε
ἐσπουδάκατον, κᾆθ', ὡς πρίων', ὁ μὲν ἕλκει, ὁ δ' ἀντενέδωκε·

οὐκ ἀποφ. ἀποκναίσι.] The
negative belongs only to the participle.
684—5 ἐλαύνων—πεζομαχῶν—
πολιορκῶν.] An explanation of v.
678.
686—90. Then too you are at
the beck and call of dissolute young
striplings. Chaereas was attacked
by Eupolis (says the Scholiast) as of
foreign extraction.
686 ἀπάγχει.] A favourite Greek
metaphor to express what annoys
one, what one cannot away with,
cannot swallow. Cf. *Ach.* 135, ταῦτα
δῆτ' οὐκ ἀγχόνη;
688 ὡδί.] He imitates the youth's
gait.
690 σημείον.] Those who came
late were shut out: cf. below, 775,
891. We find in *Thesm.* 277, τὸ
τῆς ἐκκλησίας σημεῖον ἐν τῷ Θεσμο-
φορείῳ φαίνεται: and in Andocides,
De Mysteriis, p. 6, ἐπειδὴ τὴν βουλὴν
εἰς τὸ βουλευτήριον ὁ κῆρυξ ἀνείπῃ
ἱέναι καὶ τὸ σημεῖον καθίλῃ. Whence
it is rightly inferred by Schömann

(*De Com. Ath.* pp. 149—153), that
the 'signal' was something plainly
visible, of the nature of a standard,
set up to denote when it was time to
meet, and taken down when all
were assembled, or when enough
were assembled; and that after it
was taken down no late comers
were admitted. It is of the σημεῖον
for the βουλὴ that Andocides is
speaking, but the signals whether
for council or law-courts were probably of the same nature.
691 συνηγορικόν.] 'Counsel's
fee:' double of the three-obol piece;
but not so very large. However,
his gains do not end here, for he
and some other make more by a
bribe from the defendant.
694 ἐσπουδάκατον.] 'Make a
job of it,' have settled it all between
them κατὰ σπουδήν. Cf. *Eq.* 1370,
κατὰ σπουδάς; and note on *Eq.* 926,
where this use of σπουδή is illustrated from Demosthenes.
πρίων'.] *i. e.* πρίονος, 'a pair of
sawyers.' There is a sort of mock

σὺ δὲ χασκάζεις τὸν κωλαγρέτην τὸ δὲ πραττόμενόν σε
λέληθεν.   695

ΦΙΛΟΚΛΕΩΝ

ταυτί με ποιοῦσ'; οἴμοι, τί λέγεις; ὥς μου τὸν θῖνα τα-
ράττεις,
καὶ τὸν νοῦν μου προσάγεις μᾶλλον, κοὐκ οἶδ' ὅ τι χρῆμά
με ποιεῖς.

ΒΔΕΛΥΚΛΕΩΝ

σκέψαι τοίνυν ὡς, ἐξόν σοι πλουτεῖν καὶ τοισὶδ' ἅπασιν,
ὑπὸ τῶν ἀεὶ δημιζόντων οὐκ οἶδ' ὅπη ἐγκεκύκλησαι·
ὅστις πόλεων ἄρχων πλείστων, ἀπὸ τοῦ Πόντου μέχρι Σαρ-
δοῦς,   700
οὐκ ἀπολαύεις πλὴν τοῦθ' ὃ φέρεις, ἀκαρῆ. καὶ τοῦτ' ἐρίῳ σοι

contest between the opposite parties, but they are really in collusion, and agree like a pair of sawyers, one yielding as the other pulls, πρίωθ Hirschig and Mein. πρίων, πρίωσι, πρίων, MSS. Dindorf infers the declension πρίων, -ωνος from Photius, who remarks that Cratinus uses the plural πρίωσι διὰ τοῦ ο, as if that were not the usual form.

695 κωλαγρέτην.] This officer was, among other things, paymaster to the dicasts. The derivation given by the Scholiast seems probable; though quite unconnected with the duty of the office which is here treated of: ὁ ταμίας τοῦ δικαστικοῦ μισθοῦ καὶ τῶν εἰς θεοὺς ἀναλωμάτων. νόμοι δὲ ἦν τὰ ὑπολειπόμενα τοῖς ἱερέσι λαμβάνειν ἃ εἴσω οἷον δέρματα καὶ κωλαί.

696 θῖνα ταράττει.] 'You stir my very depths.' Here θίς is of the sand at the bottom, compare Virgil's 'nigrasque alte subjeclat arenas.'

698 καὶ τοισὶδ.] Meineke first proposed ἀδστοῖσιν, 'when you and all the citizens might be wealthy:' but afterwards acquiesced in Hermann's καὶ τοισίδ'. Bentley proposed ἀγαθοῖσιν; Reiske ἴσα τοῖσιν ἄπασιν, 'because the childless are

courted by legacy-hunters.'
699 δημιζόντων.] This word is referred to by Ruhnken on δημοῦσθαι, in Timaeus' Platonic Lexicon. The two words may have been of much the same force; but in the passages we have for δημοῦσθαι and δήμωμα (Plat. Theaet. 161, and Aristoph. Pac. 796) scarcely any notion of δῆμος survives.
ἐγκεκύκλησαι.] 'A re venatoria ducla videtur metaphora.' Conz. And this seems right: 'you are encircled, hemmed in, confined, brought to bay.' The Latin version in Bekker's edition gives 'involutus ais nescio quibus angustiis.' Mitchell translates, 'Into corners you're driving (=driven, metri gratia), by the men who are thriving on the love, &c.'
701 ἐρίῳ, κ.τ.λ.] What they do give is dealt out drop by drop, like oil through wool into a man's ear. Bergler compares Dem. Olynth. III. p. 37, ἴσον ἂν ἴσον, ὦ ἄνδρες Ἀθηναῖοι, τέλειόν τι καὶ μέγα στήσαισθε ἀγαθὸν, καὶ τῶν τοιούτων λημμάτων ἀπαλλαγείητε, ἃ τοῖς ἀσθενοῦσι παρὰ τῶν ἰατρῶν σιτίοις διδομέναις ἔοικε· καὶ γὰρ οὔτε ἰσχὺν ἐκεῖνα ἐντίθησιν, οὔτ' ἀποθνήσκειν ἐᾷ, καὶ ταῦτα ἃ

ἐνστάζουσιν κατὰ μικρὸν ἀεὶ, τοῦ ζῆν ἕνεχ᾽, ὥσπερ ἔλαιον.
βούλονται γάρ σε πένητ᾽ εἶναι· καὶ τοῦθ᾽ ὧν οὕνεκ᾽, ἐρῶ σοι,
ἵνα γιγνώσκῃς τὸν τιθασευτήν· κᾆθ᾽ ὅταν οὗτός γ᾽ ἐπισίζῃ,
ἐπὶ τῶν ἐχθρῶν τιν᾽ ἐπιρρύξας, ἀγρίως αὐτοῖς ἐπιπηδᾷς. 705
εἰ γὰρ ἐβούλοντο βίον πορίσαι τῷ δήμῳ, ῥᾴδιον ἦν ἄν.
εἰσίν γε πόλεις χίλιαι, αἳ νῦν τὸν φόρον ἡμῖν ἀπάγουσιν·
τούτων εἴκοσιν ἄνδρας βόσκειν εἴ τις προσέταξεν ἑκάστῃ,
δύο μυριάδ᾽ ἂν τῶν δημοτικῶν ἔζων ἐν πᾶσι λαγῴοις

νέμεσθε νῦν ὑμεῖς οὔτε τοιαῦτά ἐστιν
ὥστε ὠφέλειαν ἔχειν τινὰ διαρκῆ, οὔτ᾽
ἀπογνόνται ἄλλο τι πράττειν ἐᾷ.

703 τοῦθ᾽ ὧν οὕνεκ᾽, ἐρῶ.] ‘And
this they do, I will tell you why,
'tis that you may.’ Meineke, omitting the comma after οὕνεκα, leaves
it doubtful whether the sense might
not be ‘and this for a reason which
I will tell you, viz. that, &c.’ ὧν
οὕνεκ᾽ ἐρῶ being = οὕνεκα τούτων ἃ
ἐρῶ.

704 τιθασευτήν.] Demosthenes
says (Olynth. III. 37) of certain statesmen τιθασεύουσι χειροηθεῖς αὑτοῖς
ποιοῦντες. Indeed there is much in
that speech that illustrates Aristophanes' strictures here.

ἐπισίζῃ.] You are kept quiet like
a dog till your master urges you on
at any one. Ruhnken's ingenious
conjecture in Theocr. Id. VI. 29,
σίξα δ᾽ ὑλακτεῖν νιν καὶ τὰν κύνα is
referred to by Brunck in illustration
of this.

705 ἐπιρρύξας.] ἐπιρύζειν εἴπας
γ᾽ ἀφιέναι καὶ ταρορμᾶν. Hesych.
ῥύζω is ‘to growl, snarl’ = Lat. hir-
rire: cf. ‘canina litera,’ (Pers. Sat.
I. 109) for the letter R. The hound
would be set on by a kind of imita-
tive growl, as well as by a hiss
(σισμόι).

708 προσέταξεν.] Dawes' alteration προσέταττεν is not necessary.
With the common text the general
sense is: ‘If the statesmen chose to
feed the people, it would be easy.
For if each one of our thousand
cities had been (some time ago) ordered to feed twenty men, twenty

thousand of our citizens would be
now living in clover;' and this plan
our statesmen might now adopt.
The imperfect προσέταττεν ‘were
each city ordered, &c.’ makes the
passage rather neater; but it is intelligible and correct as it stands.

709 μυριάδ᾽ ἄν.] Dobree's correction for μυριάδες. The particle
ἄν can hardly be dispensed with.
Richter's passages to countenance
such omission are not satisfactory.
Thuc. III. 74, ἡ πόλις ἐκινδύνευσε
διαφθαρῆναι, εἰ ἄνεμος ἐπεγένετο, is
plainly not analogous. It means
‘the city was in danger of being
destroyed (ay, and had been destroyed) if a wind had arisen.’ Nor
could ἄν have been used with ἐκινδύνευσε without a plain absurdity:
the risk was actual and real. Nearly the same may be said of Eur.
Hec. 1111, εἰ δὲ μὴ Φρυγῶν πύργους
ᾔσθομεν ἥσμεν Ἑλλήνων δορί, φόβον
παρέσχεν οὐ μέσων ὅδε κτύπος. The
noise actually did cause some alarm,
we may suppose. If any correction
be needed there, the imperf. παρεῖ-
χεν, of the incipient fear so soon to
be checked, seems to me better than
παρέσχ᾽ ἄν, δδ᾽ ἄν, the corrections of
Porson and Elmsley. And it will
be found that, in all such cases
where the past indic. without ἄν is
put, either part of the action had
taken place (or was taking place),
while the condition applies to the
completion and effect of the whole;
or, by a rhetorical emphasis of expression, what might have occurred
is represented as if it had already

καὶ στεφάνοισιν παντοδαποῖσιν καὶ πυρὶ καὶ πυριάτῃ,　710
ἄξια τῆς γῆς ἀπολαύοντες καὶ τοῦ Μαραθῶνι τροπαίου.
νῦν δ᾿ ὥσπερ ἐλαολόγοι χωρεῖθ᾿ ἅμα τῷ τὸν μισθὸν ἔχοντι.

ΦΙΛΟΚΛΕΩΝ

οἴμοι, τί ποθ᾿ ὥσπερ νάρκη μου κατὰ τῆς χειρὸς καταχεῖται,
καὶ τὸ ξίφος οὐ δύναμαι κατέχειν, ἀλλ᾿ ἤδη μαλθακός εἰμι;

ΒΔΕΛΥΚΛΕΩΝ

ἀλλ᾿ ὁπόταν μὲν δείσωσ᾿ αὐτοὶ, τὴν Εὔβοιαν διδόασιν　715
ὑμῖν καὶ σῖτον ὑφίστανται κατὰ πεντήκοντα μεδίμνους
πορεῖν· ἔδοσαν δ᾿ οὐπώποτέ σοι, πλὴν πρώην πέντε μεδίμνους,

occurred. The same condensed and graphic construction is common in Latin; *e.g.* Pons sublicius iter paene hostibus dedit nl unus vir fuisset, Liv. II. 10, Si per Metellum licitum esset, matres...veniebant, Cic. *Verr.* V. 49. Prope in proelium exarsere, ni Valens imperii admonuisset, Tac. *Hist.* I. 64. See Madvig, *Lat. Gr.* § 348. But no such explanation suits this passage, which is entirely a supposed case. The other correction by Dawes, ἴξων ἂν is unsatisfactory, because ἄν is wanted to make the phrase ἐν τ. λ. a proper parody on ἐν πᾶσιν ἀγαθοῖς.

709 ἐν πᾶσι λαγῴοις.] ἐν πᾶσιν ἀγαθοῖς, ἐν τρυφῇ. Schol. A more comical parody is the ἐν πᾶσι βολίτοις of *Ach.* 1026.

710 πυρί.] For this cf. *Pax.* 1150, ἦν δὲ καὶ πυόν τις ἔνδον καὶ λαγῷα τέτταρα.

πυριάτῃ.] A pudding made from the πυόν, they say: and the other name for it, πυρίεφθον, as well as the appearance of this word, suggests that it was made by scalding. 'Colostra' is the Latin term, Mart. XIII. 38, 2.

711 τοῦ Μ. τρ.] Cf. *Eq.* 1334. Isocrates in his Panegyric oration is fluent on the Athenians' Marathonian glories.

712 ἐλαολόγοι.] These, as the

Scholiast tells us, got small pay : and apparently kept close to the master who was to pay them to see that that same was forthcoming. The dicasts are similarly bound to their paymaster, the κωλαγρέτης mentioned above.

713 τί ποθ᾿ ὥσπερ.] The alterations adopted by many critics in this line are to suit Suidas, who on νάρκη has τί τέτοσθα· ὥσπερ νάρκη.

715. They make fine promises, which they never perform. For Euboea, cf. *Nub.* 211—13. Athens was chiefly dependent upon foreign countries for her corn. Hence (as Mitchell remarks) we find her courted by presents of it. And there were rigorous laws to ensure an adequate supply of it, as may be seen from Demosthenes' speeches against Leptines, Phormio, Lacritus, Dionysodorus.

717 ἔδοσαν.] The aorist expresses the completed action, the pres. διδόασιν only the beginning of it, 'they offer.'

πρώην.] This refers to some more recent largess of corn than that sent from Egypt by Psammetichus, twenty-three years before this play. On that occasion some four thousand aliens were found among the fifteen thousand citizens. A strict enquiry into the genuineness of the claim-

καὶ ταῦτα μόλις ξενίας φεύγων ἔλαβες κατὰ χοίνικα, κριθῶν.
ὧν οὕνεκ᾽ ἐγώ σ᾽ ἀπέκλειον ἀεί,
βόσκειν ἐθέλων καὶ μὴ τούτους   720
ἐγχάσκειν σοι στομφάζοντας.
καὶ νῦν ἀτεχνῶς ἐθέλω παρέχειν
ὅ τι βούλει σοι,
πλὴν κωλαγρέτου γάλα πίνειν.

ΧΟΡΟΣ

ἦ που σοφὸς ἦν ὅστις ἔφασκεν, πρὶν ἂν ἀμφοῖν μῦθον ἀ-
          κούσῃς,   725
οὐκ ἂν δικάσαις. σὺ γὰρ οὖν νῦν μοι νικᾶν πολλῷ δεδό-
          κησαι·
ὥστ᾽ ἤδη τὴν ὀργὴν χαλάσας τοὺς σκίπωνας καταβάλλω.
ἀλλ᾽ ὦ τῆς ἡλικίας ἡμῖν τῆς αὐτῆς συνθιασῶτα,
πιθοῦ πιθοῦ λόγοισι, μηδ᾽ ἄφρων γένῃ,
μηδ᾽ ἀτενὴς ἄγαν ἀτεράμων τ᾽ ἀνήρ.   730
εἴθ᾽ ὤφελέν μοι κηδεμὼν ἢ ξυγγενὴς
εἶναί τις ὅστις τοιαῦτ᾽ ἐνουθέτει.
σοὶ δὲ νῦν τις θεῶν

ants' citizenship was held, in cases of such distribution. Hence ξενίας φεύγων in the next line. Bdelycleon got his corn, but not without some trouble in establishing his true Athenian birth.

711 στομφάζοντας.] Cf. *Nub.* 1367, στόμφακα, κρημνοποιόν, of Aeschylus.

712 ἀτεχνῶς.] Cf. note on *Ach.* 37.

714 κωλαγρέτου γάλα.] His pay, the three obol piece, is meant : but there is also allusion to ὀρνίθων γάλα, cf. v. 508.

715—759. The Chorus join their persuasion to Bdelycleon's, but the old man cannot bring himself to do without law.

715 ἦ που σοφός.] Cf. Aesch. *Prom. Vincl.* 886, ἦ σοφὸς, ἦ σοφὸς, ὃς πρῶτος ἐν γνώμᾳ τόδ᾽ ἐβάστασε κ.τ.λ. The maxim that follows was from Phocylides : μηδὲ δίκην δικάσῃς

πρὶν ἂν ἀμφοῖν μῦθον ἀκούσῃς. Euripides in *Heracl.* 180, *Androm.* 957 adopts it. It was in the oath of the dicasts, as Bergler shews from Dem. *c. Timocr.* 746, and is urged on our dicast below at v. 919. The Chorus are now converted to Bdelycleon's (and the poet's) view. In the Clouds the chorus veer round in a somewhat similar way, and taking the honest side turn against Strepsiades.

719—36. To this correspond vv. 743—49.

730. ἀτεράμων.] ἀτέραμνος is the commoner form, *e.g.* Theocr. *Id.* x. 7, πέτρας ἀπόκομμ᾽ ἀτεράμνω, of an untiring mower.

731—36. The Chorus wish they had had the advantage of such advice, and counsel Philocleon to take it, as there is evidently some divine inspiration in Bdelycleon's words.

733 σοί.] To Bdelycleon.

παρὼν ἐμφανὴς
ξυλλαμβάνει τοῦ πράγματος,
καὶ δῆλός ἐστιν εὖ ποιῶν·
σὺ δὲ παρὼν δέχου.   735

ΒΔΕΛΥΚΛΕΩΝ

καὶ μὴν θρέψω γ᾽ αὐτὸν παρέχων
ὅσα πρεσβύτῃ ξύμφορα, χόνδρον
λείχειν, χλαῖναν μαλακὴν, σισύραν,
πόρνην, ἥτις τὸ πέος τρίψει
καὶ τὴν ὀσφῦν.   740
ἀλλ᾽ ὅτι σιγᾷ κοὐδὲν γρύζει,
τοῦτ᾽ οὐ δύναταί με προσέσθαι.

ΧΟΡΟΣ.

νενουθέτηκεν αὐτὸν ἐς τὰ πράγμαθ᾽, οἷς
τότ᾽ ἐπεμαίνετ᾽· ἔγνωκε γὰρ ἀρτίως,
λογίζεταί τ᾽ ἐκεῖνα πάνθ᾽ ἁμαρτίας   745
ἃ σοῦ κελεύοντος οὐκ ἐπείθετο.
νῦν δ᾽ ἴσως τοῖσι σοῖς
λόγοις πείθεται,
καὶ σωφρονεῖ μέντοι μεθι-
στὰς ἐς τὸ λοιπὸν τὸν τρόπον
πειθόμενός τέ σοι.   749

736 σὺ.] To Philocleon. Burges proposed τὸ δ᾽ εὖ παρὸν δέχου; Seager παρὸν, 'while you may,' which seems worthy of consideration, for σὺ δὲ παρὼν is of doubtful meaning, and comes awkwardly after παρὼν in v. 733.

738 χόνδρον.] Mentioned along with other like things in Ar. *Fr*. 364, ἀρδάουτ, πυρούτ, πτισάνην, χόνδρον, ἴειδι, ἀίρας, σεμίδαλιν.

742 προσίσθαι.] Cf. *Eq*. 359, ἐν δ᾽ οὐ προσίεται με.

743—6. He is meditating and repenting, say the Chorus.

744 τότ᾽ ἐπεμ.] The metre of this line is not satisfactory, to correspond

with v. 730 exactly. But changes to bring the metre into order are not always safe or worth the making.

748 καὶ σ. μέντοι.] 'And indeed he's wise in such change and compliance.' I can see no reason for changing (with Hirschig) to μεθεστὼς τὸν τρόπον, merely because μιθιστηχ᾽ ἂν εἶχε τρόπων occurs in *Plut*. 365. μεθίστησι is used in *Eq*. 398. The correction of πειθόμενοι to πιθόμενοι, 'metri gratia,' against all MSS. seems unsafe, as the present participle is better for the sense.

ΦΙΛΟΚΛΕΩΝ

ἰώ μοί μοι.

ΒΔΕΛΤΚΛΕΩΝ

οὗτος, τί μοι βοᾷς;

ΦΙΛΟΚΛΕΩΝ

μή μοι τούτων μηδὲν ὑπισχνοῦ.　　　　　　750
κείνων ἔραμαι, κεῖθι γενοίμαν,
ἵν' ὁ κῆρυξ φησὶ, τίς ἀψήφι-
στος; ἀνιστάσθω.
κἀπισταίην ἐπὶ τοῖς κημοῖς
ψηφιζομένων ὁ τελευταῖος.　　　　　　755
σπεῦδ', ὦ ψυχή. ποῦ μοι ψυχή;
πάρες, ὦ σκιερά. μὰ τὸν Ἡρακλέα,
μὴ νῦν ἔτ' ἐγὼ 'ν τοῖσι δικασταῖς
κλέπτοντα Κλέωνα λάβοιμι.

ΒΔΕΛΤΚΛΕΩΝ

ἴθ' ὦ πάτερ, πρὸς τῶν θεῶν, ἐμοὶ πιθοῦ.　　　760

ΦΙΛΟΚΛΕΩΝ

τί σοι πίθωμαι; λέγ' ὅ τι βούλει, πλὴν ἑνός.

ΒΔΕΛΤΚΛΕΩΝ

ποίου; φέρ' ἴδω.

750—59. The old man is in despair, and will have none of his son's gruel, &c., but in tragic pathos sighs for the law-courts.

751 κείνων ἔραμαι.] Cf. Eur. Alcest. 866, κείνων ἔραμαι, κεῖν' ἐπιθυμῶ δώματα ναίειν.

755 τελευταῖος.] Some would find a pleasure in keeping back their votes to the last. Schol.

757 πάρες, ὦ σκιερά.] Again from Euripides, parodied from the Bellerophon; of which the Scholiast gives us the following: πάρες, ὦ σκιερά φυλλάς, ὑπερβῶ | κρηναῖα νάπη· τὸν ὑπὲρ κεφαλῆς | αἰθέρ' ἰδέσθαι σπεύδω, τίν' ἔχει | στάσιν Εἰνοδία. What Philocleon addresses by σκιερά is not very definite, nor meant to be so.

759 Κλέωνα.] The dicastic character is attacked as harsh and faithless, since Philocleon keeps no faith even with Cleon, from whom his name is formed. Schol. It may however be added that now Cleon and his tribe have been exposed by Bdelycleon; whose words have had their weight (cf. v. 713), though the old dicast is not quite convinced.

760—834. As the old man cannot entirely give up law, Bdelycleon proposes that he shall hold a court at home, and points out the advantages of this plan. Philocleon consents: due preparations are made: and he takes his seat.

761 πίθωμαι.] Conjunctive of deliberation: cf. Nub. 87, τί δὲ πίθωμαι δῆτά σοι;

ΦΙΛΟΚΛΕΩΝ

τοῦ μὴ δικάζειν. τοῦτο δὲ
"Αιδης διακρινεῖ πρότερον ἢ 'γὼ πείσομαι.

ΒΔΕΛΤΚΛΕΩΝ

σὺ δ' οὖν, ἐπειδὴ τοῦτο κεχάρηκας ποιῶν,
ἐκεῖσε μὲν μηκέτι βάδιζ', ἀλλ' ἐνθάδε   765
αὐτοῦ μένων δίκαζε τοῖσιν οἰκέταις.

ΦΙΛΟΚΛΕΩΝ

περὶ τοῦ; τί ληρεῖς;

ΒΔΕΛΤΚΛΕΩΝ

ταῦθ' ἅπερ ἐκεῖ πράττεται·
ὅτι τὴν θύραν ἀνέῳξεν ἡ σηκὶς λάθρα,
ταύτης ἐπιβολὴν ψηφιεῖ μίαν μόνην.
πάντως γε κἀκεῖ ταῦτ' ἔδρας ἑκάστοτε.   770

763 "Αιδης διακρινεῖ.] 'Death will part us sooner than I will comply in this.' It seems a mixed construction of, (1) Death only shall part us (myself and the law-courts), and (2) Death shall take me (= I will die) ere I give in to this.' The Scholiast says there is reference to a passage in the *Cressae* of Euripides, where κρινεῖ ταῦτα is used. Aristophanes is indeed perpetually taking fragments from Euripides, but there is perhaps nothing in this phrase to necessitate its being a quotation.

764 κεχάρηκας.] His only joy and pleasure had come to be in courts. In *Les Plaideurs* the same plan is adopted: Act II, Sc. 13. 'Hé doucement! Mon père, il faut trouver quelque accommodement. Si pour vous sans juger la vie est un supplice, Si vous êtes pressé de rendre la justice, Il ne faut pas sortir pour cela de chez vous; Exercez le talent et jugez parmi nous.'

767 ταῦθ' ἅπερ.] i. e. ταῦτα δίκαζε ἅπερ ἑ. τ. Meineke reads πρᾶτθ' ἅπερ, perhaps because ταῦθ' ἅπερ does not fit in so well with Philocleon's interruption, περὶ τοῦ; τί

ληρεῖς; But the change is needless. Nor is it important whether ταῦθ' or ταῦθ' is read. In *Eq.* 213, ταῦθ' ἅπερ ποιεῖς ποίει is a similar phrase, where the sausage-seller is told that the new trade of politics is but a continuation of his old trade of mincing up sausage-meat. Racine continues in imitation of this part. '*Dandin*. Ne raillons point ici de la Magistrature, Vois-tu je ne veux point être juge en peinture. *Léandre*. Vous serez, au contraire un juge sans appel, Et juge du Civil comme du Criminel. Vous pourrez tous les jours tenir deux audiences: Tout vous sera chez vous matière de sentences. Un valet manque-t-il à rendre un verre net; Condamnez-le à l'amende; et s'il le casse, au fouet. *Dandin*. C'est quelque chose; encor passe quand on raisonne. Et mes vacations, qui les payera! personne? *Léandre*. Leurs gages vous tiendront lieu de nantissement. *Dandin*. Il parle, ce me semble, assez pertinemment.'

769 μίαν.] Sc. δραχμήν: that being the unit of Attic money.

770 πάντως γε, κ.τ.λ.] And the

καὶ ταῦτα μέν νυν εὐλόγως, ἢν ἐξέχῃ
εἴλη κατ᾽ ὄρθρον, ἡλιάσει πρὸς ἥλιον·
ἐὰν δὲ νίφῃ, πρὸς τὸ πῦρ καθήμενος·
ὕοντος, εἴσει· κἂν ἔγρῃ μεσημβρινός,
οὐδείς σ᾽ ἀποκλείσει θεσμοθέτης τῇ κιγκλίδι.   775

ΦΙΛΟΚΛΕΩΝ

τουτί μ᾽ ἀρέσκει.

ΒΔΕΛΥΚΛΕΩΝ

πρὸς δὲ τούτοις γ᾽, ἢν δίκην
λέγῃ μακράν τις, οὐχὶ πεινῶν ἀναμενεῖς,
δάκνων σεαυτὸν καὶ τὸν ἀπολογούμενον.

ΦΙΛΟΚΛΕΩΝ

πῶς οὖν διαγιγνώσκειν καλῶς δυνήσομαι
ὥσπερ πρότερον τὰ πράγματ᾽ ἔτι μασώμενος;   780

causes you dealt with there (says his son) were not much better. This is in contempt: but the old man would probably see nothing in it but a promise that he should have what he had before.

771—74 καὶ ταῦτα...εἴσει.] 'And these cases you will (as reason is) judge out in the sun, if the morning is fine; by the fire, if it snows; you will go indoors, if it rains.' Such appears the best way of punctuating the present text. The common punctuation gives 'if it snows, sitting by the fire, while it rains, you will take cognizance of the case,' if we take εἴσει from εἴσομαι, as the Scholiast does, who explains it by γνώσῃ τὴν δίκην. This is hardly sense. But it is, with the punctuation adopted above, rather a curious order of weather; sunshine—snow—rain: and a conjunction is wanted with ὅ. ὁ. Meineke says that in the reading of MS. V. ὕοντας 'latet aliud quid quam ὕοντος:' but what it could have been, it seems vain to conjecture: nor indeed is there enough ground for rejecting our text as corrupt.

771 ἐξέχῃ.] Cf. Ar. Fr. 346, λέξεις ἄρα, ὥσπερ τὰ παιδί', ἐξεχ' ὦ φίλ' ἥλιε.

772 ἥλ. πρὸς ἥλιον.] The derivation for ἡλιαία suggested here is countenanced by Scholiasts, though ἀλίζεσθαι is doubtless the correct origin of the word.

775 οὐδείς σ᾽ ἀπ.] You may be as late as you like. Cf. above, v. 689.

776 τουτί μ᾽ ἀρέσκει.] This accusative, in place of the usual dative, with such verbs, is called by grammarians an Attic construction. It seems worth while to compare as analogous the use in English of the directly objective case in many phrases, e.g. 'Shoot me that bird,' 'Give him the book,' and the like. And in French, 'Donnez-moi,' but 'Il m'a donné, il me donne,' when the case precedes the verb.

778 δάκνων, κ.τ.λ.] For self-biting cf. v. 374. Snappishness towards the defendant often resulted (says the Scholiast) with a hungry juror.

780—83 μασώμενος...ἀναμενοῦμαι.] We may infer that ἀναμα-

ΒΔΕΛΥΚΛΕΩΝ

πολλῷ γ' ἄμεινον· καὶ λέγεται γὰρ τουτογὶ,
ὡς οἱ δικασταὶ ψευδομένων τῶν μαρτύρων
μόλις τὸ πρᾶγμ' ἔγνωσαν ἀναμασώμενοι.

ΦΙΛΟΚΛΕΩΝ

ἀνά τοί με πείθεις. ἀλλ' ἐκεῖν' οὔπω λέγεις,
τὸν μισθὸν ὁπόθεν λήψομαι.

ΒΔΕΛΥΚΛΕΩΝ

παρ' ἐμοῦ.

ΦΙΛΟΚΛΕΩΝ

καλῶς,   785

ὁτιὴ κατ' ἐμαυτὸν κοὐ μεθ' ἑτέρου λήψομαι.
αἴσχιστα γάρ τοί μ' εἰργάσατο Λυσίστρατος
ὁ σκωπτόλης. δραχμὴν μετ' ἐμοῦ πρώην λαβὼν,
ἐλθὼν διεκερμάτιζετ' ἐν τοῖς ἰχθύσιν,
κἄπειτ' ἐπέθηκε τρεῖς λοπίδας μοι κεστρέων·   790
κἀγὼ 'νέκαψ'· ὀβολοὺς γὰρ ᾤμην λαβεῖν·
κᾆτα βδελυχθεὶς ὀσφρόμενος ἐξέπτυσα·
κᾆθ' εἷλκον αὐτόν.

σασθαι had an analogous use to the Lat. 'ruminare,' and to our own 'to chew the cud,' though this last would hardly be used of judicial reflexion. ἐκ μεταφορᾶς τῶν ἀναπεμπαζόντων τὴν τροφὴν ζώων, καὶ αὖθις ἀναμασωμένων. Schol. 784 ἀνά τοί με πείθεις.] Cf. Nub. 792, ἀπὸ γὰρ ὀλοῦμαι. 787 Λυσίστρατος.] Cf. Ach. 854, οὐδ' αὖθις αὖ σε σκώψεται Παύσων ὁ παμπόνηρος, Λυσίστρατός τ' ἐν τἀγορᾷ. Also in Eq. 1265 he is mentioned. He seems to have been a poor hungry parasite, who probably earned his dinner by his jokes. He is one of Philocleon's companions at the banquet (below, v. 1302, 1308), and we have a specimen there of his style of wit and buffoonery. 788 δραχμὴν.] That the κωλαγρέ-

ται might not have to give change, they gave a drachma (= six obols) to a pair of dicasts. 789 ἐν τοῖς ἰχθύσιν.] So ἐν τῷ μύρῳ, 'in the perfume market,' in Eq. 1375: ἐν ταῖς μυρρίναις, Thesm. 448: κἄν ταῖς χύτραις καὶ ταῖς λαχάνοισιν ὁμοίως, Lys. 557. 790 τρεῖς λοπίδας.] The three mullet scales would look like small coins at first sight. 791 κἀγὼ 'νέκαψ'.] To put coins in the mouth appears to have been a common practice. Alexis (in Athenaeus) has this very word, ὁ δ' ἐγκάψας τὸ κέρμ' εἰς τὴν γνάθον. And in Eccl. 818, μεστὴν ἀπῆρα τὴν γνάθον χαλκῶν ἔχων, is said by one who has just been marketing. 793 εἷλκον.] 'I was dragging him off (into court).'

ΒΔΕΛΤΚΛΕΩΝ
ὁ δὲ τί πρὸς ταῦτ' εἶφ';

ΦΙΛΟΚΛΕΩΝ
ὅ τι;

ἀλεκτρυόνος μ' ἔφασκε κοιλίαν ἔχειν·
ταχὺ γοῦν καθέψεις τἀργύριον, ἦ δ' ὃς λέγων.   795

ΒΔΕΛΤΚΛΕΩΝ
ὁρᾷς ὅσον καὶ τοῦτο δῆτα κερδανεῖς;

ΦΙΛΟΚΛΕΩΝ
οὐ πάνυ τι μικρόν. ἀλλ' ὅπερ μέλλεις ποίει.

ΒΔΕΛΤΚΛΕΩΝ
ἀνάμενέ νυν ἐγὼ δὲ ταῦθ' ἥξω φέρων.

ΦΙΛΟΚΛΕΩΝ
ὅρα τὸ χρῆμα· τὰ λόγι' ὡς περαίνεται.
ἤκηκόη γὰρ ὡς 'Αθηναῖοί ποτε   800

---

794 **ἀλεκτρυόνος.**] ἐπὶ πάντα πέττουσιν οἱ ἀλεκτρυόνες, θερμοτάτην κοιλίαν ἔχοντες. An ostrich is our proverbial bird for tough digestion: hence Mitchell renders it 'Health to your ostrich-coats quoth he! Hard cash, I see, disturbs not your digestion.'

795 **ταχὺ γοῦν καθέψεις.**] Hirschig reads καταψήσεις. But how the future tense is to be explained here, is not clear. With the usual text it is 'At all events you make short work of digesting money.' Lysistratus ignores the fact that he had given him fish-scales, and that he had got rid of the contents of his mouth 'exspuendo' not 'digerendo.'

ἦ δ' ὅς.] ἀντὶ τοῦ ἔφη, καὶ ἔστιν ἀπὸ τοῦ ἠμί. κέχρηται δὲ αὐτῷ συνεχῶς ὁ Πλάτων. Schol.

797 **οὐ πάνυ τι μικρόν.**] 'It is not so very small a gain.' For a thorough discussion of οὐ πάνυ see an appendix upon this phrase at the end of Cope's *Gorgias.* The irony

of the speaker, the tone of the voice &c., often make οὐ πάνυ, which strictly is 'not altogether, not quite,' a polite equivalent for 'not at all:' but there seems to me no strong reason for the rule laid down by some, that οὐ πάνυ means 'altogether not,' οὐ παντάπασι 'not altogether;' the former a negation of the whole in all its parts, the latter a negation of some one or more parts in the whole. Some passages in Plato and Aristotle are (it appears) decisive against this rule, and there are none which cannot be well explained with οὐ πάνυ = 'not quite,' which seems its natural meaning.

798 Bdelycleon goes in to fetch all that is needed to constitute a court.

799 **λόγι'.**] Frequent recourse is had to oracles, cf. *Eq.* 109 sqq., 195—201, 1030—4. Philocleon speaks these lines to himself: the slaves probably having left the stage with Bdelycleon.

δικάσοιεν ἐπὶ ταῖς οἰκίαισι τὰς δίκας,
κἂν τοῖς προθύροις ἐνοικοδομήσοι πᾶς ἀνὴρ
αὑτῷ δικαστηρίδιον μικρὸν πάνυ,
ὥσπερ Ἑκάτειον, πανταχοῦ πρὸ τῶν θυρῶν.

BΔΕΛΤΚΛΕΩΝ
ἰδοὺ, τί ἔτ᾿ ἐρεῖς; ὡς ἅπαντ᾿ ἐγὼ φέρω   305
ὅσαπέρ γ᾿ ἔφασκον, κᾆτι πολλῷ πλείονα.
ἁμὶς μὲν, ἢν οὐρητιάσῃς, αὑτηὶ
παρὰ σοὶ κρεμήσετ᾿ ἐγγὺς ἐπὶ τοῦ παττάλου.

ΦΙΛΟΚΛΕΩΝ
σοφόν γε τουτὶ καὶ γέροντι πρόσφορον
ἐξεῦρες ἀτεχνῶς φάρμακον στραγγουρίας.   810

BΔΕΛΤΚΛΕΩΝ
καὶ πῦρ γε τουτὶ, καὶ προσέστηκεν φακῆ,
ῥοφεῖν ἐὰν δέῃ τι.

ΦΙΛΟΚΛΕΩΝ
         τοῦτ᾿ αὖ δεξιόν·
κἂν γὰρ πυρέττω, τόν γε μισθὸν λήψομαι.
αὐτοῦ μένων γὰρ τὴν φακῆν ῥοφήσομαι.

---

801 ἐπὶ ταῖς οἰκίαισι.] 'At their
several homes.'
804 'Ἑκάτειον.] There were
numerous chapels of Hecate about
Athens : ὡς τῶν Ἀθηναίων ταπταχοῦ
ἱδρυομένων αὐτὴν, ὡς ἔφορον πάντων
καὶ ῥουροτρόφον. Schol. And probably they were near the entrances of
the houses.
805 Bdelycleon comes out with
his judicial apparatus.
808 ἐπὶ.] The German editors
change this to ἐκ or ἀπό. Though
these prepositions are more natural
with κρεμ., yet the vessel might
surely be said to rest on its peg.
811 φακῆ.] ὥσπερ τὸ συκῆ ἀπὸ
συκέα περιστῶσι, καὶ τὸ ἀμυγδαλῆ
ἀπὸ ἀμυγδαλέα, οὕτω καὶ φακῆ ἀπὸ
τοῦ φακέα. Schol. The plant itself
is φακός.
813 κἂν γὰρ πυρέττω.] Even

though he might be ill and sick of a
fever, he might get his pay while
sitting comfortably at home by the
fire and swallowing his gruel. For
οἱ νοσοῦντες χυλὸν πτισάνης ῥοφοῦσι.
Schol. And in a fragment of Aristophanes found in Athenaeus (Fr. 201)
we have πτισάνης διδάσκεις αὐτὸν
ἔψειν ἢ φακῆν. This explanation
seems so satisfactory that I cannot
understand Hermann's transposition
of the line to follow v. 797.
813 A cock is brought out, to
wake up the dicast, should he go to
sleep; a result not improbable. In
Les Plaideurs L'Intime, in proof of
his qualifications for an advocate,
says 'J'endormirai, Monsieur, tout
aussi bien qu'un autre.' And Dandin
accordingly does go to sleep under
the effect of the advocate's plead-
ings.

ἀτὰρ τί τὸν ὄρνιν ὡς ἔμ' ἐξηνέγκατε;   815

BΔΕΛΤΚΛΕΩΝ
ἵν' ἂν, ἢν καθεύδῃς ἀπολογουμένου τινὸς,
ᾄδων ἄνωθεν ἐξεγείρῃ σ' οὑτοσί.

ΦΙΛΟΚΛΕΩΝ
ἐν ἔτι ποθῶ, τὰ δ' ἄλλ' ἀρέσκει μοι.

BΔΕΛΤΚΛΕΩΝ
τὸ τί;

ΦΙΛΟΚΛΕΩΝ
θήρῷον εἰ πως ἐκκομίσαις τὸ τοῦ Λύκου.

BΔΕΛΤΕΛΕΩΝ
πάρεστι τουτὶ, καὐτὸς ἄναξ οὑτοσί.   820

ΦΙΛΟΚΛΕΩΝ
ὦ δέσποθ' ἥρως, ὡς χαλεπὸς ἄρ' ἦσθ' ἰδεῖν.

BΔΕΛΤΚΛΕΩΝ
οἷόσπερ ἡμῖν φαίνεται Κλεώνυμος.

ΦΙΛΟΚΛΕΩΝ
οὔκουν ἔχει γ' οὐδ' αὐτὸς ἥρως ὢν ὅπλα.

BΔΕΛΤΚΛΕΩΝ
εἰ θᾶττον ἐκαθίζου σὺ, θᾶττον ἂν δίκην
ἐκάλουν.

ἐξηνέγκατε.] Plural, because one of the slaves helped to bring out the things.

817 ἄνωθεν.] The cock was placed on a perch above Philocleon's head. Below at v. 932 he appeals to the bird to confirm his judgment.

819 εἰ πως.] This, the common text, is in every way as good as Meineke's alteration. 'If you would manage to bring out Lycus' statue' is a natural way of asking for it. Λύκου.] Cf. above, v. 389.

820 πάρεστι τουτὶ] He brings a picture of Lycus, Schol. And apparently it was a stern countenance (χαλεπὸs), and (the Scholiast says) ill-looking (δύσμορφοι). This leads to a comparison with Cleonymus; upon which it is remarked that he is like Cleonymus in not having defensive armour, with allusion to Cleonymus casting away his shield. A hero was commonly represented in full panoply.

823 οὔκουν κ.τ.λ.] Sosias is unnecessary here; to whom the line is commonly given. Bergk and Meineke corrected the arrangement. The dialogue runs thus, Bd. 'Here is Lycus'. Ph. 'What an ugly stern fellow he is.' Bd. 'He's something like Cleonymus, methinks.' Ph. 'Ay, and that's why, hero though he is, he has no shield.'

825 ἐκάλουν.] This verb is used of the presiding judge, cf. below v.

ΦΙΛΟΚΛΕΩΝ
κάλει νυν, ὡς κάθημαι 'γὼ πάλαι.   825

ΒΔΕΛΤΚΛΕΩΝ
φέρε νυν, τίν' αὐτῷ πρῶτον εἰσαγάγω δίκην;
τί τίς κακὸν δέδρακε τῶν ἐν τᾠκία;
ἢ Θρᾷττα προσκαύσασα πρώην τὴν χύτραν—

ΦΙΛΟΚΛΕΩΝ
ἐπίσχες οὗτος· ὡς ὀλίγου μ' ἀπώλεσας.
ἄνευ δρυφάκτου τὴν δίκην μέλλεις καλεῖν,   830
ὃ πρῶτον ἡμῖν τῶν ἱερῶν ἐφαίνετο;

ΒΔΕΛΤΚΛΕΩΝ
μὰ τὸν Δί' οὐ πάρεστιν.

ΦΙΛΟΚΛΕΩΝ
ἀλλ' ἐγὼ δραμὼν
αὐτὸς κομιοῦμαι τό γε παραυτίκ' ἔνδοθεν.

ΒΔΕΛΤΚΛΕΩΝ
τί ποτε τὸ χρῆμ'; ὡς δεινὸν ἡ φιλοχωρία.

1441, ἕωι ἀν τὴν δίκην ἄρχων καλᾷ.
Similar is the use of εἰσάγειν in the
next line.
827 τί τίς.] The double inter-
rogative is quite after Greek use,
and better than the common text τί
τις, though 'Who has done what?'
is in English very colloquial.
828 προσκαύσασα.] 'Burning
the pot' must here mean 'burning
or singeing the contents of it;' for
the pot would be on the fire in the
regular way of business, and would
(with the other cooking vessels) become προσκεκαυμένα, cf. below v.
939.
829 ὀλίγου.] Cf. Nub. 722, ὀλίγου φροῦδος γεγένημαι.
830 δρυφάκτου.] The only instance of the singular of this word.
831 ἱερῶν.] Cf. Thesm. 629, σὺ
δ' εἰπέ μοι, ὅ τι πρῶτον ἡμῖν τῶν
ἱερῶν ἐδείκνυτο. To the old dicast
all appertaining to the law-courts is
sacred.
832 ἀλλ' ἐγὼ κ.τ.λ.] Philocleon
posts off to fetch something for δρύ-

φακτα; his son exclaims in surprize
at the old man's quickness τί ποτε
κ.τ.λ. Then Xanthias runs in, with
the tale of the dog's theft: this is at
once seized on as the first case for
the decision of this home circuit:
then, as the old man re-enters, his
son exclaims τουτὶ τί ἐστι; The
arrangement of the speakers in Dindorf's Poetae Scenici is absurd.
The text above follows the arrangement of Richter and Meineke. The
adoption of ὅ τι ποτὲ χρῆμ' from
Hermann, to end Philocleon's speech
in v. 834, seems unnecessary. The
meaning of that would be 'I will
run in and get whatever we want'
or 'whatever article I can lay my
hands on'. The common reading
τί ποτε τὸ χρῆμ' is 'Why, what ever
ails the man? (he runs off so fast).
A wonderful thing is the love of
place!'
834 φιλοχωρία.] Philocleon has
a cat-like attachment to the law-
courts.

ΞΑΝΘΙΑΣ

βάλλ᾽ ἐς κόρακας. τοιουτονὶ τρέφειν κύνα. 835

ΒΔΕΛΥΚΛΕΩΝ

τί δ᾽ ἔστιν ἐτεόν;

ΞΑΝΘΙΑΣ

οὐ γὰρ ὁ Λάβης ἀρτίως
ὁ κύων παράξας ἐς τὸν ἰπνὸν ἀναρπάσας
τροφαλίδα τυροῦ Σικελικὴν κατεδήδοκεν;

ΒΔΕΛΥΚΛΕΩΝ

τοῦτ᾽ ἄρα πρῶτον τἀδίκημα τῷ πατρὶ
εἰσακτέον μοι· σὺ δὲ κατηγόρει παρών. 840

835—890. The first criminal to be tried is found in a dog who has stolen and eaten a cheese. His fellow dog is to prosecute. After due sacrifices and prayers from Bdelycleon and the chorus that their artifice may succeed, the trial begins.

835 βάλλ᾽ ἐς κ.] Said to the dog. τρέφειν.] Infinitive of exclamation: cf. *Nub.* 268, τὸ δὲ μηδὲ κυνῆν ...ἐλθεῖν ἔχοντα. The explanation of such a construction seems to be that the infinitive of the verb may stand for a noun, and then, the noun having been expressed, the rest of the sentence is left unsaid, the tone of the speaker plainly enough indicating what it would be. Thus, 'that I didn't even put a cap on before I came (was foolish):' and here, 'To keep such a dog (is absurd).'

836 Λάβης.] 'Griper, Nipper, Holdfast;' a natural name for a dog: the Scholiast quotes Δάκην as a dog's name used by Teleclides. But there is evident allusion to Laches and his peculations in Sicily. Cf. above, v. 240, ἔσται Λάχητι νυνὶ (ἡ δίκη). Laches went with the first Athenian expedition to Sicily, in B. C. 427. Cf. Thuc. III. 86, 88, 90. He was superseded by Pythodorus (Thuc. III. 115). The facts of the deme of

Aexone being given to the dog (Laches' real deme, cf. Plat. *Lach.* 197), and of the theft being a *Sicilian* cheese, leave no doubt that Laches is here alluded to.

837 ἰπνόν.] 'The kitchen:' for the limited sense of 'oven' will not suit. Cf. v. 139.

838 τροφαλίδα.] 'fresh curd-cheese,' from τρέφειν. Cf. Theocr. *Id.* XXV. 106, ἄλλοι ἀμόλγια εἶχ᾽, ἄλλοι τρέφε πίσσα τυρόν. One Scholiast appears to interpret it 'a round cheese;' and that the cheese was round is likely: but the explanation perhaps arises from some confusion between τρέψειν and τρέφειν. The dairy sense of τρέφειν is quite established enough to make the meaning of τροφαλὶς certain.

Σικελικήν.] πολυθρύμμων δὲ ἡ Σικελία, διὰ τυρὸν πολὺν καὶ κάλλιστον ἔχει. Schol.

839 τοῦτ᾽ ἄρα, κ.τ.λ.] Racine has a dog-trial in imitation of this. But there is not very much similarity between Aristophanes and the French dramatist here. The latter makes the tediousness and bombast of the advocates the chief feature in the trial, which ends in the judge being sent to sleep, and, on being awakened, hastily condemning the accused to the galleys.

840 εἰσακτέον.] The technical

ΞΑΝΘΙΑΣ

μὰ Δί᾽ οὐκ ἔγωγ᾽· ἀλλ᾽ ἅτερός φησιν κύων
κατηγορήσειν, ἤν τις εἰσάγῃ γραφήν.

ΒΔΕΛΥΚΛΕΩΝ

ἴθι νυν, ἄγ᾽ αὐτὼ δεῦρο.

ΞΑΝΘΙΑΣ

ταῦτα χρὴ ποιεῖν.

ΦΙΛΟΚΛΕΩΝ

τουτὶ τί ἔστι;

ΒΔΕΛΥΚΛΕΩΝ

χοιροκομεῖον Ἑστίας.

ΦΙΛΟΚΛΕΩΝ

εἶθ᾽ ἱεροσυλήσας φέρεις;

ΒΔΕΛΥΚΛΕΩΝ

οὐκ, ἀλλ᾽ ἵνα   845
ἀφ᾽ Ἑστίας ἀρχόμενος ἐπιτρίψω τινά.

ΦΙΛΟΚΛΕΩΝ

ἀλλ᾽ εἴσαγ᾽ ἀνύσας ὡς ἐγὼ τιμᾶν βλέπω.

ΒΔΕΛΥΚΛΕΩΝ

φέρε νυν, ἐνέγκω τὰς σανίδας καὶ τὰς γραφάς.

word of the judge: cf. note on v. 8:5.

844 τουτὶ] Philocleon returns, with a pig-sty fence, ἀγγεῖόν τι καρ-υωτόν, to serve for δρύφακτοι. It is called 'of Hestia,' because (says the Scholiast) they kept pigs close to their homes (if that be the meaning of ἐπὶ τῆς ἑστίας τρέφουσι χοίρους), the pig-stye adjoining the house probably. In an Irish cabin indeed the pig is more literally ἐπὶ τῆ ἑστίας. Also, at libations, they be-gan with the goddess Hestia; hence Philocleon, when charged with tem-ple-robbing, replies, 'No, it's all in the regular course; I begin with

Hestia, as our wont is, and go on to despatch my victim.' Cf. Plat. Euthyphr. 3, ἀφ᾽ Ἑστίας ἀρχεσθαι κακουργεῖν τὴν πόλιν. The phrase passed into a proverb for beginning at the very beginning.

847 τιμᾶν βλέπω.] Cf. Ach. 375, οὐδὲν βλέπουσιν ἄλλο πλὴν ψήφῳ δακεῖν. The infinitive takes the place of the noun: hence such phrases as βλέπειν νᾶπυ may be com-pared with this.

848 σανίδας.] These are certainly here what they most probably are at v. 349, tablets with notices of suits upon them; containing in a programme of the dicastic bus

ΦΙΛΟΚΛΕΩΝ

οἴμοι, διατρίβεις κἀπολεῖς τριψημερῶν·
ἐγὼ δ᾽ ἀλοκίζειν ἐδεόμην τὸ χωρίον.   850

ΒΔΕΛΥΚΛΕΩΝ

ἰδού.

ΦΙΛΟΚΛΕΩΝ

κάλει νυν.

ΒΔΕΛΥΚΛΕΩΝ

ταῦτα δή.

ΦΙΛΟΚΛΕΩΝ

τίς οὑτοσὶ
ὁ πρῶτός ἐστιν;

ΒΔΕΛΥΚΛΕΩΝ

ἐς κόρακας, ὡς ἄχθομαι,
ὁτιὴ 'πελαθόμην τοὺς καδίσκους ἐκφέρειν.

ΦΙΛΟΚΛΕΩΝ

οὗτος σὺ ποῖ θεῖς;

ΒΔΕΛΥΚΛΕΩΝ

ἐπὶ καδίσκους.

to be done. There was no strong necessity for them perhaps, when only one suit, and that a known one, was coming on; but Philocleon will insist in having all the minutest particulars of law-court furniture.

850 ἐγὼ δ᾽...τὸ χωρίον.] Meineke thinks this line corrupt. It is commonly interpreted, 'And I wanted to furrow up the ground,' i. e. to trace the line on the πινάκιον τιμητικόν. He was in a hurry to be at his work, and to condemn his man. And *Thesm.* 777—786 is brought to support such a metaphor; where Mnesilochus, meaning to write, says, ἄγε δὴ πινάκων ξεστῶν δέλτοι, δέξασθε σμίλης ὁλκούς, κήρυκας ἐμῶν μόχθων· οἴμοι τουτὶ τὸ ῥῶ μοχθηρόν· χώρει, χώρει. ποίαν αὔλακα; βάσκετ᾽ ἐπείγετε πάσας καθ᾽ ὁδούς· εἴπῃ ταύτῃ· ταχέως χρή. But is it not possible that Philocleon, who, though a dicast, is in some respects a rough old-fashioned fellow, has a farm? and that he counted on getting away to it, after despatching his law business, and doing a little farmer's work. 'You will keep me here all day,' he says, 'and I wanted to do a bit of ploughing on my farm.' χωρίον is frequently used in this sense: cf. *Ach.* 226, *Pac.* 1146, 1148. The delay of these preparations wearies him, though he is anxious to have everything correct: hence at v. 855 he will not have καδίσκοι fetched, but at once produces something to serve for them. Of course there is a little inconsistency in his wanting thus to get it over, but that is not unnatural in an old man of his sort.

ΦΙΛΟΚΛΕΩΝ

μηδαμῶς.

ἐγὼ γὰρ εἶχον τούσδε τοὺς ἀρυστίχους.   855

ΒΔΕΛΥΚΛΕΩΝ

κάλλιστα τοίνυν· πάντα γὰρ πάρεστι νῷν
ὅσων δεόμεθα, πλήν γε δὴ τῆς κλεψύδρας.

ΦΙΛΟΚΛΕΩΝ

ἡδὶ δὲ δὴ τίς ἐστιν; οὐχὶ κλεψύδρα;

ΒΔΕΛΥΚΛΕΩΝ

εὖ γ᾽ ἐκπορίζεις αὐτὰ κἀπιχωρίως.
ἀλλ᾽ ὡς τάχιστα πῦρ τις ἐξενεγκάτω   860
καὶ μυρρίνας καὶ τὸν λιβανωτὸν ἔνδοθεν,
ὅπως ἂν εὐξώμεσθα πρῶτα τοῖς θεοῖς.

ΧΟΡΟΣ

καὶ μὴν ἡμεῖς ἐπὶ ταῖς σπονδαῖς
καὶ ταῖς εὐχαῖς
φήμην ἀγαθὴν λέξομεν ὑμῖν,   865
ὅτι γενναίως ἐκ τοῦ πολέμου
καὶ τοῦ νείκους ξυνεβήτην.

ΒΔΕΛΥΚΛΕΩΝ

εὐφημία μὲν πρῶτα νῦν ὑπαρχέτω.

855 ἀρυστίχους.] ἀγγεῖον ᾧ ἐστιν ἀρύσασθαι, κοτύλη ἢ κύαθοι. Schol. 859—62. Myrtle boughs and frankincense are brought out. On μυρρίνας the scholiast says μυρρίναις γὰρ ἐστιφανοῦντο οἱ ἄρχοντες: and at most festivals these boughs appear to have been used. Cf. the well-known song on Harmodius and Aristogiton, ἐν μύρτου κλαδὶ τὸ ξίφος φορήσω. And at the merry-making in The Peace (v. 1154) myrtle-boughs are sent for. Cf. also Ran. 871 for fire and frankincense thus called (ὑσι ἴθι νυν λιβανωτὸν δεῦρό τις καὶ

πῦρ δότω, ὅπως ἂν εὐξωμαι πρὸ τῶν σοφισμάτων. 863—67. This is a system of anapaests. A strophe follows, vv. 868—873, εὔφημα...πλάτων, to which correspond vv. 885—890, ξυνευχό-μεσθα...νεωτέρων. 868 εὐφημία.] Constantly called for on similar occasions; cf. Eq. 1316, Nub. 263, Thesm. 295. This line is given by Meineke to the chorus. Richter gives the following line to Bdelycleon, making the chorus resume with τὸ πρᾶγμ᾽ δ κ.τ.λ. 869—74. The Chorus pray that

ΧΟΡΟΣ

ὦ Φοῖβ᾽ Ἄπολλον Πύθι᾽, ἐπ᾽ ἀγαθῇ τύχῃ
τὸ πρᾶγμ᾽ ὃ μηχανᾶται   870
ἔμπροσθεν οὗτος τῶν θυρῶν,
ἅπασιν ἡμῖν ἁρμόσαι
παυσαμένοις πλάνων.
Ἰήιε Παιάν.   874

ΒΔΕΛΥΚΛΕΩΝ

ὦ δέσποτ᾽ ἄναξ, γεῖτον ἀγυιεῦ τοὐμοῦ προθύρου προπύλαιε,
δέξαι τελετὴν καινὴν, ὦναξ, ἣν τῷ πατρὶ καινοτομοῦμεν·
παῦσόν τ᾽ αὐτοῦ τοῦτο τὸ λίαν στρυφνὸν καὶ πρίνινον ἦθος,
ἀντὶ σιραίου μέλιτος μικρὸν τῷ θυμιδίῳ παραμίξας·
ἤδη δ᾽ εἶναι τοῖς ἀνθρώποις
ἤπιον αὐτὸν,
τοὺς φεύγοντάς τ᾽ ἐλεεῖν μᾶλλον   880
τῶν γραψαμένων,
κἀπιδακρύειν ἀντιβολούντων,
καὶ παυσάμενον τῆς δυσκολίας
ἀπὸ τῆς ὀργῆς
τὴν ἀκαλήφην ἀφελέσθαι.

Bdelycleon's device may turn out well, and suit them all, giving them rest from their wanderings and errors in legal matters.

872 ἁρμόσαι] Infinitive, as frequently in prayers, dependent on δός, or some word of the kind.

875—885. Bdelycleon puts up his special prayer that his father may be turned to a milder mood.

875 προθύρου προπύλαιε.] Readings vary here. The MSS. are corrupt: MS. R. has προθύρου πρόσθ᾽ πύλαι: MS. V. προπύλου προσπύλαι: the rest προθύρου πρὸς πύλας. The correction in the text is Bentley's; Bergk reads πρόσθεν προπυλαίου: Meineke προπύλου πρὸς αὐλᾶς. The sense does not vary much, whichever correction we take as most probable. Meineke thinks his nearest to the Ven. MS., and that the expression is probably a fragment from Euripides.

876 καινοτομοῦμεν.] Cf. Eccl. 584, εἰ καινοτομεῖν ἐθελήσουσιν, καὶ μὴ τοῖς ἤθεσι λίαν τοῖς τ᾽ ἀρχαίοις ἐνδιατρίβειν.

877 στρυφνὸν.] From στύφειν. 'astringere:' χείλεα στυφθείς, Anth. The next word πρίνινος is applied to old men in Ach. 179, coupled with στιπτοί.

878 σιραίου.] τὸ ἡψημένον γλεῦκος, βραχὺ δ᾽ ἔχον παράπικρον ὅταν καθιψηθῇ. Schol. Instead of bitter a little sweet is to be put into the old man's composition.

880 φεύγοντάς τ᾽ ἐλ.] He had been always ready to condemn, and inexorable to piteous appeals. Cf. above, 560—70.

884 ἀκαλήφην.] 'The nettle, the sting.'   Crates in the Phoenissae used the word in the same way. Schol.

XOPOΣ

ξυνευχόμεσθά σοι * * κἀπᾴδομεν   885
νέαισιν ἀρχαῖς, ἕνεκα τῶν προλελεγμένων.
εὖνοι γάρ ἐσμεν ἐξ οὗ
τὸν δῆμον ᾐσθόμεσθά σου
φιλοῦντος ὡς οὐδεὶς ἀνὴρ
τῶν γε νεωτέρων.   890

BΔEΛTKΛEΩN

εἴ τις θύρασιν ἡλιαστής, εἰσίτω·
ὡς ἡνίκ' ἂν λέγωσιν, οὐκ ἐσφρήσομεν.

ΦΙΛΟΚΛΕΩΝ

τίς ἆρ' ὁ φεύγων οὗτος; ἴσον ἁλώσεται.

ΞΑΝΘΙΑΣ

ἀκούετ' ἤδη τῆς γραφῆς. ἐγράψατο

885 ξυνευχόμεσθά σοι] ταῦτά οτ
ταῦτά before σοι is generally accepted to fill the gap.
888 ᾐσθόμεσθα.] Corrected from
ᾐσθόμιθα of MSS. In what way
ᾐσθήμισθα, the reading of Cobet and
Meineke, is better, it is hard to say.
890 τῶν γε νεωτέρων.] τῶν γερ-
ναιοτέρων. R. V. And the Scholiast
recognizes both readings. But the
common text suits the metre, corre-
sponding with v. 873, παυσαμένοις
πλάνων; and is better for the sense.
'You love the people as no man
does of the nobler sort,' is a senti-
ment hardly intelligible. But, 'as
no man does, at least of the younger
men, of men now-a-days,' fits well
with the character of the chorus
who are approvers of an older gene-
ration. After this line Meineke
adds ἴμιν παιδν, to balance the same
in v. 874; unnecessarily perhaps; cf.
above, v. 281.
891—994. The trial begins. There
is a dog plaintiff, and a dog defendant. The charge is set forth; the
damages laid. Philocleon is eager
to condemn, before he has heard
half the case. Xanthias is spokes-

man for the prosecuting dog; shews
how the accused stole the cheese
and gave him no share. The old
dicast will hardly hear any defence,
but Ddelycleon makes him do so,
and sets forth piteously the case of
the accused, brings witnesses to
shew that the accuser is just as bad;
produces the children of the accused
as a last resource to move pity.
Philocleon is a little melted, but yet
means to condemn. Bdelycleon,
however, deceives him, and makes
him put his vote into the wrong
urn, and Labes is acquitted.
891 εἴ τις θύρασιν.] Bdelycleon
acts as thesmothetes: cf. above,
v. 775, οὐδεὶς σ' ἀνακλήσει θεσμοθέ-
την τῇ κιγκλίδι. The signal for the
gathering we may suppose now to
be taken down: cf. note on σημείου
at v. 690.
893 τίς ἆρ' ὁ φ.] Philocleon is
eager for his work; predetermined
that the defendant shall be well
trounced.
ἴσον.] Exclamatory, 'how finely,
how thoroughly?'
894—97. Bdelycleon introduces
the suit, ἀκούετ' ἤδη, 'Oyes, Oyes,'

κύων Κυδαθηναιεὺς Λάβητ' Αἰξωνέα,
τὸν τυρὸν ἀδικεῖν ὅτι μόνος κατήσθιεν
τὸν Σικελικόν. τίμημα κλῳὸς σύκινος.

ΦΙΛΟΚΛΕΩΝ
θάνατος μὲν οὖν κύνειος, ἣν ἅπαξ ἁλῷ.

ΒΔΕΛΤΚΛΕΩΝ
καὶ μὴν ὁ φεύγων οὑτοσὶ Λάβης πάρα.

ΦΙΛΟΚΛΕΩΝ
ὦ μιαρὸς οὗτος· ὡς δὲ καὶ κλέπτον βλέπει,   900
οἷ.ν σεσηρὼς ἐξαπατήσειν μ' οἴεται.
ποῦ δ' ἔσθ' ὁ διώκων, ὁ Κυδαθηναιεὺς κύων;

Mitch. Cf. the usual ἀπούετε λέῳ,
Ach. 1000.
895 **Κυδαθηναιεὺς.**] The deme
of the parties concerned is mentioned in all such formulae. Here
the deme of Cydathenus is given to
the dog, because that was (it is said)
the deme of Cleon. Cleon compares himself to a dog in *Eq.* 1023,
and is compared to one by his ad-
versaries.
Λάβητ' Αἰξωνέα.] Labes is (as
we have seen at v. 836) to represent
Laches. This deme of Aexone was
noted for the scurrilous language to
which its inhabitants were addicted,
says Stephanus; and Plato (*Laches*,
197) seems to confirm this, where
Laches says, 'I will say nothing in
reply, though I have plenty to say,
lest you should assert that I am
Aexonian not only in name but in
nature.'
897 **Σικελικόν.**] Bergler quotes
from Antiphanes in Athenaeus, τυρὸς
Σικελός, μύρον ἐξ Ἀθηρῶν, ἐγχέλεις
Βοιώτιαι. For Laches' peculations
in Sicily cf. note on v. 836.
τίμημα] The damages were first
laid by the plaintiff, who was said
τιμᾶσθαι. Against this the oppo-
nents might ἀντιτιμᾶσθαι. The judge
finally decided the amount (ἐτίμα).
κλῳὸς.] περιτραχήλιοι θεσμός.

Schol. It is of fig-wood with allusion probably to συκοφαντία: of
which Aristophanes never tires.
898 **θάνατος μὲν οὖν.**] The mild
penalty does not content Philocleon.
All his interpolations in the trial
scene are severe, and against the
defendant.
900 **κλέπτον βλέπει.**] 'He car-
ries thief in his face.'
901 **σεσηρώς.**] The 'grin,' expressed by this word, is generally
in mockery or malice, but not always
so, as Theocr. *Id.* VII. 19, εἶνε σεσα-
ρὼς ὀμματι μειδιόωντι, proves. Hence
Richter's alteration σεσηρώς (a form
perhaps not elsewhere found) is
needless. The Scholiast's explanation. κεχηνώς, διηρογμένον ἔχων τὸ
στόμα, further confirms the text.
And the broad grin would be more
immediately striking as the dog
came in, than would the wagging
of his tail. Richter quotes, *Eq.*
1029, ὃι κέρκῳ σαίνων σ', ὁπόταν
δειπνῆς, ἐπιτηρῶν ἐξέδεταί σου τοὐψον
ὅταν σύ του ἄλλοσε χάσκης.
902 **ποῦ δ' ἔσθ' ὁ διώκων.**] Dindorf
in the old Poetae Scenici had τοῦ δ'
ὁ δ., which manifestly was wrong.
In his larger edition he approves
τοῦ μοῦ διώκων, *i. e.* τοῦ μοι ὁ
διώκων, which is a curious crasis.
τοῦ τοῦ δ' ὁ δ. Mein., ποῦ δ' οὖν ὁ δ.

ΚΤΩΝ

αὖ αὖ.

ΒΔΕΛΤΚΛΕΩΝ

πάρεστιν.

ΦΙΛΟΚΛΕΩΝ

ἕτερος οὗτος αὖ Λάβης.

ΒΔΕΛΤΚΛΕΩΝ

ἀγαθός γ᾽ ὑλακτεῖν καὶ διαλείχειν τὰς χύτρας.
σίγα, κάθιζε· σὺ δ᾽ ἀναβὰς κατηγόρει.   905

ΦΙΛΟΚΛΕΩΝ

φέρε νυν, ἅμα τηνδ᾽ ἐγχεάμενος κἀγὼ ῥοφῶ.

ΞΑΝΘΙΑΣ

τῆς μὲν γραφῆς ἠκούσαθ᾽ ἣν ἐγραψάμην,
ἄνδρες δικασταί, τουτονί. δεινότατα γὰρ
ἔργων δέδρακε κἀμὲ καὶ τὸ ῥυππαπαῖ.
ἀποδρὰς γὰρ ἐς τὴν γωνίαν τυρὸν πολὺν   910

Holib. The reading of the text is in Hirschig and Richter.

903 αὖ αὖ.] μιμεῖται τὴν φωνήν. Schol. This line is variously divided. To give πάρεστιν to Bdelycleon, ἕτερος—χύτρας to Philocleon, as Dobree does, seems best. On the dicast asking for the prosecutor, he is brought forward, and barks, and Bdelycleon says, 'He is here.' The dicast remarks that he looks like a second Labes. The son rejoins that he is good at barking, &c.: and then bids his father listen in silence, while Xanthias gets up and speaks for the prosecutor.

904 διαλείχειν.] The prosecuting dog is about as bad as the other. In Eq. 1030—34 Cleon is described as a dog Cerberus, of whom Demus is to beware, and who will escape notice ξυνηδὼν νύκτωρ τὰς λοπάδας καὶ τὰς νήσους διαλείχων. The χύτραι here mean subject states or islands, as there νήσους is by way of surprise for χύτρας.

906 τηνδ᾽.] Sc. φιάλην. Cf. above,

v. 811.

907 ἣν.] It is a question whether we ought to change this to ᾗ, though this latter is certainly the more Attic construction. Richter and Meineke do, following Brunck.

909 ῥυππαπαῖ.] 'The seamen,' because ῥυππαπαῖ was the seamen's cry; for which cf. Ran. 1073; also Eq. 602, for a rhyming imitation, ἱππαπαῖ. The scholiast adds that the sailors were aggrieved by this cheese theft, ὡὶ τῶν ἐρετῶν καὶ ναυτῶν περὶ πλείστου ποιουμένων τὸν τυρόν. However this may be, the sailors are mentioned naturally enough, since Laches was in command of a fleet in Sicily.

910 γωνίαν.] This and ἐν τῷ σκότῳ the Scholiast explains ἐπειδὴ ἐν μέρει τῆι δύσεωι ἡ Σικελία. Sicily (as regards Greece) was out of the way and in a corner westward. Perhaps this is striving too much for a double meaning in all the details of the dog's theft.

κατεσικέλιζε κἀνέπλητ' ἐν τῷ σκότῳ,
νὴ τὸν Δί', ἀλλὰ δῆλός ἐστ'· ἔμοιγέ τοι
τυροῦ κάκιστον ἀρτίως ἐνήρυγεν
ὁ βδελυρὸς οὗτος.

ΞΑΝΘΙΑΣ
                    κοὐ μετέδωκ' αἰτοῦντί μοι.
καίτοι τίς ὑμᾶς εὖ ποιεῖν δυνήσεται,   915
ἢν μή τι κἀμοί τις προβάλλῃ τῷ κυνί;

ΦΙΛΟΚΛΕΩΝ
οὐδὲν μετέδωκεν;

ΞΑΝΘΙΑΣ
                    οὐδὲ τῷ κοινῷ γ' ἐμοί.

ΒΔΕΛΥΚΛΕΩΝ
θερμὸς γὰρ ἀνὴρ οὐδὲν ἧττον τῆς φακῆς.
πρὸς τῶν θεῶν, μὴ προκαταγίγνωσκ', ὦ πάτερ,
πρὶν ἄν γ' ἀκούσῃς ἀμφοτέρων.

ΦΙΛΟΚΛΕΩΝ
                    ἀλλ', ὦγαθέ,   920
τὸ πρᾶγμα φανερόν ἐστιν· αὐτὸ γὰρ βοᾷ.

911 κατεσικέλιζε.] 'He si-sliced
away.'
914 κοὐ μετέδωκ'.] That he gave
no share to the other dog (Cleon's
representative) is the chief crime.
Xanthias' complaint, as the aggrieved
dog, has an ironical meaning.
915 καίτοι κ.τ.λ.] Who can be-
nefit you, without a previous sop to
your Cerberus? It must be, 'love
me, love my dog.' Cf. the note
above at v. 904, and *Eq.* 1030—34.
917 οὐδὲν κ.τ.λ.] Meineke with
Bergk gives this and the following
line to Philocleon. Neither thus,
nor with Dindorf's arrangement,
is the connexion of θερμὸς γὰρ
ἀνὴρ with the preceding plain.
Florens says, that Philocleon, while
speaking, tries whether his lentil
porridge is ready; and, finding it

hot, says that the accused is ' as hot
(meaning 'as bold') as the lentil
porridge.' But the direct mention
of him as ἀνήρ, 'the man' (instead
of 'the dog') is curious. Nor is
θερμότητι a natural reason for with-
holding a share of anything. ἀνήρ
may indeed be compared with ἄνδρα
in v. 923; but the sense of the line
as applied to Labes or Laches is
not satisfactory. The line is better given to Bdelycleon, with
reference to some gesture of anger
and eagerness to condemn shewn
by Philocleon. Thus Bdelycleon
would say, seeing his father's hot
haste, 'Why, the man's as hot as
his lentil porridge! Pray, father, in
heaven's name don't condemn too
soon.'
920 ἀμφοτέρων.] Cf. note at 725.

ΞΑΝΘΙΑΣ

μή νιν ἀφῆτέ γ' αὐτὸν, ὡς ἔντ' αὖ πολὺ
κυνῶν ἁπάντων ἄνδρα μονοφαγίστατον,
ὅστις περιπλεύσας τὴν θυείαν ἐν κύκλῳ
ἐκ τῶν πόλεων τὸ σκῖρον ἐξεδήδοκεν.   925

ΦΙΛΟΚΛΕΩΝ

ἐμοὶ δέ γ' οὐκ ἔστ' οὐδὲ τὴν ὑδρίαν πλάσαι.

ΞΑΝΘΙΑΣ

πρὸς ταῦτα τοῦτον κολάσατ'· οὐ γὰρ ἄν ποτε
τρέφειν δύναιτ' ἂν μία λόχμη κλέπτα δυο·
ἵνα μὴ κεκλάγγω διὰ κενῆς ἄλλως ἐγώ·
ἐὰν δὲ μὴ, τὸ λοιπὸν οὐ κεκλάγξομαι.   930

ΦΙΛΟΚΛΕΩΝ

ἰοὺ ἰού.
ὅσας κατηγόρησε τὰς πανουργίας.
κλέπτον τὸ χρῆμα τἀνδρός· οὐ καὶ σοὶ δοκεῖ,

933 ἄνδρα μονοφαγίστατον.] 'Beyond all dogs a man of selfish greed.' The inconsistency of κυνῶν ἄνδρα is intentionally ridiculous. The superlative in -ίστατοι from μονοφάγοs is analogous to λαλίστατοι from λάλοs, Eur. *Cycl.* 315; cf. Ar. *Ran.* 91.

924 θυείαν.] The mortar means Sicily or the Sicilian sea, as the Scholiast says. A mortar was round (στρογγύλη): cf. *Pac.* 228.

925 σκῖρον.] Eupolis, in his *Golden Age*, has the phrase τροφαλὶs βαδίζει σκῖρον ἠμφιεσμένη. There is a play on the double meaning. Of the cheese, it is the hard under crust; of the cities, the gypsum or stucco of their buildings. And in the next line Philocleon takes it as equivalent to γῆ σκιρράs, with which they used to mend broken pitchers.

928 μία λοχμη.] There was a proverb μία λόχμη δύο ἐριθάκουs οὐ τρέφει, 'one bush does not support two redstarts'. Here Xanthias means 'one house can't keep two thieves': he himself (as the dog or

Cleon) being of course one.

929 κεκλάγγω.] Some read κεκλάγχω: but the better editors and MS. R are for κεκλάγγω.

διὰ κενῆς.] This phrase is used adverbially by Thuc. IV. 126, ἡ διὰ κενῆς ἐπανάσεισιs τῶν ὅπλων. And the Greeks often put together adverbs of nearly the same meaning. Another instance of διὰ κενῆs ἄλλωs is quoted from Plato the comic writer: and Bergler quotes ἄλλωs μάτην as combined. To which might be added αὖθις αὖ πάλιν, and similar phrases. It would be easy here to suggest a noun feminine as understood; but probably the speaker had no such definite noun in his mind, and was hardly conscious of any ellipse.

933 κλέπτον τὸ χρῆμα τἀνδρὸs] = ἀνὴρ ἐστι κλέπτηs. For τὸ χρῆμα cf. *Nub.* 2, τὸ χρῆμα τῶν νυκτῶν, and the note there.

οὐ καὶ σοί.] The dicast turns round to the cock perched up above him.

ὠλεκτρυόν; νὴ τὸν Δί, ἐπιμύει γέ τοι.
ὁ θεσμοθέτης. ποῦ 'σθ' οὗτος; ἀμίδα μοι δότω.   935

ΒΔΕΛΤΚΛΕΩΝ

αὐτὸς καθελοῦ· τοὺς μάρτυρας γὰρ ἐσκαλῶ.
Λάβητι μάρτυρας παρεῖναι, τρυβλίον,
δοίδυκα, τυρόκνηστιν, ἐσχάραν, χύτραν,
καὶ τἆλλα τὰ σκεύη τὰ προσκεκαυμένα.
ἀλλ' ἔτι σύ γ' οὐρεῖς καὶ καθίζεις οὐδέπω;   940

ΦΙΛΟΚΛΕΩΝ

τοῦτον δέ γ' οἶμ' ἐγὼ χεσεῖσθαι τήμερον.

ΒΔΕΛΤΚΛΕΩΝ

οὔκ αὖ σὺ παύσει χαλεπὸς ὢν καὶ δύσκολος,
καὶ ταῦτα τοῖς φεύγουσιν, ἀλλ' ὀδὰξ ἔχει;

ΦΙΛΟΚΛΕΩΝ

ἀνάβαιν', ἀπολογοῦ. τί σεσιώπηκας; λέγε.

934 ἐπιμύει.] 'He winks assent': and a wink from a cock is as good as a nod.

937—9 The dish, cheese-scraper, &c., are called to witness in Labes' favour. The ἐσχάρα was a portable brazier; cf. Ach. 887, δμῶες ἐξενέγκατε τὴν ἐσχάραν μοι δεῦρο καὶ τὴν κνίδα. All the kitchen vessels might have seen the theft, and seen also what the thief did with the cheese; whether he gave any to others. The ἐσχάρα was perhaps used for the toasting of the cheese.

939 προσκεκαυμένα.] 'burnt at the fire' as such utensils would be: cf. above v. 828. Dobree and Hermann read προσκεκλημένα 'subpoenaed as witnesses'; an ingenious change: but hardly needed.

941 οὐκ αὖ σὺ κ.τ.λ.] This is addressed to the old man. Bdelycleon had before asked him not to be too hasty in condemning (v. 819): he now asks it again, οὐκ αὖ σύ 'will you not, I again ask, cease &c.' Florens takes it as addressed to the prosecutor; but there is not much

sense in rebuking him for severity; severity would be reasonable in him.

943 καὶ ταῦτα τοῖς φεύγουσιν.] 'And that too against the poor defendants.' Bdelycleon wants him to have some wrath for the prosecutors. Cf. above v. 880, τοὺς φεύγοντάς τ' ἐλεεῖν μᾶλλον τῶν γραψαμένων, κ.τ.λ.

ἀλλ' ὀδὰξ ἔχει.] 'But do you hold on to them with griping teeth?' One of the expected advantages in this law-court at home was, that the dicast being not starved, but having his porridge, would cease δάπτων τὸν ἀπολογούμενον (v. 778). The αὐτοδὰξ τρόπος was a characteristic of the Athenians, cf. Pac. 607. The Scholiast strangely mistakes the meaning of this passage; and those who propose ἴχνη for ἔχει propose no improvement. The sense of the middle voice suits quite well: 'you hold fast to, cling to': it appears just the word for a bull-dog tenacity.

944 ἀνάβαιν'.] He turns to the defendant here.

ΦΙΛΟΚΛΕΩΝ

ἀλλ' οὐκ ἔχειν οὗτός γ' ἔοικεν ὅ τι λέγῃ. 945

ΒΔΕΛΥΚΛΕΩΝ

οὐκ, ἀλλ' ἐκεῖνό μοι δοκεῖ πεπονθέναι,
ὅπερ ποτὲ φεύγων ἔπαθε καὶ Θουκυδίδης·
ἀπόπληκτος ἐξαίφνης ἐγένετο τὰς γνάθους.
πάρεχ', ἐκποδών. ἐγὼ γὰρ ἀπολογήσομαι.
χαλεπὸν μὲν, ὦνδρες, ἐστὶ διαβεβλημένου 950
ὑπεραποκρίνεσθαι κυνός· λέξω δ' ὅμως.
ἀγαθὸς γάρ ἐστι καὶ διώκει τοὺς λύκους.

ΦΙΛΟΚΛΕΩΝ

κλέπτης μὲν οὖν οὗτός γε καὶ ξυνωμότης.

ΒΔΕΛΥΚΛΕΩΝ

μὰ Δι', ἀλλ' ἄριστός ἐστι τῶν νυνὶ κυνῶν,
οἷός τε πολλοῖς προβατίοις ἐφεστάναι. 955

ΦΙΛΟΚΛΕΩΝ

τί οὖν ὄφελος, τὸν τυρὸν εἰ κατεσθίει;

ΒΔΕΛΥΚΛΕΩΝ

ὅτι σοῦ προμάχεται καὶ φυλάττει τὴν θυραν

945 ἀλλ' οὐκ.] Philocleon maintains his conclusion against the defendant: thinking that he has not a word to say. His son says that it is not conscious guilt, but a sudden paralysis of the tongue.
947 Θουκυδίδης.] Son of Melesias, opponent of Pericles, accused of some misdoings in Thrace, and ostracised, B.C. 444, cf. Ach. 703, 708, where Aristophanes appears to pity him, as hardly dealt with. The policy of Pericles our poet does not approve of: cf. Ach. 530 sqq., and therefore naturally sympathizes with his rival.
949 πάρεχ', ἐκποδών.] Reiske seems to be right in thus punctuating. For πάρεχε can hardly mean 'take yourself off', or, with ἐκποδών, be equivalent to ἴθι ἐκπ., ἄναγε

ἐκπ., as L. and S. say. πάρεχε is rather 'allow me, give place, let me come', and ἐκποδών 'out of the way with you!' The Scholiast confirms this by his note λαμπρίσας τὸν κύνα φησὶν ἀναχώρει. Bdelycleon pushes aside the dog and takes the place of defendant.
952 λύκους.] τοὺς συκοφάντας. Schol. It seems rather meant that Laches was an active soldier against his country's enemies.
953 κλ. μὲν οὖν οὗτός γε.] Cf. Nub. 1112, ὠχρὸν μὲν οὖν ἔγωγε καὶ κακοδαίμονα.
955 προβατίοις.] Cf. v. 32, πρόβατα συγκαθήμενα. No doubt here too there is an idea of the Athenians being silly sheep.
957 ὅτι σοῦ.] 'The good of him is that he fights for you &c.'

καὶ τἄλλ' ἄριστός ἐστιν· εἰ δ' ὑφείλετο,
ξύγγνωθι. κιθαρίζειν γὰρ οὐκ ἐπίσταται.

ΦΙΛΟΚΛΕΩΝ

ἐγὼ δ' ἐβουλόμην ἂν οὐδὲ γράμματα,   960
ἵνα μὴ κακουργῶν ἐνέγραφ' ἡμῖν τὸν λόγον.

Philocleon had asked 'What is the good of him?' and the answer is natural enough. Dobree reads it ὅ τι; σοῦ 'you ask what good? Why he fights &c.' Either of these seems far preferable to Meineke's conjectural change in his notes, οὐ σοῦ κ.τ.λ. 'Does he not &c.'

959 κιθαρίζειν κ.τ.λ.] A curious excuse for non-appreciation of the difference between 'meum' and 'tuum'. But ignorance of the elements of music implies utter illiterateness; therefore it is as if Bdelycleon had said 'poor fellow! he's had no schooling—knows nothing—what is he to turn his hand to but thieving?' And below at v. 989, Philocleon retorts that he knows no trade but judging and condemning. In Av. 1432, τί γὰρ πάθω; σκάπτειν γὰρ οὐκ ἐπίσταμαι, is a similar excuse, given by the informer who knows no trade but his own. The scholiast quotes a proverb, to which there may be allusion, πεζῇ βαδίζω, πλεῖν γὰρ οὐκ ἐπίσταμαι, 'I trudge afoot because I cannot swim.' In the *Knights* (v. 188) the sausage-seller objects οὐδὲ μουσικὴν ἐπίσταμαι πλὴν γραμμάτων: but he is told that that is rather odds in his favour for being a statesman now-a-days; and therefore for being a thief perhaps, in Aristophanes' view of his country's statesmen at that time.

960 γράμματα.] Cf. γραμμάτων in *Eq.* 189, quoted above. After ἐβουλόμην ἂν understand ἐπίστασθαι αὐτόν.

961 ἵνα μὴ_ἐνέγραφ'.] A thorough discussion of this construction is to be found in Hermann's notes on Viger, *de Idiotismis*. ἵνα, ὅπως, ὡς, with past indicative, express a con-

sequence now impossible : 'adhibentur quum indicatur consilium, quod quis habuit, nec tamen effectum reddidit.' 'Cum indicativo praeteritorum temporum junguntur, quum significatur aliquid, quod futurum fuisset, si quid aliud actum esset, sed nunc non factum est.' Herm. They indicate something which would have been sure to follow, had something else been done, but which, as it is, has not followed, since that antecedent 'something else' was not done. Examples are, Aristoph. *Pac.* 135, Eur. *Hipp.* 645, Soph. *Oed. Tyr.* 1389—93. This last passage gives a double illustration, one for the imperfect, one for the aorist tense. οὐκ ἂν ἐσχόμην τὸ μὴ 'ποκλεῖσαι τοὐμὸν ἄθλιον δέμας, ἵν' ἦ τυφλός τε καὶ κλύων μηδέν...τί μ' οὐ λαβὼν ἔκτεινας εὐθύς, ὡς ἔδειξα μήποτε ἐμαυτὸν ἀνθρώποισιν ἔνθεν ἦν γεγώς; This past tense of the indicative may be aorist or imperfect : aorist, if a result is expressed not as lasting, but done once for all; imperfect, if lasting. Thus, ἵν' ἦ τυφλός κ.τ.λ., 'that so I might be not only blind but deaf,' the blindness and deafness being results lasting up to the time of speaking; but ὡς ἔδειξα μήποτε 'that so I might never have shewn,' the shewing being but once for all, and now over and done. 'That so' seems the closest English reading. Monk (on the *Hippolytus*) suggested 'in which case.' But this rather loses the notion of intent, purpose, &c. in ἵνα, ὅπως, ὡς. True it is that ἵνα sometimes = 'where,' with a simple relative force; but then it should be followed by οὐ (with δέ) not by μή. The English 'that' keeps the notion of purpose, &c., while the 'so' = 'in that (now impossible) case,' and

ΒΔΕΛΤΚΛΕΩΝ

ἄκουσον ὦ δαιμόνιέ μου τῶν μαρτύρων.
ἀνάβηθι, τυρόκνηστι, καὶ λέξον μέγα·
σὺ γὰρ ταμιεύουσ᾽ ἔτυχες. ἀπόκριναι σαφῶς,
εἰ μὴ κατέκνησας τοῖς στρατιώταις ἄλαβες.   965
φησὶ κατακνῆσαι.

ΦΙΛΟΚΛΕΩΝ

νὴ Δί᾽, ἀλλὰ ψεύδεται.

ΒΔΕΛΤΚΛΕΩΝ

ὦ δαιμόνι᾽, ἐλέει τοὺς ταλαιπωρουμένους.
οὗτος γὰρ ὁ Λάβης καὶ τραχήλι᾽ ἐσθίει
καὶ τὰς ἀκάνθας, κοὐδέποτ᾽ ἐν ταὐτῷ μένει.
ὁ δ᾽ ἕτερος οἷός ἐστιν οἰκουρὸς μόνον.   970
αὐτοῦ μένων γὰρ ἤττ᾽ ἂν εἴσω τις φέρῃ,
τούτων μεταιτεῖ τὸ μέρος· εἰ δὲ μὴ, δάκνει.

thus gives the right shade of meaning. Hermann observes that the
Latins have no exactly equivalent
construction, but that the Germans
have; *e.g.* in Sophocles he well
translates, '*damit* ich blind und taub
wäre,' and '*damit* ich nie gezeigt
hätte wer ich bin.' At the same time
I would urge, in favour of Monk
and his followers, that such conjunc-
tions as ἵνα ὡς ὅπως partake of the
character of relatives, and indeed
were possibly relatives originally:
compare the Latin 'quo,' which
comes to be = 'that.' And the more
common English way of putting
such a sentence is, 'why didst thou
not receive me? (or, 'would thou
hadst &c.' or, 'thou shouldest have
&c.') so had I never shewn.' Cf.
note on *Nub.* 1153, 669 for this difference of Greek and English idiom.
Shakspeare's, 'I would I were a
glove upon that hand, *That* I might
touch that cheek,' is a case for this
construction, and is so rendered in
a Porson exercise.

964 ταμιεύουσ᾽.] As a political
term this would be a dispenser of
moneys, provisions, &c. 'treasurer,'

Mitch. In a house it would be
'housekeeper, steward,' or perhaps
here 'pantler, buttery-man.'

967 ἄλαβ.] This must be a dis-
syllable in pronunciation, unless, as
Dindorf in his notes proposes, we
throw out τούς. In one edition
Dindorf writes ἔλει, 'recte, ut videtur,' says Meineke. And ἔλεινός for
ἐλεεινός rests on good authority. But
possibly some of these combinations
were monosyllabically pronounced,
and yet not monosyllabically written.
Cf. νεανίην in v. 1067, and (if the
vulg. be retained) ἀπεωσάμεσθα in
v. 1085.

968—72. Labes can eat odds and
ends and fish bones, and is here,
there, and everywhere: the other
stops at home, and wants to be well
fed. The activity of Laches and
the lazy greediness of Cleon are
contrasted.

970 οἰκουρός.] Κλέωνά φησιν ἐν-
δομυχοῦντα τὰ τῆς πόλεως κατεσθίειν.
Schol. Brunck, followed by Hirschig and Meineke, reads οἰκουρεῖν·
which seems better, but the MS.
reading is not indefensible: 'is a
sort of stay-at-home-merely.'

ΦΙΛΟΚΛΕΩΝ

αἰβοῖ, τί κακόν ποτ' ἐσθ' ὅτῳ μαλάττομαι ;
κακόν τι περιβαίνει με, κἀναπείθομαι.

ΒΔΕΛΤΚΛΕΩΝ.

ἴθ', ἀντιβολῶ σ', οἰκτείρατ' αὐτόν, ὦ πάτερ,   973
καὶ μὴ διαφθείρητε. ποῦ τὰ παιδία ;
ἀναβαίνετ', ὦ πονηρά, καὶ κνυζούμενα
αἰτεῖτε κἀντιβολεῖτε καὶ δακρύετε.

ΦΙΛΟΚΛΕΩΝ.

κατάβα κατάβα κατάβα κατάβα.

ΒΔΕΛΤΚΛΕΩΝ.

καταβήσομαι.
καίτοι τὸ κατάβα τοῦτο πολλοὺς δὴ πάνυ   980
ἐξηπάτηκεν. ἀτὰρ ὅμως καταβήσομαι.

ΦΙΛΟΚΛΕΩΝ.

ἐς κόρακας. ὡς οὐκ ἀγαθόν ἐστι τὸ ῥοφεῖν.
ἐγὼ γὰρ ἀπεδάκρυσα νῦν γνώμην ἐμὴν
οὐδέν ποτ' ἀλλ' ἡ τῆς φακῆς ἐμπλήμενος.

973 αἰβοῖ.] Philocleon is disgusted
to find that he is softening. Bdelycleon takes advantage of this, and
produces the little ones of the accused, to whine and excite com-
miseration. It was a common custom
both with Greeks and Romans to
bring the family into court, that their
tears might move the judges. Cf.
Dem. c. Mid. 574. Racine takes
this idea, 'Venez, famille désolée,
Venez, pauvres enfans, qu'on veut
rendre orphelins, Venez, faire parler
vos esprits enfantins. Oui, Monsieur, vous voyez ici notre misère.
Nous sommes orphelins, rendez-nous
notre père, &c.'
975 οἰκτείρατ'.] Plural, because
Philocleon was but one of many
dicasts.
979 κατάβα.] The customary
word for the dicasts to say, when
they had heard enough to convince

them, and bade the pleader come
down from his place and say no
more. But they sometimes deceived
the hope of acquittal thus raised.
982 ἐς κόρακας.] A curse on
either the defendant or the porridge;
perhaps on both, as Mitchell takes
it, 'Curse on yourself and curse
upon this pottage!'
983, 4 ἐγὼ γὰρ...ἐμπλήμενος.]
'For I wept freely but now, as
I think, for no earthly reason but
because I was full of the lentil porridge;' the heat of which brought
tears to his eyes. For γνώμην ἐμὴν
cf. Pac. 232, καὶ γὰρ ἐξιέναι γνώμην
ἐμὴν μέλλει. The old interpretation,
'I wept away my judgment, lost my
cool judgment in my tears,' is certainly wrong. Meineke's ἀπεδάκρυσα
is confirmed by the Scholiast's ἐπι-
δακρῦσαι τῷ τῶν παίδων ὀδυρμῷ, but
is against all MSS.

ΒΔΕΛΥΚΛΕΩΝ.

οὐκοῦν ἀποφεύγει δῆτα;

ΦΙΛΟΚΛΕΩΝ.

χαλεπὸν εἰδέναι.   985

ΒΔΕΛΥΚΛΕΩΝ.

ἴθ', ὦ πατρίδιον, ἐπὶ τὰ βελτίω τρέπου.
τῃδὶ λαβὼν τὴν ψῆφον ἐπὶ τὸν ὕστερον
μύσας παρᾷξον κἀπόλυσον, ὦ πάτερ.

ΦΙΛΟΚΛΕΩΝ

οὐ δῆτα· κιθαρίζειν γὰρ οὐκ ἐπίσταμαι.

ΒΔΕΛΥΚΛΕΩΝ

φέρε νύν σε τῃδὶ τὴν ταχίστην περιάγω.   990

ΦΙΛΟΚΛΕΩΝ

ὁδ' ἔσθ' ὁ πρότερος;

987 τηνδί.] He gives him a pebble to vote with, a pebble 'condemnatory,' καταδικάζουσαν. This he wishes him to put into the urn called ἄκυρος and also ὕστερος. The consequence would be the acquittal of the prisoner. Philocleon refuses to do that, but is so led round that he in the end mistakes the urn into which he puts his condemnatory vote, and unintentionally acquits. There were, it appears, two urns, the one called κύριος, of brass, the other ἄκυρος, of wood. There were also two kinds of voting pebble, one bored through with a hole, the other entire and solid (τετρυπημένη, πλήρης), or sometimes one black, the other white. The perforated or black were for condemnation, the solid or white for acquittal. That a vote might be used effectually it had to be dropped into the 'valid' urn (κύριος): the other vote was then put into the 'invalid' urn, and had no effect. The votes found in the 'valid' urn were counted, and the result was according to the excess or defect of one or the other. The

urns were from their position called πρότερος and ὕστερος: but what this position was exactly, is uncertain. Richter thinks the πρότερος was close to the tribunal, the ὕστερος further off, beyond where the advocate, witnesses, &c., stood, so that the dicasts put their useless vote into this just before leaving the court.

988 μύσας κ. τ. λ.] 'Shut your eyes and pass on hastily to the further urn and acquit him.' This Philocleon refuses to do, retorting on his son his own words at v. 959, 'that he is no scholar,' and knows but one trade, viz. that of condemning.

990 φέρε νύν σε.] Bdelycleon pretends to be resigned, and offers to conduct him to the πρότερος κάδισκος; but in some way so misleads him that he finds the ὕστερος where the πρότερος should, according to his idea, be, and into it he drops his condemning vote. This amounts to an acquittal; for the other vote, that of acquittal, of course goes into the 'valid' urn.

ΒΔΕΛΤΚΛΕΩΝ
οὗτος.

ΦΙΛΟΚΛΕΩΝ
αὕτη 'νταῦθ' ἔνι.

ΒΔΕΛΤΚΛΕΩΝ
ἐξηπάτηται, κἀπολέλυκεν οὐχ ἑκών.

ΦΙΛΟΚΛΕΩΝ
φέρ' ἐξεράσω.

ΒΔΕΛΤΚΛΕΩΝ
πῶς ἄρ' ἠγωνίσμεθα;

ΦΙΛΟΚΛΕΩΝ
δείξειν ἔοικεν.

ΒΔΕΛΤΚΛΕΩΝ
ἐκπέφευγας, ὦ Λάβης.
πάτερ πάτερ, τί πέπονθας;

ΦΙΛΟΚΛΕΩΝ
οἴμοι, ποῦ 'σθ' ὕδωρ;   995

ΒΔΕΛΤΚΛΕΩΝ
ἔπαιρε σαυτόν.

ΦΙΛΟΚΛΕΩΝ
εἰπέ νυν ἐκεῖνό μοι,
ὄντως ἀπέφυγεν;

993 ἐξεράσω.] Cf. Aesch. Eum. 742, ΑΘ. ἐκβάλλεθ' ὡς τάχιστα τευχέων πλ/ους, ὅσαι δικαστῶν τοῦτ' ἐπέσταλται τέλος. OP. ὦ Φοῖβ' Ἄπολλον, πῶς ἀγὼν κριθήσεται; This makes for Dindorf's text against Meineke's; for the dicast Philocleon should empty out and count the votes. But πῶς ἄρ' ἠγωνίσμεθα; does look rather as if it were an impatient question thrown in during the counting; and in the passage of Aeschylus Orestes, the defendant, puts the question. Hence I have slightly altered the arrangement of the dialogue, which now runs thus: 'Phil. Come, let me turn out the votes. Bd. How have we sped in the trial?

Phil. 'Twill soon be shewn. Bd. Labes, you are acquitted!' Bdelycleon, interested for the accused, asks, 'how have we sped?' and then sees at once the result and tells it to the defendant before the old dicast, in his astonishment and disgust, can get out a word.

994 δείξειν ἔοικε.] Sc. τοὔργον. Cf. Lys. 375, τοὔργον τάχ' αὐτὸ δείξει.

995 ποῦ 'σθ' ὕδωρ.] The old man is fainting: cf. Ran. 481, ἀλλ' ὡραπκιῶ ἀλλ' οἶσε πρὸς τὴν καρδίαν μου σπογγίαν.

996 ἔπαιρε σαυτόν.] Cf. Eur. Androm. 1076, ἆ ἆ, τί δράσεις, ὦ γεραιέ; μή πίτνε· ἔπαιρε σαυτόν. ΠΗ. οὐδέν εἰμ'· ἀπωλόμην.

ΒΔΕΛΤΚΛΕΩΝ
νὴ Δί'.

ΦΙΛΟΚΛΕΩΝ
οὐδέν εἰμ' ἄρα.

ΒΔΕΛΤΚΛΕΩΝ
μὴ φροντίσῃς, ὦ δαιμόνι', ἀλλ' ἀνίστασο.

ΦΙΛΟΚΛΕΩΝ
πῶς οὖν ἐμαυτῷ τοῦτ' ἐγὼ ξυνείσομαι,
φεύγοντ' ἀπολύσας ἄνδρα; τί ποτε πείσομαι;   1000
ἀλλ', ὦ πολυτίμητοι θεοί, ξύγγνωτέ μοι·
ἄκων γὰρ αὐτ' ἔδρασα κοὐ τοὐμοῦ τρόπου.

ΒΔΕΛΤΚΛΕΩΝ
καὶ μηδὲν ἀγανάκτει γ'. ἐγὼ γάρ σ', ὦ πάτερ,
θρέψω καλῶς, ἄγων μετ' ἐμαυτοῦ πανταχοῖ,
ἐπὶ δεῖπνον, ἐς ξυμπόσιον, ἐπὶ θεωρίαν,   1005
ἄσθ' ἡδέως διάγειν σε τὸν λοιπὸν χρόνον·
κοὐκ ἐγχανεῖταί σ' ἐξαπατῶν Ὑπέρβολος.

999 ξυνείσομαι.] 'How shall I
be conscious of this deed with myself,' *i. e.* 'how can I yet live and
know that I have done this deed,'
which almost = 'how can I pardon
myself for this?' To share in the
knowledge of a deed (if criminal),
and to make no effort to expose it,
is in effect to consent to it, or to
pardon it; hence the common
meaning of συγγιγνώσκειν. The
Latins took a different compound
to express the same thing. '*ig-
noscere*' 'to (apparently) *not* know,
to refuse to know, ignore, wink at,'
and so 'to pardon.' The one language expresses pardon by inward
acquiescence in the knowledge of a
crime; the other by outward denial
of such knowledge.

1002 κοὐ τοὐμοῦ τρόπου.] 'And
not (as a deed) fitting my character,
not after my wont.' The genitive
is the same as that in the common

phrases ἀγαθοῦ ἐστιν ἀγαθὰ πράττειν and the like. It was not δικαστικοῦ τρόπου to acquit. 'Not such
my wont, as those who know me
know' (Tennyson) Philocleon might
have said.

1003 καὶ μηδὲν ἀγανάκτει γ'.]
'Yes, yes, and don't be so over-
much grieved.' The γε gives assent
to Philocleon's excuse.

1005 θεωρίαν.] Philocleon is to
give up law and do nothing but enjoy himself at feasts and theatres.
The same kind of retirement is proposed for Cratinus in *Eq.* 536. The
'reformed' life which the old man
is to lead is not of the highest order,
and is no doubt a satire on the follies and excesses in that direction
which were prevalent at Athens in
our poet's age.

1007 Ὑπέρβολος.] Cf. *Nub.* 551,
623, 876, 1065.

ἀλλ᾽ εἰσίωμεν.

ΦΙΛΟΚΛΕΩΝ

ταῦτά νυν, εἴπερ δοκεῖ.

ΧΟΡΟΣ

ἀλλ᾽ ἴτε χαίροντες ὅποι βούλεσθ᾽.
ὑμεῖς δὲ τέως, ὦ μυριάδες   1010
ἀναρίθμητοι,
νῦν μὲν τὰ μέλλοντ᾽ εὖ λέγε-
σθαι μὴ πέσῃ φαύλως χαμᾶζ᾽
εὐλαβεῖσθε.
τοῦτο γὰρ σκαιῶν θεατῶν
ἐστὶ πάσχειν, κοὐ πρὸς ὑμῶν.
νῦν αὖτε λεῷ πρόσσχετε τὸν νοῦν, εἴπερ καθαρόν τι φιλεῖτε.

1008 Philocleon resigns himself to the change, and they go in to prepare for it, leaving the stage clear for the parabasis.

1009. The parts of this parabasis are : κομμάτιον, 1009—1014, parabasis proper (or anapaests) 1015—1050, μακρόν, 1051—1059, στροφή, 1060—1070, ἐπίρρημα, 1071—1090, ἀντιστροφή, 1091—1100, ἀντεπίρρημα, 1101—1121.

ἀλλ᾽ ἴτε χαίροντα.] Cf. Eq. 498, Nub. 510, ἀλλ᾽ ἴθι χαίρων, κ.τ.λ.

1010 μυριάδες.] To be taken rather vaguely of multitudes. Strictly speaking the 'myriads' of the audience would not be many, as Richter reminds us ; but each myriad of itself may be ἀναρίθμητοι. Plato uses μυριάδες ἀναρίθμητοι, of the numerous generations of forefathers that have preceded us, Theaet. 175, A.

1012 πέσῃ.] As did the Clouds, to the first exhibition of which he refers here and further on in this parabasis.

1013 σκαιῶν.] The exact opposite is δεξιός, a favourite word of compliment to the Athenians. Cf. Nub. 524—27, ἀπεχώρουν ὑπ᾽ ἀνδρῶν

φορτικῶν...ταῦτ᾽ οὖν ὑμῖν μέμφομαι τοῖς σοφοῖς...ἀλλ᾽ οὐδ᾽ ὡς ὑμῶν...προδώσω τοὺς δεξιούς : cf. also Nub. 521, θεατὰς δεξιούς. Euripides opposes σκαιὸς and σοφός : Med. 190, σκαιοὺς δὲ λέγων κοὐδέν τι σοφοὺς τοὺς πρόσθε βροτοὺς οὐκ ἂν ἁμάρτοις.

1015—1050. The poet complains of unjust treatment. He has done the Athenian public good service : first in the name of other poets, then in his own. He has not debased his Muse to gratify others, nor has he attacked the small ; but has boldly withstood the great and powerful, Cleon especially. Also he has exposed other plagues and corrupters of public morals. But the Athenians, though they honoured him at first, gave him up last year, and rejected the best play he had ever given them : entirely through their want of understanding, and through no fault of the poet.

1015 πρόσσχετε.] Cf. Nub. 575, Eq. 504.

καθαρόν.] Cf. above v. 631, καθαρῶς λέγοντοι. The word means here 'genuine, pure,' the real thing, as opposed to what is specious but of no real worth.

μέμψασθαι γὰρ τοῖσι θεαταῖς ὁ ποιητὴς νῦν ἐπιθυμεῖ   1016
ἀδικεῖσθαι γάρ φησιν πρότερος πόλλ' αὐτοὺς εὖ πεποιηκώς,
τὰ μὲν οὐ φανερῶς, ἀλλ' ἐπικουρῶν κρύβδην ἑτέροισι ποιη-
        ταῖς,
μιμησάμενος τὴν Εὐρυκλέους μαντείαν καὶ διάνοιαν,
εἰς ἀλλοτρίας γαστέρας ἐνδὺς κωμῳδικὰ πολλὰ χέασθαι·
μετὰ τοῦτο δὲ καὶ φανερῶς ἤδη κινδυνεύων καθ' ἑαυτόν, 1021
οὐκ ἀλλοτρίων, ἀλλ' οἰκείων Μουσῶν στόμαθ' ἡνιοχήσας.
ἀρθεὶς δὲ μέγας καὶ τιμηθεὶς ὡς οὐδεὶς πώποτ' ἐν ὑμῖν,
οὐκ ἐκτελέσαι φησὶν ἐπαρθεὶς οὐδ' ὑγκῶσαι τὸ φρόνημα,

1017 ἀδικεῖσθαι ...... πρότερος.]
'That he is the first to suffer wrong,'
not only having done the public no
wrong himself, but having done it
much good.

1018 ἐπικουρῶν κ.τ.λ.] Philonides and Callistratus were the
poets under whose names Aristophanes' earliest plays came out : viz.
the *Babylonians*, *Banqueters*, *A-
charnians*. For another mention of
this, cf. *Nub*. 530, sqq.

1019 Εὐρυκλέους.] A ventrilo-
quist and diviner at Athens, from
whom others of the same trade were
afterwards called Euryclidae. Schol.

1020 εἰς ἀλλοτρίας.] As Eury-
cles throws his voice into others, so
did I with my plays. Others seemed the utterers ; I was the real
source of the words which flowed
out.

χέασθαι.] Infin. dependent on
μιμησάμενος. ἐνδὺς χέασθαι=ἐνδύ-
ναι καὶ χέασθαι : so that the syn-
tax will be μιμησάμενος Εὐρυκλέα
(ὥστε) ἐνδῦναι εἰς ἀλλ. γ. καὶ χέασθαι.

1021 καθ' ἑαυτόν.] The *Knights*
was Aristophanes' first play exhibited in his own name. And the
Scholiast remarks that none would
run the risk of acting Cleon's
part, hence Aristophanes had to
act it himself. This would give
peculiar force to κινδυνεύων καθ'
ἑαυτόν ; but it is not necessary here
to understand anything more than

the risk of failure before the audience. And καθ' ἑαυτόν, 'by himself,' in his own name, is merely
opposed to the ἐπικουρῶν ἑτέροις.
Cf. *Eq.* 513, ὡς οὐχὶ τἀλαι χορὸν
αἰτοίη καθ' ἑαυτόν.

1022 ἡνιοχήσας.] 'Having taken on him to rein the mouths of
his own and no others' muses.' The
poet, when he had entered as it were
into others who were to utter his
thoughts, might be termed the
charioteer or controller of their
mouths, or of the strains to issue
from them. For a bold metaphorical use of ἡνίοχος, cf. *Nub*. 602,
αἴγδοη ἡνίοχοι.

1023 ἀρθεὶς δὲ μέγας.] Cf. Dem.
Olynth. II. 20, ὥσπερ οὖν διὰ τούτων
ἤρθη μέγας, οὕτως ὀφείλει διὰ τῶν
αὐτῶν τούτων καὶ καθαιρεθῆναι πάλιν.

1024 οὐκ ἐκτελέσαι κ.τ.λ.]
There is a difficulty here, which
Reiske saw, and thought ἐκτελέσαι
corrupt ; but the other commentators seem to pass it over. οὐκ ἐκτ.
φ. ἐν., must mean 'he does not—
elated by his honours—say he has
attained perfection, done everything
that there is to do.' And so the
Scholiast says : οὐκ ἐπὶ τέλος ἐδοξεν
αὐτῷ ἐλθεῖν οὔτε τῆς ποιήσεως οὔτε
τῶν ἐπαίνων. For that ἐκτελέσαι
ἐπαρθεὶς=τελέως ἐπαρθῆναι, 'to be
completely elated,' as Florens says,
following the earlier (and not very
intelligible) part of the Scholium,
is hardly possible. But οὐδ' ὑγκῶ-

ἀλλ' ὑπὲρ ὑμῶν ἔτι καὶ νυνὶ πολεμεῖ· φησίν τε μετ' αὐτοῦ
τοῖς ἠπιάλοις ἐπιχειρῆσαι πέρυσιν καὶ τοῖς πυρετοῖσιν,
οἳ τοὺς πατέρας τ' ἦγχον νύκτωρ καὶ τοὺς πάππους ἀπέ-
     πνιγον,
κατακλινόμενοί τ' ἐπὶ ταῖς κοίταις ἐπὶ τοῖσιν ἀπράγμοσιν
     ὑμῶν   1040
ἀντωμοσίας καὶ προσκλήσεις καὶ μαρτυρίας συνεκόλλων,

1037 **μετ' αὐτοῦ.**] 'With him;'
i. e. not only Cleon did he assail,
but other plagues as well. μετ'
αὐτόν 'after him' Bentley. And the
change is very slight, the confusion
between ν and ρ being frequent.
Cf. above v. 416, and *Eq.* 798.
This would give more precisely the
order of the two attacks; that on
Cleon in the *Knights*, that on the
'agues &c.' in the *Clouds.*
1038 **ἠπιάλοις.**] Explained in
the Scholiast by ῥιγοπύρετοι, and τὸ
πρὸ τοῦ πυρετοῦ κρύοι. Didymus
rather identifies the word with ἠιάλ-
ηι and ἐφάλτης 'the nightmare;'
whereas Ruhnken (on Timaeus'
Lexicon) quotes from Phrynichus
this distinction : ἠπιάλη, ὁ ἐπισί-
πτων καὶ ἐφέρπων τοῖς κοιμωμένοις
δαίμων· τὸ δὲ ἠπίαλος διὰ τοῦ ὁ
μικροῦ ἕτερόν τι σημαίνει, τὸ καλού-
μενον ῥιγοπύρετον. But whether
ἠπιάλοις mean here 'shivering fits,
agues,' or 'night-mares,' matters
little. Either might be precursors
of fever, and be naturally joined
with πυρετοῖσιν. What is more important is the general bearing of the
passage. And there can be no doubt
that it refers to the *Clouds,* and that
the ἠπίαλοι mean the sophists. Yet
whether all the details can be explained from the *Clouds,* as we have
the play, is doubtful. The Scholiast
says ἠπιάλους αὐτοὺς ὠνόμασεν ὡς
ὠχρότητα περισκώντων, but he also
notes that Aristophanes in the
Clouds uses the phrase ἅμα δ' ἠπίαλος πυρετοῦ πρόδρομος. Now this
phrase is not found in our edition of
the *Clouds,* but it may have been in
the first edition ; and there may

have been other passages and scenes
also which would explain more satisfactorily the allusions in the four
following lines, which do not appear to me to be explicable from the
Clouds as it has come down to us.
Fritzsche thinks the first *Clouds* was
very different from our play, relying
much on this passage ; and without
determining how far it differed, I
should agree that the expressions
here are too definite to refer only to
the scenes which Aristophanes' text
now gives.
1039 **οἳ τοὺς πατέρας κ. τ. λ.**]
'Throttling fathers by night,' and
'choking grandfathers,' finds no
sufficient explanation in Phidippides'
beating of his father. The 'agues
and fevers' (sophists) might be said
indeed to commit these enormities,
if they persuaded men so to do, but
a more definite reference is wanted.
1040 **κατακλινόμενοι κ. τ. λ.**]
This, again, finds no warrant in our
Clouds. The devices of Socrates,
or his disciples, or of Strepsiades,
when made to wrap himself up and
think, do not suit with this passage.
Shifts to evade payment of debt are
mentioned, but not legal traps for
the simple and unwary. Richter
renders κατακλ. 'incubantes tam-
quam incubi in cubilibus.' But
'night-mares framing legal subtle-
ties' is an odd idea. Perhaps it is
rather that the sophists were represented as lying on their beds and
devising such things.
ἀπράγμοσιν.] Cf. *Eq.* 261, κἄν
τιν' αὐτῶν γνῶι ἀπράγμον' ὄντα καὶ
κεχηνότα, κ.τ.λ.
1041 **ἀντωμοσίας, κ.τ.λ.**] 'Affi-

ὥστ' ἀναπηδᾶν δειμαίνοντας πολλοὺς ὡς τὸν πολέμαρχον.
τοιόνδ' εὑρόντες ἀλεξίκακον, τῆς χώρας τῆσδε καθαρτὴν,
πέρυσιν καταπρούδοτε καινοτάταις σπείραντ' αὐτὸν διανοίαις,
ἃς ὑπὸ τοῦ μὴ γνῶναι καθαρῶς ὑμεῖς ἐποιήσατ' ἀναλδεῖς·
καίτοι σπένδων πόλλ' ἐπὶ πολλοῖς ὄμνυσιν τὸν Διόνυσον
μὴ πώποτ' ἀμείνον' ἔπη τούτων κωμῳδικὰ μηδέν' ἀκοῦσαι.
τοῦτο μὲν οὖν ἔσθ' ὑμῖν αἰσχρὸν τοῖς μὴ γνοῦσιν παραχρῆμα,
ὁ δὲ ποιητὴς οὐδὲν χείρων παρὰ τοῖσι σοφοῖς νενόμισται,
εἰ παρελαύνων τοὺς ἀντιπάλους τὴν ἐπίνοιαν ξυνέτριψεν.
ἀλλὰ τὸ λοιπὸν τῶν ποιητῶν,   1051

davits, summonses, depositions;' legal terms explained in *Dict. Antiq.* p. 335, 336, under Δίκη.

1042 ἀναπηδᾶν.] 'So that they jumped up,' as if suddenly startled from sleep: the word rather suits the 'nightmare' explanation of ἡτίαλοι.

πολύμαρχον.] The polemarch was the protector of strangers and resident aliens. Such would be these ἀπράγμονες: see the passage from the *Knights*, referred to on v. 1040.

1043 ἀλεξίκακον.] Applied to Hermes in *Pac.* 422; but oftener as an epithet of Hercules; and Aristophanes above, at v. 1030, is compared to him. Hercules was a 'purger of the earth' from all monsters &c.; so was the poet to Attica.

1044 πέρυσιν.] When the *Clouds* was exhibited, and gained no prize.

καινοτάταις.] Cf. *Nub.* 546, οὐδ' ὑμᾶς ζητῶ 'ξαπατᾶν δὶς καὶ τρὶς ταὐτ' εἰσάγων, ἀλλ' ἀεὶ καινὰς ἰδέας ἐσφέρων σοφίζομαι, οὐδὲν ἀλλήλαισιν ὁμοίας καὶ πάσας δεξιάς.

σπείραντ'.] The metaphor is continued in ἀναλδεῖς. He had sowed good seed, but not reaped a good harvest. Bothe prefers to read διανοίας; which is simpler; Meineke mentions with approval a conjecture of Hecke, αὑτήν, 'having sown it,' *i. e.* the land. But it seems as well for this accusative to be understood, and to keep αὐτὸν, 'you sacrificed him when he sowed (the field) with

most novel ideas.'

1045 τοῦ μὴ γνῶναι.] He upbraids them with want of judgment in not appreciating his best play. The same complaints are made in the parabasis of the *Clouds*, which certainly belongs to the second edition of that play.

1046 σπένδων πόλλ' ἐπὶ πολλοῖς.] Sc. βώμοις or ἱεροῖς. With many a libation, and many a vow, he will swear that never was a better play. Cf. *Nub.* 518, κατερῶ πρὸς ὑμᾶς ἐλευθέρως τἀληθῆ νὴ τὸν Διόνυσον τὸν ἐκθρέψαντά με. οὕτω νικήσαιμί τ' ἐγὼ καὶ νομιζοίμην σοφὸς, ὡς ...ἡγούμενος...ταύτην σοφώτατ' ἔχειν τῶν ἐμῶν κωμῳδιῶν πρώτην ἠξίωσ' ἀναγεῦσ' ὑμᾶς.

1048 τοῦτο μὲν οὖν κ.τ.λ.] It is a discredit to some of you not to have appreciated me; but no discredit whatever to me in the eyes of the wise. So in *Nub.* 527 he appeals to the δεξιοί.

1050 εἰ παρελαύνων.] The metaphor is from a chariot race. If the poet's chariot has failed to win, and has been broken in the race, it was while nobly striving to beat his rivals. τὴν ἐπίνοιαν, 'the thoughts, devices, wit, &c. of the play.' τὰ ἐπινοήματα τῶν δραμάτων. SchoL

1051—59. Therefore for the future you must take better care of your good poets and their happy thoughts, if you want to be thought clever fellows.

ὦ δαιμόνιοι, τοὺς ζητοῦντας
καινόν τι λέγειν κἀξευρίσκειν
στέργετε μᾶλλον καὶ θεραπεύετε,
καὶ τὰ νοήματα σώζεσθ' αὐτῶν·   1055
ἐσβάλλετε δ' ἐς τὰς κιβωτοὺς
μετὰ τῶν μήλων.
κἂν ταῦτα ποιῆθ', ὑμῖν δι' ἔτους
τῶν ἱματίων
ὀζήσει δεξιότητος.
ὦ πάλαι ποτ' ὄντες ὑμεῖς ἄλκιμοι μὲν ἐν χοροῖς,   1060
ἄλκιμοι δ' ἐν μάχαις,
καὶ κατ' αὐτὸ δὴ μόνον τοῦτ' ἄνδρες ἀλκιμώτατοι,

1052 [ζητοῦντας...λέγειν.] 'Those
who seek out something new to
say.' The construction seems rather
[ζητοῦντας τι (ὥστε) λέγειν than ζητ.
λέγειν τι. A parallel from Av. 465
is quoted by Bergler; λέγειν ζητῶ
τρίπαλαι μέγα καὶ λαμυρὸν ἔπος τι.
1055 τὰ νοήματα σώζεσθ'.] Do
not let them fail, as our poet's ἐπί-
νοια did (v. 1050): cf. above, 1012,
μὴ πέσῃ φαύλως χαμᾶζ' εὐλαβεῖσθε.
1057 μετὰ τῶν μήλων.] εἰώθασι
γὰρ εἰς τὰ κιβώτια μῆλα βάλλειν δι'
εὐοσμίαν. Schol. By 'putting them
into their clothes' chests, that their
garments might smell of cleverness,'
it is meant that they should lay them
well to heart and so store them up,
which would give them a savour of
cleverness all the year through.
Mitchell quotes from Chaucer a
compliment to breath as sweet as
'hord of apples laid in hay or heth.'
1059 τῶν ἱμ. ὀζήσει δεξιότητος.]
Cf. Pac. 529, τοῦ μὲν γὰρ ὄζει κρομ-
μυοξυρεγμίας, ταύτης δ' ὀπώρας, and
Ach. 852, ὅζων τῶν μασχαλῶν πατρὸς
τραγασαίου.
1060—1120. In the strophe the
Chorus lament that their youth is
gone, but think that they are still
better than the foppish striplings of
the modern days. They then (in
the epirrhema) explain their wasp-
like garb, describing their deeds in

battle against the barbarian, which
gained for them the appellation of
wasps. Again (in the antistrophe)
they recal their youthful deeds; how
they won what the younger men now
steal: and (in the antepirrhema)
shew that there is a waspish element
in their behaviour at home; that
they freely use their stings; but
that there are idle drones among
them, and that this rule ought to be
enforced: 'no work, no pay.'
1060 ὦ πάλαι.] With allusion to
the proverb quoted in Plut. 1002,
πάλαι ποτ' ἦσαν ἄλκιμοι Μιλήσιοι,
of which the Scholiast on that place
gives the reported origin. It was at
any rate a proverb of those who had
formerly flourished but now did so
no longer.
1062 καὶ κατ' αὐτὸ κ.τ.λ.] This
line is corrupt in MSS., ending with
ἄνδρες μαχιμώτατοι ἀλκιμώτατοι or
ἀνδρικώτατοι, Bentley. ἀλκιμώτατοι,
Porson; and the repetition of the
same adjective seems better, and is
rather nearer in termination to the
MS. μαχιμώτατοι.
τοῦτ'.] In fighting and dancing,
as opposed to law-suits, which are
now their only strong point. Senger
thinks τοῦτο is said δεικτικῶς, point-
ing to their κέντρον. But this sting
is the weapon that they have taken
to in their old age.

πρίν ποτ' ἦν, πρὶν ταῦτα· νῦν δ'
οἴχεται κύκνου τ' ἔτι πολιώτεραι δὴ
αἴδ' ἐπανθοῦσιν τρίχες.　　　　　　　　1065
ἀλλὰ κἀκ τῶν λειψάνων δεῖ τῶνδε ῥώμην
νεανικὴν σχεῖν· ὡς ἐγὼ τοὐμὸν νομίζω
γῆρας εἶναι κρεῖττον ἢ πολλῶν κικίννους νεανιῶν καὶ
σχῆμα κεὐρυπρωκτίαν.　　　　　　　　1070
εἴ τις ὑμῶν, ὦ θεαταί, τὴν ἐμὴν ἰδὼν φύσιν
εἶτα θαυμάζει μ' ὁρῶν μέσον διεσφηκωμένον,
ἢ τίς ἡμῶν ἐστιν ἡ 'πίνοια τῆς ἐγκεντρίδος,
ῥᾳδίως ἐγὼ διδάξω, κἂν ἄμουσος ᾖ τὸ πρίν.
ἐσμὲν ἡμεῖς, οἷς πρόσεστι τοῦτο τοὐρροπύγιον,　　1075
Ἀττικοὶ μόνοι δικαίως ἐγγενεῖς αὐτόχθονες,

1063 πρίν ποτ' ἦν.] Didymus
says this is parodied from Timo-
creon of Rhodes. It is a common-
place for all poets: cf. Catullus in
the dedication of the barque 'Sed
haec prius fuere'; Virgil's 'Fuit
Ilium', &c.

1064 κύκνου...πολιώτεραι.] Cf.
Ov. Tr. 4. 8. 1, Jam mea cycnea
imitantur tempora plumas. The
chorus in Aesch. Agam. 71—82,
lament their age in a similar way.

1066 λειψάνων.] The most must
be made of what remains, though it
be but an ἰσχὺς ἰσόπαις, an ὄναρ
ἡμερόφαντον, as Aeschylus terms it.

1069 κικίννους.] 'Cincinnos.'
The long and carefully dressed hair
of the Athenian youth is continually
a mark for Aristophanes' ridicule.
He had not much to boast of in that
way himself.

1070 σχῆμα.] 'dress,' cf. Eq.
1331, ἀρχαίῳ σχήματι λαμπρός, and
below, v. 1170. But it almost includes affectation in gait; indeed it
might be here 'the mien, postures,
attitudinizing.'

1072 μέσον διεσφ.] 'Wasp-
waisted.' Probably the chorus were
tightly girded round the waist, so
as to give them a waspish contour,

cf. Plut. 561, ἰσχνοὶ καὶ σφηκώδεις,
opposed to fat aldermanic well-to-
do fellows.

1073 ἢ τίς.] ἥτις Bentley, Porson, and others. But 'if any wonders at our waspish waists, whatever is the meaning of our sting'
would identify the waist with the
sting, whereas it should rather be,
'If any wonders at our waists, or
(wonders) what means our sting.'
An 'or' or 'and' seems wanted.
Richter reads χἥτις. Unless indeed
ἐγκεντρὶς were taken to mean that
in which the κέντρον was fastened,
and so were to include the girdle
which compressed the waist.

ἡμῶν ἐστιν.] ἡμῶν ἐστιν ἡ 'πίνοια τῆσδε τῆι, vulg. Some omit
ἡμῶν, some ἐστιν, some τῆσδε.

1074 διδάξω, κἂν ἄμ.] Eur.
Sthendoea (Fr. 664), μουσικὴν δ'
ἄρα ἔρως διδάσκει κἂν ἄμουσος ᾖ τὸ
πρίν.

1076 Ἀττικοὶ κ.τ.λ.] Meineke
omits this line with a 'delevit Ha-
makerus' in his note. He omits v.
1115, οὐκ ἔχοντες...φόρον in the
antepirrhema.

ἐγγενεῖς.] So MSS. R, V. and
it is rather preferable to εὐγενεῖν.
The exaggerated self-praise in ἡμεῖς

ἀνδρικώτατον γένος καὶ πλεῖστα τήνδε τὴν πόλιν
ὠφελῆσαν ἐν μάχαισιν, ἡνίκ' ἦλθ' ὁ βάρβαρος,
τῷ καπνῷ τύφων ἅπασαν τὴν πόλιν καὶ πυρπολῶν,
ἐξελεῖν ἡμῶν μενοινῶν πρὸς βίαν τἀνθρήνια,   1080
εὐθέως γὰρ ἐκδραμόντες σὺν δόρει σὺν ἀσπίδι
ἐμαχόμεσθ' αὐτοῖσι, θυμὸν ὀξίνην πεπωκότες,
στὰς ἀνὴρ παρ' ἄνδρ', ὑπ' ὀργῆς τὴν χελύνην ἐσθίων·
ὑπὸ δὲ τῶν τοξευμάτων οὐκ ἦν ἰδεῖν τὸν οὐρανόν.
ἀλλ' ὅμως ἀπεωσάμεσθα ξὺν θεοῖς πρὸς ἑσπέρᾳ.   1085
γλαῦξ γὰρ ἡμῶν πρὶν μάχεσθαι τὸν στρατὸν διέπτατο.

ἐσμὲν μόνοι 'Α. need not be urged as an objection to the line: for praise of themselves and of their poet is with the Aristophanic chorus quite the rule. The epirrhema in the *Knights* is in a similar spirit.

1078 ἡνίκ' ἦλθ' ὁ βάρβαρος.] Isocrates describes at some length the services of Athens against the barbarian, *Paneg.* p. 58—90.

1079 πυρπολῶν.] Cf. Herod. VIII. 50, ταῦτα τῶν ἀπὸ Πελοποννήσου στρατηγῶν ἐπιλεγομένων ἐληλύθεε ἀνὴρ Ἀθηναῖος ἀγγέλλων ἥκειν τὸν βάρβαρον ἐς τὴν Ἀττικὴν καὶ πᾶσαν αὐτὴν πυρπολίεσθαι. This is of what took place after the abandonment of Athens, before the battle of Salamis. But here τύφων and πυρπολῶν may be merely of the attempt and wish to burn, for what follows refers to Marathon, which was fought ten years earlier than Salamis.

1080 τἀνθρήνια.] τὰ τῶν σφηκῶν κηρία, ἀνθρῆναι δὲ οἱ μὲν τὰς μελίττας, οἱ δὲ ἕτερον ζῶον κηροποιὸν παραπλήσιον σφηκί. Schol. Cf. *Nub.* 947. The words ἐξελεῖν, τύφειν, are specially applicable to taking wasps' or bees' nests. Cf. above v. 457, where the wasp chorus are smoked out.

1081 ὀξίνην.] Cf. *Eq.* v. 1304, ὀξίνην Τεέρβολον. Florens finds a reference to θύμον 'thyme,' a favourite food of bees, in θυμοῦ. Bergler thinks it may be so, but that it is a comic deviation from θυμὸς ὀξύς, a

common phrase.

πεπωκότες.] 'Having drunk' and so imbibed the spirit of. Cf. above v. 462, βεβρωκότες, and the note there.

1083 χελύνην ἐσθίων.] Bergler illustrates from Tyrtaeus, ἀλλά τις εὖ διαβὰς μενέτω ποσὶν ἀμφοτέροισι στηριχθεὶς ἐπὶ γῆς χεῖλος ὀδοῦσι δακών, Hom. *Od.* a. 381, ὀδὰξ ἐν χείλεσι φύντες. Dind.

1084 οὐκ ἦν ἰδεῖν.] It was before Thermopylae, according to Herodotus (VIII. 226), that 'Dieneces a Spartan, hearing from a Trachinian that, when the barbarians discharge their shafts, they hide the sun by reason of the multitude of their arrows, so numerous are they, replied undismayed—making of no account the numbers of the Medes—that the Trachinian stranger's tidings were entirely in their favour, since, should the Medes hide the sun, then would the Greeks fight in the shade.' The saying is given by others to Leonidas.

1085 ἀπεωσάμεσθα.] ἐσωζόμεσθα, V. ἐπαυσάμεσθα, R: the latter can hardly stand: the former is taken by Meineke. ἐωσάμεσθα Bergk. ἀπωσάμεσθα. Dind.

1086 γλαῦξ.] The bird of Athene, and of Athens. Cf. *Eq.* 1092, μοὶ δόκει ἡ θεὸς αὐτὴ ἐκ πόλεως ἐλθεῖν, καὶ γλαῦξ αὐτῇ 'πικαθῆσθαι. The Scholiast says that the owl bore the news of victory to the Athenians.

εἶτα δ' εἰπόμεσθα θυννάζοντες ἐς τοὺς θυλάκους,
οἱ δ' ἔφευγον τὰς γνάθους καὶ τὰς ὀφρῦς κεντούμενοι·
ὥστε παρὰ τοῖς βαρβάροισι πανταχοῦ καὶ νῦν ἔτι
μηδὲν Ἀττικοῦ καλεῖσθαι σφηκὸς ἀνδρικώτερον.   1090
ἆρα δεινὸς ἢ τόθ' ὥστε πάντα μ' ἂν δεδοικέναι,
καὶ κατεστρεψάμην
τοὺς ἐναντίους, πλέων ἐκεῖσε ταῖς τριήρεσιν,
οὐ γὰρ ἦν ἡμῖν ὅπως
ῥῆσιν εὖ λέξειν ἐμέλλομεν τότ', οὐδὲ   1095
συκοφαντήσειν τινὰ
φροντίς, ἀλλ' ὅστις ἐρέτης ἔσοιτ' ἄριστος.
τουγαροῦν πολλὰς πόλεις Μήδων ἑλόντες,
αἰτιώτατοι φέρεσθαι
τὸν φόρον δεῦρ' ἐσμὲν, ὃν κλέ-
πτουσιν οἱ νεώτεροι.   1100
πολλαχοῦ σκοποῦντες ἡμᾶς εἰς ἅπανθ' εὑρήσετε

Tacitus (*Ann.* II. 17) mentions a similar omen before an engagement with some German tribes, 'Interea pulcherrimum augurium octo aquilae petere silvas et intrare visae imperatorem advertere. exclamat, irent, sequerentur Romanas aves, propria legionum numina.'

1087 εἶτα δ' εἰπόμεσθα.] Cf. Herod. VII. 113, φεύγουσι δὲ τοῖσι Ἰλλῦροισι ἐλόντα κόντωντι.

θυννάζοντες.] κεντοῦντες ὡς τοὺς θύννους τοῖς τριοδοῦσι. Schol. Eels are now speared in a similar way, and whales harpooned. There is an evident remembrance of Aesch. *Pers.* 414, τοὶ δ' ὥστε θύννους, ἢ τιν' ἰχθύων βόλον, ἀγαῖσι κωπῶν θραύσμασίν τ' ἐρειπίων ἔπαιον ἐρράχιζον.

1089 ὥστε κ.τ.λ.] And thus we proved ourselves very wasps in the way in which we worried them, and have quite justified ourselves in assuming for our old age this waspish attire.

1091 πάντα μ' ἄν.] The vulg. πάντα μὴ is hardly defensible, for πάντα μὴ δ. must = μηδένα (or μηδὲν) δεδοικέναι. But πάντας ἐμέ, Hirschig's correction, is not quite satis-

factory. The text is Dobree's, accepted by Holden. πάντα μ' ἐκδ. might also do.

1093 ἐκεῖσε.] To Asia Minor.

1094 οὐ γὰρ ἦν ἡμῖν ὅπως.] 'The question with us was not how.'

1095—7 λέξειν ἐμέλλομεν...ἔσοιτ'] 'We were likely to speak or to accuse, but who should come to be the best rower.' μέλλω λέξειν, as nearly equal to λέξω, would answer to ἔσομαι in direct speech: hence in oblique relation ἐμέλλομεν λέξειν is tolerably parallel to the optat. fut. ἔσοιτο.

1098 πόλεις Μήδων.] Cities belonging to the Athenians, but subjected to the Medes, and now recovered, says the Scholiast. Richter understands it of allied or tributary cities now gained, which had before been under Persian dominion. No strict accuracy need be expected in this account of 'the many cities taken from the Medes,' but the mention of the φόρος immediately afterwards countenances Richter's view.

1101 πολλαχοῦ σ. ἡ.] 'If you look at us under various circum-

τοὺς τρόπους καὶ τὴν δίαιταν σφηξὶν ἐμφερεστάτους.
πρῶτα μὲν γὰρ οὐδὲν ἡμῶν ζῷον ἡρεθισμένον
μᾶλλον ὀξύθυμόν ἐστιν οὐδὲ δυσκολώτερον·   1105
εἶτα τἄλλ' ὅμοια πάντα σφηξὶ μηχανώμεθα.
ξυλλεγέντες γὰρ καθ' ἑσμοὺς, ὡσπερεὶ τἀνθρήνια,
οἱ μὲν ἡμῶν οὗπερ ἄρχων, οἱ δὲ παρὰ τοὺς ἕνδεκα,
οἱ δ' ἐν ᾠδείῳ δικάζουσ', οἱ δὲ πρὸς τοῖς τειχίοις
ξυμβεβυσμένοι, πυκνὸν νεύοντες ἐς τὴν γῆν, μόλις   1110
ὥσπερ οἱ σκώληκες ἐν τοῖς κυττάροις κινούμενοι.
ἔς τε τὴν ἄλλην δίαιταν ἐσμὲν εὐπορώτατοι,
πάντα γὰρ κεντοῦμεν ἄνδρα κἀκπορίζομεν βίον.
ἀλλὰ γὰρ κηφῆνες ἡμῖν εἰσιν ἐγκαθήμενοι,
οὐκ ἔχοντες κέντρον· οἳ μένοντες ἡμῶν τοῦ φέρου   1115

stances,' lit. 'in many places.' Their likeness to wasps on the battle-field has been shewn: it has now to be shewn at home.

1107 **ἑσμούς.**] Cf. *Lys.* 353, *ἑσμὸς γυναικῶν οὑτοσί.*

1108—1111 We swarm like wasps to our several courts. For the respective jurisdiction of the archon, the eleven, &c. see *Dict. Antiq.*, but where each court was held cannot now be fully determined.

1109 **ᾠδείῳ.**] In this building, which was properly intended for the reciting of poems, the Scholiast doubts whether courts were actually held; but it seems likely enough that the place was sometimes used for this purpose.

πρὸς τοῖς τειχίοις. It is doubtful whether this refers to any definite place, or (as Richter thinks) merely means that wherever there is anything like a wall or enclosure, dicasts are ready to sit and constitute a court, *εἴ πάντα τὸν σων εὑρήσει τις δικαστὰς ἐν 'Αττικῇ.* Schol. Cf. *Nub.* 208, *οὐ πείθομαι, ἐπεὶ δικαστὰς οὐκ ὁρῶ καθημένους.* Holden, followed by Meineke, changes **πυκνὸν** in the next line to **πυκνός**, an ingenious alteration, thus getting a definite place of meeting. The Pnyx (cf. *Dict. Ant.* p. 361) had 'a boun-

dary wall, part rock, part masonry,' which would be here meant.

1110 **ξυμβεβυσμένοι.**] 'Crammed together' so that they could hardly move. Cf. the description of the crowds in *Nub.* 1203, *ἀμφορῆς νενησμένοι.*

1111 **σκώληκες ἐν τοῖς κυττάροις.**] 'Like wasp-grubs in their cells.' **κύτταρος δὲ αἱ τῶν κηρίων κοιλότητες.** Schol. Several other kinds of holes are given to which the word may be applied: a curious use is in *Pac.* 199, *ὑπ' αὐτὸν δικ-χνῶν οὐρανοῦ τὸν κύτταρον,* explained by *τὸ κοιλότατον καὶ μυχαίτατον.*

1114 **κηφῆνες.**] The orators who stop at home and do only the talking are the drones. The Scholiast quotes from Hesiod (*Op.* 302) *μηδὲ νέεσσι κοθούροις ἴκελοι ὁρμὴν οἵτε μελισσάων κάματον τρύχουσιν ἀεργοὶ ἔσθοντες.*

1115 **οὐκ ἔχοντες κ.τ.λ.**] Meineke omitting this line takes **τόνον** for **γόνον** in the next. Twenty lines (the number as it now stands) is a number for the epirrhema, supported by the *Clouds* and *Frogs*: but there is enough variety in the number in different plays to prevent any strong argument either way on the score of the probable number of lines in an epirrhema.

τὸν γόνον κατεσθίουσιν, οὐ ταλαιπωρούμενοι.
τοῦτο δ' ἔστ' ἄλγιστον ἡμῖν, ἤν τις ἀστράτευτος ὢν
ἐκροφῇ τὸν μισθὸν ἡμῶν, τῆσδε τῆς χώρας ὕπερ
μήτε κώπην μήτε λόγχην μήτε φλύκταιναν λαβών.
ἀλλ' ἐμοὶ δοκεῖ τὸ λοιπὸν τῶν πολιτῶν ἐμβραχὺ　　1120
ὅστις ἂν μὴ 'χῃ τὸ κέντρον, μὴ φέρειν τριώβολον.

ΦΙΛΟΚΛΕΩΝ

οὔ τοι ποτὲ ζῶν τοῦτον ἀποδυθήσομαι,
ἐπεὶ μόνος μ' ἔσωσε παρατεταγμένον,
ὅθ' ὁ βορέας ὁ μέγας ἐπεστρατεύσατο.

1117 ἀστρόττωτοι.] Cf. *Nub.*
691, ἥτις οὐ στρατεύεται of Amynias: also *Eq.* 443, where the
sausage-seller threatens Cleon with
twenty indictments for ἀστρατεία.

1119 φλύσταιναν.] Cf. *Ran.*
236, ἐγὼ δὲ φλυσταίνας ἔχω. And
for other sufferings in rowing cf.
Eq. 785, ἵνα μὴ τρίβῃς τὴν ἐν Σαλαμῖνι.

1120 ἐμβραχύ.] καθάπαξ ἢ παντάπασι. Schol. Equivalent, the Scholiast says, to βραχύ, the preposition
having no force; but that it has
none, as he says, in the verb. ἐνδυ-
στυχῆσαι in Eur. *Phoen.* 727 will
not easily be granted.

1121 μὴ 'χῃ τὸ κέντρον.] Whoever is an idle drone, sting-less, and
does no work.

Mitchell notes that 'this comedy
ought to have ended immediately
with these addresses of the chorus
or even before them. The aétion
was complete; and whatever else is
added must be a mere superfeta-
tion.' And he treats the rest as
a separate piece, giving to it a separate name, 'the Dicast turned gen-
tleman.' There is certainly a strongly marked difference between the
two parts. But undoubtedly they
were one play: nor would the
latter half have had much force
except in contrast to the former.
And the representation of the Dicast converted is analogous to that

of Demus restored to youth in the
Knights. He has passed, it is true,
from one extreme to another, giving
Aristophanes occasion for satire
upon the follies of luxury and pro-
fligacy. Phidippides' conversion
from one bad course to another is a
parallel.

1122—1173 Father and son return: a discussion ensues about a
change in the old man's dress; he is
with difficulty persuaded to discard
his old doublet for a mantle of
newer fashion. Then there is a
similar dispute about shoes; which
ends in his complying, and strutting
about with the gait of the wealthy
men of the time.

1123 παρατεταγμένον] properly
of the man 'next in line.' His
cloak proved his best and trustiest
comrade in the field, when the north
wind swept down upon them.

1124 βορέας.] The Scholiast understands this of the north wind
that caused loss to the Persian fleet
at Artemisium. Probably it is
rather the whole Persian invasion
that is called 'Boreas' as coming
down from the north, while at the
same time any stormy weather that
happened then would be a reason for
Philocleon's gratitude to his trusty
cloak. Conzius thinks that βασι-
λεὺς, the great king, is especially
meant by Βορέας, and quotes in
illustration of ἐπεστρατεύσατο, 'Di-

8

ΒΔΕΛΤΚΛΕΩΝ
ἀγαθὸν ἔοικας οὐδὲν ἐπιθυμεῖν παθεῖν.

ΦΙΛΟΚΛΕΩΝ
μὰ τὸν Δί’, οὐ γὰρ οὐδαμῶς μοι ξύμφορον.
καὶ γὰρ πρότερον ἐπανθρακίδων ἐμπλήμενος
ἀπέδωκ’ ὀφείλων τῷ κναφεῖ τριώβολον.

ΒΔΕΛΤΚΛΕΩΝ
ἀλλ’ οὖν πεπειράσθω γ’, ἐπειδήπερ γ’ ἅπαξ
ἐμοὶ σεαυτὸν παραδέδωκας εὖ ποιεῖν.   1130

ΦΙΛΟΚΛΕΩΝ
τί οὖν κελεύεις δρᾶν με;

ΒΔΕΛΤΚΛΕΩΝ
                    τὸν τρίβων’ ἄφες·
τηνδὶ δὲ χλαῖναν ἀναβαλοῦ τριβωνικῶς.

ΦΙΛΟΚΛΕΩΝ
ἔπειτα παῖδας χρὴ φυτεύειν καὶ τρέφειν,
ὅθ’ οὑτοσί με νῦν ἀποπνίξαι βούλεται;

ΒΔΕΛΤΚΛΕΩΝ
ἔχ’, ἀναβαλοῦ τηνδὶ λαβών, καὶ μὴ λάλει.   1135

rus per urbes Afer ut Italas Ceu flam-
ma per taedas vel Eurus Per Siculas
equitavit undas.’ Hor. Od. IV. 4. 44.
And a comparison of v. 11 of this
play, ἐδμοὶ γὰρ ἀρτίως ἐπεστρατεύσατο Μῆδοι τις…ύπνος, confirms this
interpretation.
1127 καὶ γάρ κ.τ.λ.] For I
spoilt my cloak once with some
fish-sauce, and had to pay for its
cleaning; so I do not want a more
valuable one, lest I may spoil that.
ἐπανθρακίδων.] λεπτοὶ ἰχθύες
ὀπτοί. Schol. Cf. Ach. 670, ἠνία ἂν
ἐπανθρακίδων ὥσι παρακείμεναι, οἱ δὲ
Θασίαι ἀνακυκῶσι λιπαρόμενοι. It
was with this Thasian fish-sauce
(ἅλμη) that the garment was spoilt.
1132 τριβωνικῶς] The Scholiast
appears to have had a various reading γεροντικῶς: but τρ. seems right.

The τρίβων however we find constantly worn by the older men.
1133 ἔπειτα] ‘After this,’ mark-
ing astonishment and indignation:
cf. Ach. 126, κἄπειτ’ ἐγὼ δῆτ’ ἐνθαδὶ
στραγγεύομαι. It is not altogether
unlike πρὸς ταῦτα in the tragedians,
e.g. in Aesch. Prom. Vincl. 992,
πρὸς ταῦτα μυττέσθω μὲν αἰθαλούσσα
φλόξ. The Latins use ‘nunc’ with
the same ironical force; ‘I nunc et
versus tecum meditare canoros’ says
Horace, after describing the din of
the Roman streets.
1134 ἀποπνίξαι.] The χλαῖνα was
evidently soft, woolly, and warm,
whereas the old man’s τρίβων, however good a defence against Boreas
in days past, was probably, the
worse for wear.

ΦΙΛΟΚΛΕΩΝ

τουτὶ τὸ κακὸν τί ἐστι πρὸς πάντων θεῶν;

ΒΔΕΛΥΚΛΕΩΝ

οἱ μὲν καλοῦσι Περσίδ᾽, οἱ δὲ καυνάκην.

ΦΙΛΟΚΛΕΩΝ

ἐγὼ δὲ σισύραν ᾤμην Θυμαιτίδα.

ΒΔΕΛΥΚΛΕΩΝ

κοὐ θαῦμά γ᾽· ἐς Σάρδεις γὰρ οὐκ ἐλήλυθας.
ἔγνως γὰρ ἄν· νῦν δ᾽ οὐχὶ γιγνώσκεις.

ΦΙΛΟΚΛΕΩΝ

                                                            ἐγώ;   1140
μὰ τὸν Δί᾽ οὐ τοίνυν· ἀτὰρ δοκεῖ γέ μοι
ἐοικέναι μάλιστα Μορύχου σάγματι.

ΒΔΕΛΥΚΛΕΩΝ

οὐκ, ἀλλ᾽ ἐν Ἐκβατάνοισι ταῦθ᾽ ὑφαίνεται.

ΦΙΛΟΚΛΕΩΝ

ἐν Ἐκβατάνοισι γίγνεται κρόκης χόλιξ;

1137 Περσίδ᾽... καυνάκην.] χλαῖνα Περσικὴ ἁλιεινή, Schol. That
καυνάκη has anything to do with
καῦμα is not very likely. Conzius
gives a Persian word for a silken
texture, which he thinks may be
cognate. But this garment appears
to have been of wool, or at all
events woolly on one side, ἔχον ἐκ
τοῦ ἑτέρου μέρους μαλλούς. Philocleon takes it for a rough sheep-
skin blanket or wrapper, called
σισύρα or βαίτη.

1138 Θυμαιτίδα.] From a deme
of the tribe of Hippothoon, where
such βαῖται were made. Schol.

1139 ἐς Σάρδεις.] Where such
Persian apparel is for sale. Cf. Ach.
112, βάμμα Σαρδιανικόν.

1142 ἐοικέναι.] Meineke reads
προσεικέναι (a form found in Eccl.
1161) in deference to a rule of Cobet's, that the old Attic writers always

said εἴξασιν (Nub. 341, 343, Av. 96,
383) εἰκέναι (Nub. 185) εἰκώς. There
are not enough instances to ground
a rule upon; convenience for the
metre may have determined the
form: and there is no strong reason
against ἐοικέναι from ἔοικα (cf. below
1171), when all MSS. give it.

Μορύχου.] For whom cf. Ach.
887, Pac. 1008, and above v. 506.
It is in keeping with his character
that he should muffle himself up.
μαλλωτῷ σάγῳ ἐχρῆτο, ὡς τρυφερὸς
πλείονι θάλπει χρώμενος. Schol.

1144 κρόκης χόλιξ.] 'A tripe
of the woof or thread,' i. e. a tripe-
like texture: a curious comparison.
'Laneos floccos in panno exstantes
comparat bovis intestino, quod
crispum est, et velut pellitum.' Fl.
Chr. The same commentator suggests that the texture must have
been 'frisa, frieze'.

ΒΔΕΛΥΚΛΕΩΝ

πόθεν, ὦγάθ'; ἀλλὰ τοῦτο τοῖσι βαρβάροις　　　1145
ὑφαίνεται πολλαῖς δαπάναις. αὕτη γέ τοι
ἐρίων τάλαντον καταπέπωκε ῥᾳδίως.

ΦΙΛΟΚΛΕΩΝ

οὔκουν ἐριώλην δῆτ' ἐχρῆν αὐτὴν καλεῖν
δικαιότερον ἢ καυνάκην;

ΒΔΕΛΥΚΛΕΩΝ
ἔχ' ὦγαθέ,
καὶ στῆθί γ' ἀμπισχόμενος.

ΦΙΛΟΚΛΕΩΝ
οἴμοι δείλαιος·　　　1150
ὡς θερμὸν ἡ μιαρά τί μου κατήρυγεν.

ΒΔΕΛΥΚΛΕΩΝ

οὐκ ἀναβαλεῖ;

ΦΙΛΟΚΛΕΩΝ

μὰ Δί' οὐκ ἔγωγ'. ἀλλ', ὦγαθέ,
εἴπερ γ' ἀνάγκη, κρίβανόν μ' ἀμπίσχετε.

ΒΔΕΛΥΚΛΕΩΝ

φέρ', ἀλλ' ἐγώ σε περιβαλῶ· σὺ δ' οὖν ἴθι.

ΦΙΛΟΚΛΕΩΝ

παράθου γε μέντοι καὶ κρεάγραν.

1145 πόθεν.] 'how so?' or 'non-sense!' He does not see, or pretends not to see, what his father means by the comparison, or what there is amiss with the mantle.
1148 ἐριώλην.] Properly a violent wind: cf. *Eq.* 511, where Cleon is compared to it. Here he puns, and derives it from ἔριον and ὄλλυμι. A pronunciation of 'wool-wind' to resemble 'whirl-wind' might be a fair equivalent.
1149 ἔχ' ὦγαθέ, κ.τ.λ.] 'Steady, my good sir! and stand still while I put it on you.' He puts the cloak round his father, but the old man will make no effort to throw it gracefully over his shoulder (ἀναβάλλεσθαι), but rather throws it off; so the putting on has to be done entirely by the son.
1155—6. Well if I am to be baked or roasted (says Philocleon), let there be a flesh-hook ready to pull me out before I am done all to pieces.

ΒΔΕΛΤΚΛΕΩΝ
τιὴ τί δή;	1155

ΦΙΛΟΚΛΕΩΝ
ἵν' ἐξέλῃς με πρὶν διερρυηκέναι.

ΒΔΕΛΤΚΛΕΩΝ
ἄγε νυν, ἀποδύου τὰς καταράτους ἐμβάδας,
τασδὶ δ' ἀνύσας ὑπόδυθι τὰς Λακωνικάς.

ΦΙΛΟΚΛΕΩΝ
ἐγὼ γὰρ ἂν τλαίην ὑποδύσασθαί ποτε
ἐχθρῶν παρ' ἀνδρῶν δυσμενῆ καττύματα;	1160

ΒΔΕΛΤΚΛΕΩΝ
ἔνθες ποτ', ὦ τᾶν, κἀπόβαιν' ἐρρωμένως
ἐς τὴν Λακωνικὴν ἀνύσας.

ΦΙΛΟΚΛΕΩΝ
ἀδικεῖς γέ με
ἐς τὴν πολεμίαν ἀποβιβάζων τὸν πόδα.

1155 τιὴ τί δή.] Cf. *Nub.* 755, *Thesm.* 84.

1156 διερρυηκέναι.] πρὶν συμπεσεῖν ἀπὸ τῆι ὁττήσεωι τὰ κρέα μου. Schol.

1157 ἀνοδύου.] Hirschig proposes ὑπολύου. As MSS. R, V, have ὑποδύου, this reading is not without some warrant; but we must then take in vv. 1158, 59, 68 ὑποδοῦ, ὑποδήσασθαι, ὑποδησάμενος; the two last Scaliger's readings. However, the present text may stand. The Greeks were not bound to use, of tying on and loosing off shoes, no words save the ordinary ὑποδεῖσθαι and ὑπολύεσθαι. Richter even goes so far as to say that ἐμβάδες and Λακωνικαί were of the kind of foot covering called κοῖλα ὑποδήματα, not so much sandals as low shoes or slippers, and that ἀποδύεσθαι, ὑποδύεσθαι, suit them better than the common words. ἀποδύεσθαι 'to put off,' ὑποδύεσθαι 'to get into, slip the feet into.'

1158 ὑπόδυθι τάς.] ὑποδοῦ λαβὼν Hirschig; ὑποδοῦ τι τὰς Meineke. In this last the τι is awkward; in the former λαβὼν a violent change. ὑποδοῦ σὺ τὰς would be as likely, if it were necessary to change at all.

Λακωνικάς.] ἀστειότεραι γὰρ αὗται. Schol. They were men's shoes, as is plain from *Thesm.* 141, where they are mentioned along with χλαῖνα as a distinctive mark of a man.

1160 ἐχθρῶν κ.τ.λ.] Cf. Eur. *Heracl.* 1006, ἐχθροῦ λέοντος δυσμενῆ βλαστήματα.

1161 ἔνθες ποτ'.] ἔνθει τόδ' is Brunck's reading. 'Do pray at last put (your foot) in' is satisfactory, the ellipse being easy.

1161, 62 κἀπόβαιν'...ἐς τὴν Λακωνικήν.] 'Step out (of your own shoe) into the Laconian (shoe),' says the son: but the father understands χώραν Λ. and replies accordingly.

1163 πολεμίαν.] The ell

ΒΔΕΛΤΚΛΕΩΝ

φέρε καὶ τὸν ἔτερον.

ΦΙΛΟΚΛΕΩΝ

μηδαμῶς τοῦτόν γ', ἐπεὶ
πάνυ μισολάκων αὐτοῦ 'στιν εἰς τῶν δακτύλων.   1165

ΒΔΕΛΤΚΛΕΩΝ

οὐκ ἔστι παρὰ ταῦτ' ἄλλα.

ΦΙΛΟΚΛΕΩΝ

κακοδαίμων ἐγὼ,
ὅστις ἐπὶ γήρᾳ χίμετλον οὐδὲν λήψομαι.

ΒΔΕΛΤΚΛΕΩΝ

ἄνυσόν ποθ' ὑποδυσάμενος· εἶτα πλουσίως
ὡδὶ προβὰς τρυφερόν τι διασαλακώνισον.

ΦΙΛΟΚΛΕΩΝ

ἰδού· θεῶ τὸ σχῆμα, καὶ σκέψαι μ' ὅτῳ   1170
μάλιστ' ἔοικα τὴν βάδισιν τῶν πλουσίων.

ΒΔΕΛΤΚΛΕΩΝ

ἴτῳ; δοθιῆνι σκόροδον ἠμφιεσμένῳ.

γῆ or χώρα with the adjective is
very common.
1164. Philocleon puts one foot
in, probably the right (says Florens),
according to the Pythagorean precept, 'dextrum pedem in calceum
praemitte, laevum in ποδάνιπτρον.'
1166 οὐκ ἔστι κ.τ.λ.] Repeated
from *Nub.* 698.
1167 χίμετλον.] 'A chilblain ;'
it is put (says the Scholiast) by way
of surprise for ἀγαθὸν οὐδὲν λήψομαι.
τὰ τῶν γερόντων οὐ λήψομαι, 'I shall
not enjoy the privileges of old men,'
chilblains being among them. It
may mean, 'I shall have no chilblains, since these more luxurious
shoes will defend my feet,' as Richter says; or, 'I am not to have any
chilblains, and so be allowed the
privilege of an old man, shabby
slippers, but more comfortable than

these smart ones.' Philocleon's assertion above, that he had one toe
on his left foot a deckled Laconian-
hater, rather suggests a chilblain
already present on that toe, which
he is not to indulge.
1169 διασαλακώνισον.] From a
certain Salacon. Schol. There is
also reference to λακωνίζειν. A reading διαλυκώνισον is mentioned by the
Scholiast, and derived from Lycon.
These derivations seem but guesses.
Dindorf from Hesychius and Photius discovers a word, διασαικώνισον,
which Meineke adopts here. The
meaning is the same.
1170 σχῆμα.] Appears to include
posture, bearing, gait, &c., as well
as dress. Cf. above, v. 1070.
1172 δοθιῆνι κ.τ.λ.] An absurd
comparison, which it seems vain to
analyze. If Δοθιῆνι be read, and if

ΦΙΛΟΚΛΕΩΝ

καὶ μὴν προθυμοῦμαί γε σαυλοπρωκτιᾶν.

ΒΔΕΛΥΚΛΕΩΝ

ἄγε νυν, ἐπιστήσει λόγους σεμνοὺς λέγειν
ἀνδρῶν παρόντων πολυμαθῶν καὶ δεξιῶν;   1175

ΦΙΛΟΚΛΕΩΝ

ἔγωγε.

ΒΔΕΛΥΚΛΕΩΝ

τίνας δῆτ᾽ ἂν λέγοις;

ΦΙΛΟΚΛΕΩΝ

πολλοὺς πάνυ.
πρῶτον μὲν ὡς ἡ Λάμι᾽ ἁλοῦσ᾽ ἐπέρδετο,
ἔπειτα δ᾽ ὡς ὁ Καρδοπίων τὴν μητέρα.

ΒΔΕΛΥΚΛΕΩΝ

μή μοί γε μύθους, ἀλλὰ τῶν ἀνθρωπίνων
οἵους λέγομεν μάλιστα τοὺς κατ᾽ οἰκίαν.   1180

ΦΙΛΟΚΛΕΩΝ

ἐγᾦδα τοίνυν τῶν γε πάνυ κατ᾽ οἰκίαν
ἐκεῖνον, ὡς οὕτω ποτ᾽ ἦν μῦς καὶ γαλῆ.

ΒΔΕΛΥΚΛΕΩΝ

ὦ σκαιὲ κἀπαίδευτε, Θεογένης ἔφη

---

he were a person of known gait, it
would only remain to find why the
mantle was likened to garlic.

1174—1264. Being now dressed
properly, Philocleon is further in-
structed in the art of fashionable
talk, of deportment at a banquet.
A feast is imagined: the song is to
pass round: he shews how he would
bear his part, and succeeds tolerably
well. Both father and son then go off
to a supper at Philoclemon's house.

1176 τίνας.] From the preceding
λόγους, and the following πολλούς,
this seems almost necessary. But
most editors retain τίνα of MSS.
R, V.

1178 μητέρα.] λείπει ἔτυψεν.
Schol.

1179, 80. No long-winded tales
or fables, but common 'household'
stories are to be the rule. Richter
gives 'Kinder-und Hausmärchen' in
illustration. Philocleon at once
starts off with the most familiar and
household word he knows.

1181 οὕτω.] Cf. Plat. Phaedr.
237, ἦν οὕτω δὴ παῖς. And the
Scholiast gives ἦν οὕτω γέρων καὶ
γραῦς, as another fable beginning in
this way. Germ. 'Es war also
einmal.'

1183—85. Apparently Theogenes
(for whom cf. Pac. 928, Av. 822,

τῷ κοπρόλογῳ, καὶ ταῦτα λοιδορούμενος,
μῦς καὶ γαλᾶς μέλλεις λέγειν ἐν ἀνδράσιν; 1185

ΦΙΛΟΚΛΕΩΝ

ποίους τινὰς δὲ χρὴ λέγειν;

ΒΔΕΛΥΚΛΕΩΝ

μεγαλοπρεπεῖς,
ὡς ξυνεθεώρεις ᾿Ανδροκλεῖ καὶ Κλεισθένει.

ΦΙΛΟΚΛΕΩΝ

ἐγὼ δὲ τεθεώρηκα πώποτ᾽ οὐδαμοῖ
πλὴν ἐς Πάρον, καὶ ταῦτα δύ᾽ ὀβολὼ φέρων.

ΒΔΕΛΥΚΛΕΩΝ

ἀλλ᾽ οὖν λέγειν χρή σ᾽ ὡς ἐμάχετό γ᾽ αὐτίκα 1190
᾿Εφουδίων παγκράτιον ᾿Ασκώνδᾳ καλῶς,
ἤδη γέρων ὢν καὶ πολιός, ἔχων δέ τοι

1127, 1295), though of swinish habits, used fine words. Hence they quote his rebuke of the scavenger (perhaps for bringing something 'between the wind and his nobility') as suitable to Philocleon for venturing on such an unsavoury subject as mice and weasels in polite society. ὦ σκαὶ κάναιθευτε is of course a tragic style to begin a rebuke of a κοπρολόγοι.

1184 καὶ ταῦτα λ.] 'And that too when abusing him,' and when accordingly you would expect coarser words from such a man, especially as the Greek language is not poor in such expressions.

1185 ἐν ἀνδράσιν.] Such being 'old wives' fables.' Cf. Horace's 'garrit aniles ex re fabellas' of just this style of fable.

1187 ξυνεθεώρεις.] Sacred embassies, which should be given to the honourable and noble, are mentioned in connexion with these worthless men, to reprove the Athenians for placing such rascals in high office.

Androcles appears to have been attacked as a beggar and profligate by other comic writers; Cleisthenes is often assailed by Aristophanes.

1189 ἐς Πάρον.] What expedition to Paros is meant, is uncertain. It was not, at any rate, a θεωρία; but he went merely as a μισθωτὸς στρατιώτη, as the Scholiast says. Richter interprets τεθεώρηκα ἐς Π. 'stipendium merui ad Parum otiose spectando, non fortiter pugnando.'

1191 ᾿Εφουδίων...᾿Ασκώνδᾳ.] It is not necessary that these should be real persons: but it is more likely that they were real pancratiasts, or fictitious names for such, than that they were effeminate persons thus ridiculed, as Richter thinks. What Aristophanes' satire is pointed at is the trifling nature of the conversation, when they could find nothing better to talk of than the details of such athletic contests. Horace gives 'Hora quota est? Thrax est Gallina Syro par?' as an instance of small talk.

πλευρὰν βαθυτάτην καὶ χέρας λαγόνας τε καὶ
θώρακ' ἄριστον.

ΦΙΛΟΚΛΕΩΝ

παῦε παῦ', οὐδὲν λέγεις.

πῶς δ' ἂν μαχέσαιτο παγκράτιον θώρακ' ἔχων; 1195

ΒΔΕΛΤΚΛΕΩΝ

οὕτως διηγεῖσθαι νομίζουσ' οἱ σοφοί.
ἀλλ' ἕτερον εἰπέ μοι· παρ' ἀνδράσι ξένοις
πίνων, σεαυτοῦ ποῖον ἂν λέξαι δοκεῖς
ἐπὶ νεότητος ἔργον ἀνδρικώτατον;

ΦΙΛΟΚΛΕΩΝ

ἐκεῖν' ἐκεῖν' ἀνδρειότατόν γε τῶν ἐμῶν, 1200
ὅτ' Ἐργασίωνος τὰς χάρακας ὑφειλόμην.

ΒΔΕΛΤΚΛΕΩΝ

ἀπολεῖς με. ποίας χάρακας; ἀλλ' ὡς ἢ κάπρον
ἐδιώκαθές ποτ', ἢ λαγών, ἢ λαμπάδα
ἔδραμες, ἀνευρὼν ὅ τι νεανικώτατον.

ΦΙΛΟΚΛΕΩΝ

ἐγῷδα τοίνυν τό γε νεανικώτατον· 1205

1194 θώρακ'.] 'The chest,' a sig-
nification of the word which is found
in later Greek, but, we may infer,
was fashionable in a certain class at
this earlier time. Philocleon does
not understand it, and takes θώραξ
to mean 'breastplate.' The pancra-
tion only included wrestling and
boxing, for neither of which would
a breastplate be needed or allowed.
1196 οὕτως.] Such was the style
of narrative among the clever young
fellows of the time. Bdelycleon then
goes on to instruct him that he must
be prepared with some boastful
story about himself.
1197 ξένοις.] ἔθος γὰρ ἐπὶ τοῖς
ξένοις καυχᾶσθαι Schol.
1201 Ἐργασίωνος.] Some countryman. Deeds of thieving are not
unfrequently boasted of; cf. above,

v. 236.
1203 λαμπάδα.] They used to
run bearing torches in the Cerami-
cus. Schol. Cf. Ran. 129—133. The
torch-race is frequently mentioned
by Attic writers, and gives rise to
some striking metaphorical expressions: e.g. Plato's καθάπερ λαμπάδα
τὸν βίον παραδιδόντες ἄλλοις ἐξ ἄλλων; whence Lucretius, 'quasi cur-
sores vitai lampada tradunt.' But
the precise rules of the race are
difficult to ascertain.
1204 νεανικώτατον.] The word
from the sense of 'youthful, vigor-
ous, mettlesome,' comes to mean
'violent, overbearing;' as below at
v. 1307. νεανιεύσθαι has similar
meaning.
1205—7 ἐγῷδα.] If races and
chaces are to be the order of the

ὅτε τὸν δρομέα Φάϋλλον, ὢν βούπαις ἔτι,
εἷλον διώκων λοιδορίας ψήφοιν δυοῖν.

ΒΔΕΛΤΚΛΕΩΝ

παῦ'· ἀλλὰ δευρὶ κατακλινεὶς προσμάνθανε
ξυμποτικὸς εἶναι καὶ ξυνουσιαστικός.

ΦΙΛΟΚΛΕΩΝ

πῶς οὖν κατακλινῶ; φράζ' ἀνύσας.

ΒΔΕΛΤΚΛΕΩΝ

εὐσχημόνως.   1210

ΦΙΛΟΚΛΕΩΝ

ὡδὶ κελεύεις κατακλινῆναι;

ΒΔΕΛΤΚΛΕΩΝ

μηδαμῶς.

ΦΙΛΟΚΛΕΩΝ

πῶς δαί;

ΒΔΕΛΤΚΛΕΩΝ

τὰ γόνατ' ἔκτεινε, καὶ γυμναστικῶς
ὑγρὸν χύτλασον σεαυτὸν ἐν τοῖς στρώμασιν.
ἔπειτ' ἐπαίνεσόν τι τῶν χαλκωμάτων,
ὀροφὴν θέασαι, κρεκάδι' αὐλῆς θαύμασον   1215

day, then, thinks the old dicast, my prosecuting Phayllus is the right sort of exploit. He puns on the double meaning of διώκειν, as in *Ach.* 700, *Eq.* 969, διώξει Σμικύθην καὶ κύριον. Phayllus is mentioned as a great runner in *Ach.* 215, οὐκ ἂν ἐν' ἐμῆι γε νεότητος ὅτ' ἐγὼ φέρων ἀνθράκων φόρτιον ἠκολούθουν Φαύλλῳ τρέχων. See note and Scholiast there. And even if this be another Phayllus (for the Scholiast on the *Acharnians* says there were three, and the third a λωποδύτηι), yet there is plainly some reference to the Olympian name-sake, when it is said of him that 'for all he ran so fast, he was (pur)sued and caught at last.'

1210 κατακλινῶ.] Aor. 2. conj. of the passive voice: cf. κατακλινεὶς above.

εὐσχημόνως.] Dengler quotes from Euripides Silenus' directions to the Cyclops (*Cycl.* 563), θὲς δὴ τὸν ἀγκῶν' εὐρύθμως, κᾆτ' ἔπειε ὥσπερ μ' ὁρᾷς πίνοντα.

1213 ὑγρὸν χύτλασον.] 'Throw yourself in loose easy posture.' L. and S. refer to Hippocrates for ὑγρὸς κεῖσθαι. Cf. Pindar's ὑγρὸν νῶτον αἰωρεῖ of the eagle (*Pyth.* 1. 17). About χύτλασον the Scholiast appears to be wrong, taking it of anointing. The context here shews that it must be a description of a certain way of lying.

1214 ἐπαίνεσον.] Compliment-ary remarks on the plate, tapestry, &c. would be usual. But the para-site in Diphilus (quoted by Athe-naeus) holds a rather different view: ὅταν με καλέσῃ πλούσιος δεῖπνον

ὕδωρ κατὰ χειρός· τὰς τραπέζας ἐσφέρειν
δειπνοῦμεν ἀπονενίμμεθ'· ἤδη σπένδομεν.

ΦΙΛΟΚΛΕΩΝ

πρὸς τῶν θεῶν, ἐνύπνιον ἐστιώμεθα;

ΒΔΕΛΤΚΛΕΩΝ

αὐλητρὶς ἐνεφύσησεν. οἱ δὲ συμπόται
εἰσὶν Θέωρος, Αἰσχίνης, Φανὸς, Κλέων,
ξένος τις ἕτερος πρὸς κεφαλῆς Ἀκέστορος.
τούτοις ξυνὼν τὰ σκόλια πῶς δέξει;

1220

ΦΙΛΟΚΛΕΩΝ

καλῶς.

ποιῶν, οὐ κατανοῶ τὰ τρίγλυφ' οὐδὲ
τὰς στέγας· οὐδὲ δοκιμάζω τοὺς Κοριν-
θίους κάδους· ἀτὰρ δὴ τηρῶ τοῦ μα-
γείρου τὸν κατρόν.
1216. ὕδωρ κατὰ χειρός.] Cf.
Av. 463, καταχεῖσθαι κατὰ χειρὸς
ὕδωρ φερέτω ταχύ τις. E. δειπνήσειν
μέλλομεν; ἢ τί;
ἐσφέραν] imperatively used.
The tables were actually brought in
in ancient times. See Dict. Ant.
p. 613.
1217. ἀπονενίμμεθ'.] μετὰ τὸ
δειπνῆσαι ἔθος λέγειν ἀπονίψασθαι
ὅδι, ὦ ταῖ. Schol.
1219. αὐλητρίς.] Music and
dancing were usual after a banquet.
Cf. Homer's μολπή τ' ὀρχηστύς τε
τὰ γάρ τ' ἀναθήματα δαιτόs. (Od. a.
152). In Ach. 1090—93 many details of a banquet are enumerated,
dancing girls among them.
1220. Θέωρος κ.τ.λ.] Phanus,
a dependant of Cleon's, is mentioned in Eq. 1256. Cf. note there.
For Theorus and Aeschines cf. vv.
42, 325.
1221. ξένος τις…Ἀκέστορος.]
Another foreigner lying above Acestor. Acestor appears from the Scholiast here and on Av. 431 to have
been of Thracian extraction, and called Σάκας 'the Sacian.' In Av. 31,
νόσον νοσοῦμεν τὴν ἐναντίαν Σάκα· ὁ
μὲν γὰρ οὐκ ὢν ἀστὸς ἐσβιάζεται·
ἡμεῖς δὲ…ἀνεπτόμεθ' ἐκ τῆς πα-
τρίδος.

1222—3. There are different
ways of arranging the dialogue. The
text is Richter's: Dindorf's (in the
Poetae Scenici) hardly makes sense,
καλῶς is better given to Philocleon,
and ἄλφθει, to Bdelycleon. Meineke
further puts οὐδ' εἰ Δ. for οὐδεὶς Δ.,
meaning Diacrion to be a proper
name, I suppose, and his reading
would mean 'I shall take up the
song well, so that not even if Diacrion were to take it could he take
it better.'
1222. σκόλια.] It was the old
custom at a banquet for the guests
to follow whoever led off first, with
the song, continuing the song where
he left it. For the leader held a
branch of bay or myrtle and sang a
song of Simonides or Stesichorus,
as far as he pleased, and then passed
it on to whom he would, in no
particular order; and he who received it from the first continued the
song and then again passed it on.
Schol. Various explanations are
given of the word σκόλιον: that the
songs were so called from the irregular nature of the metre and music;
from the zig-zag manner in which
the song might pass this way and
that way about the table; from the
irregular arrangement of the couches.
The fact that the song passed according to no rule seems to shew that
it is lost labour in this passage to
attempt to arrange the guests, to

ἄληθες;

ΦΙΛΟΚΛΕΩΝ

ὡς οὐδεὶς Διακρίων δέξεται.

ΒΔΕΛΥΚΛΕΩΝ

ἐγὼ εἴσομαι· καὶ δὴ γάρ εἰμ᾽ ἐγὼ Κλέων,
ᾄδω δὲ πρῶτος Ἁρμοδίου· δέξει δὲ σύ.   1225
οὐδεὶς πώποτ᾽ ἀνὴρ ἐγένετ᾽ Ἀθηναῖος

ΦΙΛΟΚΛΕΩΝ

οὐχ οὕτω γε πανοῦργος κλέπτης

ΒΔΕΛΥΚΛΕΩΝ

τουτὶ σὺ δράσεις; παραπολεῖ βοώμενος·
φήσει γὰρ ἐξολεῖν σε καὶ διαφθερεῖν
καὶ τῆσδε τῆς γῆς ἐξελᾶν.

ΦΙΛΟΚΛΕΩΝ

ἐγὼ δέ γε,   1230

account for some not singing, to suppose (as one commentator does) that the text is corrupt or deficient on that account. It is plain that Aristophanes might take just as many singers as suited his purpose.

1223. Διακρίων.] The old division of the Athenians was into Diacrians, Pediaeans, Paralians. Richter observes that Marathon was in the Diacrian district, and Philocleon has termed himself Μαραθωνομάχας: so of the old-fashioned divisions, which, as a lover of old customs, he keeps to, he chooses that.

1224. ἐγὼ εἴσομαι.] Cf. above v. 416, and Nub. 901.

καὶ δή.] 'For now suppose me Cleon:' as in Eur. Med. 386, καὶ δὴ τεθνᾶσι. He begins with Cleon, as the most important person at table, and giving a ready handle for a parody.

1225. Ἁρμοδίου] sc. μέλοι. Cf. Ach. 980, τὸν Ἁρμόδιον ᾄσεται, whence Reiske inferred Ἁρμόδιον should be read here. But in Lysistr. 1237 ᾄδοι Τελαμῶνος seems a genitive of the same kind.

1226. οὐδεὶς...'Αθηναῖος.] This line does not suit well with the ἐν μύρτου κλαδὶ τὸ ξίφος φορήσω κ.τ.λ. in metre. Meineke's change improves it, but is uncertain. Bergk and Dindorf propose ἐγένετ᾽ Ἀθήναις, which Holden adopts. In the next line something is wanted before κλέπτης. Bentley supplies ὡς σὺ, Bergk οὐδέ. This first line was apparently to end in praise of Harmodius, but is turned off to abuse of Cleon.

1227. κλέπτης.] By Cleon's own confession (Eq. 1252) his successor would be κλέπτης μὲν οὐκ ἂν μᾶλλον εὐτυχὴς δ᾽ ἴσως.

1228. τουτὶ σὺ δράσεις;] Porson reads τοῦτ᾽ εἰ σ. δ. παραπολεῖ βοώμενος φήσει γάρ. Dobree takes this, but punctuates after βοώμενος. But the separate short sentences of the common text are satisfactory. βοώμενος is to be taken passively 'bawled down.' Cleon's loud voice is constantly spoken of.

1228. παραπολεῖ.] 'You will be ruined by the way, into the bargain,' you will get with your song more than you ever bargained for.

ἐὰν ἀπειλῇ, νὴ Δί' ἕτερον ᾄσομαι.
ὤνθρωφ', οὗτος ὁ μαιόμενος τὸ μέγα κράτος,
ἀντρέψεις ἔτι τὰν πόλιν· ἁ δ' ἔχεται ῥοπᾶς.   1235

ΔΔΕΑΤΚΑΕΩΝ

τί δ', ὅταν Θέωρος πρὸς ποδῶν κατακείμενος
ᾄδῃ Κλέωνος λαβόμενος τῆς δεξιᾶς,
'Αδμήτου λόγον, ὦταῖρε, μαθὼν τοὺς ἀγαθοὺς φίλει,
τούτῳ τί λέξεις σκόλιον;

ΦΙΛΟΚΛΕΩΝ

        ᾠδικῶς ἐγώ,   1240
οὐκ ἔστιν ἀλωπεκίζειν,
οὐδ' ἀμφοτέροισι γίγνεσθαι φίλον.

ΒΑΕΑΤΚΑΕΩΝ

μετὰ τοῦτον Αἰσχίνης ὁ Σέλλου δέξεται
ἀνὴρ σοφὸς καὶ μουσικός· κᾆτ' ᾄσεται·
χρήματα καὶ βίαν   1245

1231. **ἕτερον ᾄσομαι.**] As the MSS. have ἑτέραν ᾄσομαι Dobree corrects to ἕτερ' ἀντᾴσομαι. With ἕτερον must be supplied μέλος or σκόλιον.

1232. **ἄνθρωφ'.**] From Alcaeus, the Scholiast tells us. The lines as he gives them are rather different and hardly intelligible : μαιόμενοι stands in place of μαιόμενος. They are meant here as a rebuke to Cleon's grasping ambition.

1235. **ἔχεται ῥοπᾶς**] 'is near the turning of the scale,' wants but little to decide its fall.

1236. **πρὸς ποδῶν**] 'at the feet of, next below.' Cf. above v. 1221.

1238. **'Αδμήτου.**] The Scholiast supplies another line of this song : τῶν δειλῶν δ' ἀπέχου γνώς ὅτι δειλῶν ὀλίγα χάρις. But whether this praise of bravery, and caution against cowardice, is concerned with Admetus' spiritless conduct, or with his wife's bravery, and who is supposed to speak it, is uncertain. Here it gives occasion for a hit at Theorus' cowardice

and flattery. The metre of this song is that of Horace's 'Tu ne quaesieris (scire nefas) quem mihi, quem tibi.'

1240. **ᾠδικῶς.**] Dindorf's proposed reading in his notes ὠδὶ πῶς is apparently as good. The MSS. and old edd. have ᾠδικὸς or ᾠδικός. Meineke (with Hamaker) ejects the line.

1240. **ἀλωπεκίζειν.**] The fox was the emblem of cunning and flattery, of old, as now. Cf. Pind. *Pyth.* II. 141, where such persons are called ἀλωπέκων ἴκελοι.

1245. **χρήματα κ.τ.λ.**] There was a well-known song of Clitagora : cf. *Lys.* 1237, Κλειταγόρας ᾄδειν δέον. She was a poetess, and a Thessalian acc. to one Scholiast, a Laconian acc. to another. But what the original bearing of the song was does not appear. The Thessalians helped the Athenians in the war against their tyrants. βίαν is read for βίαν by some editors. As concluded by Philocleon, the song is

Κλειταγόρᾳ τε κἀ-
μοὶ μετὰ Θετταλῶν

ΦΙΛΟΚΛΕΩΝ

πολλὰ δὴ διεκόμισας σὺ κἀγώ.

ΒΔΕΛΥΚΛΕΩΝ

τουτὶ μὲν ἐπιεικῶς σύ γ᾽ ἐξεπίστασαι·
ὅπως δ᾽ ἐπὶ δεῖπνον ἐς Φιλοκτήμονος ἴμεν.   1250
παῖ παῖ, τὸ δεῖπνον, Χρυσέ, συσκεύαζε νῦν,
ἵνα καὶ μεθυσθῶμεν διὰ χρόνου.

ΦΙΛΟΚΛΕΩΝ

μηδαμῶς.
κακὸν τὸ πίνειν· ἀπὸ γὰρ οἴνου γίγνεται
καὶ θυροκοπῆσαι καὶ πατάξαι καὶ βαλεῖν,
κἄπειτ᾽ ἀποτίνειν ἀργύριον ἐκ κραιπάλης.   1255

ΒΔΕΛΥΚΛΕΩΝ

οὔκ, ἢν ξυνῇς γ᾽ ἀνδράσι καλοῖς τε κἀγαθοῖς.
ἢ γὰρ παρῃτήσαντο τὸν πεπονθότα,
ἢ λόγον ἔλεξας αὐτὸς ἀστεῖόν τινα,
Αἰσωπικὸν γέλοιον ἢ Συβαριτικόν,

meant to ridicule Aeschines for his boasting : especially his boasting of wealth which he never had. Cf. *Av.* 921, ἆρ᾽ ἐστὶν αὐτηΐ Νεφελοκοκκυγία, ἵνα καὶ τὰ Θεογένους τὰ πολλὰ χρήματα τά τ᾽ Αἰσχίνου γ᾽ ἅπαντα ; Hence Burges' διεκόμπασαι for διεκόμισας has great probability, and is approved by several editors. Thus, whatever the song was going to say about the wealth &c., Philocleon retorts that Aeschines had nothing to do with wealth, save in bragging of it.

1250 Φιλοκτήμονος.] ἄσωτος οὗτος. Schol.

1251 τὸ δεῖπνον συσα.] εἰ δέ τοῦ τις ἐκαλεῖτο εἰς ἄριστον ἢ εἰς δεῖπνον, τὸ ἄριστον ἢ τὸ δεῖπνον ἑαυτοῦ ἔφερε. Schol.

1253—55. The old dicast retains

as yet his old caution, and thinks that drinking leads to brawls and damages to pay next morning.

1257. παρῃτήσαντο.] As in Eur. *Heracl.* 1025, κτεῖν᾽, οὐ παραιτοῦμαί σε, and Herod. V. 33, VI. 24. Cf. also *Eq.* 37, ἣν δ᾽ αὐτοὺς παραιτησώμεθα : and this double acc. construction is common. The verb also takes simply the accusative of the penalty, *e.g.* παραιτεῖσθαι ζημίαν : as well as the acc. of that which you rescue, παραιτεῖσθαι τὴν ψυχήν : resembling in this the Lat. 'deprecari'.

1259 Αἰσωπικόν.] Cf. above v. 566. The Aesopic were (acc. to the Scholiast) about beasts, the Sybaritic about men. The father follows his son's advice below at v. 1401.

ἃν ἔμαθες ἐν τῷ συμποσίῳ· κᾆτ' ἐς γέλων   1260
τὸ πρᾶγμ' ἔτρεψας, ὥστ' ἀφεὶς σ' ἀποίχεται.

ΦΙΛΟΚΛΕΩΝ

μαθητέον τἄρ' ἐστὶ πολλοὺς τῶν λόγων,
εἴπερ ἀποτίσω μηδὲν, ἢν τι δρῶ κακίν.
ἄγε νυν ἴωμεν· μηδὲν ἡμᾶς ἰσχέτω.

ΧΟΡΟΣ

πολλάκις δὴ 'δοξ' ἐμαυτῷ δεξιὸς πεφυκέναι,   1265
καὶ σκαιὸς οὐδεπώποτε·
ἀλλ' 'Αμυνίας ὁ Σέλλου μᾶλλον οὐκ τῶν Κρωβύλου,
οὗτος ὅν γ' ἐγώ ποτ' εἶδον ἀντὶ μήλου καὶ ῥοᾶς
δειπνοῦντα μετὰ Λεωγόρου.
πεινῇ γὰρ ἥπερ 'Αντιφῶν.   1270

1260 **ἐς γέλων κ.τ.λ.**] 'Solvuntur risu tabulae: tu missus abibis.' Hor.

1261 **ἀφείς.**] sc. ὁ πεπωθών.

1262—3. Philocleon's spirit here is rather like Stepsiades' in the *Clouds.*

1265—1291 Here follows a kind of second short parabasis, consisting of a strophe and epirrhema, and an antepirrhema : the antistrophe being lost. There are second parabases in the *Knights, Peace, Birds,* each of four parts: in the *Acharnians* there is only a commation with strophe and antistrophe. The Chorus here attack and ridicule certain worthless characters, and explain the poet's conduct with respect to Cleon.

1267 **'Αμυνίας κ.τ.λ.**] Amynias was the son of Pronapus really, but is called son of Sellus, that he may be made out brother to Aeschines son of Sellus, and as poor as was Aeschines. He was an effeminate coward (*Nub.* 691—93), and was foppish in his way of dressing his hair (cf. v. 466, κομῃταμυνίαι), hence he is called οὐκ τῶν Κρωβύλου. The general sense of the passage (which is rather obscure) seems to be 'I

thought myself dexterous and clever, but that poor beggar Amynias beats me; whom I saw, instead of his frugal meal, enjoying a feast with the epicure Leogoras. But then he did go on an embassy to Thessaly, and there held conference with the Penestans, being himself a Penestan (beggar-man) equal to any.' The ἀλλὰ γὰρ seems to be put as if to account for the sudden change in Amynias' meals and mode of living; but, as the sentence is turned off with a pun which implies they were all poor together; we are left to conclude that his δεξιότης was but that of a hungry parasite, and what begun as praise is thus turned to satire. The Scholiast says we ought to supply σκαιός ἐστιν after μᾶλλον; but what then is the bearing of the whole passage?

οὐκ τῶν Κρωβύλου.] 'Of the family of *Chignon.*' For this mode of dressing the hair cf. *Thuc.* I. 6 : and *Eq.* 1331, note on τεττιγοφόραι. The Scholiast here describes it εἶδος πλοκῆς ἐπ' ἀνθρῶν εἰς ὀξὺ ληγούσης.

1269 **Λεωγόρου.**] Cf. *Nub.* 109, and note there.

1270 **'Αντιφῶν.**] An orator of

ἀλλὰ πρεσβεύων γὰρ ἐς Φάρσαλον ᾤχετ'· εἶτ' ἐκεῖ
μόνος μόνοις
τοῖς Πενέσταισι ξυνῆν τοῖς
Θετταλῶν, αὐτὸς πενέστης ὢν ἐλάττων οὐδενός.

ὦ μακάρι' Αὐτόμενες, ὥς σε μακαρίζομεν,   1275
παῖδας ἐφύτευσας ὅτι χειροτεχνικωτάτοις,
πρῶτα μὲν ἅπασι φίλον ἄνδρα τε σοφώτατον,
τὸν κιθαραοιδότατον, ᾧ χάρις ἐφέσπετο·
τὸν δ' ὑποκριτὴν ἕτερον, ἀργαλέον ὡς σοφόν·
εἶτ' Ἀριφράδην, πολύ τι θυμοσοφικώτατον,   1280
ὅντινά ποτ' ὤμοσε μαθόντα παρὰ μηδενός,
ἀλλ' ἀπὸ σοφῆς φύσεος αὐτόματον ἐκμαθεῖν
γλωττοποιεῖν ἐς τὰ πορνεῖ' εἰσιόνθ' ἑκάστοτε.

. . . .

εἰσί τινες οἵ μ' ἔλεγον ὡς καταδιηλλάγην,

some note. He was attacked by the comic writers as receiving money for speeches written for others.

1271 πρεσβεύων.] The Scholiast tells us that Eupolis mentioned this embassy, and attacked Amynias as παραπρεσβευτήν. Perhaps some bribery is hinted at here as the possible reason of his sudden luxury.

1272 μόνος μόνοις.] A favourite Greek collocation, ξυνῆν μόνος μόνῳ = 'he had a tête-à-tête:' here perhaps it means 'he had some private talk with them,' he and they laid their heads together.

1273 Πενέσταισι. The lower class among the Thessalians. δέον οὖν εἰπεῖν μετὰ τῶν πολιτευομένων ξυνῆν, εἶπε μετὰ τῶν Πενεστῶν. Schol. and there is a play on πένη and Πενέστης.

1278 τὸν κιθαραοιδότατον.] Arignotus, spoken of in Eq. 1277, as ἀνὴρ φίλος, as well known to all, and as not a brother in nature though in name to Ariphrades (τοὺς τρόπους οὐ ξυγγενής). Why Richter includes Arignotus as 'turpissimis usus moribus' in the face of these two passages is inexplicable.

1279 ὑποκριτήν.] The name of this actor is unknown.

ἀργαλέον ὡς σοφόν.] Compare the phrases θαυμαστὸν ὅσον, ἀμήχανον ὅσον.

1280 θυμοσοφικώτατον.] Cf. Νυb. 877, θυμόσοφός ἐστιν φύσει.

1281 ὤμοσε.] Supply ὁ πατήρ, says the Scholiast: but it is awkward to do so. ὤμοσα Bentley. ὁ πατὴρ ποτ' ὤμοσε Bergk.

1284—91 The transactions between Cleon and Aristophanes, to which this antepirrhema alludes, are not known. Apparently Cleon had attacked the poet—perhaps had brought him into court—after the exhibition of the Ἱππῆς, as we know he did on an earlier occasion referred to in Ach. 3;6. The antistrophe is lost after v. 1283; perhaps this might have explained something. Bergk thinks that it consisted of a violent attack on Cleon, to make up for any previous leniency, and to justify the proverb in v. 1291. This antepirrhema is short by one line.

1284 καταδιηλλάγην.] In the Clouds Cleon had been spared; or

ἡνίκα Κλέων μ' ὑπετάραττεν ἐπικείμενος   1285
καί με κακίαις ἔκνισε· κᾆθ' ὅτ' ἀπεδειρόμην,
ἐκτὸς ἐγέλων μέγα κεκραγότα θεώμενοι,
οὐδὲν ἄρ' ἐμοῦ μέλον, ὅσον δὲ μόνον εἰδέναι
σκωμμάτιον εἶποτέ τι θλιβόμενος ἐκβαλῶ.
ταῦτα κατιδὼν ὑπό τι μικρὸν ἐπιθήκισα·   1290
εἶτα νῦν ἐξηπάτησεν ἡ χάραξ τὴν ἄμπελον.

ΞΑΝΘΙΑΣ

ἰὼ χελῶναι μακάριαι τοῦ δέρματος,
καὶ τρισμακάριαι τοῦ 'πὶ ταῖς πλευραῖς τέγους.
ὡς εὖ κατηρέψασθε καὶ νουβυστικῶς

al all events was not the principal object of attack; for *Nub.* 586, 591, are not complimentary to him.

1287 ἐκτὸς.] This seems to rest on better MS. authority than the common reading οὗκτόι. Indeed what can οὗκτόι mean? 'Those who were without,' *i.e.* those who were out of the scrape themselves?

1288 οὐδὲν ἄρ' ἐμοῦ μέλον.] The absolute use of the participle μέλον is analogous to that of ἐξὸν, παρὸν, and the like.

1290—91. When Aristophanes saw that he received no help from those who only cared for the amusement to be got out of him, he played the flatterer awhile, but afterwards turned on Cleon.

1290 ἐπιθήκισα.] The ape is often the emblem of flattery. Cf. Pind. *Pyth.* II. 132, καλὸς τοι πίθων παρὰ παισίν· ὁ δὲ Ῥαδάμανθυς... φρενῶν ἔλαχε καρπὸν... οὐδ' ἀπάταισι τέρπεται.

1291 ἡ χάραξ.] This was a proverb of those deceived in what they believed to be their prop or stay. Thus Cleon rested secure that Aristophanes would not, after once giving in, return to the attack, but was quite deceived in this hope. Cleon is the vine, Aristophanes the vine-prop. To trust in a reed, which breaks and pierces the hand of him

that leans on it, is a similar expression. Cf. 2 Kings xviii. 21.

1292—1449. Xanthias comes in smarting from blows, and tells how Philocleon bore him at the banquet; how he outdid all in tipsy revelry, and is laying about him with his staff. Philocleon soon enters, tolerably drunk, and with a flute-girl. His son follows, and tries to check him; but to little purpose, the father retorting on him some of his own instructions. A baker-woman demands compensation for spoilt loaves, a man assaulted threatens law-proceedings; but they only get mocked at, and absurdly put off with fables; till at last the son prepares to take his father indoors out of harm's way.

1292 χελῶναι.] Cf. above, v. 429, ὀστρακόδερμα is given by the Scholiast as applied to animals protected by such shells.

1293 τέγους.] This correction (for MS. ἐμαῖς and στέγεω) is due to Bentley. The general sense of the passage and the following κατηρέψασθε κερδμῳ leave hardly any doubt that Aristophanes wrote τέγους.

1294 νουβυστικῶς.] τοῦ πεπληρωμένου. Schol. This curious compound occurs again in *Eccl.* 441, γυναῖκα δ' εἶναι πρᾶγμ' ἔφη νουβυστικόν.

9

κεράμῳ τὸ νῶτον ὥστε τὰς πληγὰς στέγειν.   1295
ἐγὼ δ᾽ ἀπόλωλα στιζόμενος βακτηρίᾳ.

ΧΟΡΟΣ

τί δ᾽ ἔστιν, ὦ παῖ; παῖδα γὰρ, κἂν ᾖ γέρων,
καλεῖν δίκαιον ὅστις ἂν πληγὰς λάβῃ.

ΞΑΝΘΙΑΣ

σὺ γὰρ ὁ γέρων ἀτηρότατον ἄρ᾽ ἦν κακὸν
καὶ τῶν ξυνόντων πολὺ παροινικώτατος;   1300
καίτοι παρῆν Ἵππυλλος, Ἀντιφῶν, Λύκων,
Λυσίστρατος, Θούφραστος, οἱ περὶ Φρύνιχον.
τούτων ἁπάντων ἦν ὑβριστότατος μακρῷ.
εὐθὺς γὰρ ὡς ἐνέπλητο πολλῶν κἀγαθῶν,
ἐνήλατ᾽, ἐσκίρτα, πεπόρδει, κατεγέλα,   1305
ὥσπερ καχρύων ὀνίδιον εὐωχημένον·
κἄτυπτεν ἐμὲ νεανικῶς, παῖ παῖ καλῶν.
εἶτ᾽ αὐτὸν ὡς εἶδ᾽, ἤκασεν Λυσίστρατος·
ἔοικας, ὦ πρεσβῦτα, νεοπλούτῳ τρυγὶ

1295 στέγειν.] This is commonly used of water, 'to keep it out, or in,' to be water-proof or water-tight. Here it is of the cudgel-proof shell of the tortoise.

1297 τί δ᾽ ἔστιν, ὦ παῖ.] Cf. Them. 582, τί δ᾽ ἔστιν, ὦ παῖ; παῖδα γάρ σ᾽ εἰκὸς καλεῖν, ἕως ἂν οὕτω τὰς γνάθους ψιλὰς ἔχῃς.

1300 παροινικώτατος.] In Ach. 981 παροίνιοι is given by MSS. Some change that to παροινικός. It is quite possible there were two forms.

1301 Ἵππυλλος κ.τ.λ.] Of three of these guests we know nothing. For Antiphon cf. above, v. 1270; for Lysistratus, v. 787, Ach. 855, Eq. 1265. There seem to have been several of the name of Phrynichus: a tragic poet, a comic poet, and an actor. For analogous forms to Thuphrastus (=Theophrastus) cf. Eq. 1103, Θουφάνης, 1267, Θούμαντις.

1303 ὑβριστότατος.] The regular

comparative and superlative of this word are confirmed by several examples. See L. and S. But Cobet, Meineke, and others adopt ὑβρίστατος.

1305 ἐνήλατ᾽.] Some MSS. have ἐνήλλατ᾽: whence Meineke reads ἐνήλλετ᾽, Lenting ἀνήλλετ᾽. Certainly ἐνάλλεσθαι rather requires an object, and the imperfect tense suits with the other verbs. But it may be ἐνήλατό (μοι), of the first insulting attack, followed by the imperfects, to describe the rest of his tipsy frolic.

1306 ὥσπερ κ.τ.λ.] Like a full-fed donkey he began to frisk. Bergler compares Xen. Anab. v. 8. 3, εἰ ἐν τοιούτῳ καιρῷ ὕβριζον ὁμολογῶ καὶ τῶν ὄνων ὑβριστότερος εἶναι, οἵ φασιν ὑπὸ τῆς ὕβρεως κόπον οὐκ ἐγγίνεσθαι.

1307 νεανικῶς.] Cf. below, v. 1333, νεανίας; and above, note on v. 1204.

1309 ἔοικας.] Absurd and hardly intelligible comparisons: cf. those

κλητῆρί τ' εἰς ἀχυρὸν ἀποδεδρακότι.   1310
ὁ δ' ἀνακραγὼν ἀντήκασ' αὐτὸν πάρνοπι
τὰ θρῖα τοῦ τρίβωνος ἀποβεβληκότι,
Σθενέλῳ τε τὰ σκευάρια διακεκαρμένῳ.
οἱ δ' ἀνεκρότησαν, πλήν γε Θουφράστου μόνου·
οὗτος δὲ διεμύλλαινεν ὡς δὴ δεξιός.   1315
ὁ γέρων δὲ τὸν Θούφραστον ἤρετ', εἰπέ μοι,
ἐπὶ τῷ κομᾷς καὶ κομψὸς εἶναι προσποιεῖ,
κωμῳδολοιχῶν περὶ τὸν εὖ πράττοντ' ἀεί;
τοιαῦτα περιύβριζεν αὐτοὺς ἐν μέρει,
σκώπτων ἀγροίκως καὶ προσέτι λόγους λέγων   1320
ἀμαθέστατ', οὐδὲν εἰκότας τῷ πράγματι.
ἔπειτ' ἐπειδὴ 'μέθυεν, οἴκαδ' ἔρχεται
τύπτων ἅπαντας, ἤν τις αὐτῷ ξυντύχῃ.
ὁδὶ δὲ δὴ καὶ σφαλλόμενος προσέρχεται.
ἀλλ' ἐκποδὼν ἄπειμι πρὶν πληγὰς λαβεῖν.   1325

of Bdelycleon at v. 1171. The compliments exchanged between Sarmentus and Messius in Horace (*Sat.* i. 5. 56) are somewhat similar.

νεσηλούτῳ τρυγλ.] Δίδυμός φησιν ὅτι ἀδιανόητα σκώπτει. Schol. And indeed it seems so. 'Solent recens ditati esse insolentes.' Bergler. Richter thinks it means 'one newly made rich,' but adds 'loquuntur bene poli.'

1310 κλητῆρί κ.τ.λ.] κλητῆρι is put where ὅτῳ should be (cf. above, v. 189); for the Scholiast gives a proverb ὄνος εἰς ἄχυρον. The ass that had made its way to the strawyard would (probably) pick up a good feed there, and wax skittish. And 'bailiff' is put for 'ass' with reference to the dicast's employment.

1311 τὰ θρῖα τ. τ. d.] 'That has lost the leaves of its cloak,' *i. e.* its leaf-like covering, or its wings. Lyaistratus (a poor man) is reproached with his threadbare cloak, and compared to a locust which has cast or lost its wings. The outer wings

of locusts are sufficiently leaf-like to make θρῖα τ. τ. intelligible, though of course the simile is meant to be ridiculous.

1313 Σθενέλῳ.] Sthenelus was a tragic actor, who from his poverty had to sell all his stage dress and furniture. Schol.

1315 διεμύλλαινεν.] ὑπερηφάνως τὰ χείλη διέστρεφον ὡς χλευάζων καὶ μὴ ἠσθείς τῷ λελεγμένῳ. Schol.

δεξιός.] As if such rude commoi jests were beneath him.

1318 κωμῳδολοιχῶν.] Cf. *Nub.* 451, ματτυολοιχός, for the termination of this compound. It must mean 'playing the fool to amuse, and so earning a dinner;' 'punster and parasite.'

1319 περιύβριζεν.] L. and S. give only the sense 'to insult exceedingly;' but both here and in *Thesm.* 535, τοιαῦτα περιυβρίζειν ἡμᾶς ἄνδρας, it perhaps means 'to insult all round.'

1321 οὐδὲν εἰκότας.] Of which we have specimens 1309—10.

ΦΙΛΟΚΛΕΩΝ

ἄνεχε, πάρεχε·
κλαύσεταί τις τῶν ὕπισθεν
ἐπακολουθούντων ἐμοί·
οἷον, εἰ μὴ 'ρρήσεθ', ὑμᾶς,
ὦ πονηροί, ταυτῃὶ τῇ   1330
δᾳδὶ φρυκτοὺς σκευάσω.

ΚΑΤΗΓΟΡΟΣ

ἦ μὴν σὺ δώσεις αὔριον τούτων δίκην
ἡμῖν ἅπασι, κεἰ σφόδρ' εἶ νεανίας.
ἀθρόοι γὰρ ἥξομέν σε προσκαλούμενοι.

ΦΙΛΟΚΛΕΩΝ

ἰὴ ἰεῦ, καλούμενοι.   1335
ἀρχαῖά γ' ὑμῶν· ἀρά γ' ἴσθ'
ὡς οὐδ' ἀκούων ἀνέχομαι
δικῶν; ἰαιβοῖ αἰβοῖ.
τάδε μ' ἀρέσκει· βάλλε κημούς.
οὐκ ἄπει σύ; . . ποῦ 'στιν   1340

1316 **ἄνεχε, πάρεχε.**] Cf. *Av.*
1720, ἄναγε, δίεχε, πάραγε, πάρεχε.
In Eur. *Troad.* 308, ἄνεχε, πάρεχε
is said by Cassandra, and in Eur.
Cycl. 202, ἄνεχε, πάρεχε by Silenus.
Plainly it is an exclamation of ex-
citement and of drunkenness ; 'stop
there ! make way !' Philocleon is
making tipsy demonstrations to those
who are following him to get redress
for insults. And for πάρεχε cf. note
above on v. 949.

1329 **οἷον.**] Cf. *Eq.* 367, οἷόν σε
δήσω 'ν τῷ ξύλῳ.

1331 **φρυκτούς.**] οἱ φρυκτοί or
τὰ φρυκτά were specially small fish
for frying. The Scholiast says ὡς
ἰχθύδια πεφρυγμένα φρυκτοὺς σκευάσω
ὀπτήσαι.

1332 **ἦ μὴν κ.τ.λ.**] These lines
should be given to one of those following Philocleon, as Bergk and
Lenting suggest. Bdelycleon, to
whom they were given, should not

come in till v. 1363 : nor have they
much force in the mouth of the
chorus, who have been on the stage
while Philocleon has been feasting.

1333 **νεανίας.**] 'Insolent.' Cf.
above, v. 1307.

1335—9. Philocleon scorns the
idea of a summons, and cannot bear
even the word.

1336 **ἀρχαῖά γ' ὑμῶν.**] ' 'tis
out of date—your plan.

1339 **τάδε.**] 'this,' viz. the life
I now lead, one of mirth and jollity.

βάλλε κημούς.] βάλλε δὲ κόρακας
τὰ δικαστικὰ σκεύη. Schol.

1340 **οὐκ ἄπει σύ.**] Addressed to
the departing κατήγορος. Meineke in
his notes proposes ἀπολέσει: the MSS.
have ἄπεισι. After ἄπει σύ something is wanted to complete the line.
Meineke reads ποῦ 'στιν ἡμῖν. Dindorf in his notes ποῦ 'στι, ποῦ 'στιν,
which may be acquiesced in.

ἡλιαστής; ἐκποδών.
ἀνάβαινε δεῦρο χρυσομηλολόνθιον,
τῇ χειρὶ τουδὶ λαβομένη τοῦ σχοινίου.
ἔχου· φυλάττου δ', ὡς σαπρὸν τὸ σχοινίον·
ὅμως γε μέντοι τριβόμενον οὐκ ἄχθεται.
ὁρᾷς ἐγώ σ' ὡς δεξιῶς ὑφειλόμην   1345
μέλλουσαν ἤδη λεσβιεῖν τοὺς ξυμπότας·
ὧν οὕνεκ' ἀπόδος τῷ πέει τῳδὶ χάριν.
ἀλλ' οὐκ ἀποδώσεις οὐδὲ φιαλεῖς, οἶδ' ὅτι,
ἀλλ' ἐξαπατήσεις κἀγχανεῖ τούτῳ μέγα·
πολλοῖς γὰρ ἤδη χἀτέροις αὔτ' εἰργάσω.   1350
ἐὰν γένῃ δὲ μὴ κακὴ νυνὶ γυνή,
ἐγώ σ', ἐπειδὰν οὑμὸς υἱὸς ἀποθάνῃ,
λυσάμενος ἔξω παλλακήν, ὦ χοιρίον.
νῦν δ' οὐ κρατῶ 'γὼ τῶν ἐμαυτοῦ χρημάτων.
νέος γάρ εἰμι καὶ φυλάττομαι σφόδρα.   1355
τὸ γὰρ υἴδιον τηρεῖ με, κἄστι δύσκολον
κἄλλως κυμινοπριστοκαρδαμόγλυφον.
ταῦτ' οὖν περί μου δέδοικε μὴ διαφθαρῶ.
πατὴρ γὰρ οὐδείς ἐστιν αὐτῷ πλὴν ἐμοῦ.
ὁδὶ δὲ καὐτός· ἐπὶ σὲ κἄμ' ἔοικε θεῖν.   1360

1341 ἡλιαστής.] He calls the man by this name perhaps in a tipsy confusion of ideas. 'Where's our heliast? our man who is for the courts and for summoning.' 'Oh! I see now he's taken himself off.' Philocleon then turns to the girl.

1342 χρυσομηλολόνθιον.] Cf. Nub. 763 for the μηλολόνθη, and the practice of letting it fly by a string.

1348 φιαλεῖς.] Cf. Pac. 432 for this rare word.

1352 ἐπειδὰν κ.τ.λ.] He speaks of his son as a son might speak of his father: as expecting his death, and as under strict tutelage. But when his own master, then he will (he says) free this girl from slavery and make her his mistress.

1354 κρατῶ 'γώ.] Elmsley proposed κρατῶ συ, 'rightly,' says

Meineke: but it is questionable whether such change is needed. The pronoun is naturally enough expressed 'but at present I am not master myself of my own property.'

1357 κυμινοπρ.] Alexis in Athenaeus has κυμινοπρίστης ὁ τρόπος ἐστί σου πάλαι. Hesychius explains κυμινοπρίσται· οἱ φειδωλοί· ὁμοίως καὶ οἱ πρδαμογλύφοι.

1359 πατὴρ γάρ.] A ridiculous reversal of the usual order of things: 'he has no son but me' would be ordinary enough from a son to a father.

1360 ὁδὶ δὲ καὐτός.] This 'and here comes his very self' shews that Bdelycleon did not return with his father at v. 1326; therefore the lines 1332—4 cannot be rightly assigned to him.

ἀλλ' ὡς τάχιστα στῆθι τάσδε τὰς δετας
λαβοῦσ', ἵν' αὐτὸν τωθάσω νεανικῶς,
οἵας ποθ' οὗτος ἐμὲ πρὸ τῶν μυστηρίων.

ΒΔΕΛΤΚΛΕΩΝ

ὦ οὗτος οὗτος, τυφεδανὲ καὶ χοιρόθλιψ,
ποθεῖν ἐρᾶν τ' ἔοικας ὡραίας σοροῦ.   1365
οὔ τοι καταπροίξει μὰ τὸν Ἀπόλλω τοῦτο δρῶν.

ΦΙΛΟΚΛΕΩΝ

ὡς ἡδέως φάγοις ἂν ἐξ ὄξους δίκην.

ΒΔΕΛΤΚΛΕΩΝ

οὐ δεινὰ τωθάζειν σε, τὴν αὐλητρίδα
τῶν ξυμποτῶν κλέψαντα;

1361—2 **δετὰς λαβοῦσ'**. The girl is to take the torch, that the old man may make his absurd assertions, vv. 1371—7.

1363 **οἷαι**.] Better, as following νεανικῶς, than οἵαις of MSS. R. V.

πρὸ τῶν μ.] It appears to have been the custom for those already initiated to frighten those who were preparing to be so. Schol. 'When I was simple and ignorant, my son played on my fears and made a fool of me: now that I am grown wiser, I will pay him in kind.' I was, as it were, a child and minor then: now I am come of age.

1364 **τυφεδανὲ.**] The Scholiast explains this as equivalent to τυφογέρων, a word used twice by Aristophanes (Νub. 908, Lys. 335), with a possible play on the similarity in sound to τυμβογέρων. But the Scholiast's further comment ἄξιοι τετύφθαι is curious. The word cannot surely have anything to do with τύπτειν. Richter suggests that the Scholiast wrote ἄξιοι τεθάφθαι: but, though that suits the context here, τυφεδανὸς cannot be conneĉed with θάπτω. Might not τυφεδανὸς mean 'inflamed' with passion, or love, amorous'? Compare Lys. 221, ὅπως

ἀν ἀνὴρ ἐπιτυφῇ μάλιστά μου: and Plat. Phaedr. 230 A, θῆριον Τυφῶνος πολυπλοκώτερον καὶ μᾶλλον ἐπιτεθυμμένον. The opposite is denoted by ἄτυφος, ἀτυφία, 'modest, modesty.' See Thompson's note on the passage in the Phaedrus. This sense of τυφεδανὸς suits the context far better than that given by L. and S., 'smoky-witted, a dullard.' And indeed τυφογέρων may as well mean 'puffed up, excited, inflamed,' as 'stupified, dull.'

1365 **ὡραίας σοροῦ.**] By surprise for ὡραίας κόρης: but also with the sense of 'an early bier.' Cf. Lys. 601, σὺ δὲ δὴ τί μαθὼν οὐκ ἀποθνήσκεις;...σορὸν ὠνήσει.

1367 **ὡς ἡδέως φάγοις ἄν.**] He tells his son that no doubt he would like to sue and punish his father, a suit would be a sweet morsel to him. Bdelycleon is now twitted as φιλόδικος, Philocleon is μισόδικος. For description of pleasures as eatables cf. above, v. 511, and Eq. 706, φέρε τί δῶ σοι καταφαγεῖν; ἐπὶ τῷ φάγοι ἥδιστ' ἄν; ἐπὶ βαλλαντίῳ; Also we have a fragment of the Gerytades (Fr. 91), καὶ τῶν ἐγὼ Σθενέλου φάγοιμ' ἂν ῥήματα, εἰς ὄξος ἐμβαπτόμενα ἢ ξηροὺς ἅλας;

ΦΙΛΟΚΛΕΩΝ

ποίαν αὐλητρίδα;

τί ταῦτα ληρεῖς, ὥσπερ ἀπὸ τύμβου πεσών;   1370

ΒΔΕΛΤΚΛΕΩΝ ·

νὴ τὸν Δἴ, αὕτη πού 'στί σοί γ' ἡ Δαρδανίς.

ΦΙΛΟΚΛΕΩΝ

οὔκ, ἀλλ' ἐν ἀγορᾷ τοῖς θεοῖς δᾲς κάεται.

ΒΔΕΛΤΚΛΕΩΝ

δᾲς ἥδε;

ΦΙΛΟΚΛΕΩΝ

δᾲς δῆτ'. οὐχ ὁρᾷς ἐστιγμένην;

ΒΔΕΛΤΚΛΕΩΝ

τί δὲ τὸ μέλαν τοῦτ' ἐστὶν αὐτῆς τοὖν μέσῳ;

ΦΙΛΟΚΛΕΩΝ

ἡ πίττα δήπου καομένης ἐξέρχεται.   1375

ΒΔΕΛΤΚΛΕΩΝ

ὁ δ' ὄπισθεν οὐχὶ πρωκτός ἐστιν οὑτοσί;

ΦΙΛΟΚΛΕΩΝ

ὄζος μὲν οὖν τῆς δᾳδὸς οὗτος ἐξέχει.

ΒΔΕΛΤΚΛΕΩΝ

τί λέγεις σύ; ποῖος ὄζος; οὐκ εἶ δεῦρο σύ;

ΦΙΛΟΚΛΕΩΝ

ἆ ἆ, τί μέλλεις δρᾶν;

1370 **ἀπὸ τύμβου πεσών.**] This is a variation on *Nub.* 1273, τί δῆτα ληρεῖς ὥσπερ ἀπ' ὄνου καταπεσών; where the fall ἀπ' ὄνου is meant to suggest a fall ἀπὸ νοῦ, 'from the wits, mind, sense.' ἀπὸ τόμβου here seems put for the same. Philocleon is making out himself to be young, his son an old τυμβογέρων, everything being now reversed. But the phrase is very curious, 'fallen from a tomb.' The general meaning is 'Why have you come out of your grave (in which you ought to be) to talk such rub-

bish?' He ridicules the idea of its being a flute-player, and would fain persuade his son that his eyes deceive him. In the Jacobite song 'Hame came our gudeman at een' the wife says to her lord, 'Ye're an auld doited carle, and unco blind ye be,' when trying to make him believe that the horse, plume, and sword of the concealed cavalier are a milch-cow, hen, and parritch-stick.

1371 **Δαρδανίς.**] Phrygia was noted for its flute-players,

ΒΔΕΛΥΚΛΕΩΝ
ἄγειν ταύτην λαβὼν
ἀφελόμενός σε καὶ νομίσας εἶναι σαπρὸν   1380
κοὐδὲν δύνασθαι δρᾶν.

ΦΙΛΟΚΛΕΩΝ
ἄκουσόν νυν ἐμοῦ.
Ὀλυμπίασιν ἡνίκ' ἐθεώρουν ἐγὼ,
Ἐφουδίων ἐμαχέσατ' Ἀσκώνδᾳ καλῶς,
ἤδη γέρων ὢν εἶτα τῇ πυγμῇ θενὼν
ὁ πρεσβύτερος κατέβαλε τὸν νεώτερον.   1385
πρὸς ταῦτα τηροῦ μὴ λάβῃς ὑπώπια.

ΒΔΕΛΥΚΛΕΩΝ
νὴ τὸν Δί' ἐξέμαθές γε τὴν Ὀλυμπίαν.

ΑΡΤΟΠΩΛΙΣ
ἴθι μοι παράστηθ', ἀντιβολῶ πρὸς τῶν θεῶν.
ὁδὶ γὰρ ἀνήρ ἐστιν ὅς μ' ἀπώλεσεν
τῇ δᾳδὶ παίων, κἀξέβαλεν ἐντευθενὶ   1390
ἄρτους δέκ' ὀβολῶν κἀπιθήκην τέτταρας.

ΒΔΕΛΥΚΛΕΩΝ
ὁρᾷς ἃ δέδρακας; πράγματ' αὖ δεῖ καὶ δίκας
ἔχειν διὰ τὸν σὸν οἶνον.

ΦΙΛΟΚΛΕΩΝ
οὐδαμῶς γ', ἐπεὶ

1382 Ὀλυμπίασιν κ.τ.λ.] He
begins to put in practice his son's
precepts on polite conversation. Cf.
above, v. 1190.
1388—91. The baker-woman
comes in to recover compensation
for her lost loaves.
1390 ἐντευθενὶ.] Perhaps she
points to her basket.
1391 ἄρτους δέκ' ὀβολῶν.] 'ten
loaves worth as many obols:' or
'loaves—ten obols' worth,' the number of loaves being left indefinite.
Dobree's and Cobet's τέτταρων would
make this last rendering necessary,

though indeed it may be so taken
even with the common text.
κἀπιθήκην τέτταρας.] 'And four
given in:' ἐπιθήκη is explained as
'additamentum, superpondium.' It
seems a large proportional addition,
a liberal 'baker's ten.' But ἐν.
τέτταρων, 'a further lot worth four,'
after d. δ. d. is a clumsy way of ex-
pressing fourteen obols' worth.
1392 πράγματ' αὖ.] Again they
will have trouble, lawsuits, &c., from
which Bdelycleon hoped he had set
them both free.

λόγοι διαλλάξουσιν αὐτὰ δεξιοί·
ὥστ' οἶδ' ὅτι ᾗ ταύτῃ διαλλαχθήσομαι.　　　　1395

ΑΡΤΟΠΩΛΙΣ

οὔ τοι μὰ τὼ θεὼ καταπροίξει Μυρτίας
τῆς Ἀγκυλίωνος θυγατέρος καὶ Σωστράτης,
οὕτω διαφθείρας ἐμοῦ τὰ φορτία.

ΦΙΛΟΚΛΕΩΝ

ἄκουσον, ὦ γύναι· λόγον σοι βούλομαι
λέξαι χαρίεντα.

ΑΡΤΟΠΩΛΙΣ

μὰ Δία μὴ μοί γ', ὦ μέλε.　　　　1400

ΦΙΛΟΚΛΕΩΝ

Αἴσωπον ἀπὸ δείπνου βαδίζονθ' ἑσπέρας
θρασεῖα καὶ μεθύση τις ὑλάκτει κύων.
κἄπειτ' ἐκεῖνος εἶπεν, ὦ κύον κύον,
εἰ νὴ Δί' ἀντὶ τῆς κακῆς γλώττης ποθὲν
πυροὺς πρίαιο, σωφρονεῖν ἄν μοι δοκοῖς.　　　　1405

ΑΡΤΟΠΩΛΙΣ

καὶ καταγελᾷς μου; προσκαλοῦμαί σ' ὅστις εἶ,
πρὸς τοὺς ἀγορανόμους βλάβης τῶν φορτίων,
κλητῆρ' ἔχουσα Χαιρεφῶντα τουτονί.

1394 **λόγοι κ.τ.λ.**] Cf. above, 1258.

1396 **μὰ τὼ θεώ.**] An oath much used by women; and therefore of most frequent occurrence in the Lysistrata, Thesmophoriazusae, Ecclesiazusae: *e.g. Lys.* 51, 112, 148, *Thesm.* 383, 566, *Eccl.* 155, 156, 158.

1399. He begins upon fables: cf. above, v. 1260.

1402 **ὑλάκτει.**] Note the ῠ long in an augmented tense: whereas at v. 904 ἀγαθὸν γ' ὑλακτεῖν begins a verse; the υ is therefore short.

1405 **πυρούς.**] To make bread with, and so repair the loss of her loaves. Schol. Such will be the force of πυρούς in the intended application of the story. In the story itself it is not quite clear whether the κύων is a literal one or not. The μεθύση does not suit the animal: but the tale is of course intentionally absurd.

1406 **καὶ καταγελᾷς.**] 'Do you also (or even) laugh at me;' do you add insult to injury? Cf. *Eq.* 274, καὶ κέκραγας.

1407 **ἀγορανόμους.**] Cf. *Ach.* 723. τοὺς ἐπισκοποῦντα τὰ τῆς πόλεως ὤνια καὶ διακοῦντα αὐτά. Schol.

1408 **Χαιρεφῶντα.**] One of the pale scholars of Socrates in the *Clouds.* Cf. *Nub.* 103, 504, τοὺς ὠχρ-

ΦΙΛΟΚΛΕΩΝ

μὰ Δί', ἀλλ' ἄκουσον, ἤν τί σοι δόξω λέγειν.

Λᾶσός ποτ' ἀντεδίδασκε καὶ Σιμωνίδης·   1410
ἔπειθ' ὁ Λᾶσος εἶπεν, ὀλίγον μοι μέλει

ΑΡΤΟΠΩΛΙΣ

ἄληθες, οὗτος;

ΦΙΛΟΚΛΕΩΝ

καὶ σὺ δή μοι, Χαιρεφῶν,
γυναικὶ κλητεύειν ἔοικας θαψίνῃ,
Ἰνοῖ κρεμαμένῃ πρὸς ποδῶν Εὐριπίδου,

ΒΔΕΛΤΚΛΕΩΝ

ὁδί τις ἕτερος, ὡς ἔοικεν, ἔρχεται   1415
καλούμενός σε· τόν γέ τοι κλητῆρ' ἔχει

ΚΑΤΗΓΟΡΟΣ

οἴμοι κακοδαίμων. προσκαλοῦμαί σ', ὦ γέρον,
ὕβρεως.

ὦνται...λέγειτ, and ΣΩ. οὐδὲν διαί-
σειτ Χαιρεφῶντοι τὴν φύσιν. ΣΤ.
οἴμοι κακοδαίμων, ἡμιθνὴς γενήσομαι.
1409—12. Lasus and Simonides
were rivals, and had a contest.
Lasus said he cared little for his
opponent: nor do I care for your
summons and lawsuit. This is
apparently the application, if it has
any. Lasus of Hermione was an
early writer on music, and origina-
tor of the Dithyrambic contest.
Simonides, the lyric poet of Ceos,
is well known.
1411 ὀλίγον μοι μέλει.] τοῦ Σι-
μωνίδου δηλώστι. Schol.
1412 ἄληθε οὗτος.] Cf. Eq. 89.
1413 κλητεύειν.] Meineke follows
Dobree in reading κλητεύων. Chae-
rephon would then be compared to
a sallow woman : cf. note on v. 1408.
But προσπολῶν, in the next line, does
not suit so well with this as with
κλητεύειν.
θαψίνῃ.] Cf. Theocr. Id. 11.
88, καὶ μευ χρὼν μὲν ὁμοῖοι ἐγίνε-
το πολλάκι θάψῳ. One Scholiast
thinks there is an allusion to θά-
πτειν.

1414 Ἰνοῖ, κ.τ.λ.] Ino threw
herself from a rock, and was (the
Scholiast says) ὠχρὰ ὑπὸ τῆς κακο-
παθείας. How Ino in Euripides'
play was κρεμαμένη πρὸς ποδῶν is not
clear : but προσπολῶν, an alteration
of Hermann's, accepted by some
editors, does not make such un-
doubted good sense as to be un-
hesitatingly taken : 'attending on
the hanging Ino of Euripides.' κρ.
ἐκ ποδῶν (or κρ.) must refer apparently to Ino when about to
throw herself over. Euripides (Med.
1288) describes her as αὐτὴς ὑπερ-
τείνασα ποντίας πόδα, and in the
play of Ino there may have been
some phrase justifying κρ. ἐκ ποδῶν
here. That the Ino was a play full
of distress, tears, &c. we may infer
from Ach. 434, where Ino's and
Thyestes' rags have between them
those of Telephus.
1417 οἴμοι κακοδαίμων.] Holden
gives this to Bdelycleon. But after
an assault (ὕβρεω) the plaintiff might
well say the words. See the behaviour of the old man described at
v. 1323.

ΒΔΕΛΥΚΛΕΩΝ

ὕβρεως; μὴ, μὴ καλέσῃς πρὸς τῶν θεῶν.
ἐγὼ γὰρ ὑπὲρ αὐτοῦ δίκην δίδωμί σοι,
ἣν ἂν σὺ τάξῃς, καὶ χάριν προσείσομαι.　　　　1420

ΦΙΛΟΚΛΕΩΝ

ἐγὼ μὲν οὖν αὐτῷ διαλλαχθήσομαι
ἑκών· ὁμολογῶ γὰρ πατάξαι καὶ βαλεῖν. ·
ἀλλ' ἐλθὲ δευρὶ πρότερον, ἐπιτρέπεις ἐμοί,
ὅ τι χρή μ' ἀποτίσαντ' ἀργύριον τοῦ πράγματος,
εἶναι φίλον τὸ λοιπὸν, ἢ σύ μοι φράσεις;　　　　1425

ΚΑΤΗΓΟΡΟΣ

σὺ λέγε. δικῶν γὰρ οὐ δέομ' οὐδὲ πραγμάτων.

ΦΙΛΟΚΛΕΩΝ

ἀνὴρ Συβαρίτης ἐξέπεσεν ἐξ ἅρματος,
καί πως κατεάγη τῆς κεφαλῆς μέγα σφόδρα·
ἐτύγχανεν γὰρ οὐ τρίβων ὢν ἱππικῆς.
κᾆπειτ' ἐπιστὰς εἶπ' ἀνὴρ αὐτῷ φίλος·　　　　1430
ἔρδοι τις ἣν ἕκαστος εἰδείη τέχνην.
οὕτω δὲ καὶ σὺ παράτρεχ' ἐς τὰ Πιττάλου.

·ΒΔΕΛΥΚΛΕΩΝ

ὅμοιά σου καὶ ταῦτα τοῖς ἄλλοις τρόποις.

1420 προσείσομαι.] Better thus
than separately, πρὸς εἴσομαι, as Dindorf's earlier editions have it.
Richter compares Soph. *Oed. Tyr.*
232, τὸ γὰρ κέρδος τελῶ 'γὼ, χἡ
χάρις προσείσεται.
1421—26. Philocleon gets the
man to come and listen quietly in
hopes of compensation, and then
puts him off with a Sybaritic fable :
following in this to the letter his
son's precept at v. 1260.
1423 ἐπιτρέπεις ἐμοὶ ὅ τι χρή.]
'Do you leave it to me (to name)
what sum I am to pay you and be
friends, or will you name it?'

1428 κατ. τῆς κεφαλῆς.] Cf.
Ach. 1180, and *Pac.* 71, ξυνετμήβη
τῆς κεφαλῆς.
1430—31. He got no pity, but
a proverb. 'Quam quisque norit
artem, in hac se exerceat.' Cic.
Tusc. I. 18.
1432 οὕτω δὲ κ.τ.λ.] And so
you, as you will get no pity, had
better get a plaister for your head.
Meineke, following Hamaker, places
this line after v. 1440.
ἐς τὰ Πιττάλου.] Cf. *Ach.* 1222,
which Elmsley would reduce to
exact correspondence with this
phrase ; unnecessarily.

ΚΑΤΗΓΟΡΟΣ
ἀλλ᾽ οὖν σὺ μέμνησ᾽ αὐτὸς ἀπεκρίνατο.

ΦΙΛΟΚΛΕΩΝ
ἄκουε, μὴ φεῦγ᾽· ἐν Συβάρει γυνή ποτε   1435
κατέαξ᾽ ἐχῖνον.

ΚΑΤΗΓΟΡΟΣ
ταῦτ᾽ ἐγὼ μαρτύρομαι.

ΦΙΛΟΚΛΕΩΝ.
οὑχῖνος οὖν ἔχων τιν᾽ ἐπεμαρτύρατο·
εἶθ᾽ ἡ Συβαρῖτις εἶπεν, εἰ ναὶ τὰν κόραν
τὴν μαρτυρίαν ταύτην ἐάσας ἐν τάχει
ἐπίδεσμον ἐπρίω, νοῦν ἂν εἶχες πλείονα.   1440

ΚΑΤΗΓΟΡΟΣ
ὕβριζ᾽, ἕως ἂν τὴν δίκην ἄρχων καλῇ.

ΒΔΕΛΤΚΛΕΩΝ.
οὔ τοι μὰ τὴν Δήμητρ᾽ ἔτ᾽ ἐνταυθὶ μενεῖς,
ἀλλ᾽ ἀράμενος ἐγώ σε

ΦΙΛΟΚΛΕΩΝ.
τί ποιεῖς;

ΒΔΕΛΤΚΛΕΩΝ.
ὅ τι ποιῶ;
εἴσω φέρω σ᾽ ἐντεῦθεν· εἰ δὲ μὴ, τάχα
κλητῆρες ἐπιλείψουσι τοὺς καλουμένους.   1445

ΦΙΛΟΚΛΕΩΝ
Αἴσωπον οἱ Δελφοί ποτ᾽

1434 ἀλλ᾽ οὖν.] Addressed to the κλητήρ.

1436 ἐχῖνον.] The Scholiast tells us this word meant at Athens a vessel for holding depositions of witnesses. It is not likely that here it means more than 'a pot, pitcher,' or the like.

1437 ἐπεμαρτύρατο.] Philocleon continues his story, but neatly adopts the other's word.

1438 τὰν κόραν.] δωρίζει ἐπίτηδες. Schol. The Sybaritic woman would use some such dialect: and the oath was specially a Sicilian one.

1443 ἐγώ σε.] ἐγωγε Brunck. οἴσω σε vulg. εἴσω σε Reisig, Richter.

1446 Αἴσωπον κ.τ.λ.] The Delphians were going to throw Aesop down from a rock for his

ΒΔΕΛΥΚΛΕΩΝ

ὀλίγον μοι μέλει.

ΦΙΛΟΚΛΕΩΝ

φιάλην ἐπῃτιῶντο κλέψαι τοῦ θεοῦ·
ὁ δ' ἔλεξεν αὐτοῖς ὡς ὁ κάνθαρός ποτε

ΒΔΕΛΥΚΛΕΩΝ

οἴμ' ὡς ἀπολεῖ σ' αὐτοῖσι τοῖσι κανθάροις.

ΧΟΡΟΣ

ζηλῶ γε τῆς εὐτυχίας   1450
τὸν πρέσβυν, οἷ μετέστη
ξηρῶν τρόπων καὶ βιοτῆς·
ἕτερα δὲ νῦν ἀντιμαθὼν
ἦ μέγα τι μεταπεσεῖται
ἐπὶ τὸ τρυφῶν καὶ μαλακόν.   1455

supposed theft, when he told them the fable of the beetle. How it saved him does not appear, nor how Philocleon meant to apply it here, for his fabling is cut short. This fable is again spoken of in *Pac.* 129.

1449 ἀπολεῖ σ'.] 'He (this plaintiff) will ruin you, you and your beetles.' The MSS. have ἀπολεῖς: whence the above text may be inferred. 'Your tale of a beetle will not save you though it saved Aesop.' It is perhaps more usual to omit the definite article in this use of αὐτοῖς, but cf. above, v. 170, τὸν ὅσον ἄγων αὐτοῖσι τοῖς κανθηλίοις. The other readings of the editions ἀπόλοι', ἀπολῶ σ' are further from the MSS. And the son did not want to destroy, but to save, his father. Richter suggests ἀπολεῖς μ', 'you will ruin me.' But this would require as a continuation 'with your beetles,' not 'beetles and all.' Meineke's τοῖς σοῖς for ταῖσι is unnecessary, if it is to avoid the def. art. with κανθάροις: if it be thought that ταῖσι crept in wrongly because of αὐτοῖσι preceding, then we might

as well fill it up αὐτοῖσι κανθάροις ᾧδε, to gain a subject to ἀπολεῖ.

1450—1473. The chorus, having now quite changed their views (compare the conduct of the chorus in the *Acharnians, Clouds,* and *Peace*), praise the old man for his altered mode of life, and his son for his cleverness in bringing about this result. The song is antistrophic: vv. 1450—1461 = 1462—1473. The metre of most of the lines is a monometer iambic followed by a choriambus; but the last lines of strophe and antistrophe have a cretic in place of a choriambus. The reading and metre of v. 1454 are uncertain.

1452 ξηρῶν.] The old man certainly was well moistened by liquor now.

1454 μεταπεσεῖται.] This reading is fairly satisfactory both for sense and metre. The MSS. vary much. Dobree proposed ἀντιμαθὼν ἤθη μεταν. The line seems to be a sort of Anacreontic. It should correspond to v. 1466. Strophe and antistrophe seem thus to be broken up into two parts of five and seven lines.

τάχα δ' ἂν ἴσως οὐκ ἐθέλοι.
τὸ γὰρ ἀποστῆναι χαλεπὸν
φύσεος, ἣν ἔχοι τις ἀεί.
καίτοι πολλοὶ ταῦτ' ἔπαθον·
ξυνόντες γνώμαις ἑτέρων   1460
μετεβάλλοντο τοὺς τρόπους.
πολλοῦ δ' ἐπαίνου παρ' ἐμοὶ
καὶ τοῖσιν εὖ φρονοῦσιν
τυχὼν ἄπεισιν διὰ τὴν
φιλοπατρίαν καὶ σοφίαν   1465
ὁ παῖς ὁ Φιλοκλέωνος.
οὐδενὶ γὰρ οὕτως ἀγανῷ
ξυνεγενόμην, οὐδὲ τρόποις
ἐπεμάνην, οὐδ' ἐξεχύθην.
τί γὰρ ἐκεῖνος ἀντιλέγων   1470
οὐ κρείττων ἦν βουλόμενος
τὸν φύσαντα σεμνοτέροις
κατακοσμῆσαι πράγμασι;

ΞΑΝΘΙΑΣ
νὴ τὸν Διόνυσον, ἄπορά γ' ἡμῖν πράγματα

1456 **τάχα δ' ἄν.**] Perhaps he
may not complete the change: nature is difficult to overcome, 'expel-
las furca, tamen usque recurret.'
Hor.
1462 **παρ' ἐμοί.**] 'With me,' in
my estimation, in my mind. Passages constantly occur where we
should in English say 'from' rather
than 'with;' but of course the strict
meaning of παρά with dative is
'with.'
1469 **ἐξεχύθην.**] Cf. above, v.
744. τράγμαθ' οἷς τότ' ἐπεμαίνετο.
ἐξεχύθην.] No exact Greek parallel is quoted. 'Effundi,' effuse lae-
tori in Latin is common. Collo-
quially we use 'to gush, gushing.'
1473 **κατακοσμῆσαι.**] Meineke's
κατακομῆσαι (to suit with μετεβά-
λοντο in v. 1461, which seems right,
as no reason can be given for the
imperfect tense μετεβάλλοντο) is very

doubtful. The word κατακομᾶν is
given by L. and S. intransitive, 'to
wear long hair.' But κατακομῆσαι
σ. π., 'to plume himself on grander
things,' is not very good: τὸν φύσαντα
is more naturally the object than
the subject of the verb. And κατακοσμῆσαι is satisfactory in sense: nor
is it certain that the first part of such
a line might not consist of anapaest
and spondee. For the general meaning compare *Nub.* 515, νεωτέροις τὴν
φύσιν αὐτοῦ πράγμασιν χρωτίζεται.
A various reading κατακηλῆσαι, 'to
charm,' is proposed by one Scholiast.
1474—1537. Xanthias enters with
an account of the wonderful pranks
his master is now playing. He is
gone mad upon dancing. Philocleon follows, and begins his wild
measures, challenging all the world
of tragic dancers. The challenge is

δαίμων τις ἐσκεκύκληκεν ἐς τὴν οἰκίαν.   1475
ὁ γὰρ γέρων ὥς ἔπιε διὰ πολλοῦ χρόνου
ἤκουσέ τ' αὐλοῦ, περιχαρὴς τῷ πράγματι
ὀρχούμενος τῆς νυκτὸς οὐδὲν παύεται
τἀρχαῖ' ἐκεῖν' οἷς Θέσπις ἠγωνίζετο·
καὶ τοὺς τραγῳδοὺς φησιν ἀποδείξειν κρόνους   1480
τοὺς νῦν, διορχησάμενος ὀλίγου ὕστερον.

ΦΙΛΟΚΛΕΩΝ

τίς ἐπ' αὐλείοισι θύραις θάσσει;

ΞΑΝΘΙΑΣ

τουτὶ καὶ δὴ χωρεῖ τὸ κακόν,

ΦΙΛΟΚΛΕΩΝ

κλῇθρα χαλάσθω τάδε. καὶ δὴ γὰρ
σχήματος ἀρχὴ   1485

taken up by three sons of Carcinus successively, who come on and dance, their name being made the subject of various punning allusions. Philocleon joins them, and the chorus, after a brief song, depart escorted by the dancers, and probably dancing off the stage themselves. This 'ballet' was quite a novelty: introduced to make as strong a contrast as possible between Philocleon's present habits and his former judicial life. At the same time a travesty of certain tragic dancing was probably intended.

1475 ἐσκεκύκληκεν.] Properly ἐσκυκλεῖν is the opposite of ἐκκυκλεῖν: to bring in by means of the machine called ἐκκύκλημα. Thus in *Thesm.* 265 the man who had been wheeled out says, εἴσω τις ὡς τάχιστά μ' ἐσκυκλησάτω. A word of rather tragic sound is chosen, as a fit prelude to Philocleon's heroics.

1476 διὰ πολλοῦ χρόνου.] Wrongly translated in the Latin version 'diu multumque,' and by Mitchell, 'had given long time to his cups.' It means 'after a long time:' *i.e.* after long abstinence from such drinking, for his habits had

been ξηροί (v. 1452). Cf. *Plut.* 1045, διὰ πολλοῦ χρόνου ἑορακέναι, and above at v. 1252, ἵνα μεθυσθῶμεν διὰ χρόνου, cf. *Pac.* 570, 710. Florens remarks 'videntur facilius inebriari qui contra morem bibunt.'

1479 τἀρχαῖ' ἐκεῖν'.] As an old man that dances would be old-fashioned: those in use with Thespis. But this does not prevent him from charging others with being κρόνοι, for which word cf. *Nub.* 398, 929. No other Thespis than the well-known founder of tragedy need be supposed.

1481 διορχησάμενος.] So MSS. R. V. vulg. διορχησόμενος. Either may be satisfactorily rendered: the aorist by 'he will prove them fools by dancing a match with them;' the future by 'he will prove them fools, for he means to dance, &c.' For the sense of διὰ in the compound compare διαπίνειν, to which there is allusion in *Ach.* 751, διαπεισθμες.

1482 τίς κ.τ.λ.] Tragic style: and below κλῇθρα χαλάσθω is illustrated from Eur. *Hipp.* χαλᾶτε κλῇθρα, πρόσπολοι, πυλωμάτων, and *Hel.* 1196, *Iph. Taur.* 1304.

ΞΑΝΘΙΑΣ

μᾶλλον δέ γ' ἴσως μανίας ἀρχή.

ΦΙΛΟΚΛΕΩΝ

πλευρὰν λυγίσαντος ὑπὸ ῥώμης,
οἷον μυκτὴρ μυκᾶται καὶ
σφόνδυλος ἀχεῖ.

ΞΑΝΘΙΑΣ

πῖθ' ἐλλέβορον.

ΦΙΛΟΚΛΕΩΝ.

πτήσσει Φρύνιχος ὥς τις ἀλέκτωρ,   1490

ΞΑΝΘΙΑΣ

τάχα βαλλήσεις.

ΦΙΛΟΚΛΕΩΝ

σκέλος οὐράνιόν γ' ἐκλακτίζων.
πρωκτὸς χάσκει.

ΞΑΝΘΙΑΣ

κατὰ σαυτὸν ὅρα.

1487 λυγίσαντος.] Cf. Theocr. *Id.* I. 96, τὸ θὴν τὸν ἔρωτα κατεύχεο, Δάφνι, λυγιξεῖν; where it is of one wrestler bending down by force and so throwing the other. Here the dance is said to bend or twist the side. 'The twisted side the forceful motion owns; Lows the wide nostril, and the back-bone groans,' Mitchell.

1489 πῖθ' ἐλλέβορον.] The common cure for madness. Philocleon continues his speech, regardless of Xanthias' interruptions.

1490 πτήσσει Φρύνιχος.] The old commentators seem in the wrong to take πτήσσει here of fear. Whether this Phrynichus be the well-known tragic poet, as is probable enough (for the old man uses the measures of Thespis (v. 1479), and so, naturally enough, those of Phrynichus), or a dancer of the name, it it is plain that there was some dance called Phrynichean (v. 1524), in which the leg was kicked out. This

fling the old man begins to execute, and describes himself as 'Phrynichus throwing out his leg heaven-high,' to the imminent danger of Xanthias, who interpolates τάχα βαλλήσεις. This throwing out the leg is compared to the stroke of a cock when fighting. But πτήσσει need not be discarded for πλήσσει, as Bentley and Porson wished; πτήσσει means 'crouches, gathers himself up,' in act to spring. Cf. Eur. *Andr.* 753, for πτήξαντες of such crouching: ὅρα δὲ μὴ νῷν εἰς ἐρημίαν ὁδοῦ πτήξαντες οἶδε πρὸς βίαν ἄγωσί με. But Dindorf's note is 'fingitur trepidare Phrynichus, quippe victus a meliore saltatore, Philocleone.' Of course there are abundant examples to illustrate πτήσσει used of a bird crouching in fear; but I do not see that this interpretation makes good sense in connexion with v. 1491 compared with v. 1524.

1493 κατὰ σαυτὸν ὅρα.] 'Do look where you're going.'

ΦΙΛΟΚΛΕΩΝ

νῦν γὰρ ἐν ἄρθροις τοῖς ἡμετέροις
στρέφεται χαλαρὰ κοτυληδών. 1495
οὐκ εὖ ;

ΒΔΕΛΤΚΛΕΩΝ

μὰ Δί᾽ οὐ δῆτ᾽, ἀλλὰ μανικὰ πράγματα.

ΦΙΛΟΚΛΕΩΝ

φέρε νυν ἀνείπω κἀνταγωνιστὰς καλῶ.
εἴ τις τραγῳδός φησιν ὀρχεῖσθαι καλῶς,
ἐμοὶ διορχησόμενος ἐνθάδ᾽ εἰσίτω.
φησίν τις, ἢ οὐδείς ;

ΒΔΕΛΤΚΛΕΩΝ

εἷς γ᾽ ἐκεινοσὶ μόνος. 1500

ΦΙΛΟΚΛΕΩΝ

τίς ὁ κακοδαίμων ἐστίν ;

ΒΔΕΛΤΚΛΕΩΝ

υἱὸς Καρκίνου
ὁ μέσατος.

ΦΙΛΟΚΛΕΩΝ

ἀλλ᾽ οὗτός γε καταποθήσεται·
ἀπολῶ γὰρ αὐτὸν ἐμμελείᾳ κονδύλου.

1495 κοτυληδών.] τὸ δὲ ἐν ᾧ
στρέφεται ὁ μηρός, κοτυληδών. Aristot.
1496 οὐκ εὖ ;] This is Dobree's
arrangement : better than the common one.
1498—9 εἴ τις κ.τ.λ.] Con-
trast with this εἴ τις θύρασιν ἡλιαστής,
εἰσίτω, v. 891.
1501 Καρκίνου.] He had three
(some say four) sons : their names
are rather variously given ; cf. Nub.
1263. They were dancers; but one
of them wrote tragedy. They are
ridiculed in Pac. 781—9, ὄρνιγαι
οἰσογενεῖς γυλιαύχεναι ὀρχησταὶ να-
νοφυεῖς, σφυράδων ἀποκνίσματα, μη-
χανοδίφαι.
1502 "ὁ μέσατος.] This implies

that there were but three : though
the Scholiast on this passage asserts
there were four : three dancers, one,
Xenocles, a poet. But plainly the
poet was one of the dancers, v. 1511:
so that we may content ourselves
with three, Xenocles, Xenotimus,
and Xenarchus. The other names,
Demotimus and Xenoclitus, perhaps
are in some way mistakes for Xenotimus and Xenocles.
1503 ἐμμελείᾳ κονδύλων.] ἐμμέ-
λεια τραγικὴ ὄρχησις, Schol. But
destroying him in the ' knuckle measure' also means correcting him with
blows. Cf. Eq. 1236, κονδύλοι
ἡρμοττόμην.

10

ἐν τῷ ῥυθμῷ γὰρ οὐδέν ἐστ'.

ΒΛΕΛΤΚΛΕΩΝ

ἀλλ' ὤζυρέ,
ἕτερος τραρῳδὸς Καρκινίτης ἔρχεται,   1505
ἀδελφὸς αὐτοῦ.

ΦΙΛΟΚΛΕΩΝ

νὴ Δί' ὀψώνηκ' ἄρα.

ΒΛΕΛΤΚΛΕΩΝ

μὰ τὸν Δί' οὐδέν γ' ἄλλο πλὴν γε καρκίνους.
προσέρχεται γὰρ ἕτερος αὖ τῶν Καρκίνου.

ΦΙΛΟΚΛΕΩΝ

τουτὶ τί ἦν τὸ προσέρπον; ὀξὶς, ἢ φάλαγξ;

ΒΛΕΛΤΚΛΕΩΝ

ὁ πιννοτήρης οὗτός ἐστι τοῦ γένους,   1510
ὁ σμικρότατος, ὃς τὴν τραγῳδίαν ποιεῖ.

ΦΙΛΟΚΛΕΩΝ

ὦ Καρκίν', ὦ μακάριε τῆς εὐπαιδίας·
ὅσον τὸ πλῆθος κατέπεσεν τῶν ὀρχίλων.
ἀτὰρ καταβατέον γ' ἐπ' αὐτούς μ', ὤζυρέ
ἄλμην κύκα τούτοισιν, ἢν ἐγὼ κρατῶ.   1515

1504 ἐν τῷ ῥυθμῷ κ.τ.λ.] 'For
he is not at all in rhythm :' he does
not keep time or measure in his
dancing, and therefore requires a
regular knuckle-rapping to keep him
in order.
1505 ἕτερος.] Number two of
Carcinus' sons.
1506 ὀψώνηκ' ἄρα] 'I'm well
found, methinks, in fish :' the καρ-
κίνοι coming under the class ὄψον.
1507 μὰ Δί'...καρκίνους.] Xanthias objects that all the ὄψον he
has got is crabs, for now enters
number three.
1509 ὀξίς.] Some variety of
crab is thought to be meant; or a
shrimp. Brunck quotes Av. 1103,
ὄνομα δέ σοι τί ἐστι, πλοῖον ἢ κυνῆ;
as an analogous passage. It is not

clear how a vinegar-cruet and a
spider could be suggested by the
same person. The smallest of the
three Carcinites, who were perhaps
in some way put on the stage so as
to resemble crabs, might be something like a spider, by a stretch of
imagination.
1510 πιννοτήρης.]   A small
kind of crab. Some write the word
πινοτήρης.
1511 ὃς τ. τραγῳδίαν τ.] Xenocles. Cf. note at v. 1502.
1513 ὀρχίλων.] 'Wrens' probably : cf. Av. 568. As being of
diminutive stature these sons of
Carcinus are so called : but there is
reference to ὀρχηστῶν, 'dancers.'
1515 ἄλμην.] In which they
are to be dressed ; ἐπειδὴ ἄλμην

ΧΟΡΟΣ

φέρε νυν ἡμεῖς αὐτοῖς ὀλίγον ξυγχωρήσωμεν ἄπαντες,
ἵν᾿ ἐφ᾿ ἡσυχίας ἡμῶν πρόσθεν βεμβικίζωσιν ἑαυτούς.
ἄγ᾿, ὦ μεγαλώνυμα τέκνα
τοῦ θαλασσίοιο,
πηδᾶτε παρὰ ψάμαθον   1520
καὶ θῖν᾿ ἁλὸς ἀτρυγέτοιο.
καρίδων ἀδελφοί·
ταχὺν πόδα κυκλοσοβεῖτε,
καὶ τὸ Φρυνίχειον
ἐκλακτισάτω τις, ὅπως   1525
ἰδόντες ἄνω σκέλος ὦ-
ζωσιν οἱ θεαταί.
στρόβει, παράβαινε κύκλῳ καὶ γάστρισον σεαυτὶν,
ῥῖπτε σκέλος οὐράνιον· βέμβικες ἐγγενέσθων.   1530
καὐτὸς γὰρ ὁ ποντομέδων ἄναξ πατὴρ προσέρπει
ἡσθεὶς ἐπὶ τοῖσιν ἑαυτοῦ παισί, τοῖς τριόρχοις.

παρασκευάζουσιν ἐπὶ τὸ φαγεῖν ἰχθύδια ἢ καρείονι. Schol.
1516 **φέρε νυν**] The Chorus clear
a space for this Phrynichean ballet,
in which they perhaps join, but the
Carcinites were the chief performers.
1517 **βεμβικίζωσιν**.] Cf. *Av.*
1465, **βεμβικιᾶν**. And these same
dancers are called **Καρκίνου στρόβιλοι**
Pac. 864. The Scholiast quotes the
well-known epigram οἱ δ᾿ ἄρ᾿ ὑπὸ
πληγῆσι θοαὶ βέμβικας ἔχοντες ἐστρέ-
φον εὐρείῃ παῖδες ἐνὶ τριόδῳ.
1518—23. Rather epic in style
and language; hence the termination
-οιο in v. 1519.
1519 **θαλασσίοιο**.] Vulg. θαλασ-
σίου: to which many editors add
θεοῦ, to be scanned as a mono-
syllable. But the Scholiast on *Pac.*
792 quotes from Plato *Com.* Ξενο-
κλῆς ὁ δωδεκαμήχανος, ὁ Καρκίνου
παῖς τοῦ θαλαττίου. 'Children of
him of the sea' seems rather better
than specifying that he was θεός.
Besides the epic form is quite in place.
1521 **ἀτρυγέτοιο**.] It does not

appear well to change this to ἀτρυ-
γέτου that it may correspond metrically with v. 1526: for it seems
likely that the Homeric phrase would
have been taken as it was. Richter
reads ὦ ὦζωσιν at v. 1526; where
MS. Rav. has ὦζωσιν, which Bergk
approves. We cannot be quite certain that this song is antistrophic.
1524 **Φρυνίχειον**.] Cf. note on
v. 1490. δῆλον ὡς σημειωθεῖ τι ἦν
τὸ Φρυνίχειον, τὸ εἰς ὕψος ἐν τῇ
ὀρχήσει ἐκλακτίζειν. Schol.
1530 **βέμβικες ἐγγ.**] 'Let there
be pirouettes,' top-like spinnings
round and round. The Scholiast
rather implies that a certain dance
was called βέμβιξ or βεμβικισμός.
1534 **τριόρχοις.**] 'His dancing
triad of sons.' Whether the other
sense of τριόρχης (a kind of falcon,
cf. *Av.* 1181, 1206) is played upon,
is doubtful. But as ὀρχίλοι above
means a bird, perhaps it is so.
These dancers might be falcons in
their gyrations.

ἀλλ' ἐξάγετ', εἴ τι φιλεῖτ' ὀρχούμενοι, θύραζε   1535
ἡμᾶς ταχύ· τοῦτο γὰρ οὐδεὶς πω πάρος δέδρακεν,
ὀρχούμενον ὅστις ἀπήλλαξεν χορὸν τρυγῳδῶν.

1535—7. The Chorus request the
Carcinites, if they like dancing so
much, to conduct them off the stage
with a dance: an unheard of novelty,
for the Chorus entered indeed with a
dance, but did not make their exit so.
1536 ἡμᾶς.] I can see no reason
for preferring ὑμᾶς, Bentley's alteration.
1537 ὀρχούμενον ὅστις.] Whether ὀρχούμενω or ὀρχούμενοι be
taken, matters little. ὀρχούμενός τις
MSS. The Chorus are conducted

off the stage by the dancers, but it
seems probable they in some sort
joined the dance themselves. The
whole line is explanatory of οὐδεὶς
πω δέδρακεν. 'This no man ever
yet did. I mean—no man has there
been who took his chorus off with a
dance.' And the accusative is perhaps rather preferable. Bentley's
rendering, 'no-one (who has escaped
with impunity for such innovation)
ever took off his chorus dancing,'
seems awkward.